14 × 12/13   LT 12/13

THE
DEAD DETECTIVE
by WILLIAM HEFFERNAN

Published by Akashic Books
©2010 William Heffernan

ISBN-13: 978-1-936070-61-9
Library of Congress Control Number: 2010922716

First Printing

Akashic Books
PO Box 1456
New York, NY 10009
Akashic7@aol.com
www.akashicbooks.com

This book is for Karyna, Cheryl, Alisa, Taylor, Max, and Parker, young men and women who are always there for me. Love you guys.

AUTHOR'S NOTE

Great liberties were taken in the portrayal of the Pinellas County Sheriff's Department and the Tarpon Springs Police Department. Those liberties were needed to produce a certain dramatic effect and should not be taken as a condemnation of either police agency or the people who run them.

Prologue

The mirrored ball rotating above the stage sent small patches of light spiraling about the room, and together with the grinding beat of the music it seemed to accent the faint film of sweat that covered the dancer's body. She was a beautiful woman, young and lithe and erotically proportioned, and she was dressed in the skimpiest of thongs with a bikini top so small it failed to cover the aureoles of her breasts. Yet none of that staged eroticism found its way to her dancing, and the perspiration on her body came from the heat of the stage lights rather than any degree of exertion.

Darlene Beckett studied the woman and tried to think of a single word that would describe her performance. Somnambulistic was the only one that came to mind, and she wished she could go up on the stage and push the woman aside; show her how to arouse the men who sat staring up at her; show her how to use her body, how to put that little pout in her lips, how to make her eyes call out with an open invitation, how to use all of it until she had them slipping their hands under the table and reaching for themselves.

A faint smile played across Darlene's lips as she thought of doing just that. But of course she couldn't. The media would jump on any misstep she made, and the courts would be right behind, just waiting for a chance to slap her down. Darlene had been able to get rid of the ankle monitor she was supposed to wear. That was no longer a problem. She had bedded her probation officer within a month of her sentencing to house arrest, and he had helped her remove it on two conditions. First, that she always wear slacks to hide its absence, and second, that she keep it with her at all times, so she could claim it had just fallen off if she was ever questioned about it. She smiled again. She had ignored that second condition from the very start. The monitor sat atop her bedroom dresser, deactivated, and there it would stay. As far as the courts and the probation department were concerned she was home asleep in her bed.

"Hello, there, pretty lady."

Darlene turned to the sound of the male voice. It was the man who had been watching her most of the evening, and she had been wondering when he would get up the courage to approach her. She had even asked one of the dancers about him, just to make sure he wasn't a well-known creep. He was certainly young enough. He was also tall and lean and fairly good looking. He was wearing a cowboy hat, western-style boots, and a wide belt with a large silver buckle to hold up his jeans. There were a great many horse ranches scattered across the nearby counties, but he didn't carry with him that always lingering smell of horse. Just a barroom cowboy, she decided.

"Hi there," she said, thinking that despite the costume this one just might do.

"The name's Clint. You who I think you are?" he asked.

"Who do you think I am?"

"That lady who was on TV all the time a few months back."

"You have a good memory for faces, Clint. My name's Darlene in case you forgot that part."

"I didn't forget." He flashed a wide, very white smile. "I just never thought I'd get a chance to meet you."

Darlene put some sparkle in her eyes and allowed her lips to play with the idea of a smile. "And now you have."

He gave a long, slow nod of his head. "You like this place?" He raised his chin indicating the room.

"I like to watch the dancers," Darlene said. "The good ones anyway." She let her eyes go to the woman on the stage and gave a small shake of her head, letting him know this one wasn't one she enjoyed.

"I like everything about it." Clint drew a deep breath. "Place smells like sex."

Darlene took a long, slow, less obvious breath, filling her lungs with the intermingling odors of stale liquor and cigarettes and sweat. She let her playful smile return. "Hmm, it does," she said.

The cowboy leaned in close. "You wanna take a little ride? I could pick up whatever you're drinkin' and maybe we could head over toward the beach. How's that sound?"

Darlene's hands began to tremble. She reached for her purse and squeezed it between them to hide that small display of fear. She drew a long breath; then hit him with the full force of her deep green eyes. "That might be nice," she said. The smile that followed glittered under the rotating lights.

Clint leaned in even closer. "Darlene, honey, I promise you it's gonna be very, *very* nice."

CHAPTER ONE

Harry Doyle sat in his car outside the front gate of the Central Florida Women's Correctional Facility. He remained nearly motionless except for the occasional rise of one hand to bring a cigarette to his lips. He seemed to be staring ahead at the white brick buildings as if studying them for flaws. The main building was a long, low, sprawling structure with a collection of smaller buildings off to one side, all of it surrounded by eighteen-foot chain-link fences, set in two rows with a twenty-foot no-man's-land between them. Both rows of fences were topped with three additional feet of razor wire, the edges of which glistened in the bright Florida sun. Escape was possible, of course, as it was from any detention facility. But anyone who made it over those fences would carry the gift of that razor wire, and would leave a blood trail that pursuing dogs would easily follow.

Harry looked beyond the edge of the road where he had parked his car. The prison was set in a patch of Central Florida wilderness. In every direction thick scrub land and swamp met his eye. It would be hard territory to cross, filled with all manner of danger. A game warden had once told him that anyone walking through a patch of Florida wilderness would pass no less than one hundred venomous snakes per mile traveled, and while most would try to get out of the way, sooner or later you would meet one that could not or would not. There would also be countless gators in the deeper swamps, and while the patches of dry open land would hold scorpions and fire ants, the thicker woods would offer up a variety of creatures you wouldn't care to meet unarmed, even the occasional Florida panther, black bear, or wild boar.

Harry took a long drag on his unfiltered Camel and ground out the butt in an overflowing ashtray. It was his fourth cigarette since he'd arrived. He had given up smoking five years ago, and had only smoked on this one day every year since.

When he looked back at the prison he noticed two guards standing just inside the main gate staring back at him. After a few minutes, the gate opened and one of the guards walked slowly toward Harry's car. He was a tall, angular man with a large nose and thin, pinched lips. He looked to be about twenty-five and he walked a bit stiffly, as if he were tightly wound and ready to react. His hand was on the butt of his holstered Glock automatic. It was a touch of hoped for intimidation that almost made Harry smile.

Harry lowered the window on the driver's side. The guard stopped, his eyes scanning what he could see of the car's interior. They settled on the police radio.

"You a cop?" the guard asked.

Harry raised his shield and credential case. The guard bent over to look at it more closely.

"Pinellas County," he said, a slight grin coming to his lips. "That don't carry a lot of weight out here in the boonies." There was a smirk on his face that Harry didn't like; an unearned arrogance. Harry was six-one, with enough lean, well-conditioned muscle to fill out a fairly large frame, and he had little compunction about using it. People often misjudged him. He had craggy features that made him seem a bit older than his thirty-one years, wavy brown hair and soft green eyes that made him appear almost docile. It was a misconception that usually disappeared as soon as Harry opened his mouth.

"I guess you didn't hear me," the guard snapped. He shifted his weight and tightened his grip on the butt of his weapon, clearly irritated by Harry's lack of response. "I said that Pinellas County don't carry a lot of weight out here."

Harry studied the man's name tag. It said, *L. Bottoms.* "What's the "L" stand for?" he asked.

The guard hesitated, uncertain if an answer might cost him control of the situation. Finally, he gave in. "Leroy," he said, accenting the second syllable of his name.

Harry nodded. When he spoke it was in a slow, soft, well-modulated voice. "Well, Le-*roy*, how much weight would it carry if I got out of my car, took hold of that Glock you keep playing with, and shoved it eight inches up your ass?"

Leroy's jaw dropped, and his face paled. Then he began to stammer. "Now wait . . . now wait . . . a . . . a damn minute."

"No, you wait, Le-*roy*. Then you turn your skinny ass around and get back to work. I showed you my tin and that's all you need to see. So, fuck off. And fuck off fast."

"Well . . . well . . . fuck you too," Leroy snapped. He hesitated, trying to decide what to do. Then he cursed Harry once more, made a quick pivot, and headed back toward the main gate.

Harry watched him walk away. Leroy seemed a little deflated at first. Then he stiffened his back and added a bit of swagger. Harry assumed it was a touch of bravado for the other guard who was still watching from inside the gate.

Ten minutes later another figure emerged from the gate. He was tall and slightly overweight, the bulge of a belly hanging over his belt, and he wore lieutenant bars on his shirt collar. His name was Walter Lee Hollins and Harry had known him for more than ten years.

"How ya doin', Harry?" he offered as he reached the car window.

"I'm good, Walter Lee, how about yourself?"

"Tolerable. Better on days when I don't have to put up with assholes like Leroy. He give you a hard time?"

"He was just playing badass, and I just wasn't in the mood."

"Shouldn't have to be. Not once you showed him your tin. You did, right?"

Harry nodded. "He saw the police radio and asked. So I showed him."

"That's what I figured. Anyways, he's makin' a big stink."

"To you?"

"Oh, no, he knows better'n that. He's talkin' to the captain. He's new, and on the young side, and almost as stupid as Leroy. Just thought I'd warn you to expect to hear about it."

Harry nodded again. "Thanks, Walter Lee."

"Oh, and in case you were wonderin', your mama's still inside, still healthy. You ever change your mind about wantin' to see her, I can arrange it to happen out of the way and real quiet."

Harry nodded but said nothing, and Walter Lee gave the top of the car a light rap and headed back toward the prison.

Harry watched him go; then turned his attention back to the surrounding landscape. Little had changed in all the years he had come here, which was exactly as he wanted it to be. He came once each year, always on the anniversary of his brother Jimmy's murder. He never saw his mother on any of these visits. He only saw the place where she was caged. It was a necessary trip; one that only he could make. He had lived and Jimmy had not. On his way home he would stop at Jimmy's grave and tell him that their mother was still behind bars.

"I'll make sure she stays there, Jimmy," he would promise, as he did each year. "I'll make sure she's there until she's dead."

Harry Santos and his brother Jimmy died on June 7, 1985, on a hot, humid Florida morning. The boys were ten and six years old and on the morning of their deaths they were seated in the kitchen of their home waiting for their mother to join them at the breakfast table. Jimmy, the youngest and the family clown, was imitating their three-year-old next-door neighbor who sang the same song day after day while playing in his backyard. It was a simple, childish song about a spider and a water spout, but Jimmy's hand gestures and facial expressions perfectly mimicked the three-year-old and produced gales of laughter from his older brother Harry. Across the kitchen their mother Lucy smiled at their antics. Then she turned her back to them and began crushing four sleeping pills into a fine powder. She divided the powder, put equal amounts into two glasses of freshly squeezed orange juice, and brought the glasses to the table. Twenty minutes later, when the boys were unconscious, Lucy dragged them into the garage and placed them on the floor side-by-side next to the exhaust pipe of her five-year-old Chevrolet. As both boys slept she carefully folded their hands across their chests, placed small silver crosses on their foreheads, and covered their eyes with hand towels, then stood quietly for a moment, viewing the scene she had created. Slowly, a look of pleasure crept into her eyes and she turned and walked quickly to the car, opened the driver's-side door, slipped inside, and started the engine. Finished, she went back into the house and closed the door to the garage behind her. After placing a folded towel at the base of the door to confine the exhaust fumes, she smiled again, collected her Bible, and walked the two short blocks to the evangelical church she attended each Sunday. There, she prostrated herself on the floor of the altar, just below a large stained-glass window depicting the three crosses of Golgotha, and asked God to deliver her sons to His heavenly peace.

While Lucy was praying an elderly neighbor walked past her house, heard the car running inside the garage, and became concerned. He knocked on the front door and after getting no response, hurried home and called 911. Two patrol cops arrived at the scene minutes later and forced their way into the garage. They found Harry and Jimmy just as their mother had left them and carried them outside. Both boys had stopped breathing and neither had a heartbeat. The two officers called for emergency service backup and immediately began CPR. Harry, who was big for his age, was brought back to life before the EMTs arrived. Jimmy, who was much smaller and quite frail, never regained consciousness.

When she returned home from church, Lucy Santos was arrested and charged with the murder of her son Jimmy, and the attempted murder of her son Harry. Under questioning she admitted drugging the boys, placing them on the floor next to her car, and starting the engine. She told the arresting officers that she was making sure her sons would be waiting for her in heaven. When asked why, she said that June 4 had been her thirty-third birthday, as if that alone explained her actions. A psychiatrist hired by Lucy's court-appointed attorney theorized that Lucy, as a devout Christian, believed that Jesus Christ had been crucified, died, and was buried shortly after his thirty-third birthday, and then had risen from the dead and ascended into heaven three days later. He said Lucy believed that God had chosen her to follow that exact same path, and that she had not wanted to abandon her sons to the care of strangers.

The state's attorney, who was eyeing a future run for governor, told the press that he wasn't buying any of it, and announced that he would seek the death penalty and would have ten-year-old Harry testify that his mother had been perfectly rational in the days—even the hours—leading up to the murder. Harry, who was now in state custody, became an instant media darling. Reporters swooped in like seagulls at a picnic, easily manipulating the child into a series of sensational quotes. The few child welfare workers who tried to intervene were pushed aside by the state's attorney, who insisted that Harry was under the protective custody of his office. With that door opened wide, the media played its part and gave the state's attorney just what he wanted. The initial headline in the *St. Petersburg Times* read: *Ten-Year-Old Ready to Put Mom on Death Row*, while the *Tampa Tribune* intoned: *Harry Says Killer Mom Must Die.*

After the initial barrage of outrageous quotes and comments, the story made its way to the back pages and a year passed in relative quiet before the case was ready for trial. By that time, closely held psychiatric evidence had begun to build indicating that Lucy Santos was insane. Two days before the trial was set to begin, the state's attorney held a press conference with Harry at his side. There, surrounded by the media, he announced that a plea bargain had been reached that would send Lucy to prison for the rest of her natural life. Harry, now eleven, was asked how he felt about the decision and the fact that he would not have to testify against his mother. The young boy, well coached by prosecutors, stared back at the reporters with very lost, very empty eyes and told them that he had been prepared to testify. Then he paused, and in words that had not been scripted for him, said: "I just want to be sure my mother never gets out of prison."

Three weeks after his mother was sentenced, the county agency that had taken charge of Harry placed him in permanent foster care. The foster family's name was Doyle. The father, John—Jocko to his friends—was a sergeant with the Clearwater Police Department. The mother, Maria, was a Cuban exile, who ran her home with endless amounts of love, and the efficiency of a Marine drill instructor. There were no other children, and after two years Jocko and Maria Doyle petitioned the courts to adopt Harry and make him their son. Harry had no objection and the courts saw no reason to deny the request. Harry had never known his father, he was simply a man he vaguely remembered who had occasionally come into his mother's life, remained awhile, and then left again. They had never married and by the time Jimmy was born he was gone for good.

Harry remained with the Doyle's for eleven years. Over time he learned to care for them, but he never allowed himself to love them, or to look on them as his parents. His affection tended more toward respect and gratitude for the care and love they had generously given him. Trust was never an issue for Harry. Throughout the time he lived with them, Harry Santos Doyle never went to sleep without first locking his bedroom door.

* * *

Harry arrived at the Pinellas County sheriff's office at three-thirty, parked his unmarked car in the lot reserved for police vehicles, and headed for a rear door that would take him to the second-floor offices of the homicide division. He was working four to midnight, which meant he'd probably finish up at three or four in the morning if the night turned busy. But the extra time didn't matter. It was his favorite shift, one that his fellow detectives, most of whom had families or lovers, preferred to avoid. It also encompassed the hours when the most complicated murders took place. Daylight killings, and those that happened after midnight, usually turned into ground balls—simple, straightforward homicides that often left the perpetrator standing at the scene, murder weapon still in hand. Those, anyone could handle. It was the more difficult, more intricate cases that Harry loved, and as far as the other homicide dicks were concerned, if the dead detective wanted the more complex cases, and the extra, unpaid hours they inevitably involved, it was fine with them. The job was tough enough and dangerous enough as it was.

They had been calling Harry the "dead detective" ever since his appointment to the division. During his time in a patrol car he had kept a fairly low profile about his past. But once he reached homicide the cat quickly left the bag. Detectives have a tendency to remember cases, especially the big ones, and when Harry was promoted to homicide five years earlier at the tender age of twenty-six, there were still older cops who remembered the case of the two murdered brothers. They also remembered that a Clearwater patrol sergeant named Jocko Doyle had adopted the one who came back to life. Given the morbidity of cop humor, Harry's new name was immediately set in stone.

Harry had joined the sheriff's department shortly after graduating from the University of South Florida. Everyone thought it was a tribute to his adoptive father, who had become a stabilizing force in his life. To some small degree that was true, but there was also another more driving reason that Harry never spoke about. The sheriff's department handled most of the homicides throughout the county, and Harry had one very personal goal: to devote his life to the pursuit of murderers.

As Harry approached the rear door of the sheriff's office, a small, lean figure stepped out from behind a thick pineapple palm. He was dressed in an oversized basketball shirt and baggy basketball shorts, with a Miami Heat cap sitting slightly askew on his head. Even though the boy was squinting into the afternoon sun, Harry recognized the size and shape of his favorite twelve-year-old gangsta, Rubio Martí.

"Hey, Doyle. Wassup?" Rubio offered.

Harry shielded his eyes and saw that Rubio was grinning up at him. It was an infectious grin and Harry had to force himself not to smile back. "What's up with you, you little weasel," he said. "And why aren't you in school?"

"School's out, man. It's been out for three weeks. Where you been at? Maybe they still goin' ta school up north, but not in Florida."

"I thought you'd be in summer school," Harry said, playing a game they always played about Rubio's school work.

"Hey, man, I'm too smart for summer school. You know that. That's truth."

"The only thing smart about you is your ass," Harry snapped back. "And that's truth."

"Don't you be dissin' me. You do, I'll have to whoop you good."

Harry put a hand on the boy's shoulder and gave it an affectionate squeeze. Two years ago he had stumbled across the kid while investigating the murder of a Cuban crack dealer. Rubio, who was ten at the time, was working for the man as a lookout, and being paid in both money and drugs. The dealer had been trying to get the kid hooked—something he had succeeded in doing with a number of others. It was a way of guaranteeing both dependence and loyalty from the children who comprised his last line of defense against the police. But Rubio had sold the drugs he had received and given the money to his mother in a vain effort to keep her off the streets. Harry had befriended him and talked him into going back to school. A year later he found himself investigating the murder of the boy's mother. She had been found in an alley beaten and stabbed fourteen times. It had been a ground ball that ended with the arrest and conviction of her pimp. It had also been one more devastating blow in Rubio's young life. Now he lived with his grandmother and peddled information to the police—mostly Harry—whenever he could.

"So you down here to have a late lunch with me, or what?" Harry asked.

"Naw," Rubio said. "I got sumthin' for you." He jabbed the index finger and thumb of each hand at the ground as he spoke, playing the gangsta wannabe to the hilt. But with his soft brown face, liquid brown eyes, and strands of curly hair sticking out from beneath his cap, he looked more like a wayward cherub. This time Harry couldn't keep the smile off his face.

"So whaddaya got, hotshot?" he asked.

The boy kept using his hands and shoulders to emphasize his words. "Hey, you know that woman down in my hood got herself offed? That scaggy ol' junkie broad?"

"Yeah, it's not my case, but I know who you're talking about."

"Hey, I know it's not your case, man. It belongs to that tall, skinny dude you work with. The one with the fat partner who's such a mean-assed mutha."

"Weathers and Benevuto," Harry said. "What about it?"

"Yeah, well, they tryin' to pin it on that scaggy ol' junkie's boyfriend."

"And he didn't do it," Harry said.

"You bet you ass he din'." Rubio was grinning again.

"But you know who did."

"You got that straight."

"So who did it?"

"You tell that skinny cop—don't you tell that mean, fat one—that he oughta check out the ol' lady lives next door. The real ol' one."

"The old lady killed her?"

Rubio shook his head. "Nah. Was her son. That scaggy ol' junkie broad was robbin' that ol' lady's Social Security checks. Pissed the son off real bad."

"You sure about this?" Harry asked.

Rubio jabbed his index fingers and thumbs at the ground for emphasis. "Truth, man. You check it out. You see." He grinned up at Harry. "You know, you shoulda had this case. You coulda solved it right off, usin' that power you got."

Harry suppressed a smile. "What power is that?"

"You know what I'm talkin' about. That way you have to talk to dead people. The way you can look in a dead person's eyes and see stuff there, because you was dead once yerself."

"Who told you that?"

"I heard other cops talkin' about it." Rubio grinned. "I hear lots a stuff you cops say."

"Well that one's a fairy tale."

"Yeah, yeah, I know," Rubio said. "You jus' don't wanna let on about it."

Harry put his hand in his pocket and took out a fold of bills, slipped a twenty off the top, and handed it to the boy. "You put that to good use," he said. "Buy a couple of books. Do something for your brain."

"Yeah, yeah," Rubio said. He shrugged his shoulders, becoming the tough guy again.

"And come see me later in the week so we can grab something to eat," Harry said.

"I will. I will."

"No, you won't. But think about it, anyway. And say *hola* to your grand-mother for me. Tell her I'll be by someday to check up on your ass."

Harry watched the boy head across the parking lot, then turned and entered the building. When he reached the homicide office, he found John Weathers and passed along Rubio's tip, without explaining where he had gotten it. Weathers didn't seem that interested. Harry decided not to push it. At least not until they arrested the boyfriend.

Harry spent the first hour working at his desk, reviewing the paperwork on a case he had closed the previous day. It hadn't been a particularly satisfying one—an elderly man killed during a robbery gone sour. Harry had tracked down the killer within forty-eight hours. It turned out to be a teenage boy raised in a home that the ASPCA wouldn't have allowed to keep a dog or cat. It was a case where everyone had lost except the people who really deserved to. A voice barked across the room, interrupting his thoughts: "Doyle. In here."

He looked up and saw Pete Rourke, the division captain, going back into his office, a trailing finger beckoning Harry to follow. When he entered the office Rourke was already behind his desk. There was also an attractive, dark-haired woman, somewhere in her late twenties or early thirties, seated in one of the two visitors' chairs.

"Doyle, meet your new partner," Rourke snapped. "This is Vicky Stanopo-lis. She's new to the division, just came up from sex crimes. She also claims she can work with anybody." Rourke looked at each of them, then shook his head. "We'll see if she can work with you. God knows, nobody else wants to."

Harry fought off a smile. "Thanks, cap."

"No problem." Rourke turned to Vicky. "Harry doesn't have a life, so he likes to work long hours. You don't have to try and keep up when he goes crazy that way. But you might learn a few things working with him. Including things you *shouldn't* do. But it's like I told you before he came in, he seems to have a special talent, let's call it an intuition about killers—an intuition that some people consider a little spooky. Other partners he's had claimed that the victims . . . told him things." He gave Harry a long look as if awaiting some confirmation. When none came he turned his attention back to Vicky. "He's also an enormous pain in the ass." He threw Harry a stern look. He was a big man with a square, fleshy face, unruly black hair, and piercing blue eyes. His voice, as usual, was gruff, the words sharp and to the point. "I got a call from the women's prison . . . a corrections captain who said you threatened one of his men."

"It wasn't much of a threat," Harry said. "The guy was a professional jackass. I just let him know that I knew he was a jackass." Amusement flickered in Harry's eyes. "I guess he complained."

"Yes, he did."

"Sort of proves my point."

Rourke glared at him. "Next time, try a nice, warm smile when you tell somebody you're gonna shove their Glock up their ass. It's good public relations."

"Yes, sir."

Rourke shook his head as if the entire conversation had been pointless. He pulled some papers from a pile, ready to get back to work. "Take Vicky out to the bullpen and introduce her around. The desk across from you is empty, right?"

Harry nodded.

"Now it belongs to her."

Introducing Vicky to the other detectives proved easy duty. She was tall and slender and shapely, with long brown hair that fell almost to her shoulders, pale brown eyes that looked like they could swallow you whole, a straight nose, and a mouth that seemed just a bit large, a bit sensual. None of that had registered in Rourke's office. Now, confronted with the wide-eyed stares of his fellow detectives, Harry couldn't help but notice.

Most of the male detectives were overly friendly but respectful. They had been taught respect from the only other woman in the division, Diva Walsh, the sergeant in charge of assigning cases. Diva was a heavyset black woman, who could probably kick half the asses in the room, maybe more than half, and she easily kept most of the detectives in line. One of the few exceptions now followed Harry and Vicky back to their desks.

Nick Benevuto was a silver-haired lothario with an expanding waistline. To his fellow detectives he was known as Nicky the Pimp, owing to the fact that he had once worked vice and most of his snitches were still aging hookers. He also had a reputation as one mean son of a bitch just as young Rubio Martí had claimed earlier. Right now he was busy playing office Romeo. Vicky seemed to have his number from the start.

"So, Vicky, honey," Nick began, only to be cut short.

"Don't call me honey," Vicky said. She hardened the words with a cold smile; then added: "I have a gun, and I'm good with it."

Nick raised his hands defensively. "Hey, darlin', I was only—"

"Don't call me darlin' either."

"Okay, okay. No offense. Jesus, you Greek women are hard."

"You bet your bippy," Vicky said.

Nick drew a long breath, turned, and started back across the room. "You're gonna get along just great with the dead detective," he muttered.

When Vicky turned back to her desk Harry was already seated across from her, a smile playing at the corners of his mouth. His eyes told her it would be a nice smile if he ever let it grow.

"I guess Rourke will be talking to *you* soon," Harry said.

"About what?"

"About how you treat jackasses."

Vicky fought off her own smile. "So why did he call you the dead detective?" she asked, as she slid into her chair.

"I died once," Harry said. "It was a long time ago."

"Duty related?"

"No. I was only a kid."

"You wanna tell me about it?"

Harry gave her an indifferent stare. "No, I don't. In time you'll hear all about it from them." He inclined his head toward the room, indicating the other detectives. "It's a better story when they tell it."

Harry went back to his paperwork, sorting out reports for two cases that were now set for trial. Vicky watched him. She was more than a little curious about the man, about this "spooky" intuition he was supposed to have about killers. She had already dismissed Rourke's comment about victims talking to him as little more than cop shop nonsense and she wondered how it all tied into this dead detective business. But she was also smart enough to know that it was a subject she couldn't push. There was a sense of intensity about Harry Doyle that seemed to infuse everything he did, the way he moved and spoke; even the way he looked at you. She wasn't certain why, but she found it very appealing. Too much so, she told herself. And it didn't help that she liked the way he looked. He was tall and lean, just a bit over six feet, she guessed, with wavy brown hair, penetrating green eyes, and a strong jaw. He wasn't a pretty boy by any means. Ruggedly handsome would better describe him. But those strong features seemed to soften when that sense of playfulness came to his eyes and that small smile toyed with the corners of his mouth.

Vicky thought about that. She didn't want to get involved with Harry Doyle or anyone else. Her personal life was a shambles at the moment, and she didn't need to make it worse by falling for her partner.

"Doyle. Stanopolis."

It was Diva. Harry got up quickly and headed for her desk. Vicky followed.

"Whaddaya got?" Harry asked.

"We got a woman in the Brooker Creek Preserve, a very dead woman. Some old lady out on a bird watching jaunt found her and started screaming for the park rangers. They called it in and we sent two units. First car at the scene said the vic's throat's been sliced. Also said she's been posed and that it looked like a fresh kill."

"They seal off the area?" Harry asked.

"Deputy said he did," Diva answered. "Couple more cars were dispatched just to make sure it stayed that way. The preserve's got a lot of groups hiking the trails this time of year."

"You call the crime scene techs, or is that something we should do?" Vicky asked.

"Already did it," Diva said. "But thanks for asking. Most of the honchos around here would just assume Diva got it done for them, and then bitch and moan if for some reason the call didn't get made." She offered up a small laugh. "Hell, I got three kids at home who don't need their noses wiped as much as these clowns do."

"Not their fault," Vicky said. "They're men. They're all born with that 'Hey, baby, bring me a beer' gene."

This time Diva barked out a loud laugh. "You got *that* right, honey."

Harry cut the conversation short by spinning on his heels and heading for the stairs. Vicky hurried to catch up.

"Hey, you two be careful," Diva called after them. "Sounds like you might have a psycho on your hands."

"Slow down, the vic's not going anywhere," Vicky said.

"Yeah, but there's always the chance somebody else might get there ahead of us. I like to get to a crime scene when it's still fresh, before anybody screws it up," Harry said, taking the stairs two at a time. When they reached the parking lot he glanced back and grinned. "How come Diva gets to call you honey?" he asked over his shoulder.

"'Cause I want her to," Vicky said. "But don't let that give you any ideas."

"Never happen," Harry said. "I won't even ask you to bring me a beer. And I won't ask you to drive either," he added as he slid behind the wheel of their unmarked car.

Vicky got in, slipped on her sunglasses, and looked at him over the tops. "That's good, Harry. I don't want your feminist side to start running amok."

The Brooker Creek Preserve is 8,000 acres of raw Florida land, a mixture of sandy pine forest and cypress swamp that sits on the northern edge of Pinellas County in a densely populated and pricey residential community known as East Lake. A series of wetlands in neighboring Hillsborough County flow lazily across fifteen miles, constantly feeding the preserve, and only a three-building environmental education complex and two and a half miles of hiking trails mar a landscape that was once prime hunting grounds for Seminole Indians.

Harry pulled up to the preserve's open iron gates, stopping at a sign that listed the hours it was open to the public. He jotted them down in his notebook—*Wednesday, 9 a.m. to 8:30 p.m.; Thursdays through Sundays, 9 a.m. to 4 p.m. Closed Monday and Tuesday.* It was now five-thirty on a Wednesday afternoon. Harry studied the gate. It was electronic, run from a keypad so it would have to be opened each morning and closed each night by someone who either knew the code or had an override key like the ones police, fire, and rescue personnel carried. He turned to Vicky.

"We won't know until the autopsy, but if our victim was killed here, or dumped here right after the park opened, whoever was in charge of this gate may have seen our perp entering the preserve. We need to find out who that was."

Vicky stared into the forest that spread out from the gate. "Sure is a lot of cover for a dirty deed."

Harry started to laugh. "A dirty deed?"

"What's wrong with that?"

Harry shook his head. "What's next, 'Curses, foiled again'?"

"I'm saving that for when Nick Benevuto kicks me out of his bed," Vicky quipped.

"Nicky the pimp has never kicked anyone—or thing—out of his bed," Harry said.

"Well it's true then," Vicky snapped back. "God *is* good."

Harry put the car in gear and started down the mile-long macadam road that led to the Environmental Education Center. Two hundred yards in he pulled off to the right behind two sheriff's patrol cars that had been parked on each side of a partially overgrown hiking trail leading into the forest. A uniformed deputy stood guard at the head of the trail.

Harry left his coat on the front seat, walked to the rear of the car, and opened the trunk. He took out the small crime scene case he carried to all homicides, then removed a pair of rubber boots and slipped them on. He glanced at Vicky, who had come to the rear of the car and was watching him intently.

"You should get a pair of these boots, or something similar," he said. "We can have the size and sole prints on file with forensics. It'll save time eliminating your footprints at crime scenes. It'll also save you from replacing three or four pairs of ruined shoes every year."

Vicky grinned at him. "I'll do it." She glanced at his rubber boots. "But something a bit more stylish, I think."

Harry smirked. "Whatever," he said, as he turned and walked toward the deputy guarding the head of the trail, looking him up and down as he did.

The deputy was tall and lanky with a country boy's raw-boned strength, but behind a pair of intense blue eyes a good amount of intelligence looked back. Harry was certain they had never met before and made a mental note of the man's name tag, which read, *Morgan*.

"What's your first name, Morgan?" he asked as he came up beside him.

Morgan's eyes drifted to the detective's badge attached to Harry's belt. "Jim," he said.

Harry extended his hand. "Harry Doyle. I'm with homicide." He tilted his head toward Vicky. "This is my partner, Vicky Stanopolis. I understand you've got a body for us."

"Sure do," Morgan said. "Back up that trail about a quarter of a mile at the edge of a cypress swamp. It's a weird one for sure."

"How so?" Harry asked.

"Lady's all posed . . . sexually posed. And she's wearing a mask and all. Like one of those they wear at Mardi Gras."

Harry nodded and studied the ground. Fresh tire tracks ran off into the trail. "You guys drive in there?" he asked.

The deputy shook his head. "No way. I was the first one here and I saw the tracks right off. I asked the ranger who called us if he drove in, but he said he didn't. Said they never do unless they're running a work crew. He said they haven't worked on this particular trail since last spring. After I heard all that I made sure nobody else drove in."

They'd lucked out, Harry thought. Morgan was sharp, much more so than a good percentage of deputies.

"Okay," Harry said, "when the crime scene boys get here, tell them I want photographs and casts on those tracks. Tell them I want all four tires if they can get them. They'll probably have to do it on a curve in the trail, but they'll know that. Anybody else going in, you tell them to keep to the sides of the trail. And no smoking, no candy bars, no anything that'll screw up my crime scene. You got all that?"

"I got it."

Harry looked Morgan in the eye. "One more thing, Jim. You did a nice job. Thanks."

Harry and Vicky slipped on latex gloves and started in, each one us-ing a different side of the eight-foot-wide trail, which was little more than heat-hardened earth, covered in dry, matted grass. A heavy growth of pines rose on each side, obscuring much of what lay beyond . . .

The deputy called after them: "Be careful when you get to that cypress swamp. There's a nine-foot gator back there thinks it's his."

"Thanks again," Harry called back.

They walked in slowly, checking the trail for any discarded items that might have been left by the killer, finding only three scattered cigarette butts, a chewing gum wrapper, and a number of shoe impressions. Close to where the tire tracks ended they found an empty book of matches ad-vertising a topless bar in Tampa. Harry made a note of the name. All in all the items they found could have been dropped by anyone too lazy to stick them in a pocket to discard later. But every item had to be checked, so they took their time, placing small orange marking flags next to each one. This was only preliminary, an effort to save them time. The crime scene unit would do a far more thorough job; they would literally sweep the area around each flag that Harry had left and comb the entire area in much greater depth, carefully looking for hair, clothing fibers, anything that might be linked to the crime. Still, Harry gave the trail a reasonably thorough search. He didn't want to wait several hours for the CSI unit to give him an obvious clue.

It took them twenty minutes to reach the cypress swamp where the land and vegetation suddenly changed. There was a long, narrow pool at the swamp's center, dotted with water lilies, and it forced the hiking trail, which now turned into black, loamy earth, to veer to the left. A green heron strutted along the bank of the pond hunting frogs, its sharp dagger beak and snakelike neck poised to strike. Harry saw no sign of the gator he had been warned about. Thirty yards ahead, where the trail skirted the pond, he could see two uniformed deputies standing guard over something unseen. He motioned Vicky to his side of the trail, away from the edge of the pond.

"Don't wanna use me as gator bait, huh?" she said.

"I'll wait for gator season," Harry shot back.

"That's my new partner. Just a sweet, sensitive guy."

"Always," Harry said.

When they reached the deputies they could just make out one leg of the body. It extended out past a rotting cypress stump located ten feet off the trail.

The deputies were a Mutt and Jeff combination, one tall and slender, the other short and beefy. Harry introduced himself. Vicky did the same, as Harry studied the ground leading to the body. It was soft and spongy and there were footprints leading in and out. He counted four or five sets, some appeared to be the same size, making the exact number hard to determine on first glance. He turned back to the deputies.

"How many of you went in there?" he asked Jeff, who seemed to have the sharper eyes of the pair.

"Let's see," Jeff said, counting mentally. "We went in." He nodded toward the other deputy. "So did Morgan, the deputy you met coming in. And so did the park ranger. He was first. He went straight in after the bird watcher told him there was a body out here. Then he called us."

"What about the bird watcher?" Harry asked. "Do you know if she went in?"

"When Morgan questioned her, she told him she didn't. Just saw the leg stickin' out and went for the ranger. But she's still up at the preserve office with another deputy if you want to talk to her."

"The deputy at the office, did he go in?"

Both deputies shook their heads. "He came later—after us; after the crime scene was set up. He was sent to guard the witness; never got out here at all."

Harry nodded. "Okay, good work. Now, I'd like one of you to call the office and make sure our witness stays put. I'm also gonna need to get the shoe sizes of everyone who went in to the body, and later, when the crime scene techs gets here, I'm going to want casts and photographs of the soles of everyone's shoes. We'll have to eliminate all of you from any prints the perp might have left. Also, I need to know if anyone touched the body."

This time it was Mutt, shaking his head. "None of *us*," he said. "Morgan was the first one here and he made sure no one did. The park ranger said he felt her wrist for a pulse. I don't know why he bothered. Her throat's cut back almost to her spine. Same as O.J.'s wife." Mutt shrugged, suddenly embarrassed by the comparison he had just made; then added: "At least that's what they said at Simpson's trial."

Vicky looked away and rolled her eyes. "Morgan told us she's wearing a mask. Did anybody touch *it*?" she asked, turning back to the two deputies.

"Not after we got here," Jeff said, taking over again. "Morgan got here first and made sure nobody touched anything. I can't swear about the ranger, but he *says* he only touched her wrist."

"Okay," Harry said. "We're going in to check the body, but we'll circle wide to avoid adding our footprints to the mix."

"Watch where you step," Jeff warned. "There's a few cottonmouths around these swamps."

Vicky wrinkled up her nose and gave a small shudder. "Snakes, alligators, and a dead woman in a Mardi Gras mask—I'm really starting to love this case."

Harry studied her for several moments. The toughness was well established behind her eyes, and that charnel house humor was a definite plus, a necessary survival tool for a cop working homicide. Yeah, he thought, she'll do just fine. He gave her an amused smile. "Tomorrow we get vampires," he said.

"I've got to wait until tomorrow?"

"They only show themselves on Thursdays."

"What about werewolves?" Vicky said.

"Never saw one in Florida—too hot for all that fur."

"Damn. And I could've sworn I'd dated a few."

They moved toward the body in a wide circle, looking not only for the snakes the deputy had warned of, but also for any evidence the killer might have tossed out into the thick undergrowth from the immediate crime scene. The walk in proved uneventful, but a more thorough, wider search would be made later. Right now they needed to learn all they could from the body.

The body lay on its back on a rich, dark bed of rotting vegetation. The woman had been clothed in a straight black dress that would have stopped just above the knees had someone not used a knife to slice open the entire front. Black thong underwear was the lone undergarment and it had been pulled aside exposing a neatly trimmed blond pubis, the same shade as the woman's hair. Her breasts were also exposed and they were full and round and pointed rigidly up.

"Implants," Harry observed.

"You betcha," Vicky said. "Even when all the muscles go soft and slack, these boobs will not sag or lose their shape. Plastic surgeons should use that line in their advertising."

"I thought they already did," Harry said.

The flip words didn't carry to their eyes. Each pair remained grim and focused. It was the charnel house humor again, two detectives forced to witness daily human carnage, trying to maintain their personal sanity.

Harry took a Polaroid camera from his crime scene case and took two photos of the body in situ. He took another of the woman's feet, which were shoeless and relatively clean except for a dusting of beach sand, indicating both that she had been carried into the swamp and had recently visited a beach. Then he took a minute to study the area around them. It seemed peaceful and threatening at the same time, the way only a primal forest can, and except for the intrusion of the body of a young, modernly dressed woman he might have been standing in a place that had remained unchanged for hundreds of years. He let his eyes roam. Spread out before him were several large cypress stumps, like the one that stood next to the body, each one rotting with age; each probably there since the turn of the last century when loggers scoured Florida lands searching out and cutting all the mature cypress they could find. To the left were several Southern live oaks, their boughs heavy with Spanish moss. Between the oaks were small groupings of young pond cypress, many with butterfly orchids and resurrection ferns attached to their trunks. Larger patches of swamp fern grew in dense clusters across the black, spongy ground, their toothed edges providing protective shelter for small animals, and as Harry watched a cotton rat scurried from one patch to another, scaring up a pair of common yellowthroat, the small birds darting off in search of safer cover. In the distance he could hear the gooselike grunts of tree frogs and the high-pitched chirping of cicadas, and up in the trees he could see several parula warblers and white-eyed vireos flying from tree to tree.

He felt a hand on his arm and turned back. Vicky was staring at him strangely.

"You lost in thought, or just enjoying a Discovery Channel moment?" she asked.

Harry ignored the question and asked one of his own. "Why bring her here? We can be reasonably sure the killer drove a car in, at least as far as the swamp. But why risk it? Why risk being seen? He could have been spotted by a park ranger driving on a trail, or by any number of hikers. Why risk any of it when there are so many places to dump a body? The beaches, at night; all the thick pine forests in the middle of the state. He obviously didn't kill her here. He brought her body here and posed it in this setting. Why? Why was that part of the overall plan, or does this place have some special significance?"

Vicky looked back at the body and the area around it. It was as the deputy had said. The woman's throat was cut so deeply that the head was nearly severed from the body. It told her that the killer was either very powerful or very angry to use that degree of cutting force. But there was no blood splatter on the cypress trunk or the cluster of swamp ferns that grew beside it. Somewhere there was a large pool of blood that had pumped from her body when the carotid arteries had been severed, and had kept on pumping until her heart stopped beating. When they found that pool of blood—*if* they found that pool of blood—they would have the real crime scene. Harry's voice brought her back.

"You're the sex crimes expert. You see any indication she was raped?"

Vicky looked at the body more closely. "I see what looks like a small amount of dried semen in her pubic hair. But I don't see any signs of violence. There's no bruising or cuts or scratches." She pointed to the woman's right hand. "She's got two broken fingernails, but that could have happened while she was being killed. I'm just not seeing what's usually there when somebody's raped. Maybe the autopsy will tell us more."

Harry nodded. He was squatting next to the body, studying the Mardi Gras mask that covered the woman's face. He took out the Polaroid again and took two more photos. Vicky squatted on the other side, joining him. The mask was a deep iridescent purple, with highlights of silver. There were cat's ears at the top and whiskers sprouting from the cheeks and small, dark red plumes rising from high on the forehead. Clouded green eyes looked out blindly through the holes in the mask, giving the only hint of the face that lay beneath. The mask was not held in place by any band. It had simply been placed on the face, so Harry carefully lifted it, using one finger of each hand, and laid it on the woman's chest.

When the woman's face was exposed an audible gasp escaped Vicky's throat and Harry's head snapped back. They knew this woman. Like most of the people in the United States they had seen her picture countless times in newspapers and magazines and television screens, although now the ex-quisitely beautiful face had been altered. A single word had been carved in her forehead with a very sharp knife—the word *EVIL*. The mutilation jolted Harry, his mind immediately flashing to the small silver crosses his mother had placed on his and Jimmy's foreheads; the way she had covered their eyes with towels.

"It's really her," Vicky said, bringing Harry back to the present. There was no trace of a question in her voice.

"Yeah, it's her." Harry felt his fists tighten into balls.

Vicky rose slowly, shaking her head. "Holy shit, it is gonna be a circus out here. We better call the captain. If this gets out we're gonna have me-dia moving through here like Sherman through Georgia."

"Back out the same way you came in," Harry said. "Try to step in your own footprints where you can."

Vicky started to move carefully away. Harry stood there for a moment, staring down at the body of Darlene Beckett. He picked up the camera and took two more photos with the mask removed. Even then he didn't move. He could almost feel the killer standing next to him, the last person to see her without the mask. He continued to stare at the body, bringing back the last image he had of the woman. She was standing before the TV cam-eras, giving them that slightly sly, very self-absorbed little smile she had displayed so often when appearing in court. Slowly, almost imperceptively, Harry nodded his head. Evil, he thought. Yes, you were definitely that. But somebody finally got to you. Somebody finally presented the bill and told you it was time to pay. He continued to stare at the woman's face, uncon-trolled words racing through his mind. The word *religion* kept returning, but he couldn't tell if it came from Darlene Beckett or memories of his mother. He drew a long, steady breath as he took in the look of disbelief on her face—a disbelief that had begun to change into abject terror as the life rushed from her body. Then it all stopped—that mix of disbelief and terror frozen on her face as her life ended. He stared into her eyes. They had begun to cloud, but it was still there as well, that same mixture. Who was it you saw and why did it surprise you so? He drew another deep breath. It was all there in her eyes, but it was fading fast. He crouched down, still staring into her eyes, thinking about what the woman had done. The word *evil* played over and over in his mind and the image of a cross began to form. Was that it? he wondered. He continued to stare into her eyes. "Talk to me, Darlene," he whispered. "It's alright. You belong to me now." He closed his eyes and drew a long breath. Now it's my job to find out who put that disbelief and that fear in your eyes. And I'll find him. I promise you I'll find him. His jaw tightened and he opened his eyes and once again stared at her beautiful face. And when I find him, Darlene, maybe I'll give the son of a bitch a medal.

The figure watched the trail that the two detectives entered. He stood in the shadows, his back to a line of trees, and he knew he was invisible, or as close to invisible as a person could be. Just one of many shadows in the preserve, blending into his surroundings like he had planned, into the foliage, the earth itself; completely unnoticed by anyone who could pose a threat. It was the way it had to be. He had become a lone branch on the spreading boughs of a large oak, a part of the whole, indistinguishable from all the rest. There for anyone to see and yet invisible. He fought off a smile. They would never find him unless he made a mistake, and he was much too smart to let that happen.

By now the detectives would have reached her body. And they would know. They would *know* who it was; know who had been made to answer for her sins. The small smile began to return but was quickly forced away. The dead woman was not the only one who had to wear a mask. Masks were necessary right now, very necessary. Another smile began to form but it, too, was driven away. Patience was also necessary. Just wait and watch.

That is all you can do now. Wait, watch, and take pleasure in the fruits of your labor. But don't let anyone see your pleasure. And soon you will be able to do even more.

CHAPTER TWO

Darlene Beckett was tall, statuesque, blond, and beautiful. She was a former bathing suit model, whose picture had appeared in various magazines, primarily those devoted to motorcycles and automobiles. At twenty-four she left modeling, married, and entered the teaching profession. Her first job was teaching health at a Tampa middle school. Two months into her new career she took a fourteen-year-old student home with her and had sex with him. The sexual encounters continued for several months. They took place in the home she shared with her husband of six months, in her school classroom, and in the backseat of her car. Like the good health teacher she was, she always provided the boy with condoms. Her undoing came when she performed repeated acts of sexual intercourse with the boy as his fifteen-year-old cousin drove her car along county roads and watched through the rearview mirror. The fifteen-year-old was later overheard telling a friend how he had watched this beautiful teacher "screw the shit" out of his cousin. And all the time she did it, he told his friend, "she kept watching me watch her, and she kept smiling at me."

Darlene was subsequently arrested and after a year of legal haggling, the state's attorney agreed to a modest plea bargain. To save the boy from testifying, prosecutors allowed Darlene to plead guilty to sexual assault of a minor and accept the following penalty: registration as a sex offender, surrender of her teaching certificate for life, the inability to live within 1,000 feet of a church, school, or playground, and three years of house arrest, which required her to wear an ankle monitor and to be inside her home by ten o'clock each evening.

Harry thought about the woman as he stared out into the pond at the side of the hiking trail. He had just completed a cell phone call to his captain, Pete Rourke, and had been told not to proceed with his investigation until he got further instructions. That meant Rourke was calling the chief of detectives, which meant that the crime scene would soon be overrun with brass. Harry wasn't sure which he liked less, fighting off the media or fighting off the brass. He'd probably end up with both. The chance of the story leaking from a commander's office was even greater than it leaking from the field.

"What are you thinking about?" Vicky asked.

"That nine-foot gator," Harry said. "I finally spotted it."

"Where is it?"

Harry elevated his chin toward the other side of the pond. "It's in that patch of duckweed just opposite us."

Vicky stared at the duckweed, a floating emerald-green plant so tightly formed that it makes the water it covers look like solid ground. Tourists have been known to step on it unawares and come up sputtering for air and covered in a green film. In the center of the weed bank she could just make out the gator. "He is a big boy," she said. "I'm surprised he didn't sniff out our corpse."

"He would have by tonight," Harry said. "And if he didn't the vultures would have for sure."

Vicky inclined her head toward the gator. "What do we do if he decides to come across the pond?"

"We shoot him." Harry took in the slightly shocked look on her face and smiled. "Back when I was on patrol, I was sent out to back up a deputy who was trying to keep a four-footer from crossing a highway. Ten minutes later we were calling for backup again. There were five of us before it was all over, four deputies and an animal control officer. This little four-footer chewed up the pants leg of one deputy and beat the hell out of the rest of us with its tail. The animal officer finally got a capture wire around its jaws, but it still took all of us twenty minutes to wrestle it back into the retention pond it had crawled out of. And that pond was only fifty feet away."

Vicky nodded her head. "I knew they were nasty, but alligator wrestling . . . I missed that little thrill during my time on the street." She gave him an impish smile. "But you just got my vote, Harry Doyle. That nine-footer comes over here, we shoot it."

The brass arrived twenty minutes later. Pete Rourke led them in, keeping everybody to the side of the trail. You'd think they'd know that without being carefully directed, Harry thought. But he knew this wasn't the case. He had endured enough compromised crime scenes at the hands, and feet, of senior commanders to know better. Above squad commander, which was Rourke's level, promotions were based purely on politics—who had most ingratiated himself in Florida's political quagmire. And the sheriff's department offered some of the biggest political plums to be had. At the county level the department commanded more jobs, more authority, and a bigger share of the budget than any other. That made the elected office of sheriff one of power personified. And promotions to the upper levels of his department were reserved for those who had served the sheriff politically and could be considered trusted allies. It was mostly a question of earned patronage rather than competence, although occasionally you found someone who was a clever politician and who also knew the job. But it was rare. In Harry's view, the three men who Rourke now led into the crime scene did not fall into that rarified category.

Marching along directly behind Rourke was Kyle Rothman, the chief of department, a man who had jumped to that post from a lieutenancy in patrol after working tirelessly for the election of Dave Oberoff, the incumbent sheriff. Oberoff, himself, had never seen the inside of a patrol car. Prior to taking control of the county's police force, he had headed one of the state's largest real estate firms—a multimillion-dollar company that was now operated by his wife. Rothman supposedly ran the department for him. In reality, Rothman, a tall, slender, hatchet-faced fifty-year-old with fast receding black hair, contented himself with issuing the sheriff's directives and planning press conferences that would make his boss seem like an "in charge" police executive, while assuming that the real cops under him would keep the department functioning. And that's what Harry assumed he was doing here now—evaluating the crime scene for press potential—that and amusing himself by playing detective, a rank he had never achieved.

Following directly behind the chief was his right-hand man, Rudy Morse, whose main job was to drive the chief's car and open his doors. Morse was in his late thirties, a weightlifter gone to seed, with a square head shaved in a high and tight military cut, who despite a questionable I.Q. had been hired into the newly created post of assistant to the chief. He did have one essential qualification: he was the sheriff's nephew.

Last in line was Jim Mabrey, a fifty-five-year-old former assistant editor for the *Tampa Tribune*, and now the department's public information officer. Mabrey would probably have been competent at his job if he was allowed to do it unimpeded. But that was never the case where the press was concerned. Especially in a politically charged situation, where one ranking officer or another always thought they knew how to best handle the media. Mabrey was tall and paunchy, with thick salt-and-pepper hair, a large nose, and heavy bags under his eyes, all of which made him look a bit like a bassett hound. He considered his job part of his retirement, and looked at it with a world-weary eye. If the higher-ups didn't want him to do the job the right way, he would do it the way they wanted and smile all the way to the bank.

"Okay," Rourke began, as the quartet came to a halt in front of Harry and Vicky, "you're in charge of the crime scene, Harry. Tell us where we can and can't go."

Harry gave Rourke a look that asked if he really wanted an honest reply. Rourke gave him a stern look of warning in return.

"I really don't want anyone to go any further than this," Harry began. "The more people allowed in, the greater the chance of compromising the scene." He inclined his head toward Vicky. "My partner and I can fill you gentlemen in and show you the Polaroids we took of the body."

Rourke let out a heavy sigh, knowing what was coming.

Rothman glared at Harry, bristling at the rebuke. "I'm going in and you're taking me," he snapped.

"You're the chief," Harry said.

"That's right, I am," Rothman replied.

"Then why don't you follow me and step exactly where I step," Harry said as he turned and started back into the swamp.

That's my partner, Vicky thought, as she fought back a smile. Mr. Personality.

Rothman uttered a string of expletives. Harry assumed that one of the chief's highly polished, dress cordovans had slipped into a soft spot in the swamp's surface. His back was to the chief, so it was safe to smile without risking the man's ire, but Harry knew he would have done it even if they were face-to-face. He decided to find another soft spot on the way out, one that would take the chief down to his ankle.

When they reached the body Harry stopped four feet away and extended an arm to keep the chief from stepping any closer. Then he dropped his arm and pointed to the mask that rested on the victim's chest.

"The mask was on her face when we got here," Harry said. "So I think it's safe to assume that we're the only people, aside from the killer, who know her identity. I'm hoping we can keep it that way a bit longer."

The chief let out a grunt. "That won't be easy, detective. The media turned this woman into a national celebrity over the past year. We try to hide who it is, they'll have our livers for lunch."

"I just need the department to hold it back until we clear the crime scene," Harry said. "We stand to lose a lot of evidence if an army of reporters and photographers come marching through here or start hovering overhead in helicopters."

The chief's eyes hadn't left the victim's body, and now seemed concentrated on the thong underwear that had been pulled aside, exposing Darlene Beckett's trimmed pubis. "You guys pull that underwear away like that?" he asked.

"No, sir, that's the way we found her," Harry said. "About keeping her identity quiet . . ." he started again.

"You think she was raped?" the chief asked, ignoring him.

"We can't be sure until the M.E. conducts an examination. I think she had sex recently, but I don't see any indication it was rape. About her identity . . ."

The chief let out another grunt. "We can seal off the trail and keep the press out," he snapped. "I can get as many men in here as you need to get it done."

"Chief, there are 8,000 acres in this preserve, and as many ways in. We can't seal off the whole thing. And we can't stop helicopters from flying over and telling reporters on the ground where we are. These guys are resourceful as hell when they smell something big. The only way to keep them out is by not telling them until we're ready."

Rothman glared at him, his voice turning to ice. "You tell Captain Rourke how many men you need. He'll tell me, and I'll send them. That's what I want from you, detective. End of subject."

Harry gritted his teeth but kept silent. Nothing he could say to this man would make any difference. Behind him he could hear Vicky briefing the others about the crime scene. She might as well do it on a bullhorn, he thought.

"I've seen enough," Rothman said. "I'm ready to go back."

Harry stepped past him and began the long circle around to the hiking trail. "Try to step in the same footprints you left coming in," he said over his shoulder.

Rothman ignored him. Harry tightened his jaw and looked for another soft spot that would swallow Rothman's shoes.

Harry, Vicky, and Pete Rourke stood next to the pond and watched the two deputies who had been guarding the body lead the brass out.

"Lovely day for a walk in the woods," Vicky said.

"Don't you start on me too," Rourke warned. "We have what we have, and we deal with it."

"Yes, sir," Vicky said.

Rourke turned to Harry. "Okay, Doyle, let's get it over with. Say what you have to say."

Harry looked at him, his face expressionless. "I'd like to keep all information about the mask and the mutilation away from the media as long as possible."

Rourke drew a long breath, but it was clear his frustration was not directed at them. He kept his gaze on Harry. "I'll do what I can, and I'll do it as forcefully as I can." He waited for Harry to respond and when he didn't, continued: "While you were in there with the chief we got a call from the deputy at the head of the trail. The crime scene unit is here. They're working their way back right now. When I get to my car I'll call the M.E. and tell him to stop screwing around and get his ass out here; I want that broad's body out of here as fast as possible. I'll also tell him to keep his mouth shut. The damn woman's as much trouble dead as she was alive." He gave each of them a sharp look. "Now get to work and process the goddamn scene."

Harry sent Vicky to interview the woman who had found the body and the park ranger who was the first officer on the scene. Then he took his crime scene case and went back in to the body. Squatting beside Darlene Beckett he studied the wound in her throat. Because of the depth and the angle of the cut he decided she had been attacked from behind, that the killer had pulled back her head and drawn the blade across her throat. The cut also appeared to have gone from right to left, indicating the killer had used his left hand. It could also mean that fingerprints from the killer's right hand might be found on the woman's face.

Next he studied each of the woman's hands. There was no clear indication of anything beneath the nails, but as they'd noticed earlier, two nails on the right hand were broken. Clearly Darlene Beckett had tried to fight off her killer. A more detailed examination of what might still be lodged beneath her nails could prove valuable, but that was the medical examiner's job. Harry took two paper bags out of his crime scene case and bagged each hand, making sure nothing that was still under the nails would be lost when the body was transported to the morgue. In the process he noted that rigor mortis had fully set in. Right now he needed to know an approximate time of death, and he knew rigor was the least likely way to get it. He tried a simpler, more accurate test and inserted a hand into Darlene Beckett's underarm. It was cold and clammy to the touch, telling him she had died eighteen to twenty-four hours ago. That time period would be narrowed during the autopsy, when the M.E. examined the contents of the gastrointestinal tract. He also checked for postmortem lividity and found that Darlene Beckett had probably been transported on her back after being killed.

Next he moved on to check the pubic area for any stains of a stiff, starchy texture indicating dried semen. There was some in the blond pubic hair, as Vicky had noted earlier, and some on the inner thigh. He jotted those locations in his notebook. At the morgue the M.E. would use ultraviolet light to do a more extensive check. He would also take vaginal, anal, and oral swabs to collect any semen still in the body, and send it off for DNA testing. Although in and of itself, it would not prove murder, it would place a suspect in intimate contact with the victim.

Harry turned to the sound of his name and saw Mort Janlow, an assistant county medical examiner, standing on the trail next to the pond. Janlow, a short, pudgy, balding man closing in on fifty, asked how Harry wanted him to enter the scene.

"I'll come and get you," Harry called back.

Janlow glanced nervously over his shoulder. "Never mind that," he shouted back. "Just tell me. There's a goddamn alligator in this pond, looking at me like I'm his lunch."

Harry pointed to the area he had used with the chief, making a circular gesture with his arm. "You'll see a set of tracks over there. They're ours. Try to follow them in."

When the M.E. arrived a few minutes later, he set his own case next to Harry's and squatted beside the body.

"Christ, it is her," he said. He stared at the mutilation of her forehead. "*Evil.*" Janlow nodded his head, but Harry couldn't tell if it was in agreement with the sentiment, or just an acknowledgment of the killer's opinion. "We'll fingerprint her at the morgue to make sure it's her. But I sure as hell don't have any doubts. If I remember correctly her ex-husband lives in Clearwater and her parents are up in Port Richey. We'll have to get one of them for a positive." He glanced up at Harry, his round, cherubic, normally smiling face now filled with concern. "Deep down I was hoping you guys were wrong." He looked back at the body and shook his head. "This circus is going to be a three-ring Lollapalooza, my lad. I hope you know that."

"It's why we wanted you here as soon as possible," Harry said. "One other thing. I'd like to keep the mask and the mutilation under wraps."

"I know. I know. I already listened to Rourke snap and growl about all of it," Janlow said. "But I'm here, and understand the situation, and I know we can't afford to screw this one up. So don't rush me. Just tell me what you already found."

At eight o'clock the body of Darlene Beckett was being carried down the hiking trail on its way to the morgue wagon, and crime scene techs were in the last stages of their investigation. The sheriff, under arrangements made by Chief Kyle Rothman and Jim Mabrey, the public information officer, had held a press conference at seven to insure getting plenty of face time on the eleven o'clock news. The first news helicopter appeared over the crime scene thirty minutes later, creating a downdraft that dislodged any remaining evidence and diminishing its value in any future prosecution.

Harry walked down the trail, a look of resigned disgust on his face. He let out a long breath and willed himself to get past the self-serving stupidity that seemed to emerge in every major investigation. You just work past it, he told himself. And you hope for the best. You've done it before; you'll do it again now.

When he reached the bottom of the trail he found Jim Morgan, the deputy he had met when he arrived, still guarding the way in. He had been joined by three others.

"Still at it, I see," Harry said. "Where are the reporters?"

"They're being held at the main gate." Morgan grinned. "We've had a dozen or so try to sneak in through the brush, but it's so thick we could hear 'em coming a hundred yards off. Then one of them stepped on a rattler and we ended up calling in the rescue squad. Didn't stop the others from trying, though."

"How's the snake?" Harry asked.

Morgan laughed. "Probably died."

Harry made his way to the car and headed up to the education center to reconnect with Vicky. He found her in an office with the elderly bird watcher who had discovered the body and the park ranger who had been first on the scene. He introduced himself, thanked them for their help, and then took Vicky out into the hall.

"Anything worthwhile?" he asked.

"I interviewed everybody who was working here today and no one remembers seeing anything unusual," Vicky began. "The woman who found the body isn't much help either. All she can remember is seeing the leg sticking out from behind the cypress stump. She may remember something later when she calms down, though right now she's so shaken she can hardly remember her own name. But the park ranger remembered something interesting."

"How so?"

"Three or four days ago he noticed that somebody else had driven into the same area, and went all the way back to where the body was found. It's rained a lot since then, so those tracks are probably gone. But he said it's really unusual to have somebody drive in on one of the trails. There are signs letting people know they are off limits to vehicles, and getting caught on one gets you a citation. It's also pretty easy to go too far and get stuck. He checked it out when he saw those earlier tracks, but whoever had driven in there had already left."

"So it could have been the perp scouting the area," Harry said.

"That's what I'm thinking."

Harry paused to consider what Vicky had said. "We need a list of everyone who's worked here in the past year," he said at length. "Paid employees, volunteers, everybody. It could have been somebody who knew the patrol routine, knew when he could drive in with the least chance of being seen."

"And then did a test run to be sure," Vicky said.

Harry nodded, then paused again. "Damn, I wish we had that second set of tracks to compare to the ones there now."

"It would be nice," Vicky said.

"We better tell the CSI techs to look for old tracks, just in case there are traces still there," Harry said. "Even a partial would help. Then we could be reasonably sure our perp was here earlier getting the lay of the land. And that would increase the chances that somebody saw him."

"We can stop and talk to them on the way out of here," Vicky said. "Speaking of which, where *do* we go from here? Darlene's home?"

"You got it. We search her place, and we talk to her neighbors; start putting together a list of her friends, relatives, lovers, anybody we can find out about. Then I want to check out that empty book of matches we found on the trail."

"You mean the bar in Tampa?"

Harry nodded.

"The *topless* bar in Tampa?"

Harry gave a small shrug and fought to hold a deadpan expression. "Sorry, but a good detective has to go where the evidence leads him."

"Yeah," Vicky said, her voice turning mildly sarcastic. "And sometimes it's even fun." She gave him a long look. "This time it will be more fun for you than for me."

CHAPTER THREE

Harry knew from newspaper accounts of her trial that Darlene Beckett lived in Tampa, but since no ID was found on her body he called in and asked for a computer check of the sex offender's registry to get a current home address. A computer technician radioed back five minutes later, and as the information came through the radio's speaker, Vicky noticed Harry's hands visibly tighten on the steering wheel. She resisted her natural curiosity and just stored the information away.

The place that Darlene Beckett had called home turned out to be a slightly rundown garden apartment complex in northern Tampa, a mixed neighborhood both racially and economically with a smattering of college students thrown in from the nearby University of South Florida.

The apartment was a half hour drive from the Brooker Creek Preserve and throughout the trip Harry hadn't spoken a word. Again, Vicky said nothing. She simply concentrated on the passing scenery.

"Darlene wasn't exactly living high, was she?" Vicky observed as they pulled up in front of the address listed on the registry. It was an end unit in a two-story apartment building, one of four built in a square surrounding a central green. Each apartment had its own entrance, driveway, and garage, making them seem more like town houses. The original intention was a quaint village effect, but the buildings' white painted bricks were now flaking badly, and the grass front yards of several units had patches of heat-hardened earth showing through. Darlene's was simply overgrown and dotted with weeds.

They tried the front and rear doors, found them locked, and located the building super, a short Latino about thirty years old with a ragged goatee and cynical eyes. He answered their questions, telling them the little he knew about Darlene. When told she was dead he simply shrugged, and asked when her apartment could be shown to prospective tenants.

"Nobody goes in until the crime scene tape is taken down," Harry said, nodding to the roll of yellow tape Vicky carried.

The super, who had given his name as Juan Vasquez, sneered at the answer. "Owner's gonna want it rented. Gonna be all over my ass about it."

"Anybody goes in before the tape comes down they get busted," Vicky said. "You tell the owner that goes for him too. In fact, you tell him he sees the tape's down he better call us anyway. Make sure it was us who took it down."

The warning produced another sneer. "Doan know why anybody gives a shit. Broad was nothin'. Jus' a fuckin' short eyes."

Harry noted the prison term for a child molester and looked at the man more closely. Detecting something at the bottom edge of his T-shirt sleeve, he reached out and raised it, exposing a crude prison tattoo of a dagger piercing a heart. "Where'd you do your bit?" Harry asked.

Juan stared up at him. He was short and stocky with a swarthy complexion and dark brown eyes. His mouth twisted into a sneer that held a lifetime of hard-earned cynicism. He looked away and shook his head.

"Up north. New York." He shook his head again. "So now I'm a fuckin' suspect."

Vicky took a step forward. "Hey, Juan, it's like they say on TV. Everybody's a suspect." She gave him an innocent smile, and then let her eyes slowly harden. "So fish out your driver's license."

Vicky copied his name, address, and date of birth, then asked for his Social Security number and added that to her notebook. It would all be used later for a computer check at the National Crime Information Center.

Finished, she gave him another smile. "Now open the damn door."

Juan took out a massive ring of keys, found the one to Darlene's front door, and opened it.

"You can go back to your apartment," Harry told the super. "When we're finished somebody will come and get you, so you can lock up."

"How long?" Juan asked.

"It'll be a couple of hours."

Harry watched the man shuffle away, jotted his name in his own notebook with the words *New York* beside it, then got on his cell and called the CSI team.

"They still at the preserve?" Vicky asked when he had finished.

"They're just loading up. Be here in half an hour."

Darlene Beckett's apartment was immaculate. Not a thing out of place; not a dirty dish in the sink. Even the bath off the master bedroom was scrubbed clean. Except for the full closets it looked like a model apartment; as if no one really lived there. Harry and Vicky donned latex gloves and cloth shoe coverings like those worn in hospital operating rooms and moved slowly through the apartment. They found the ankle monitor on the first pass through her bedroom.

"Somebody had to help her get that off," Vicky said. "And that somebody is going to have some heavy questions to answer."

They continued with the walk through.

"You think Darlene was this much of a neat freak?" Harry asked when they had been in every room.

"If she was, she was like no single woman I ever met." Vicky paused and thought about what she'd said. "Actually, she *was* like no single woman I ever met." She turned to Harry. "You think the perp came in here and cleaned up? Like maybe he'd been here before and wanted to make sure there was nothing for us to find?"

"There's always something," Harry said.

"Yeah, but maybe the perp doesn't know that."

They spent an hour looking through Darlene Beckett's personal effects—clothing, bills, letters, books and magazines, makeup, food supplies, and prescription drugs—drawing together a picture of what the woman had been like, her personal needs and tastes.

Vicky concentrated on Darlene's bedroom. Like the rest of the apartment the closets and dressers were neat and carefully arranged. Even so, they were close to overflowing. The woman had owned twice the amount of clothes and shoes as Vicky herself.

In the top drawer of a small bedside table Vicky found a collection of sex toys and a plain white envelope that held what appeared to be five Viagra tablets. She pointed them out to Harry.

"No prescription bottle," she noted. "Probably bought on the street, either by her boyfriend or maybe she bought them herself. There's a regular black market on stolen E.D. pills."

"A boyfriend's not gonna leave them here, unless he's a pretty regular boyfriend," Harry said. "According to Juan there were plenty of guys, but nobody special."

"So you think *she* bought them?"

"Just a guess. Maybe she wanted to make sure her lovers could handle seconds or thirds."

Vicky gave him a wide-eyed, innocent look. "Guys can do that?"

"You're a regular comic."

"I try," Vicky said, turning away to hide an impish grin that had broken through.

"There's something even more interesting in the kitchen," Harry said, causing her to turn back.

"What's that?"

"Come and see."

Vicky followed him into the small, galley-style kitchen.

Harry opened a drawer next to a battered gas range. Inside Vicky saw a collection of red paper matchbooks, each identical to the one they had found on the Brooker Creek hiking trail, each bearing the name *The Peek-a-Boo Lounge*.

"Looks like Darlene had a favorite bar," Vicky said.

"Looks like," Harry agreed.

Vicky studied the floor, then raised her eyes to Harry. "I told you I never met a single woman like her. You can put a big star next to that line. I guess we better check that place out tonight. And bring some pictures of her with us."

The CSI team arrived just as Harry and Vicky finished their search and were preparing to hit the streets to interview neighbors. Martin LeBaron, the deputy sergeant who headed up the unit, collected Harry and Vicky's shoe coverings and bagged them so they could be processed for any trace evidence they had picked up.

"So tell me what you found," LeBaron said.

Reading from his case notebook, Harry gave him a detailed list.

"Matches from a tits-and-ass bar, huh," LeBaron said. "I've driven by that joint. It's the pits. That broad, she was a piece of work, wasn't she?"

Harry ignored the comment and reminded LeBaron that he needed a complete workup on the apartment as quickly as possible.

"I know, I know," LeBaron said. "I already got that *be thorough, be fast* crap from your captain, as well as some clown in the chief's office." LeBaron was tall and slender and somewhere in his forties, with unruly black hair, a large nose, and eyes that seemed perpetually tired. "You guys seem to think we'll do a half-assed job if you don't stay on top of us. I promise you that won't happen."

"It's a big case," Harry said.

LeBaron grinned at him. "Harry, all your cases are big cases, and every time you have one you tell me the same thing." He looked at Vicky. "You his new partner?"

"I am," Vicky said.

"God help you." LeBaron laughed and waved a hand at them. "So go canvass the neighborhood and let me do my work."

Like Juan, the building super, most of the neighbors seemed unmoved by news of Darlene's death. One woman even expressed relief that she was "finally out of the neighborhood," and several others said they had kept a close eye on who visited Darlene's apartment. According to the neighbors there had been a steady stream of men, but no one visitor who seemed to come more than the others. There was also an older man and woman, who neighbors had assumed were Darlene's parents. Several emphasized that none of the visitors had been children, with one woman flatly stating that she would have called the police "if anyone under eighteen had gotten within ten feet of her front door."

At an apartment directly across the small green from Darlene's unit, a man in his mid- to late-seventies confessed to keeping an even closer eye on his notorious neighbor.

"I watched her good," he explained with a clear element of pride in his voice. His name was Joshua Brown and he was short and slender, almost frail, with a white beard masking his chocolate-colored face. He was the kind of witness that Harry both loved and hated—someone with enough time on his hands to watch what was going on very closely, but who also might not live long enough to testify at a trial.

Brown grinned and nodded his head as he spoke. "Whenever she had a visitor I took my dog Junie for a walk," he explained. "So's I'd get a better idea of what was goin' on."

Harry looked past the man and saw an ancient tan mongrel sleeping on the floor next to a battered leather recliner. The dog had not stirred when they rang the doorbell, or even opened its eyes while he and Vicky interviewed the man. Harry smiled to himself, thinking how the old man must have dragged the dog out the front door every time he felt the need to spy on Darlene Beckett.

"You think you could identify the men who visited Ms. Beckett?" Harry asked.

"Kin do better than that," Brown said. "I kin give you a list of the license plates on their cars, and the dates I saw them parked in her driveway."

Harry was seldom shocked by what came out of a neighborhood canvass, but this time he was. "Why did you keep a list like that?" he asked.

"Figured somebody might need it if they turned out to be a bunch of perverts like she was," Brown said.

When the door closed, he turned to Vicky and shrugged. "That old man just saved us a day or two of work."

Vicky nodded absently, and then shook her head.

"What?" Harry asked.

"I just realized what a fishbowl that woman was living in." She watched Harry's eyes harden.

"Don't waste your time feeling sorry for her," he said. "If she was living in a fishbowl, it was one she made for herself."

Harry went back to their car with the list of tag numbers and dates that Joshua Brown had given him and called in the plates. Since Darlene's garage was empty he also asked for information on any vehicle registered to a Darlene Beckett at the north Tampa address. A short time later he had a description and plate number for a green 2004 Ford Taurus registered to Darlene Beckett, along with the names, addresses, and dates of birth of the owners of the vehicles on Joshua Brown's carefully compiled list. He then placed a second call and ordered a check of wants and warrants on each of those persons, as well as a rundown on any criminal histories. He asked for the same for the building super. With a little luck—meaning the state computers wouldn't go down—they should have all the information he had requested by the end of their shift.

"Where to now?" Vicky asked. "The strip club?"

"First we check the street for Darlene's Taurus, then the strip club," Harry said.

Vicky paused a beat. "While we're checking for the car, let's drive around the neighborhood a little more? I'm not familiar with this part of Tampa and I'd like to be."

"I'm familiar with it," Harry said. "I lived a couple of streets away until I was ten years old."

Vicky wondered if this was why he had seemed so tense while coming here. She decided now was the time to find out. "Show me," she said.

Harry drove through the neighborhood, his mood suddenly distant; his body language setting up a shield between them. You'd make a lousy criminal, Harry Doyle, Vicky thought. Your emotions come off you like sweat.

Vicky studied the streets as they drove. It was a typical lower-middle-class neighborhood, each house, each apartment building in a varying state of repair, each announcing the degree of affluence of the people who lived within its walls. The main streets were much the same, a neat block adjacent to one where the sidewalks and gutters were littered with debris. There were lower-end shops and Mom-and-Pop stores, all announcing sales in their windows. There were fast-food chains and discount clothing and shoe stores, all still open late into the evening, racks of clothes and tables of shoes out on the sidewalks. Harry slowed as they passed a small evangelical church and Vicky looked across the front seat and saw that he was staring at it.

"Your church as a kid?" she asked.

"My mother's church. She was always there for something."

"She didn't drag you along?"

She watched as Harry shook his head, saying nothing.

"You're lucky. We were Greek Orthodox, and there was always something going on. My mother dragged me to everything. When I was a teenager it drove me nuts." She laughed. "Now I don't go at all. Probably the result of being dragged there so much." She smiled at the memory. "So where did you live?"

She was still smiling when she looked back at Harry, but the smile died quickly when she saw the cold, hard look in his eyes.

"What?" she asked.

"What's all this crap about wanting to see where I lived?" They were stopped at a light, and he was looking straight into her eyes. His voice was still soft, but so cold Vicky could almost feel the icy vapor rising from the words.

"Hey, it's nothing special. I was just curious," she said.

"You wanna see where the dead detective got his name, is that it?" Again, the ice in his voice almost made her shiver.

Vicky began to stammer. "Jesus, no . . . I mean . . . I didn't know it had anything to do with that."

"Alright, forget it," Harry said. The light had turned green, and he turned his attention back to the road and drove. "Let's get back to work and forget all the other crap."

They drove in silence for almost ten minutes before Vicky spoke again. "Look, Harry, I didn't know I was getting into your baggage back there. I'm sorry if I went someplace I shouldn't have gone. We've all got baggage we don't want to talk about."

She could see his jaw tighten, and wondered if she had gone too far again.

"So what's *your* baggage?" he said at length.

His words had a challenge in them, and she knew if they were going to have any success as partners she had to answer. She was sure Harry knew that too.

"A week from Saturday I was supposed to get married in that Greek Orthodox church I was telling you about."

"So you decided not to." Harry spoke the words dismissively.

Vicky paused. "No, I didn't decide anything. *He* decided."

Harry glanced at her, then back at the road. There had been a look of regret in his eyes and she realized that it was as much of an apology as anyone would ever get from Harry Doyle.

"Guy was obviously a jerk," Harry said at length.

"Thanks," Vicky said. "But I think he just realized that a cop who made a lousy girlfriend because she was never available, well, the chance of her becoming a good wife and mother down the road just wasn't in the cards."

Harry was quiet again, then said: "Maybe wives and mothers are over-rated."

There was another long pause and Vicky allowed it to draw out.

"The house back there, the one I grew up in," Harry finally said. "My mother murdered my brother and me in that house." He drew a long breath, almost as if he needed it to steady himself. "One morning she just decided we had to die. So she drugged our orange juice and dragged us into the garage. Then she laid us out, side-by-side, put small silver crosses on our foreheads, and covered our faces with hand towels. Then she started her car and left." He shook his head. "She went to that church you saw." He punctuated the sentence with a mocking breath. "Anyway, a neighbor heard the car running and called the cops. Two Tampa uniforms forced the garage door open and found us. We had both stopped breathing; no heartbeat; nothing. They worked on us anyway, and they were able to bring me back. But my brother was younger and smaller. They couldn't help him."

Now Vicky drew a long breath. "When was that?"

Harry kept his eyes on the road. "Twenty-one years ago. Twenty-one years ago today."

"Where's your mother now?"

Harry glanced at her briefly. "Central Florida Women's Correctional Facility. She copped a plea to avoid the death penalty. She got life."

And that's where you were today, Vicky thought. On the anniversary of your brother's murder. And that's where you told that correctional officer you were going to take his Glock and shove it.

"Do you ever see her?" Vicky asked.

"Never have, never will. She writes to me once a year. Always makes sure it arrives on this date. There should be a letter waiting for me when I get home." He turned and stared at her. "I don't answer the letters."

No, you just visit the prison and sit outside, she thought. "She have any shot at parole?"

"Not if I can help it," Harry said.

They were quiet for several minutes. Then, as they pulled up at a stop light, Harry turned to her.

"Did you notice the look on Darlene's face?" he asked. "The look of surprise that seemed to be changing into terror as she realized that her throat had been cut and she was going to die? Then how it froze, halfway between those two sensations, as she lost consciousness?"

Vicky nodded, unable to form any response.

"Well, I remember that. I remember lying on the garage floor, starting to wake up from the drug my mother had given me, but still too knocked out to pull myself together and get up. I remember seeing the exhaust fumes coming out of the back of her car; smelling them, but being too weak to force myself up so I could pull my brother and myself out of there. And then I remember the terror I felt when I knew I was going to die . . . how everything started to cloud up and fade away as I lost consciousness again. It was like my head was suddenly being filled with cotton." He stared at Vicky for a long moment. "That's how it was for Darlene. That's how it is when you know you're going to die and there's nothing you can do to stop it."

The light changed and they drove on in silence, Vicky thinking about what Harry had told her. She couldn't even imagine what a heavy weight he carried around inside. But she did know it was heavy enough to be a problem in the case they were working. She also knew it was a concern she couldn't voice, at least not yet. But there was no getting around the fact that Harry Doyle might be the wrong cop to be working the murder of a child-harming monster like Darlene Beckett.

The dark sedan stayed three car lengths back in the far right lane. Traffic was light so it was easy to maintain a safe, unobtrusive pace, to speed up whenever it was needed to make a light; then fall back and blend into the traffic again.

He had almost missed them. He had gotten tied up by things he couldn't avoid, and it had taken longer than expected, and he had rushed out to Darlene's apartment complex, assuming it would be one of the first places they would visit after finding her body. The local radio and television stations were full of the news; were already running special reports reliving every detail of her corrupt life, and he had no doubt the networks would soon pick up the story, if they hadn't already done so. It was the only part of her murder that displeased him, giving her more of the notoriety that she had so clearly enjoyed. But that couldn't be helped. He couldn't dwell on that, had to force himself to ignore it. Now he had to concentrate on the detectives who were working the investigation. He had to know what they were doing so he could stay one step ahead. One of the news reports he had heard claimed the sheriff's department had assigned one of its top homicide investigators to handle the case. Harry Doyle. Well, we'll see, won't we? We'll just see just how good Harry Doyle is.

When the car carrying the two detectives made a turn on to Nebraska Avenue, he knew exactly where they were going. One point for you, Harry Doyle, he thought. You got here faster than I thought you would. Now we'll see if you're good enough to find anything. But I don't think you will be. Oh, no. In fact, unless I'm very much mistaken, you won't ever find what you're looking for, not here, not now, not ever. You see, I'm very sure that all traces of the whore's killer have already disappeared.

The Peek-a-Boo Lounge was located on Nebraska Avenue in an area dominated by street walkers and their pimps. It was a windowless white cinder-block building with a massive air conditioner hovering above a wooden front door that had been painted red. On each side of the door the name of the bar had been painted in large, block red letters along with the silhouette of a naked dancer. The only other decorative touches were the four scraggly cabbage palms that lined the adjacent crushed-shell parking lot. All in all it was a depressing sight and Harry and Vicky both knew it would be even more so in daylight.

Harry pulled the car into the parking lot, gathered up a photo of Darlene Beckett that they had taken from her apartment, and headed for the front door. Vicky hurried to catch up.

"You always in such a hurry to get into a place like this?" she asked his back.

"I lead a lonely life," Harry said over his shoulder.

"Don't we all."

Harry pulled open the door and stepped aside. "Ladies first," he said.

"You're cute," Vicky snapped back.

* * *

The interior of the Peek-a-Boo Lounge was as original as its name, a central stage with two fireman's poles stretching from floor to ceiling, a battered collection of tables and chairs gathered before it, and a long bar off to one side. There were two dancers working the poles, each wearing only the briefest of thong underwear, the tops of which were stuffed with currency. The dancers glistened with sweat and the smell of that sweat and the sweat of those who had preceded them mixed with the odor of cigarettes, spilled booze, and stale beer, and seemed to permeate the room. The heavy beat of rap music pulsated from speakers set above the stage.

"Nice place," Vicky offered. "I wonder if they do wedding receptions."

It took a moment for their eyes to refocus as the door closed behind them. Except for the stage, which was engulfed in lights that presented a continuous change in color, the room was dimly lit and filled with a haze of cigarette smoke. Through that haze they could make out men sitting at the tables set before the stage. The men stared dully at the women who gyrated before them, occasionally luring one closer by extending a hand that held a folded bill. When the dancer reached the edge of the stage, squatted and rolled her hips to the beat of the music, the men would stuff the bill into the string of her thong.

There were men at the bar, filling half the stools, most turned toward the dancers, some just staring blindly into their drinks like drunks the world over. Harry moved toward the bar with Vicky at his side, stopping at the far end and raising his shield for the bartender when their eyes met.

The bartender, a thickly built thirty-something with a shaved head and one gold earring, gave a heavy sigh to let Harry know he wasn't pleased to have cops in his bar, then moved slowly toward them.

"You need somethin'?" he asked.

Closer up Harry could make out part a barbed-wire tattoo that showed through the open collar of his shirt and appeared to encircle his neck. There were matching tattoos encircling each arm.

"I need you to look at a picture," Harry said.

"I'm not too good with pictures," the bartender replied in the raspy voice of a heavy smoker.

"What's your name?" Harry asked.

"Name's Jack."

"Well, Jack, if you're not good with pictures, it's probably the lighting in this pisshole of a joint." Harry made a show of looking around the room and squinting. "I think it might help if we took you someplace where the light is better."

"I'm workin'," Jack offered.

"Yeah, so are we," Vicky said. "And guess whose work comes first."

Jack turned his head away to demonstrate his disgust. "Show me your picture," he said. "I'll light a match if I need to."

Harry handed him the photo of Darlene Beckett.

Jack looked at it and snorted. "This is who you wanted me to ID? Shit, that's Darlene."

"How do you know her?" Harry asked.

"I know her 'cause she's here a couple times a week," Jack said.

"She's a regular?" Vicky asked.

"As regular as they get here. Hell, she was here last night." Jack jerked his head toward the front entrance. "Her car's still in the parking lot. I saw it there when I came to work." He gave them an evil smile. "She musta got lucky and found somebody to take her home last night. Not that it would take much. I mean she's a good-lookin' broad." He grinned again. "And, what the hell, she's a fuckin' celebrity, am I right?" The grin widened and returned to its distinctly evil quality. "I mean a real *fuckin'* celebrity."

Harry and Vicky ignored the comment.

"You ever take her home?" Harry asked.

Jack shook his head. "Never got that lucky."

"You sure?" It was Vicky this time.

"Yeah, I'm sure."

"How come you know what her car looks like?" Now it was Harry. They had Jack's head swiveling between them as though he were watching a tennis match, and small beads of sweat had formed on his upper lip.

"Hey, I helped her get it started once, that's all."

"Just a good Samaritan, huh?" Vicky said. "Just the kind of a guy who offers to help when a lady finds herself in a tough spot, is that right?"

"That's right."

"Bullshit," Harry snapped.

"Hey, what the fuck is goin' on here? What's this all about?"

"Who was Darlene with last night?" It was Vicky again. "Who was she talking to?"

"How the hell do I know? I mean she was a friendly broad. She sat here at the bar and talked to lots of people."

Harry leaned in closer. "*You* better talk to *us*, Jack. You better stop the shit, and *talk* to us."

"Hey, look, I don't want no trouble, alright? I don't remember who she was talkin' to, not what guys, anyway. I know she was talkin' to Jasmine. She's one of our dancers. Darlene likes to talk to the dancers. I always thought maybe she goes that way too." He tried a knowing sneer; then gave it up when he saw it wasn't working.

"Is Jasmine here?" Harry asked.

"Yeah. She's in back." He inclined his head toward a black velvet curtain between the stage and the bar. "She's doin' a private lap dance."

"Get her," Vicky ordered.

"Hey, that's a fifty-buck gig for her. Maybe more, you know what I mean? She ain't gonna be too happy I break it up."

"Guess what, Jack? We're not here to bring sunshine into your lives," Vicky said.

"Get her," Harry said. "Get her . . . *now*." As Jack moved away Harry leaned in close to Vicky. "While we're waiting, check the parking lot and make sure Darlene's car is there." He jotted down the plate number the DMV had given him and handed it to her. "If it's the right car, call the CSI unit and tell them we have another job for them. Then give Tampa P.D. a call and tell them we need backup. At least four uniforms. When we get through with Jasmine we're gonna shake this place down."

Jasmine was dressed in her thong, a white see-through rayon beach robe, and a sour expression when she came to the bar a few minutes later.

"You just cost me money," she snapped.

"Life is hard," Harry said. He matched Jasmine's stare. "Sit down," he ordered.

Vicky returned from the parking lot just as Jasmine eased herself on to a stool. Harry moved to one side of her, Vicky to the other, effectively pinning her between them.

Harry glanced at Vicky. "You find it?"

Vicky nodded. "The team is on the way. So's the backup."

They both turned their attention to Jasmine.

"Now, you're going to answer some questions," Harry began. "And if I think you answered them straight you get to go back to work. If I don't think you answered them straight that cute little butt of yours is going to be sitting in the back of a patrol car headed for the Pinellas County sheriff's office. You got that?"

"I got it," Jasmine said.

"Be sure you got it," Vicky said. "Because if you screw with him, you're gonna find out *this* policeman is not your friend."

Jasmine raised her hands and let them fall back to her lap in a gesture of surrender. "Alright, alright. You ask, I'll answer. I just wanna get back to work. It hasn't been a very good week, okay?"

Jasmine was a beautiful woman, hard around the eyes and with far too much makeup, but someone who would be eye-catching if she cleaned herself up. She had a lean sensuous body, with full breasts and long shapely legs. Her hair was short and black, and her eyes were a vivid blue and seemed to jump out of a sharply defined face. She was also chewing gum with her mouth open, snapping and popping it with each movement of her jaw, which for Harry destroyed whatever sensual effect she hoped to achieve.

Harry showed her the picture of Darlene Beckett. "You know her?"

"Yeah, that's Darlene. She was here last night."

"What time did she get here, and what time did she leave?" Harry asked.

Jasmine shrugged, then seemed to think better of it. "When she comes, she usually gets here around nine and stays for about an hour. She has a curfew, you know . . . because of her . . . because of the trouble she had."

"You know who she left with?" Vicky asked.

"No. I mean I can't be sure. I was in the changing room when she left. But she was askin' me about this one particular guy. Askin' if I knew him, if I thought he was safe."

"Did you know him?" Harry asked.

Jasmine shook her head. "I mean I saw him. He was young, kind of cute, not like most of the creeps we get in here. But I never met him or nothin'. But I got the impression from her that he'd been watching her." She shrugged to confirm her uncertainty. "Darlene liked it when guys watched her."

"Has he been in tonight?"

"No, I haven't seen him tonight. In fact, I never saw him before, either."

"Tell us about him," Vicky said.

"Like what? I told you I never met him."

"Start with what he looked like, how he was dressed," Harry said.

"Well, like I said, he was cute. He had short hair, what I could see of it, 'cause he was wearin' a cowboy hat, you know? But no beard or mustache. He just looked kinda clean, kinda neat."

"What was he wearing with the hat?" Vicky asked.

"He was neat that way too. Nothin' special. Just jeans with a big ol' silver belt buckle and a T-shirt. But the clothes were good, expensive, you know, and real clean, like everything had just been washed and ironed."

"What kind of shoes?"

"I dunno. I didn't see his shoes."

"Glasses, anything like that?"

Jasmine shook her head.

"What color was his hair, his eyes?"

"His hair, I guess it was brown, what I could see of it. I never saw his eyes."

"How tall was he? How heavy?"

"I remember that he wasn't a big guy, but he wasn't short either, kind of just above average I guess. Maybe five-ten, five-eleven." She shrugged.

"Weight?"

"He wasn't fat, or real skinny, but I don't remember him looking real strong. Just kind of normal, you know? Like medium, maybe a hundred and sixty, a hundred and seventy pounds. I'm not too good with weight on guys."

"Do you know what kind of car he was driving?" Vicky asked.

Jasmine shook her head.

"Did Darlene leave with him?"

"I dunno. Like I said, she left when I was in the dressing room. But come to think of it, I didn't see him when I came out. So she could have, I guess."

"Did Darlene usually pick up guys when she came here?" Vicky asked.

Jasmine gave them another shrug. "Sometimes. I mean Darlene liked to have guys look at her, liked to know they liked what they saw, maybe wanted her, you know what I mean?" She let out a little laugh. "Like that would be a surprise. The guys who come here are all horny. Hell, that's why they're here, to look at the dancers. But I think Darlene liked to have them want her even more than they wanted the dancers, almost like it was some kind of competition—her against us—you know what I mean?"

"That's a little sad," Vicky said.

Jasmine looked at her, thinking about what she had said. "Yeah, it is." She shook her head. "God, if I didn't have to come here I wouldn't walk through those doors. But I got a kid at home who likes to eat, and she's got a bum for a father who never sends his support checks, so I'm here doing what I have to do."

Harry wanted to tell her there were other jobs, jobs where her life wouldn't be at risk, but knew it would be a waste of breath. An uneducated woman could never find a straight job where she could make the kind of money she could in a place like this. At least until her body gave out. "Somewhere down the road I'll want you to look at some mug shots, maybe a lineup, so I need your full name and current address," he said instead. "I also want you to give a description of this guy to a police artist. You willing to do that?"

Jasmine nodded.

"Is your real name Jasmine?" Vicky asked.

"No, my real name's Anita Molari."

"Pretty name," Vicky said.

Jasmine looked at her as though she had said something strange. "You think so? I never liked it."

When the Tampa P.D. backup arrived Harry ordered the bartender to kill the music and turn on all the lights, then to bring all the dancers out to the main room. When that was done, and as the backups moved in to block all exits, he announced who he was and explained that everyone in the room would have to submit to a police interview as part of an official investigation. He also assured them that the stage shows would resume as soon as they were finished. Groans filled the room, but no one attempted to leave.

The interviews with the patrons and dancers proved useless. All the men sitting at the tables and the bar insisted they had not been there the previous evening, and while several acknowledged having seen Darlene on earlier occasions, none remembered seeing her with any one particular individual. The dancers also provided little information, although most said they had talked with Darlene over the past few months, with several commenting that Darlene clearly had her eye out for good-looking men. Harry was certain some of the men had lied to him about being there the previous night, but there was little he could do about that. He took down names and addresses in case any further interviews proved necessary. He also planned to run criminal record checks on everyone present. Any hits would be followed up with a more intense interrogation.

"Well, it wasn't a complete loss," Vicky said as they returned to the parking lot. "We know where she was last night; we have a description of a man she may have left with; and we found her car. That's a lot of pluses."

"It's a start," Harry said as they headed toward Darlene's 2004 green Taurus, which was now cordoned off with yellow crime scene tape and bathed in portable high-intensity light.

They stopped outside the tape and watched Martin LeBaron dust the passenger's-side door. When he saw them he beckoned them inside the tape. "We finished with everything around the car," he said. "In fact, when I finish with this door, we'll have done everything we can here. I'll be towing it back to the garage to finish up there."

"You find anything?" Vicky asked.

"Nothing that jumps out at me," LeBaron said. "Plenty of prints inside and out, just as you'd expect. We'll have to run them; see what comes up."

Vicky turned to Harry. "What now?"

"Now we go back to the office, write up what we found, and get our murder book started. I also want to go back to DMV and have them send us copies of the driver's licenses of all the people whose cars we ran earlier. I want to see if any of them match up to the description of the guy Jasmine told us about. If any of the photos fit that description we'll show them to Jasmine tomorrow, see if she can ID him."

"We gonna see everybody on that list?"

"That's the drill." He gave her an amused half smile. "You thought homicide was going to be all glamour, huh?"

Vicky shook her head. "No, I've been a cop too long to think that."

It was three a.m. when Harry slipped his key in the front door of his two-bedroom beach house off Mandalay Avenue on Clearwater Beach. He had bought the house ten years earlier, well before Clearwater Beach property had gone through the roof. He had put himself in hock to the tune of $200,000, and now found himself the owner of a "beach shack" worth five or six times that. It wasn't the house of course; it was the property, sitting as it did directly behind a small dune with a clear view of the Gulf of Mexico. For the past five years he had fended off realtors with ever-escalating offers—each one representing a buyer who wanted to tear down his beach shack and build some glass-and-stucco monstrosity like all the others that now lined the beach. Harry told them all that he planned to wait for the hurricane that would eventually level the house, and then decide whether to rebuild or sell the land and the pile of sticks that sat on it. He was certain the realtors left hoping the next hurricane season would get him.

The house was a simple one-story wood-frame dwelling with a living room, kitchen, two bedrooms, and a bath. It had a screened lanai off the living room facing the gulf, and a deck off the master bedroom that also overlooked the water. If he left the bedroom's sliding glass doors open he could go to sleep each night to the sound of the waves rolling up on the beach. The house was his private bit of heaven, the one thing that kept him sane.

He had been thinking about Darlene Beckett's mutilated face when he found the annual letter from his mother waiting in the mailbox. Just one more bit of *EVIL* to end his day with, he thought, as he collected it and tossed it, unopened, on a small side table just inside the front door. He kicked off his shoes, also leaving them near the front door as he always did, just under the longboard and helmet that hung on a rack behind the door. He used the board—a longer, more elegant version of a skateboard—as a form of exercise, racing along the sidewalks and streets early in the morning, or late at night, testing the tolerance of pedestrians whose comments often followed him down the street. He loved the board, loved the exercise it gave him, loved how it brought back memories of riding alongside his brother Jimmy, on the battered skateboards they had as kids, always together back then.

Harry cut three oranges in half, squeezed a glass of juice, and went out on the lanai. It was high tide and a light breeze coming in off the gulf sent a steady line of waves against the shore. He took a deep breath to let the ugliness of the day drain away. He knew it wouldn't work, not today. Darlene Beckett was too fixed in his mind, the image of her lifeless body with its catlike Mardi Gras mask, the seedy strip club she had visited so regularly, all relentlessly coming back at him, all unreasonably mixed together with the letter that waited in the living room.

"Hi, Harry."

He looked toward the screen door of the lanai and found Jeanie Walsh standing there.

"What are you doing up so late, or early, or whatever?" he asked.

"Couldn't sleep, so I went for a walk on the beach."

"Dangerous," he said. "I've told you that before."

"I know. Can I come in?"

"Sure."

Jeanie entered and took a seat next to him, facing the water. She was a few years younger than Harry, five-five and slightly underweight, but in a pleasing sort of way, with short, curly blond hair and very soft, very gentle brown eyes. He had met her early one morning while he was terrorizing the neighborhood on his longboard. He had come around a corner far too fast, startling her and causing her to drop a container of coffee she had just purchased. He had apologized, walked her back to the coffee shop and bought her another. Within fifteen minutes they had become friends.

Jeanie lived in the blot-out-the-sun condo next to Harry's house. She was a stockbroker, financially secure, recently separated, and lonely. Within a week they had become casual lovers, a matter of comfort and convenience for each of them—Harry who wanted no emotional commitment in his life, and Jeanie who was still in love with her long gone husband, even though he was addicted to sweet young things and had cheated on her repeatedly while they were together.

"So why the solo beach walk? Just trying to tempt the homeless psychos who sleep there at night?"

Jeanie leaned her head back, turned her face toward him, and smiled. Harry thought it was a beautiful smile.

"Just brooding about my soon-to-be ex-husband." The smile faded and she looked back toward the water. "It's like I told you when we first met. I'm just a born sucker."

"So stop," Harry said. "Look, maybe you'll get lucky, or unlucky, or whatever, and that clown will wake up some morning and realize what a great lady you are. Maybe he never will. But in the meantime you're still a great lady. Enjoy being one. You're part of a rare and exclusive breed."

"Not so rare, Harry. You just don't trust women."

"I don't trust men either. Kids, well, they're so, so."

Jeanie laughed. "If people ever find out what a softie you really are, you're going to have a hard time selling yourself as a big, bad detective."

"So don't tell anybody."

"Don't worry, your secret's safe with me."

They sat quietly for several minutes; then Jeanie reached out and took his hand. "Can I stay here with you, Harry? I don't want to be alone for the rest of the night. I don't want anything. I really couldn't handle anything. I just want to climb into your bed and lie next to you."

"Sure. I'd like that." Harry thought about the letter from his mother that awaited him in the living room, and he thought about Darlene Beckett and what awaited him there. He squeezed Jeanie's hand, turned to her, and nodded. "I don't really want to be alone either," he said.

CHAPTER FOUR

Harry ran the gauntlet of reporters and cameramen who had gathered at the rear door of the sheriff's department, awaiting the arrival of any detective who might give up information about Darlene Beckett's murder. He gave them a few shrugs, a grunt or two, but offered nothing. Based on the shouted questions, they seemed to know almost as much as he did, even the fact that the woman's face had been covered by a mask. When he reached the office upstairs he was met by a blare of telephones, the calls either from out-of-town reporters or people offering mostly valueless opinions about Darlene's life, or murder, or state of grace. As he walked past Diva Walsh's desk she drew a long breath and shook her head. She pointed at the front pages of the two local newspapers that lay on her desk. Each carried a hauntingly beautiful photograph of Darlene Beckett.

"I've had five people call to tell me what part of hell that woman is in," she said.

"What part?" Harry asked.

"I can't remember the name, but they all said it's very, very hot."

Harry grinned at her. "Good thing she used to model bathing suits. Anything else shaking?"

"Body on the beach at Frank Howard Park in Tarpon Springs. Benevuto and Weathers are on it."

"Let me know if anything worthwhile comes in on Beckett. Is Vicky in yet?"

"She's in with the captain. He wants you in there too." She shook her head again. "You know I grew up down here, and my mama always took me to church when I was a kid. But the church folk you got down here now—especially the white church folk—they scare the bejesus out of me."

"Why is that?"

"Because they're all nuts, Harry. Every damned one of them."

When Harry reached Pete Rourke's office, Vicky Stanopolis was already occupying one of the two visitors' chairs. Harry took the other. It was only eight a.m., but they had each agreed to work double shifts until Darlene Beckett's murder was cleared.

"I've got CNN, FOX, local TV, and every damned newspaper I've ever heard of calling," Rourke said. "Hell, there are newspapers I *never* heard of calling. Some of the out-of-town papers are playing the story inside or below the fold, but they're still pushing for every bit of information they can get, and I've got some producer for *Court TV* calling every five minutes. On top of that, the brass is meeting in the conference room upstairs trying to decide if we need a task force to handle this."

"A task force would be a good idea. The more bodies we have working this the better," Harry said. He paused a beat. "Providing . . ."

"That you're the lead detective," Rourke said.

"It's my case," Harry said.

"When the brass gets involved, it's *their* case." Now it was Rourke's turn to pause. "Unless something goes wrong. *Then* it's yours."

"Same as always," Harry said.

"Okay, let's all stop whining. Tell me where you're at."

Harry briefed him on everything they had come up with. "Right now we're going to push on the cars that were seen in her driveway. One belonged to her ex-husband, so he's number one on the list. Another belonged to an old boyfriend, who the local newspapers said she was dating again during her court appearances. He ranks right behind the husband for now. But I gotta tell you, cap, this doesn't have the feel of an angry husband or a pissed-off boyfriend."

"What does it feel like?" Rourke asked.

"Retribution," Harry said.

"Why?"

"The fact that the word *evil* was carved in her forehead; then covered by a mask." Harry shook his head. "The message is too bizarre and too simplistic. My gut tells me the killer is a fanatic. Probably a religious fanatic, somebody who needed some very public payback for what she did to that kid, and who wanted to make sure that everybody understood why she had to die."

"Okay, that makes sense." Rourke leaned forward. "But let me say this to both of you right up front. This is a high-profile case—they don't get much higher—and the state's attorney needs cold, hard, irrefutable evidence to take to the grand jury. That means he isn't going to give a fiddler's fuck about Harry Doyle's gut."

Before Harry could respond Diva stuck her head in the office. "The body in Tarpon Springs. Looks like it may have been part of the Beckett murder. Benevuto just called it in asking that Harry and Vicky get out there."

Rourke looked at each of them. "Go," he said.

Frank Howard Park sits on the Gulf of Mexico at the western edge of Tarpon Springs, a once sleepy fishing village noted for the Greek sponge divers who migrated there early in the last century. Now a vibrant tourist attraction, the village maintains its Greek flavor with a glut of restaurants and shops, many of which still sell sponges brought up from the seabed by descendents of the original immigrants. The park, like the village itself, is immaculately maintained and begins with a winding road that meanders past picnic groves and ends in a causeway leading to an island beach a quarter of a mile from the mainland. The body—a male Caucasian, late twenties to early thirties—was found by a maintenance crew on the eastern end of the causeway. It was laying on a jut of sand hidden from view by a dense patch of sea grape.

"Welcome to the love nest," Nick Benevuto said as Harry and Vicky ducked under the yellow crime scene tape that delineated the killing ground.

Harry took in the blanket that had been spread on the sand, the now melted bucket of ice, the margarita mix, the bottle of tequila, and the plastic cups that were scattered near the body, all of it giving off the feel of a romantic liaison—all except for the man's already decomposing body, the forehead pushed in from repeated blows with a club or rock, the front of his western shirt stiff with dried blood; all except for the other large pool of blood that had soaked into the sand several feet away from the blanket and a lone pair of women's shoes that had been left behind.

"Looks like we found the place Darlene was killed," Vicky said.

"That's what hit us first off," John Weathers replied.

"I'd bet the mortgage on it," Nick Benevuto said. "We found the victim's car. It's parked out on the road near the park entrance. They close off the entrance at sunset so nobody can drive in and camp for the night. CSI has already been told to dust it."

Harry didn't say anything. He walked to the blanket and squatted next to the man's body. The body had been in the sun for a day and land crabs and seagulls had already picked at the soft tissue. The eyes were gone. There was nothing to see there and the body was not pleasant to be near. Still, he needed to get a closer look at the wound.

"I'd say the blows were struck from left to right," Harry said at length. The victim's hands had already been bagged so he couldn't tell if he had fought his attacker. "Did you find anything under his fingernails?"

"Nothing I could see, so I just bagged them," Benevuto answered. "My guess is the first blow caught him by surprise and knocked him cold. The others were administered later. Probably after the other murder," he added, catching Harry's drift. "And I think you're dead-on about the blows coming left to right. Any sign Darlene's killer was left-handed?" he asked

Harry nodded as he walked to the blood pool. His movements were slow and careful, giving his eyes time to scan the ground ahead of him so he wouldn't inadvertently disturb any evidence.

"There are no footprints leading here, or away from here," he pointed out. "Looks like the sand could have been brushed clean."

"That's our guess," Weathers said.

Harry saw a very small glint in the sand and squatted next to it. The glint was no bigger that a few grains of sand, but sand didn't shine that way. He took a pen from his pocket and began to clear the area around it. Gradually a gold cross emerged.

"Vicky, hand me some tweezers and a plastic bag from my crime scene kit," he said.

When he had the tweezers and the bag, he carefully lifted the cross and held it at eye level. It was thick and heavy, definitely gold. He turned it over and saw a stamped 18K on the rear. Above the mark there was a faint engraving, so badly worn it was unreadable, almost as if it had rubbed against the wearer's body for so long it had begun to disappear. Again, he had the same feeling he had experienced at the Brooker Creek crime scene, one of the killer standing next to him.

"Can you make this out?" Harry asked, holding the cross out for Vicky to see.

"No. It's too faint. Maybe the lab can bring something up. If not ours, we can send it to the FBI lab in Washington."

"Would you say this belonged to a woman?" Harry asked.

Vicky gave her head a slight shake. "Eighteen karats, so it's good stuff. The kind of gold any woman would like. But it's too heavy for a woman. I'd say it's a man's. You think it was torn off when the killer cut Darlene?"

"Be a good guess," Harry said. "But it could also have been here for months. Just something somebody lost."

"I'm betting it's from this murder," Vicky said. "This place isn't exactly a popular picnic spot. It isn't much good for anything but what they were using it for."

"I'm with you on that," Benevuto chimed in. He was grinning at her.

Vicky gave him ice in return.

Benevuto let out a long breath. "Look, when you got here I was just heading out to get some coffee for me and Weathers. You guys want any?" He shrugged when Harry and Vicky declined, then turned to go. "Be back in ten minutes."

Harry slipped the cross into the evidence bag and handed it to Weathers. "Yours for now," he said. He raised his chin toward the blood pool and the women's shoes. "At least until we're sure the blood and the shoes are Darlene's."

He drove the car past the park, nodded to the two uniforms guarding the entrance, then turned left into a side street and headed south, blending into the background yet again. There had been four cars, two marked and two unmarked, which meant there were at least four detectives at the scene. And that could only mean they knew they had found the place where the whore had been punished. It would also mean they would soon be intensifying their investigation; adding more detectives and deputies. But that was something that would serve well. It was something that could be used if he was clever and artful. But he knew everything was not as perfect as he would have liked it to be. A hand went to the chain where the cross had once hung. Its loss had not been planned, and he had not discovered it until that morning. It was a bit of carelessness that could not be repeated. He had hoped to get to it before the body was found, but he'd been too slow. He'd hesitated about coming back to the place she had died, and that hesitation had been costly. His jaw clenched at the thought. That's one point for you, Harry Doyle. Still, he doubted the cross could be traced back to him. It was far too old, something he had worn since childhood, given to him by that other bitch who so enjoyed harming the children in her care. But that debt had already been paid in full ten long years ago. Now Darlene Beckett could be added to that list. And as long as he kept the police bumbling along, missing the truth that stood right in front of them, he would be safe. And if he remained safe, then there would be others.

It was almost noon before CSI reported back that prints in the male victim's car were a positive match to Darlene Beckett, and the blood in the sand matched her blood type. DNA would take longer, but there was little doubt what the results would be. The male victim had also been identified as Clint Walker, a software salesman with no known previous ties to Darlene. He had simply picked her up in a topless bar, taken her to a deserted beach, and paid for it with his life.

When Harry received word on the results, he and Vicky were back at headquarters questioning Jordon Beckett, Darlene's estranged husband. Beckett had just identified his former wife's body and he still seemed to be in shock. Either that or he was the best actor Harry had seen in a long time. Now, sitting in the homicide division conference room, Beckett lowered his eyes and shook his head. He was average height, with sun-bleached hair and bland features. He worked as a yacht broker and appeared to do pretty well at it.

"You know, she wasn't a bad person," he said, his voice barely audible. "In court she claimed she was bipolar. But I don't buy that. She just needed to be the center of attention; always needed to know she was the woman that every man in the room wanted. I found out too late that she only knew one way to get that."

"So what are you telling us?" Vicky asked. "She was the slut with the heart of gold?" Her voice was harsh, intentionally so.

"No. I'm not telling you anything like that." Beckett kept his eyes down as he spoke.

"So what is it?" Harry asked, making sure his voice was slightly softer, less threatening than Vicky's. "You telling us you're not bitter about everything she did to you? That all the public humiliation you went through was okay? That you don't care that she went to bed with a fourteen-year-old student, when she had you at home? The man she had just married six months earlier?"

"Even did it in your own bed," Vicky threw in harshly.

The questions snapped out at Jordan like the strokes of a whip, and Harry watched the man's jaw tighten with each one. When Beckett's eyes finally rose to meet Harry's they were not friendly.

"At the time I was too shocked to feel anything," he said. "Later, yeah, I hated her guts. Every court appearance was like a knife in my heart. Every time she was on the front page of the newspapers, or the news on TV, I felt like puking. I filed for divorce and stayed as far away from the court and the press as I could. Then it was finally over and I met somebody else and my life started to get back to normal. All I wanted was to move on, forget all of it." He stared hard at Harry. "Now she's even taken that chance away. Now I'm back in the same cesspool, with the same spotlight shining on me. And, yeah, deep down it pisses me off. But I never wanted her dead, not ever, not one time."

"You're sure?"

Beckett stared back at Harry. "Yeah, I'm sure."

"Where were you two nights ago?"

"I was on my sailboat, anchored off Venice."

"Alone?"

"No. My fiancée was with me. We got the news when a friend called my cell to tell me. It was a great way to end a romantic cruise. Darlene even managed to ruin that."

Vicky moved in close, her eyes ice cold. "Let's cool it with the pity party. Tell me about this fourteen-year-old boy and why your wife might want to go to bed with him."

Beckett glared at her, then dropped his eyes to his lap. "It wasn't him; it wasn't that she was crazy attracted to him or anything like that. I saw the guy in court and he was just a skinny little kid with scraggly hair and a mild case of acne."

"Then why?" Vicky pressed.

Beckett shook his head. "I've thought about it a lot, and the only thing I can come up with is that Darlene was in trouble at the school."

"What kind of trouble?" Harry asked.

"The principal was an older woman, who didn't like anything about Darlene—from the way she dressed, to the way she ran her classroom, just about everything. She particularly didn't like what she said was Darlene's inability to control the kids in her class." He shook his head. "You know what seventh and eighth grade kids are like. You need a whip and a chair to keep them in line. Anyway, the principal was all over her about it. Said she needed to find a way to control these kids, that if she couldn't she didn't belong in a classroom."

Harry gave Beckett a bewildered look. "So you think she used sex as a way to control her class?"

Beckett shook his head. "No. As way to prove to herself she could control a kid that age." He stared back at Harry. "Sex was the way she got control over everything in her life. It was the only way she knew."

"Give me your fiancée's name and address," Vicky said.

The next interrogation involved one of Darlene's old boyfriends. According to newspaper accounts, Billy Smithers had been a high school sweetheart who suddenly reappeared in Darlene's life during one of her early court appearances. Harry remembered the news reports. They had had a bit of a smirk to them. Old boyfriend becomes Darlene's new beau. Smithers, he recalled, had seemed to revel in the notoriety of it all. Now, as he sat in the interrogation room, he seemed to be enjoying it all over again.

"Look, it was never anything serious between Darlene and me. Not even back in high school. She was just, like, you know, the great-looking girl who put out." Smithers finished off the comment with a cavalier shrug.

He was in his late twenties, tall and lanky with chiseled features, long sandy hair, and a body that spoke of regular trips to the gym. Harry imagined that women would find him attractive, but there was a hint of arrogance in his eyes, and in his tone of voice, that would be off-putting to men.

"So you dated her in high school because she had a reputation of being an easy lay," Vicky said.

"Yeah, that's about it. I mean she was fun in other ways too. But the main reason was she was pretty free and easy about sex." He grinned at Vicky as if offering some type of apology. "Look, I'm just trying to be honest here."

"We appreciate that," Harry said. He wanted to keep the man talking.

"So when you read the newspapers and saw the kind of trouble Darlene had gotten herself into, you weren't surprised," Vicky said,

Smithers let out a short laugh. "Hell no. I wasn't surprised at all. I mean that was what Darlene was all about. In high school there was a rumor that she was screwing one of *her* teachers."

"And so when you saw her on the news, you remembered how easy she was and decided to jump right back in," Vicky pressed.

Smithers twisted in his chair. "Well, yeah. I mean she looked pretty good on TV, you know. And I remembered how good she was . . . well, you know."

"In bed," Vicky said.

"Yeah." He paused a beat. "Yeah, she was wicked in bed."

"And you figured she didn't have anybody taking care of her right then. Taking care of her in bed that is."

"Well, yeah, I guess that too."

"So you called her."

"No, actually, I went by her house. I mean I heard her husband had split, and like I didn't have her number or anything. So I just dropped by."

"To be supportive," Vicky said.

"Yeah."

Harry had no idea where Vicky was going with the line of questioning, but he decided to let her run with it for the moment. Smithers had the feel of a clown to him, not a killer.

"So how supportive were you?" Vicky asked.

Smithers stared at her, a blank look on his face. "Well, you know."

"No, I don't know," Vicky snapped. "Tell me."

Smithers twisted in his chair again. "I just kind of offered her a shoulder. I mean I gave her what she needed."

"And what was that? Tell me, Mr. Smithers, what is it you have that every girl needs?"

"Hey, what the hell is going on here? I mean, I'm just trying to help." He glared at Vicky, and then turned to Harry. "Look, do I need a lawyer here?" His voice held both concern and anger now.

"You think you need a lawyer?" Vicky said.

"Where were you two nights ago?" Harry asked, stopping her.

"I was at a Rays game at the Trop," Smithers said.

"Alone?" It was Vicky again.

"Alone?" Harry said, letting her know he was doing the questioning now.

"No, I was with two buddies. We go to every home game we can get to."

Harry picked up a pen and turned to a fresh page in his notebook. "I'll need their names, addresses, and phone numbers," he said.

When Smithers left, Harry drew a breath and stared at Vicky for several moments.

"I guess I went a little over the top," she said at length.

"Yeah, a little. What happened?"

"He was just such a jerk." She stared at the other side of the room, avoiding Harry's eyes. "I saw so many guys like him when I was in sex crimes. The big studs, the guys who prey on every woman they consider vulnerable, and who assault or rape the ones who reject them." She paused as if thinking about what she had said, analyzing it. "No, what really pissed me off is that I've dated creeps like that." She shook her head as if dismissing past mistakes. "Sometimes a guy's so good looking, or has such a great line of B.S. that it takes you awhile to see past it. Smithers is that kind of guy, and realizing it, just being in the same room with him, pissed me off."

Harry nodded. "It happens," he said at length. "Next time use your anger . . . use it like a rapier not a bludgeon."

CHAPTER FIVE

At two o'clock Harry and Vicky were back in Rourke's office.
"First the good news," Rourke said. "We're getting a task force. Four detectives from this squad, and six uniforms we're bringing up to work in plainclothes." He paused and stared at Harry for a long moment. "Harry, you'll be lead detective. But I gotta tell you, the brass didn't want you as lead. You're not popular upstairs, which is something you know. And it's mainly due to your big mouth." He raised a hand, stopping any comment before it could be made. "They wanted Nick Benevuto. Their argument was that he's senior to you in homicide, which is true. I said I wanted you. So my ass is on the line. You screw up and I lose a big chunk of it; you'll wish you were never born."

Again, he held up his hand. "Now the bad news. Tarpon Springs P.D. is screaming that we came in and snatched a major case from them."

"That's bullshit," Harry said. "Vicky and I already had the case. They know that."

"Sure they do. But their chief sees all the media the sheriff is getting, while he's just standing around with his dick in his hand." He glanced at Vicky. "Sorry."

"That's okay, cap, I've met the chief. It's a lovely image. The man's a fourteen-karat asshole."

Rourke gave her a long look. "Yeah, well anyway, the sheriff agreed to put two of his detectives on the task force and hold a little press conference this afternoon to announce the joint operation. It's all politics, but we have to live with it."

"Should be a great press conference," Vicky said. "Sort of a two-man circle jerk."

Rourke stared at her again, longer this time. "You're talking about the sheriff, you know. *Our* sheriff."

"Goodness, what came over me," Vicky answered.

"How long have you worked with Doyle?" Rourke snapped. "Two days? And already I got this?"

Harry fought off a smile. "Who are the two Tarpon dicks we're supposed to take on?" he asked.

Rourke looked at a note on his desk. "Bob Davis and Jerry Deaver."

"I know them," Harry said. "The other cops call them the *two D's.*" He offered up a small shrug. "They have the rep of not being very imaginative, but very thorough, so it could be worse." Harry took out his notebook and wrote down the names of the Tarpon Springs detectives. "Who are the uniforms?" he asked.

Rourke rattled off six names, the last of which was Jim Morgan, the deputy who had done such a good job at the Brooker Creek crime scene. Rourke noticed Harry nodding approval at the mention of Morgan's name.

"I picked Morgan based on what you put down in your report," Rourke said. "You wrote that he'd done an excellent job. He also pushed hard for the assignment and I thought you could use an eager beaver on the team."

"Meaning that the rest of us aren't?" Vicky teased.

Rourke leveled a finger at her. "Don't start with me. I get enough from your partner." He turned back to Harry. "I just sent word out on their new assignments about an hour ago, so they should be learning about it as we speak. They're all due in here at three on a 'forthwith' to get their specific assignments from you, so you've got an hour to figure out who you want doing what. Your team can work out of the conference room next to my office."

At three o'clock Harry stood before the team and began handing out assignments. It was basically grunt work for now, much of it going over ground already covered in the initial investigation, looking for anything that might have been missed. Nick Benevuto and John Weathers were sent to interview Darlene's parents and Clint Walker's friends and family. Uniforms were assigned to verify the husband's and boyfriend's alibis. Others were sent out to interview the men whose cars were parked in Darlene's driveway in the months leading up to her death. Jim Morgan was told to do another canvass of Darlene's neighbors. The Tarpon Springs detectives, the two D's, were sent to canvass the residences around Frank Howard Park, where the "cowboy's" body had been found. Vicky, because of her background in sex crimes, was told to dig up whatever information she could about the boy Darlene had molested, his family, his friends, along with any psychological treatment he may have received. Harry would take on the unpleasant task of Darlene's autopsy, as well as reviewing all forensic evidence that had been collected. The following day he was scheduled to meet with Jasmine, the dancer from the Peek-a-Boo Lounge, to view driver's license photos of men who had visited Darlene's apartment. It was a massive amount of work, but Harry was convinced he had the manpower to get it done quickly and efficiently. It was now a question of finding that one key piece of evidence that would break the case open.

Darlene's autopsy was scheduled for four p.m. It was originally planned for early that morning, but had been delayed when Mort Janlow, the assistant M.E. assigned to the case, was sent out to the Tarpon Springs crime scene. Now Janlow stood before the body, snapping on a pair of latex gloves. Harry stood across from him, watching a grin spread across the medical examiner's face.

"Still don't like these slice-'em-and-dice-'em jobs, eh, Harry?"

Harry gave Janlow a flat stare and held it until the assistant M.E. was forced to look away. "Not my favorite part of the day," he finally said. What he didn't say was that it made him think of his six-year-old brother Jimmy lying on a similar autopsy table twenty years ago. He had never seen his brother then, of course, but that had been the overriding image he'd had as a young deputy witnessing his first autopsy, and it was one that rushed back at him each succeeding time. He believed then, as he believed now, that no one who had ever witnessed an autopsy would want one performed on someone they loved.

He stared into Darlene Beckett's dead face, the slightly opened eyes, the parted lips. But most of all he stared at the single word that someone had carved into her forehead, denouncing her as evil. Was she? Or was she a woman fighting her own inner demons. He wondered if he'd ever know the answer, or any part of it.

"Let's get to it," Janlow said, picking up a scalpel for the initial cut. Then he paused and looked at the body. "She was an extraordinarily beautiful woman, wasn't she?" The question wasn't directed at Harry, even though he was the only other person in the room. Now Janlow looked at Harry as if embarrassed by the comment. "Most people, even the ones who are extremely attractive in life, don't carry their looks to this table. The muscle tone is gone; the clear, glowing complexions have turned pale and gray, the eyes are clouded. It makes you realize that it's not the superficial exterior that we all work so hard at getting right, it's that spark of life that makes people truly appealing." He paused. "But every so often there's one who's beautiful even in death."

"Maybe it's because that's all they ever had," Harry said.

Janlow inclined his head to one side. "Never thought of it that way. Maybe you're right, Harry. Maybe you're right."

Janlow reached up and turned on the overhead microphone that would record his observations. He gave the date and time, followed by routine statements. "We are about to begin the postmortem examination of Darlene Beckett, a twenty-six-year-old white female. The body is well developed, and shows no identifying scars or tattoos. There is bruising about the arms and shoulders indicating that she struggled before death. There is only one exterior wound, a deep cut across the throat that severed the thyroid cartilage, the trachea, and the right carotid artery, causing a massive loss of blood, which would have continued until the heart stopped beating. The wound appears to have been administered from behind in a right-to-left motion, indicating the killer used his left hand."

Harry noted Janlow's caution. He had avoided stating flatly that the killer was left-handed. Several years earlier Janlow had performed an autopsy on another of Harry's cases. It involved a young woman who was beaten to death with a metal softball bat owned by her husband. The blows had come from left to right, and Janlow had declared during the autopsy that the direction of the blows indicated that the killer was left-handed. At trial the defense ripped into Janlow's report, demonstrating beyond doubt that the husband—the man Harry had arrested—was right-handed. The case seemed certain to fail, until Harry went back into the field and came up with several softball teammates of the accused, each of whom testified on redirect that the husband, though signing his name and throwing a ball with his right hand, always batted left.

"The wound goes back to the spine and caused a nick in the third vertebrae, indicating a heavy-bladed knife, possibly a hunting knife," Janlow continued. He paused again, thought over what he had said and then nodded to himself. "Okay, let's open her up," Janlow said, bringing himself and Harry back as he began the Y-shaped incision that went from each shoulder to the sternum, then ran in a straight line to the pubis.

Harry always handled the early stages of an autopsy well. The opening of the body cavity never bothered him. There was Vicks to dab under the nostrils to keep the odor of putrefaction at bay, and the inner organs, when explored and removed, never seemed quite real to him. His difficulties came later when the craniotomy was performed. It began with the sound of the scalp being ripped away from the skull; then pulled down over the face, followed by the buzz of the small electric saw as it cut around the skull; then the popping sound as the skull cap was pulled away, exposing the brain. It was at this point that Harry was always forced to think about what he had just witnessed. And he always came away with the same conclusion: it was the final indignity one human being could force upon another, not much more than a cruel joke, a stripping away of the last vestige of humanity, even if it's done with a noble intention, a search for the final truth of that person's life.

Darlene Beckett's autopsy took an hour and a half to complete. There would still be microscopic analyses of various organs, and subsequent toxicology reports, but the initial evidence was fairly clear. She had died because someone slit her throat.

As he prepared to leave the autopsy suite, Harry paused and looked back at the body. It was the last time he would see Darlene Beckett. He would see her in photographs, of course. They would fill his office until the case was solved. But this was the last time he would see *her.* He stared at her face. The look of surprise and terror were gone now, as if washed away by the autopsy, and Harry again realized how little sympathy he felt for this woman; how much he truly disliked her, even in death. But as he stared at her profile he offered an unspoken promise, just as he had to all those who had come before her: to find her killer and bring that person to trial. It's what I do, he thought. It's what I am, what I was made to be. He continued to stare at Darlene Beckett for several drawn-out moments until he realized that Mort Janlow was watching him. Then he turned and briskly walked away.

* * *

Harry returned to headquarters and went immediately to the CSI lab. He found Sergeant Marty LeBaron in his office, and dropped into a chair facing his desk.

"So . . ." Harry began.

LeBaron grinned at him. "Believe it or not, Harry, I *was* going to call you."

"No need. I'm here."

"I was trying for sarcasm," LeBaron said.

"Yeah, I know. Sarcasm accepted. So what have you got?"

"On the cross?"

"Especially the cross."

"The engraving is barely readable, but we were able to bring it up a bit with an acid bath. It's a line from the Lord's Prayer. It says: *And deliver us from evil . . .*"

"*For Thine is the kingdom and the power and the glory forever,*" Harry finished.

"Harry, I didn't know you were religious."

"I'm not." Harry stared at him across the desk. "Anything else?"

"Just confirmation of what we already knew. Tire tracks were all standard over-the-counter all-season tires. One set of Firestone; couple of sets of Bridgestone just like the ones we use on our police vehicles. Nothing that was special order, nothing that's going to help us identify a particular car, just common treads. In Tarpon Springs that software salesman parked his car off the road and carried the blanket and booze onto the beach. But the killer drove around the gate and in to where they were—like he knew he was going to need the car to load up the body."

"Or he parked on the road, followed them in, killed them, and then drove in to pick up Darlene's body," Harry said.

"Yeah, that makes sense. Oh, one thing more. The killer, we think, wears a size eleven shoe."

"Just like I do," Harry said. "And half the people who were at the crime scene," he added as an afterthought.

LeBaron lifted one foot and placed it on the edge of his desk. "Join the club," he said.

At seven o'clock the team was gathered in the conference room. Harry knew that cops were quick to feel slighted if they thought their work was being pushed aside for someone else's. So to keep everyone happy he advised the group that he'd be taking reports by order of seniority. That put Nick Benevuto first up. He and his partner, John Weathers, had checked out the alibis of Darlene's ex-husband, Jordan Beckett, and her high school boyfriend, Billy Smithers.

"The ex was out on his sailboat with his new girlfriend," Benevuto began. "The marina where he keeps the boat said he filled it up with diesel in the late afternoon on the day of the murder, and told the guy who filled it that he was heading south in the gulf for a few days. The girlfriend confirms that she was with him every minute right up to the time he got the call that Darlene was dead. His office also confirms that he took the time off from work." He gave Harry a shrug. "Of course, there's no way of being certain he didn't have a car stashed somewhere along the route, where he could get back, do his ex-wife, and return to the boat. So I checked for any traffic citations or parking tickets he might have gotten between here and Venice, along with the area north of the marina in case he lied about where he took the boat. I also checked car rentals for him and his girlfriend. Nada. If it went down that way the girlfriend would have to be in on it, and she honestly doesn't seem the type. She comes across as pretty much of a straight arrow."

"What did you find out about her?" Harry asked.

"She's an emergency room nurse at Tampa General. They've got nothing but good things to say about her—dedicated, caring, all the usual bullshit. I thought I was listening to a goddamn commercial."

"Did you have time to check his credit cards to see if he made any gasoline purchases on land at the same time he was supposed to be on the boat?"

"Not yet, but I planned to do that in the morning."

Benevuto said it a bit sheepishly and Harry knew he had caught him out. "Okay, let's leave Jordan Beckett for now. What about the old boyfriend, Billy Smithers?"

"Same story," John Weathers chimed in. "He's got three buddies who say he was at a Rays game at Tropicana Field the night of the murder. All of them said they stayed to the end then went to a bar for a few beers before heading home. It was at least one a.m. before they left St. Petersburg, so that puts him about thirty miles from the crime scene until well after Darlene was iced. Oh, and Smithers also has his ticket stub from the game. It was still in his wallet."

"Why would he keep the ticket stub?" Harry asked.

"These guys buy reserved seats near the Rays' dugout. The attendants check tickets every time you go out and try to come back in. So he just stuck the stub in his wallet. It was still there."

"Okay, we'll cross Mr. Smithers off the list for now. When you get a chance check out the bar they were at. Take a driver's license picture with you and see if the bartender can confirm their story." Harry turned to the Tarpon Springs detectives, the two D's, Bob Davis and Jerry Deaver. "What did you guys come up with at the murder sight?"

Davis and Deaver looked like Tweedle Dum and Tweedle Dee. They were the same height, about five-ten; both had the same blocky builds, with thick necks and square faces, and each had out-of-date crew cuts. If they had worn fedoras they would have fit into a 1940s detective flick, Harry thought.

Davis took the lead: "Our canvass of the neighbors around the park pretty much drew a blank. One guy," he paused to consult his notebook and rattle off a name and address, "he was out walking his pooch a little before midnight and he remembers two cars being parked near the entrance to the park. He didn't pay a lot of attention to them because kids park there sometimes and walk into the park to fool around. The work crews claim they pick up a lotta used condoms around the picnic areas, especially on weekends."

"At least your local kids are practicing safe sex," Vicky offered.

"Yeah, there's that," Davis said. "But it doesn't make me want to eat my lunch on one of those picnic tables."

"Did this neighbor remember the make and model of either of the cars?" Harry asked.

"No. He's so used to seeing cars there, he didn't pay much attention. He just noticed they were there. He did remember that both of them looked pretty new for kid's cars. But other than our dog walker nobody saw anything or heard anything unusual. It's a pretty quiet neighborhood. On work nights most people are in bed by the time our murder went down. One thing that's curious is that a car did drive around the gate. CSI has casts of the tires, but there doesn't seem to be anything special about them. And we can't be certain it happened around the time of the murder. Could have been earlier, or later. All we know for certain is that they're Bridgestone tires. Same tread as the car that drove into Brooker Creek."

"Yeah," Harry said. "I already got a report from Marty LeBaron on that. I think we can lean toward the idea that this was the killer's car. That he drove it in to pick up Darlene's body. So I'd like you to stay on it. If the cars are new they probably have factory tires on them. So check and see what makes and models came out of the factory with those treads, or better yet what dealers might offer those tires as options."

"You got it," Davis said.

Harry turned to Vicky. "What did you come up with on the abuse victim and his family?"

Vicky opened her notebook. "The kid's name is Billy Hall, but that's something we can't let out to the media. His identity is still protected as a juvenile. He's fifteen years old—he was barely fourteen when Darlene abused him."

Nick Benevuto let out a snort. "I wish somebody like Darlene had abused me when I was fourteen."

Soft laughter filled the room.

Vicky inhaled and let out a long breath. "Alright, guys, let's get something straight. It is abuse whether it's done to a male or female. And it does cause harm. Trust me. I saw enough of it in sex crimes." She could tell she wasn't getting through to most of them. "Look, I know it's hard for all you macho guys not to think that what Darlene did wasn't all that terrible. I've heard the *Who did she hurt?* argument over and over in cases like hers. But try to think of it as a male teacher doing what she did to a fourteen-year-old girl. Trust me, it's the same power trip and it's just as damaging. This kid is shell-shocked from all the notoriety. He just wants it to go away and he wants a hole to hide in until it does. His parents are two hard-working, blue-collar types, and they just want the same thing. They've got friends and neighbors who have turned their backs on them because they refused to let the kid testify. And it doesn't matter that they did that based on a psychologist's recommendation. The friends and neighbors are salt-of-earth types themselves, and they all wanted Darlene hung out to dry. When she was allowed to cop a plea, so the kid wouldn't have to testify, they took it out on the parents. The parents told me that even the people in the church they attended turned their backs on them."

"So there had to be a lot of resentment toward Darlene," Harry suggested.

"A ton of it," Vicky said. "The boy's mother flat out said she was glad Darlene was dead—that she'd like to thank whoever killed her."

"They have alibis for the night of the murder?" Harry asked.

"Just each other," Vicky said. "They all claim they were home that night, that they watched a little television, then went to bed around eleven. But even if that's true, it doesn't rule out that another member of their family, a neighbor or friend, or somebody from their church, won't qualify as a suspect. There's a lot more checking to do there."

"I agree," Harry said. "It's a promising lead. Let's talk about it some more later." Harry now turned to the uniforms, taking them one at a time, starting with those who were checking out the owners of cars seen parked in Darlene's driveway. The one person who had visited most often was her probation officer. He had visited her like clockwork every Thursday night. Her other visitors all seemed to have alibis, some stronger than others, but they still had to be checked out. Harry told the deputies to keep at it until they had all the alibis nailed down one way or the other.

The last man he called on was Deputy Jim Morgan, who had been asked to recanvass Darlene's neighbors.

"I just came up with one new thing, but I think it could be important," Morgan began. "The elderly neighbor, the one who kept track of the cars in her driveway, Joshua Brown, well, it seems he withheld two plate numbers when he gave you the list he compiled."

Harry cocked his head to one side, surprised by the information. He couldn't understand why the old man would do that and he was a little embarrassed that he hadn't pressed him enough to draw that information out during his initial interview. "Tell me about it," he said.

"Well, it was all his doing." Morgan was obviously uncomfortable that he had put Harry on the spot. "He just threw it out while I was talking to him—that he was surprised we didn't already have all the plate numbers since we were watching her so closely. When I asked him what he meant, he told me he had seen two unmarked cars in front of her house and figured we were watching her pretty close."

"How did he know they were unmarked police cars?"

"He said he saw the radios through the windows. He had already written down the license numbers, but he didn't include the cars on the list after he saw the police radios."

"But he kept the numbers," Harry said.

"Sure did. All the numbers were in a small notebook he carried when he took his dog out for walks. Then he transferred the numbers to the list he gave you. These two numbers were still in his notebook with lines drawn through them."

Harry couldn't help but smile. A notebook, transferring plate numbers to another list. The old coot had embarrassed him, but thank God he had so much time on his hands. "So did you run those new plates?"

"Yes, I did. And here's the kicker. Both cars are registered to us, to the Pinellas County Sheriff's Department. And according to the motor pool there's no record of who took either of those cars out." Morgan paused. "And there should be."

"Sounds like we have some more work to do," Harry said, then turned to Vicky. "I'd like you to work with Jim on this. I'd also like one of you to run a computer check on past murders—local and federal. See if you can come up with anytime where the victim's face was covered by a mask or where words were carved in the flesh. And don't limit the check to this county or even to Florida."

Vicky's eyebrows rose. "You thinking serial killer here?"

"No. But I don't want to overlook the possibility either, and then get second guessed about why we never checked. While you're doing that I'll pick up where you left off with the kid and his family. Everybody else just keep working on what you've got." He looked back at Morgan. "Helluva nice job."

Morgan tried to suppress a grin. Harry took it in and decided that the young deputy, like most cops, had an oversized ego. And he likes it fed with as much praise as he can get.

* * *

Harry was back at his desk jotting the information Vicky had gathered into his notebook, while she dictated it from hers.

"Why do you want me working with Morgan?" she asked when they had finished.

"This is new for him," Harry said. "I just want to make sure he follows through on it. I have no reason to believe he won't, but then I don't know how he feels about investigating other cops, and I just want to make sure I've got somebody more experienced looking over his shoulder." He gave Vicky a long look. "This is something that could come back and bite us if it's not handled right. Even if it doesn't prove to be part of the case, we've got to be able to show we investigated it thoroughly. I also want you to check out Darlene's probation officer. Find out why he spent so much time at her town house and what the hell she was doing without her ankle monitor—"

The phone on Harry's desk rang, interrupting him.

"Doyle," he said as he answered it.

"Harry, it's Walter Lee Hollins, over at the prison."

Harry's stomach tightened and seemed to rise toward his throat. It had to be news about his mother, and news about her was never good. "Hey, Walter Lee, something going on?"

"Yeah, I'm afraid there is. Your mama just got notified that she's been put up for a parole hearing. I wanted to make sure you heard about it, in case those assholes on the parole board or in the state's attorney's office forget to tell you. It's happened before."

"When will it be?" Harry's voice had gone dead cold and most of the color had left his face. He could feel Vicky staring at him, but refused to look at her.

"They ain't set a date yet, far as I know. But it could be as soon as next week. If she don't make the list for that parole hearing, it'll probably be the next one. I'm not sure how close they're scheduling them right now. There's a lot of pressure from Tallahassee to parole as many as we can to ease up on overcrowding. I never thought it would affect your mama though. Not with what she's in here for."

"No, I didn't either. Thanks for the information."

"No problem, Harry. You take care, hear?"

When Harry ended the call Vicky was still staring at him. "Bad news?" she asked.

"Just some personal stuff."

CHAPTER SIX

Harry sat on the lanai, a box of letters before him, a few already yellowing with age. The letters had been written by his mother, one each year, stretching back to when he was eleven years old. Each was written and carefully mailed so it would arrive on a specific day—the anniversary of the day she had killed her two small sons. Now, twenty years later, it was odd to think that he had died on that day. But it was a simple fact. He had not been breathing and had lacked a heartbeat when the two Tampa cops broke into the garage and started CPR on the two small boys they found there. But it only worked for one . . . only one had come back.

Harry picked up the last letter he had received, the only one he hadn't yet read. Each year he had to force himself to read her latest letter. This time it was taking longer than usual. But he knew once he read it, he would read it over and over again, sickened by the madness he would find there. He also had to force himself to read *all* the letters again, hoping he'd find enough in each to present a strong, clear argument to the parole board, something that would keep them from turning his mother loose.

His hands trembled slightly as he opened the letter. He looked at his hands and gave a slight shake of his head. There were criminals on the street who would love to see that hint of fear, that slight crack in will that they could pounce on, something that made him vulnerable, another potential victim rather than a threat. But they wouldn't see it. He'd make certain that never happened. And if the day ever came that he could no longer hide his fear, he knew he would walk away from the job and never look back.

He removed the letter from the envelope. It was plain, prison-issue stationery, the writing paper lined, the return address on the envelope just a name and inmate number. It began as it always did; the same first line that never varied except for the number of years since Jimmy's death.

My Darling Son,

Your brother Jimmy has been with Jesus for twenty-one years now. How I wish you were there too, sitting before Him in His everlasting glory, receiving the reward that comes to all who lead a life of goodness. I tried my best, but things don't always happen the way God wants. I've learned that sometimes the evildoers have their way. Sometimes the devil steps in and stops even the plans of the Lord.

I have suffered here in man's purgatory for twenty-one years now. But this year there is some good news, finally some hope. The doctor who they made me see says he will recommend that I be sent home. I had to tell him that I am sorry about what I did. For years I tried to tell people that I needed my sons to be with Jesus, to be there waiting for me when I arrived. But this was something very few people could ever understand. For the last few years I have stopped trying, except with my minister, who visits me often. He tells me it is alright to be sorry that Jimmy died and to also be happy he is with the Lord. So that is what I tell people now. The important thing is that I will soon come to you. I know they have been hiding the letters you have written to me. It is an evil act, but it is their way of punishing me for my sins. Maybe when I am sent home they will give me those letters they have hidden away. I promise, if they do, that I will read each and every one. I often wonder if you are married now, and if you are, if you have children of your own. I would like very much to be a grandmother who can sit with her grandchildren and tell them the story of Jesus and Mary and Joseph. It is what grandmothers should do. They should make sure that all children

*are ready to go to God and to sit before His wondrous goodness, to live
in His house forever and ever. But we will talk about that when I see
you. I pray to the Lord Almighty that it will be very, very soon. I miss
you and Jimmy so very much.*

Pray for me, my son,
Your loving mother

The letter had been written in a neat, precise cursive, each letter so
small it was barely an eighth of an inch above the line on which it was
penned. Harry stared at it, thinking about those small, precise letters coming out of that twisted mind, flying like insects to gather on the paper as
she willed them to be. He remembered his mother from childhood, always
affectionate, especially when he was younger, then later as he approached
adolescence becoming strangely aloof, almost as though she were living in
a world apart from him. He remembered when he was nine and she began
standing outside the bathroom door whenever she knew he was inside,
asking him what he was doing that was taking so long, warning him not to
do things that were wrong. He had not known what she meant. Puberty
was still years away. It was the madness slowly growing. He knew that now.
But at the time he thought it was because he had come to displease her. He
didn't pay much attention to it. He thought it was something that would
pass. She was his mother, and he therefore believed she had to love him. It
was just the way things were. Jimmy had noticed the change in her as well.
He had called it her strange time. But to him it was more of a joke. *Mama's
in her strange time,* Jimmy would say, and then he would giggle.

There was a light rap on the screen door, and when he looked up he
saw Jeanie Walsh standing there smiling at him.

"Are you working?" she asked. "I don't want to interrupt you if you
are. I heard all about your new case on the news. That you're heading up

the investigation, I mean. It sounds awful." She drew a breath. "God, I'm babbling."

It was a bright night with a full moon high in the sky. A clear stream of moonlight illuminated one side of her face, making her short, curly blond hair sparkle; leaving the other side deep in shadow. It made her look beautiful and elusive, he thought; some pixie who had floated in on the gulf wind.

"No, it's not work," he said. "Come in."

He gathered the letters, returning them to the shoe box where he stored them.

She took a chair at the round outdoor table where he was seated, her eyes going to the old box.

"My mother's letters," he said. "I heard today that she'll be coming up for parole, and I wanted to be able to show the parole board that she hasn't changed, no matter what the prison shrinks say."

"Is that what you want . . . to keep her in prison?" Jeanie asked.

"That's what I want."

"It must be hard, coming at a time when you've got this big case."

"It would be hard if I was on vacation on some quiet Caribbean island. I just don't want her back in my life. I don't want her to have any part in my life ever again."

Jeanie looked at him and nodded slowly. Then her eyes drifted back to the box of letters. Oh, Harry, she thought, my sweet Harry. She's here right now whether you see it or not, and she always will be whether you want it or not. And all the letters in the world, and all the parole boards, won't be able to change it.

She spoke none of it. Instead she smiled and said, "Would you like to go for a walk on the beach?"

Harry nodded. "Sure. Just let me put these letters away."

Jeanie smiled at him and wondered if he ever would.

* * *

The car was parked under a small palm just up the street from Harry's house, the driver slouched behind the wheel, his eyes roaming the street before returning to the house. Not bad for a cop, the watcher thought. The house, old and inelegant as it was, would still be worth a cool million even as a teardown. He had wanted to see where the detective lived. He would be running the investigation and you never knew when an unexpected visit might become necessary. It had been easy to follow him home. Still, he had been cautious, had remained well back, careful not to give himself away. It had been more caution than had probably been needed. Criminals seldom go after cops for revenge, so it's usually dirty cops who worry about being followed, and he had no reason to believe that Harry Doyle fell into that category.

He started the car and made a quick U-turn. No point in hanging around and risk being seen. He had what he needed. Now it was better to play it smart and blend back into the scenery. Just like always: the little branch on the big tree, too insignificant to be noticed, but there all the same.

CHAPTER SEVEN

Harry knocked on the door and waited for someone to answer. It was nine in the morning and the day was already beginning to heat up. It was expected to reach ninety by midday, and based on the trickle of perspiration he could feel under his shirt it already seemed well on its way. The house was a single-story rectangle, built close to the street so the small lot could provide some semblance of a backyard. Like most of Florida's homes it was a cinder-block construction with the exterior walls covered in stucco, all of it a quiet nod to the yearly hurricane season. Of course, if a big enough hurricane hit, the cinder blocks would be all that was left. Once the windows were broken by flying debris the roof would be ripped away and everything inside the house would become part of the tempest.

The house was located in Temple Terrace on the northern outskirts of Tampa, less than a mile from the home that Darlene Beckett had once shared with her husband. It was on a short street that ended in a cul-de-sac, a working-class neighborhood where each house offered up bicycles, skateboards, or doll carriages stranded on the front lawns. Every other driveway seemed to be graced with a basketball hoop. On the surface it was a neighborhood of hard-working families with plenty of children to love and care for and support.

Harry rang the bell a second time before it was finally answered by a short, solidly built woman dressed in a T-shirt and shorts. She had unruly brown hair and a plain face absent of makeup. She also seemed short of breath. Vicky's notes said she and her husband were both thirty-five, but right now the woman looked considerably older.

"Sorry to leave you waiting. I was in the back of the house making up the beds."

Harry held up his shield and introduced himself.

The woman's face deflated. "I just had another detective here yesterday. Is it about the same thing, that bitch who hurt my son?"

"It's about Darlene Beckett," Harry said. "Are you Mrs. Hall?"

"That's me. Betty Hall, mother of the victim." There was a weary sarcasm in her voice as if she were repeating a phrase she had heard and read too often.

"There are some things I have to go over with you, your husband, and your son."

"My husband's at work and my son's asleep, and I'm not waking him up for *this*." Her voice was uncompromising and Harry knew better than to fight her on the position she had just staked out.

"Then I'll talk to you now, and I'll come back to talk to your husband and son later today. What time do you expect your husband home?"

She let out a long, weary breath. "Six, six-thirty. Not before that."

"Can you arrange to have your son available then too?"

"Why not?" She looked past him and shook her head. "Why not give him another sleepless night."

She led him through the air-conditioned house, through a set of sliding glass doors, and out on to a lanai that held a small pool. She explained that she didn't want her son waking up and overhearing yet another conversation about Darlene Beckett. Then she let out a breath as if finally giving in to the inevitable and asked Harry if he'd care for some coffee.

"Thank you, I'd love some," he responded. He really didn't want coffee or anything else, but now that he had her in a giving mood he wanted to keep her there.

"Cream? Sugar?"

"Black is fine."

She went back into the house and returned minutes later with two hot mugs. Even before he tasted it the aroma told Harry it would be good.

Taking his time, Harry eased into the interrogation. "Mrs. Hall, I don't have any children, myself, so I can't fully appreciate the pain this has caused you and your family. And I'm sorry I have to revive it for you all. But we have a murder to investigate, and as you know it's captured a lot of attention from the media. Now, right or wrong, this puts pressure on the people above me, and believe me, that pressure rolls downhill. So I need to solve this case as quickly as possible, which, if I can do that, will serve your interests as well. The sooner I can find out who killed Darlene Beckett, the sooner the focus of the media will turn away from you and your son. Okay?"

"Are you going to protect my son and my family from the media?" Her eyes bore into him.

"As best we can. I'm the lead investigator on this case and I don't want the media in contact with *any* of our witnesses. But I can only control it from our end. If you or any member of your family, or any of your friends, chooses to talk to the media, I can't control that. But no information will come from us." Harry didn't say that he also couldn't control what the brass in his own department might do.

"We've already had them calling," she said, "and right off we changed our phone number. *Again.*" The line of her mouth hardened, but Harry could tell she was fighting to keep tears from her eyes. "We sold our old house six months ago and moved here. I loved our old house. We all did. Our kids were born there; most of our friends were there. But that woman—what she did and all the madness it brought down on us—didn't leave us much choice. My son was scared every time he went out of the house, scared that some reporter or some fanatic was gonna jump out of the bushes and start in on him." The tears began to well in her eyes. "The school system even made him change schools. He got *thrown out* of his school because of what that woman did to him. One of their own employees." Both her fists had clenched now. "Oh, they said it was for his own good, but they just wanted to be rid of him, be rid of what they let happen to him. And he saw it for what it was: a punishment." She shook her head violently. "How else *could* he see it? Even the church he'd gone to all his life turned against us."

Harry opened his notebook, which held the notes Vicky had taken. He had to turn the questions to areas where he needed answers and hoped the woman was ready for it. Cooperation, he knew, even among the innocent, was a matter of will.

"Mrs. Hall, when Detective Stanopolis was here yesterday you folks told her that you were all at home together at the time Ms. Beckett was killed."

"That's right. My husband and I were in the living room watching a show we like. The kids were in the family room watching something different. We even told her what the shows were about," she added.

"I know you did," Harry said. "But according to Detective Stanopolis's report, no one other than the people who were here could confirm that you were all here together."

"Well, that's not true," she snapped. She shook her head. "I don't mean that the detective didn't tell the truth. What I mean is that after she left I realized that my husband's mother had called that night to say she couldn't find her medicine. She's got heart trouble and her husband just passed away a few months ago, so she calls Joe every time something goes wrong. I think she just needs to know someone's there to help her." She smiled, weakly. "Anyway, I answered the phone when she called at about ten o'clock and gave the phone to Joe. Then, when she called back an hour later, I answered the phone again, and gave it to Joe."

"Did she talk to her grandchildren?" Harry asked.

Betty Hall's jaw tightened. "No, she didn't. You'll just have to take our word that they were here." Her voice was ice.

"It's good to have whatever confirmation we can get. It'll just spare you more questions down the road." Harry offered her a small smile that wasn't returned. "Can I get your mother-in-law's name, address, and phone number?"

Mrs. Hall rattled off the information.

Harry consulted the notebook. "Was there anyone in particular who seemed unusually upset about what happened to your son or the fact that Ms. Beckett was allowed to plead to a lesser charge?"

"You mean that she walked away pretty much scot-free?" Her eyes became fierce. "Yeah, there were Joe and me for starters. I don't think my son cared. I think he was just glad it was over. At least he thought it was."

"Anyone outside your family?" Harry pressed. "How about anyone at your husband's job, or friends of yours?"

"No, our friends either tried to be supportive, or just avoided the subject . . . and us too—at least some of them did. The guys on my husband's job, well, they all thought it was real funny. Or they were telling him how lucky his kid was, especially after they saw that bitch on television. The only people who really wanted to see her hung out to dry were some of the people at our church. They couldn't understand why we were willing to let her off the hook without a trial. But they didn't have to listen to Billy crying in his room, they didn't have to see him afraid to go out of the house. Even the psychologist we sent him to said to let it go. He said having to testify and live it all over again, plus dealing with all the publicity that a trial would bring, could cause him serious emotional stress. So I said to hell with all of them, I was gonna put my son first. So I just told the prosecutor to kiss my grits and we stopped going to that damned church. My husband never wanted to go to the church anyway. He just did it for the kids, and because I wanted it."

"What's the name of the church?" Harry asked.

"The First Assembly of Jesus Christ the Lord." She pushed back an unruly strand of hair that had fallen across her forehead. "I've got a church bulletin. There's something in it I want to show you, anyway."

She retrieved the bulletin and gave it to Harry. It was professionally printed and slickly laid out, filled with church information, some short feature articles, and a column by the minister, the Reverend John Waldo. Betty Hall had underlined a comment in that column relating to Darlene Beckett. She jabbed a finger at it. "Just read it. That's what we were living with every time we went to church."

Harry read the minister's column. In it, Reverend Waldo urged his parishioners to *fulfill your Christian duty and do whatever you can to bring justice to Darlene Beckett and thereby free the boy she has led astray so he can be returned to the loving arms of Jesus Christ.*

"And that s.o.b. pressed for that every chance he got," she said.

Vicky decided that she and Jim Morgan would take on Darlene's probation officer before they ventured into the quagmire of the department's computer systems. Morgan, apparently a closet computer geek, raised a mild objection, but Vicky refused to be swayed.

"People before machines," she said. "People have heart attacks or get hit by buses. Machines will be there the next day."

Morgan pointed out that machines caught deadly viruses and had fatal crashes too. Then he laughed and agreed that he couldn't fight her logic. He had a nice laugh, she thought, one that went well with his outgoing, easy manner. He was tall and lean, well put together, but not the type who wore his shirts a size too small to accent his biceps. There were enough of those in the department and she had no interest in working with someone who had to check himself out in every mirror he passed. Before today she had only seen Morgan in uniform. Now, dressed in casual civilian clothes, there was a youthful quality about him that she found very appealing. He had short, sandy hair, striking blue eyes, and a wide, sensual mouth, and she couldn't help but notice that he wasn't wearing a wedding band. She caught herself and pushed that thought away. She had no intention of getting involved with anyone. She'd been dumped by her last boyfriend and had no interest in having a rebound love affair with somebody on the job. She found herself smiling. But you can look, she thought.

Darlene's probation officer was an eighteen-year veteran named Bennie Rolf. His office was adjacent to the Hillsborough County Courthouse in a featureless 1960s building. The interior was much the same, cookie-cutter offices filled with drab, institutional furnishings that were one step above those found in most prisons.

Bennie Rolf fit the offices perfectly. Just under six feet, he carried two hundred and forty pounds layered over a frame designed for one-eighty. He was in his early forties with fast receding brown hair and a badly trimmed beard that was flecked with gray. Just looking at him, Vicky would have bet the rent money that he had a nasty case of bad breath.

The man also looked a little twitchy, Vicky thought, as they took chairs in his cramped office. She decided she'd have to watch his eyes throughout the interview, looking for the *tell* that would let her know when he was lying.

The office was a mess with client folders and papers piled haphazardly. There was a lone window that looked out onto a parking lot and the glass in the window was the only part of the office that appeared clean.

Vicky started off slow and friendly. "So Bennie, did Darlene ever tell you about any threats she'd received, or anyone in particular that she was afraid of—like maybe her ex-husband, or boyfriend, or somebody she met while she was out bar hopping?"

"She wasn't allowed in bars," Rolf said. "That was part of her probation agreement."

Vicky smiled across the desk. "Well, let me clue you in, Bennie. The lady was a regular at one bar we know of for sure. And we've got witnesses who'll swear to it. In fact, the guy who was killed with her picked her up in that bar."

"I know. I read it in the papers." Rolf shook his head as if even now he found it hard to believe. "We can't follow clients around twenty-four-seven. We can only do the best we can."

"Well, you sure seemed to be trying." She watched Rolf nod agreement. "You sure made enough visits to her apartment."

"Not that many," Rolf protested.

Now it was Vicky's turn to shake her head in disbelief. "Bennie, Bennie, Bennie, we got a neighbor who was a regular hawk about Darlene. He literally kept a book on every car that was parked in her driveway. And he was home day and night, so he didn't miss many. In the past nine months, which is ever since she started reporting to you, he's got you there thirty-nine times. That's at least once a week. Seem about right to you?"

Bennie began to stutter. "Wa . . . Wa . . . Well, I don't know about that. I don't think my case file would show that many visits."

"Maybe you didn't write them all down," Morgan suggested.

"Oh, no. Oh, no. I always record every visit."

"Is it normal to visit a client that many times?" Vicky asked.

Rolf raised his hands defensively. "Look, this woman was notorious, a very high-profile case. Sure, I visited her more than usual. If anything went wrong with her, if she got involved with another kid, say, well, my butt would be on the carpet big time."

Bennie was sweating now. His eyes were blinking rapidly and his stutter wasn't about to go away. The man had so many tells going you could hardly keep track of them, Vicky thought. She remained silent, knowing instinctively that Bennie would fill the void. She glanced at Morgan, letting him know she wanted him to follow her lead. The silence didn't last long.

"Look," Bennie said, "if this was a drug dealer, or some petty hood that somebody offed, you guys wouldn't even be here. I've had plenty of clients who've ended up dead, but I can count on one hand the number of times you guys have come to me with questions."

Vicky and Morgan continued to stare at him. Finally, Vicky leaned forward as if expecting him to say more.

Rolf obliged. "Okay, maybe I was a little intrigued with her too. For crissake, she'd become a media star, hadn't she? So just like everybody else, I took a special interest in her."

Vicky nodded as if she understood completely. "Tell us about the ankle monitor, Bennie."

"Oh, no. Oh, no." Bennie waved both hands in front of himself as if it would ward off what Vicky was suggesting. "I've got no idea how she got that off. The last time I visited her I checked it—just like I did every time I saw her—and she had it on just like she was supposed to. That's right there in every one of my reports."

"How do you think she got it off?" Morgan asked.

"How the hell do I know?" Bennie caught himself and made his voice less defensive. "Look, this isn't the first case I've had of somebody getting one of those off. It's not foolproof, for crissake."

Vicky looked toward the window. Disbelief mingled with disgust and Bennie picked up on it immediately.

"Hey, if you're trying to say that I had something to do with the monitor coming off, that's bullshit. Why would I risk my career, my pension, everything I have, for that slut?"

"You married, Bennie?" Vicky asked.

"What? No. What does that have to do with anything?"

"Yeah, law enforcement, it's a lonely life outside the job," Vicky said. "Sometimes that's all you've got, the job and the people you work with every day." She looked back at him. "You find that to be true, Bennie?"

"Hey, I don't like where you're going here," Rolf snapped. "You've got no proof I did something wrong. If anything, what you've got shows I worked extra hard to keep an eye on Darlene. And that's *all* it shows." Perspiration began to gather on his upper lip. "But if you even suggest what you're hinting at here, you could cause me a lot of grief. You know that. We have the equivalent of an internal affairs division in our department too. And they get on your case, they start going through *all* your files, interviewing *all* your clients. And when they do that, they can always come up with something. Hell, the clients will claim you did all kinds of shit. You've been breaking their chops and suddenly they have a chance to get back at you, and they take it. You better believe they take it."

"We don't want to cause you any trouble, Bennie. We just need to know what went down with Darlene Beckett." Vicky made the claim with as much sincerity as she could muster.

"Nothing went down with her. Not with me. I did my job the way I was supposed to. If anything, I did it too well, and now I'm getting slammed for it." Bennie took out a handkerchief and wiped the sweat from his face. "God it's hot in here," he said defensively. "That damned air-conditioning system must be on the fritz again."

"I was just thinking it's a bit chilly," Vicky said. "But forget about that, Bennie. Let's get back to our original question. Did Darlene ever express any fear about anybody—ex-husband, boyfriend, the guy next door, anybody at all?"

Bennie shook his head emphatically. "All she ever did was whine about the restrictions the court put on her."

"Did she ever express any remorse about what she did to that young boy?" Morgan asked.

"Darlene? Are you kidding? She never expressed remorse about anything. She was just like all the others I deal with every day. The only thing she regretted was getting caught."

Vicky stared at him, wondering if the man saw that the same description fit him as well.

"I need a complete rundown on where you were and who you were with on the night Darlene was killed," Vicky said, her voice becoming very cold.

Bennie Rolf closed his eyes momentarily and nodded. "Sure," he said, "whatever you want."

Back in their car, Vicky took a few minutes to jot down some additional observations in her notebook. When she finished she glanced at Morgan. The line of his jaw had a hard set to it. "So, what do you think?" she asked.

Morgan stared straight ahead. "I think Darlene Beckett talked her P.O. into taking that monitor off, and I think she paid him off with sex whenever he came by."

"Yeah, I agree. I think she made him the proverbial offer he couldn't refuse. It was probably a dream come true for that poor, pathetic slug. But I don't think we'll ever prove it."

Morgan turned to face her. "Are we at least going to recommend that his department investigate him? He's probably doing the same thing with every female client he has."

"Could be. But that'll be up to the state's attorney when we close the case and hand over our final reports. I'll sure include my suspicions. But after that it will be up to powers greater than me." She let Morgan chew on that before adding, "Just don't be surprised if nobody wants to raise that issue. Law enforcement agencies don't like to piss on each other. They all worry about being tarred by the same brush. So, unless there's some political advantage to be had, or they're forced to do something, they usually prefer to look the other way."

"That stinks," Morgan said.

"Yeah, it does."

* * *

Harry returned to the Halls' Temple Terrace home promptly at six-thirty. He had spent the intervening hours confirming Mrs. Hall's alibi, running background checks on all members of the family, and trying to trace the origin of the gold cross he had found at the Tarpon Springs crime scene.

Mrs. Hall opened the door, looked at him, and sighed. "My mother-in-law told me you stopped by to see her," she said.

"Just routine, Mrs. Hall," Harry said. "I'm just dotting all the I's. Are your husband and son at home?"

"As promised," she replied. "Come in. My husband's out on the lanai cooking some burgers. You know the way. I'll tell my son you're here."

"I'd rather talk to your husband alone and talk to your son when we're finished."

Betty Hall eyed him suspiciously. "Back when this all started, our lawyer told us we had the right to be present whenever Billy was interviewed by the police."

"That's true," Harry said. "And if that's the way you want it, that's the way it will be. But I do want to talk to your husband without your son being there. I think he'll be able to talk more freely if we do it that way. I can take him to my office if you'd rather."

Betty Hall glared at him. "Do it your way. That's the way it's been since this whole thing started."

Joe Hall was a big, burly man, who worked as a supervisor for one of the area's larger construction firms. He was easily six-three, a good two hundred and forty pounds, and dressed as he was now in shorts and a T-shirt, he looked like someone who could have played middle linebacker for a Division I football team. There was no question in Harry's mind that he could have overpowered both the "cowboy" and Darlene Beckett. But all of that was dispelled when he turned to greet Harry. He had a high widow's peak over the softest brown eyes Harry had ever seen in a man, and his voice was so equally soft and gentle that Harry had to listen carefully to be sure he caught every word. He was as far from homicidal as any man Harry had ever met.

"I hope you'll take it easy on my son Billy when you talk to him," Hall began. "He tries to cover it up, but all this has hit him pretty hard. We thought he was starting to come out of it, but now with her being murdered and all, it's just started up for him all over again."

"I'll do my best not to make it worse," Harry said. "But right now I need to ask you some questions."

"Sure. Fire away."

Harry took him through their activities on the night of Darlene's murder, and the alibi he had already established. All of Hall's answers squared with what he already knew.

"At any time since this all began, did anyone ever say anything to you that made you feel they wanted to do harm to Darlene Beckett?"

Hall shook his head. "No, never. The only people who really spouted off about her were the people at our church." He let out a weary breath. "But they spout off about a lot of things. It wasn't like they were ready to burn her at the stake or anything."

"What do they spout off about?" Harry asked, more to keep him going than to get any specific information.

"Oh, you know, they're anti stuff. They're anti-gay, anti-abortion, anti-immigrants, anti the way kids dress today, especially girls, anti the music they listen to. It's like they know just how the world should be, and anything less than that is sinful."

"So why go to the church if you find it offensive?" Harry asked.

"I just never worried about it that much; I sort of tuned it all out. My wife liked the church. They had a really good youth program and she thought it was helpful for the kids to have that religious influence." He shook his head. "I guess it didn't take for my son. But God knows, I don't know what I would have done if I'd faced that same situation at fourteen. I'm pretty sure I'd have been just as scared as he was."

"He was frightened?"

"He told me he was," Hall said. "And I believe him. But I don't expect him to admit that to you. That would break the code. You know what I mean?"

Harry thought of his gangsta friend Rubio Martí. "Yeah, I know what you mean. When was the last time you saw Darlene Beckett?" Harry asked, changing tack.

"In court, the day the plea deal was approved by the judge." Anger came to Mr. Hall's eyes for the first time since they had started talking. "She walked out of that courtroom and she smiled at us. Can you believe it? She hurts my son like that, and she turns all of our lives to shit, and she smiles about it." Hall drew a deep breath. "I'll tell you, Detective Doyle. Right then I wanted to hurt that woman, and if I was ever gonna kill her I would have killed her right then and there. And I would have done it with my bare hands."

Billy Hall sat at the small outdoor table, flanked by each of his parents. Through the sliding glass doors Harry could see his six-year-old sister peaking out at them from far back in the house. Harry studied the boy closely. Because of his age, no photographs of him had ever run in area newspapers, so this was the first time Harry had seen him. He looked like a typical fifteen-year-old Florida teenager, thin and lanky with tanned skin and sunbleached hair. He had none of his father's size, although his bone structure hinted that he might one day grow into it. His blue eyes came from his mother as did a longish nose and wide mouth. There was nothing exceptional about him. He was neither particularly attractive nor unattractive. Right now his eyes were wary, almost frightened, and his lips trembled slightly when he spoke.

"Billy, when was the last time you saw Darlene Beckett?" Harry asked.

"In court," Billy said. "The last time she was in court."

"Did you speak to her?"

The boy shook his head vehemently.

"When was the last time you spoke to her?"

"In school." The boy blushed deeply. "You know, just before the police got involved and arrested her."

"What did you talk about?"

"She told me we both had to deny everything, and that I had to get my cousin to take back the stuff he told the cops."

"Did you do that?"

Another shake of the head. "My mom and dad told me I had to play it straight with the police, and that I'd just get Randy—that's my cousin—in trouble if I got him to lie."

"And you never spoke to her again."

"No."

"Did she ever try to get in touch with you?"

"No, not after that last time in school."

"Did you ever hear anyone make threats against Ms. Beckett?" Harry asked.

The boy shrugged. "I heard some people say some bad things about her." He glanced furtively at his mother. "But I never heard nobody say they were gonna kill her or beat her up or anything. Some people at the church said she'd burn in hell for what she did." He twisted nervously in his chair. "They said I'd burn in hell too, if I didn't repent. I told them I already had, but they said I had to do it publicly, like in front of the whole congregation. I told them, no way."

"Okay, Billy." Harry handed him a business card. "That has my office phone and my cell numbers on it. If you think of anything else, I want you to call me. Straight?"

Billy lowered his eyes and nodded. Harry doubted the boy would ever call, but he was certain he'd be seeing him again.

Harry was alone in the conference room going over his notes and the reports filed by the other members of the team, when the door flew open and Vicky breezed in.

"You missed one heck of an interview," she said. "Morgan and I just finished up with Bennie Rolf, Darlene's P.O. The man started peeing his pants so hard I thought we were gonna need a rowboat."

She was grinning; her eyes dancing with pleasure. Harry fought back his own smile. "Sounds like you had a chance to play Wicked Witch of the West. And it looks like you enjoyed it."

"Oh, I did indeed."

"Did you let Morgan play good cop to your bad cop?"

Vicky took a chair opposite him. "Well, that was a little odd," she said. "Don't get me wrong, he handled the interview just fine. But later . . ."

"Later, what?" Harry asked.

"Well, it was pretty clear to us that all those visits Bennie made to Darlene's crib weren't completely kosher. When we pushed him on it and hinted that he might have helped lose her monitor, he really freaked out. I mean the man just oozed guilt. By the time we walked out of his office we were pretty convinced that old Bennie had helped Darlene out in exchange for some very serious nookie. But his alibi for the night she died checks out. He was with his mother, if you can believe it."

"He was visiting her?"

"No, he lives with her," Vicky said. "The same house he grew up in. Seems old Bennie never left home and hearth."

"And I bet he doesn't want Mama to know about his little tryst with Darlene."

"You bet your bippy. When I told him we'd have to confirm his alibi with her, well, like the song says, he turned a lighter shade of pale."

Vicky paused and Harry thought she seemed suddenly reluctant to say more. "So what about Morgan?"

Vicky wished she hadn't brought it up; she hadn't anticipated Harry's reaction. But it was too late to backtrack. "Well, when we got to the car I could see he was pissed off. He didn't like the idea of Rolf giving in to her—Darlene being able to use sex to get around the restrictions the court had placed on her. What can I say, he's a real by-the-book cop." She smiled at Harry and added: "Just like we're all supposed to be. I think it just ticked him off that Rolf let himself be used that way and he wanted to know if we were going to report it to anyone. He was pretty adamant that we should."

"And what did you tell him?"

"I told him it would be noted in my report, but that someone else would decide whether to pursue it or not. I also told him I didn't think the chances were very good." She paused. "That didn't make him a happy camper, but he knows he has to live with it." She watched Harry think that over, then quickly added, "Look, Harry, this guy's just very intense about his job. And he's very good. I don't think there's anything to worry about. He's just like most patrol cops. He doesn't see gray. He's a black-and-white kind of guy."

Harry stared at her. "It still concerns me," he said. "Not a lot yet, but it concerns me. I don't want this investigation tainted by anyone's preconceived notions about morality. We have to remain above that or we'll end up going down a lot of wrong paths. So I want you to keep working with him and keep a close eye on what he does. At least for a while. What's he doing now?"

Vicky's jaw tightened. Her anger was directed more at herself than at Harry. She should have just kept her mouth shut. "He's trying to find any deleted information in the department's motor pool records. And he seems to know what he's doing. Like I said, I'm not worried about him at all. He may be a little straight-laced, but from what I've seen he's got good instincts as an investigator." She paused, then pressed on. "Harry, I've got to be up front with you. If I was running this case I'd be more concerned about *your* personal hang-ups than I would be about his."

Harry was jolted by the comment, but fought not to let it show. "Your concern's noted. I promise you I'll keep my hang-ups in check."

CHAPTER EIGHT

D r. Lola Morofsky was a seventy-year-old psychiatrist who refused to retire. After a forty-year career as a therapist she no longer accepted private patients; now she devoted her efforts strictly to law enforcement, working exclusively with the various police agencies in Pinellas and Hillsborough counties. When Harry called seeking an appointment, she agreed to see him immediately.

"So you've got the big one," she said, peering up at him from the large executive desk chair that enveloped her body like a cocoon.

She was a tiny woman, no more than five feet tall and well under one hundred pounds. She had short, kinky brown hair, obviously dyed, a long nose, and thick lips. Heavy makeup did its best to cover the sea of wrinkles on her face. She had never married, and had no children, and although she'd lived in Florida most of her adult life, she still carried with her the Brooklyn accent of her childhood.

"So you're coming to me with Darlene Beckett?" she asked as Harry slipped into a visitor's chair.

"I am. I need a psychological profile on the woman and, if possible, on the type of men she would attract. Plus, if you can tell me something about the killer—like his name, address, and Social Security number, it would be good." Harry's face broke into a grin. He had worked with her many times and both liked and respected the woman.

Lola brought her tiny hands together with pleasure. "So you need me. Even with Harry Doyle's famous intuition, his ability to hear the whispered words of the dead, he needs an old lady to help him." She laughed at herself, at both of them. "In any event, I'm delighted. Ever since this woman appeared on the scene, I've been dying to study her." She leaned forward. "This, I think we will find, is a complex lady, Harry. Not the simple bimbo the media has made her out to be. Understanding her, understanding how her mind worked, will be a challenge." She waved her small hands as if dismissing what she had just said. "As far as your other questions go, I can tell you right off that any heterosexual man with a living member between his legs would be attracted to her. Not every one would act on that attraction, but they would all desire her. This, Harry, was a *very* alluring woman, and one who worked hard at being so. Regarding your killer, I think I can help you. Not a name and address, of course, but at least a strong profile. But for that I'll have to see your entire case file. Darlene's as well, of course."

Harry placed the two folders he had brought with him on her desk. "The top one is a copy of the entire murder file," he said. "I really need you to look at that first, and tell me anything you can about the killer. The other folder is the child abuse case file. I just got it from the Hillsborough County state's attorney last night and had it copied for you."

"So it's a copy I can keep?"

Harry nodded, and again Lola brought her tiny hands together. "A treasure, a virtual treasure trove." She shook her head. "It will be difficult to concentrate on the murder file with this sitting here waiting for me."

"Please," Harry said.

Lola raised her hand like a traffic cop. "I will. I will."

As Harry watched, Lola began poring over the murder file. The office was designed to provide a soothing, relaxed atmosphere. The lighting was subdued; the furniture—a sofa and two chairs—was oversized and covered in soft, plush fabric. Even Lola's desk was not intimidating, a Queen Anne style, something more suited to a home than an office. There were no diplomas or certificates on the walls—those had been relegated to the reception area—only soothing pastels. It was a place designed to make frightened, insecure people feel safe. It was something that didn't work for Harry. Instead he felt a lingering inner tension that he knew would stay with him until Darlene's murder was solved. It was something he lived with on every complex case, something that drove him to find the answers that eluded him, or so he believed.

Lola was studying the in situ photographs of Darlene's body. She glanced up at Harry. "Implants?" she asked.

"Yes."

"Interesting. A woman so beautiful and still she had to offer herself up to the surgeon's knife to become even more appealing." She opened the other file and found an earlier photograph of Darlene in a cheerleader's costume. "Look here," she said. "She didn't have a flat chest as a child. She was perfectly normal, absolutely lovely." She shook her head. "There was a deep psychological need here. I would bet my license that this woman's psyche was severely brutalized at a very young age—something that made her obsessive about her looks and her desirability as a woman. She would also want to be desirable to other women," she added. "I'm not saying she was a lesbian, or bisexual. This was an obsession, and the need to be wanted would not be limited to one sex." She shook her head again. "But that's only a guess for now. Give me time and I'll find more. This was a complex woman, a very disturbed woman. Your case will undoubtedly be solved before I understand her completely . . . if I ever do."

"Any initial sense about the killer?" Harry asked.

"Well, here we obviously have obsessive behavior of a different kind. I would guess that our killer is young. No more than late twenties, early thirties. Very religious to the point of obsession. Intelligent, but blinded by his own convictions. Not willing to question those beliefs, or be tolerant of anyone who doesn't accept them with the fervor that he does. Without question, a true believer in every meaning of that phrase." She raised her hands and let them fall back to the desk. "This business of carving the word *evil* on his victim's forehead, then covering it up with a mask, is so direct it's a bit unnerving. There is no subtlety in this man. He believes and therefore he acts. His mind is organized and yet it isn't." She nodded to herself. "It shows me someone who is not quite as smart as he thinks he is; someone who has convinced himself that other people are so unable to grasp what he sees that he must give them a message that is blatantly simplistic. This is someone who has no respect or tolerance for his fellow man; someone with no feeling of moral responsibility other than to himself, although he *believes* he has great moral responsibility to everyone, even to the world at large, perhaps even to the point of having a savior complex, if you will . . . Harry, my friend, you are dealing with a pure sociopath. And he may be very hard to spot, because he is extremely good at hiding. He has practiced that art for years. He has had to."

"Could he have been the victim of abuse himself?" Harry asked.

"Very possibly. But if so, I think he would believe that he—himself— had sinned. He may believe that he was led into sin by someone even more evil than himself, but he would still carry great guilt for his part in it."

"And deliver us from evil," Harry said.

"Exactly." Lola nodded her head emphatically. "That is exactly how he would now feel."

"You haven't gotten to it yet in the file, but we found a gold cross at the murder scene with that quote from the Lord's Prayer engraved on it."

"I would be surprised if that cross had not been torn from the killer's neck," she said.

"The young boy who was abused by Darlene, he and his family be- longed to an evangelical church that shunned them when his family re- fused to let him testify. The minister also urged the parishioners to do everything they could to bring Darlene to justice." Harry stared at her. "It was an unqualified statement, as far as I've been able to determine, almost an invitation for someone to take the law into his own hands."

"An invitation our killer would not have needed, but one he would have taken very, very seriously." She paused and stared into Harry's eyes. "Did you get anything from the victim . . . anything about religion?"

"Yes."

"It was a strong . . . sensation?"

"Very."

Lola paused again, considering what Harry had said. Then she nodded to herself. "I would look at this church closely, Harry. Very closely indeed."

As Harry began to rise from his chair, Lola leaned forward and studied him closely. "What's new with you, Harry? You seem very tense. Any personal problems you'd like to talk about?"

Harry hesitated, then shook his head. He had talked to Lola in the past about his mother, and whenever they met she inquired without specifically asking about her.

"Nothing?" Lola persisted.

"My mother's coming up for parole," Harry finally conceded. "But I don't need to talk about it."

She smiled up at him. "You probably do. But I won't press the matter. I *will* ask you to consider one thing: consider that this case may not be right for you; that perhaps someone else should investigate this woman's murder." She waved off any objection before it came and continued, "I don't mean you won't be able to do a good job. You're probably the best homicide detective in the state. I mean this case may not be right for *you*."

"I can't let it go," he said.

"I know you can't." Lola gave him a long look. "What does your intuition tell you about the killer, Harry? I can sense that you feel something."

Harry shook his head. "Very little, except that at times he feels very close. Sometimes it's almost as though he's standing right next to me. I've never felt that before."

"Maybe it's your past that's standing next to you, Harry," Lola said. "Think about that possibility, Harry. Think about it very seriously."

The First Assembly of Jesus Christ the Lord was located on Keystone Road, close to the Pinellas-Hillsborough county line. That also placed it only a few miles from the Brooker Creek Preserve. The church was a sprawling complex that included the church itself, an elementary school, a gymnasium, and several smaller buildings, including one clearly marked as a teen center. All the buildings were connected by a covered outdoor walkway. There was also a sizable parking lot, attesting to a large congregation. As a young deputy Harry had occasionally been assigned to Sunday traffic control at various large churches throughout the county. The congestion created by those churches prior to and at the conclusion of services rivaled that of weekday rush hours. Harry called ahead but was told the Reverend John Waldo was in the sacristy "preparing" Sunday's service. He decided to come early and catch the reverend when those preparations ended.

Harry climbed a wide cement stairway that led to a series of glass doors opening into a reception area. Across a twenty-foot expanse were another set of doors that opened into the church proper. Beyond those interior doors Harry found himself standing beneath an enormous arch that ran the entire length of the sacristy. But the focal point of the church was a vast stage that took up one entire end and faced out to rows of pews that would hold well over five hundred parishioners. There were lights suspended above the stage, and only the pews and the arched ceiling and a large golden cross that hung on the rear wall made him feel he had entered a church. Without them he would have felt he'd just walked into a large theater.

A man stood center stage his body fixed in a spotlight. Above him, to his right and left, his image was projected on two massive television screens, as the words he spoke ran in a scroll beneath. To his left, well off to the side, a group of musicians listened respectfully. Harry noted the instruments—organ, piano, three guitars, a drum set, a conga drum, two saxophones, two trumpets, and a flute. To the man's right stood a choir of twelve men and women, each appearing equally intent on hearing every word the man spoke. At the front of the church, high above the pews, Harry could see a director's booth hidden behind darkened glass. He assumed that the projection screens and all the stage lighting were run from there, an assumption that was confirmed when the man standing center stage interrupted his sermon at several points and spoke directly to the booth, asking that the cameras be brought in tight for close-ups at those specific points. As far as church services went, it was beyond anything Harry had ever envisioned, and he realized he was watching a rehearsal worthy of a professional theater.

The man at the crux of that rehearsal, who Harry assumed was Reverend Waldo, was railing against a gay pride parade that would be held in St. Petersburg the following Sunday, terming it a "celebration of sodomy" and urging his flock to join protestors throughout the county to speak out against "this public glorification of sin."

Harry felt a hand on his shoulder, the pressure light but distinct. He turned and found a man, perhaps in his late twenties, standing behind him. He had blond hair of an unnatural color that fell almost to his shoulders. He was tall and slender, dressed in jeans and a T-shirt that bore the logo *Jesus Now and Always*. He had a square face and a flattened nose that looked as if it had been hit more than once; his eyes were cobalt-blue and despite a wide smile were clearly unfriendly.

"Can I help you?" he said, his tone holding no offer of help in it.

"I don't know," Harry said. "I'm looking for Reverend John Waldo. Are you him?"

The smile faded. "Who are *you?*"

Harry took out his credential case and held it up.

"A cop," the man said.

"Good reading," Harry responded. "Now who are *you?*"

"Bobby Joe Waldo," the man said with a smirk. "I'm Reverend Waldo's son and one of the associate ministers here. Reverend Waldo's the man up on the stage."

"How long before Reverend Waldo will be finished with his rehearsal?" Harry asked.

"We don't call it a rehearsal."

"What do you call it?"

"We call it preparing the way."

Harry nodded, as if digesting a heavy bit of information. "Well, when do you suppose he'll be through preparing the way?" Now it was his turn to smirk.

The younger Waldo glanced at his watch. Harry's tone had turned his face into a sneer. "About ten minutes. Right now I have some stuff to do up on the stage. If you want, you can stay here and I'll let him know you're waiting on him. But don't start wandering around. It distracts him, and he doesn't like it when that happens." He hesitated, offering as hard a look as he could muster. A bit of face saving, Harry thought. "He'll wanna know what it's about," the man added for effect.

Harry smiled up at him, thinking how pleased Pete Rourke would be. "Just tell him it's police business," he said in an unmistakable *fuck you* tone. Maybe Rourke wouldn't be pleased.

"I'll be sure to give him that message," the young minister snapped back.

Harry watched him as he headed toward the stage, trying to keep a bit of swagger in his walk. He made a note to check Bobby Joe Waldo for a rap sheet. Instinct told him he'd find something.

Ten minutes later, as predicted, Reverend Waldo wrapped up his *preparation*, and Harry watched his son walk up to him and whisper in his ear. The older minister nodded and looked out to where Harry was seated. After giving some final instructions to the director's booth and the people on the stage, he started toward Harry. Almost immediately the choir began its preparation of "Amazing Grace."

Waldo wore a broad salesman's smile when he reached Harry. But the smile never carried to his eyes which were narrowed and wary. He was a short, rotund man, no more than five-seven, Harry guessed, and he was pushing two hundred pounds hard. His son obviously got his height, slender frame, and sneer from a different member of the family. Waldo was easily in his mid- to late-fifties but there was no visible gray in his full head of hair. He was wearing a vibrant Tommy Bahama floral print shirt and sharply creased tan linen trousers that broke over gleaming, glove-soft Italian loafers, and there was a gold Tag Heuer watch on his wrist. It was high-end casual and Harry estimated that Waldo was wearing more money on his back than Harry spent on clothing in an entire year, maybe two.

"Well," the minister began, "deputy is it?"

"Detective," Harry said, opening his credential case. "The name's Harry Doyle."

"Well, Detective Doyle, my son tells me you need to speak to me on police business."

"That's right, reverend. It's about Billy Hall. I believe the boy was once a member of your church."

"Still is, far as I know." A sudden edge came into the minister's voice and he quickly masked it with another faux smile.

Harry took out his notebook and wrote the time, the date, and the minister's name. When he looked up Waldo was shifting impatiently from one foot to the other. "If this is going to take some time, why don't we adjourn to my office where we'll both be more comfortable? The church secretary brews a good cup of coffee and I can always use one after a long session of preparing the way."

Waldo's office was like the man himself, oversized and expensively furnished. After passing through an outer office that housed a secretary and two assistants, they entered a twenty-by-twenty-foot room. With his first step Harry sank into a full inch of thick Berber carpet and his nostrils were filled with the scent of expensive leather and recently applied furniture polish. The room was dominated by a massive desk that was easily eight feet across, the surface empty except for a leather blotter and a gold pen set. Behind the desk was an equally large credenza that held a telephone console, a flat-screen computer monitor and keyboard, a photograph of a middle-aged woman who Harry assumed was the minister's wife, and a solitary, well-worn Bible. Above the credenza a large picture window looked out on a pond that had been meticulously designed. There were bulrushes at one end and flowering lily pads at another. One bank held a large royal poinciana tree, its wide branches and flaming red flowers reflecting in the pond's surface; another offered a white crape myrtle and a golden rain tree, while a third held a towering jacaranda, heavily laden with purple bell-shaped flowers and rich fernlike leaves. If the landscape architect was shooting for serenity, Harry decided he had hit the mark squarely.

The office interior offered its own sense of design, this time aimed at the minister's image. To the left of the desk photographs of Reverend Waldo with various politicians and civic leaders filled an entire wall, including one that showed Waldo shaking hands with Harry's ultimate boss, the Pinellas County sheriff. A second wall was filled with awards and plaques citing the minister for various meritorious acts. The final wall held a large portrait of Jesus Christ. Oddly, it was the only item that seemed out of place, and Harry immediately thought of the Bible quote that spoke of a camel and the eye of a needle.

Waldo settled himself into a high-backed leather desk chair that let out a discernable creak under his weight. He gestured toward one of two visitors' chairs and Harry found himself sinking into soft leather. Almost immediately the office door opened and the secretary entered carrying a tray of coffee. Waldo thanked her, using the name Emily, but withheld any introduction to Harry, who jotted the woman's name in his notebook. When the woman left, Waldo sipped his coffee, then sat back and brought his hands together like a man preparing to pray. "Now, what can I tell you about Billy Hall?" He offered Harry another smile.

Harry leaned forward and held the minister's eyes. "Billy's mother told us the boy was under a great deal of pressure to 'repent his sins.'"

Waldo nodded. "Indeed he was."

"She also said the congregation was encouraged to 'seek justice' for Darlene Beckett."

Again, Waldo nodded. "Equally true."

"Was there anyone in your congregation who showed a particular interest in doing so?"

Waldo let out a soft chuckle. "If you mean, did anyone try to get together a group to light torches and march on the courthouse, the answer would be no. I'm afraid I'm not that powerful a preacher. If you're asking if anyone wrote letters to the court, or the state's attorney, or even to Ms. Beckett herself, I would have to say I'm sure some might have, although I have no personal knowledge of any such letters. But I do know that we have a very committed congregation. Committed to the repentance of sin, committed to the punishment of sin, and also committed to the forgiveness of sin, I might add."

"Was Billy Hall forgiven his sin?" Harry asked.

Now it was the minister's turn to lean forward, his eyes harder. "Billy Hall would have been forgiven had he repented. But you must have one to have the other. Billy Hall did *not* repent his sins. He did *not* testify against that woman, as he should have. And his parents yielded to his refusal to do so. Because of that, a truly evil woman escaped justice."

"I notice that you use the word *evil*." Harry watched the man's eyes.

"It's clearly what she was," he said. "Not that she, too, couldn't have repented, forsaken her evil ways and received the Lord's forgiveness."

Harry stared at the minister for several moments. "Did you or anyone on your staff have any contact with Ms. Beckett?"

"Certainly not," Waldo snapped.

"You're sure you can speak for your entire staff on that?"

"I don't directly supervise the staff. My son Bobby Joe, who is an associate minister here, does that. I'm sure he would have told me if that had been the case. But why leave it open to speculation? Let's have him in so he can tell us directly."

Harry waited while Waldo got on the office intercom and asked his secretary to locate his son. When he finished, Harry opened a fresh page in his notebook. "Exactly what denomination is your church?"

"We're not part of any particular denomination. We're an independent evangelical church," Waldo answered.

"So your ministers aren't ordained?"

"I ordain our ministers myself . . . after a suitable course of study and work within the church, of course. I, myself, was ordained the same way by my predecessor."

Their conversation was interrupted as Bobby Joe Waldo entered the office. Harry noticed the smirk he had been treated to earlier was now missing and he wondered if Bobby Joe knew better than to cop that kind of attitude in front of his father.

"The detective here just hit me with a question I couldn't rightly answer," Waldo began. "He wants to know if anyone on our staff ever had any contact with that woman who molested young Billy Hall."

Bobby Joe thought for a moment, then shrugged his shoulders. "Why would they?" There was a slight movement of his eyes to the left when he answered, which Harry picked up on. It was a classic tell. It didn't mean the young minister was lying, but it did indicate that he was not answering the question in a completely truthful manner.

Apparently his father picked up on it as well. He leaned forward in his chair again. "Just tell us if you know of anyone who had contact with that woman."

Bobby Joe shifted the position of his feet—another tell—and shook his head. "I don't know anyone who had any contact with her," he said.

"How many ministers and staff do you have working here?" Harry asked before either man could say any more.

"That depends what you mean by staff," the minister said. "My first associate minister, a man named Justin Clearby, and Bobby Joe here are the only ordained ministers. We have several lay ministers, who have regular jobs outside the church. Our music director, for example, is considered a lay minister even though he's not ordained. And we have several folks who work with the children's programs who we refer to as assistant lay ministers. As far as full-time paid staff goes, we have our regular ministers, my secretary and one assistant—the other is a part-time volunteer—the director of our school and three teachers, and a custodian. The folks who run the lighting and sound for our services are paid part-time employees."

"I'd like to speak with any staff people who are here now," Harry said. "And I'd like a list of both paid and unpaid staff with their home addresses and phone numbers."

"Is all that really necessary?" Bobby Joe chimed in. "I already told you that nobody from here had any contact with that woman."

Harry stared at the young man, but before he could say anything else, Reverend Waldo gave his son a clear and direct order: "You do what the man asked, Bobby Joe. It's our job to help if we can. You have Emily put together a list and you see to it that Detective Doyle gets it."

Bobby Joe seemed to shrink in size as he nodded his head. "I'll do it right now," he said, and headed back to the outer office.

Waldo rose from behind his desk, a smile fixed on his face again. "Come with me and I'll introduce you to the people who are here," he said.

They passed through the outer office and out onto the covered walkway that led back to the church and the other buildings. They had only gone a half dozen steps when the minister stopped. "Just a minute, I forgot to tell my secretary something that's a bit pressing. I'll be right back."

Before Harry could say anything he had spun around and reentered the office.

Back inside, Waldo led Bobby Joe away from the secretary's desk, then leaned in close so he could speak without being overheard.

"Now you listen to me, son. You sure this detective isn't gonna find anything out that's gonna come back and embarrass this church?"

"I'm sure, Daddy."

"I'm countin' on you to make sure it stays that way, hear? And you also better check that list Emily's putting together and keep anybody off it who might be a problem."

"I'll see to it, Daddy."

"Make sure that you do. You also make sure everybody else knows that's how I want it to be."

"I will."

Waldo caught his son's eyes moving toward the exterior door of the office, and he turned and saw Harry standing there.

"Hot out there," Harry said. "Thought I'd come back to the air-conditioning while I waited."

The ready-made smile returned to Waldo's face. "Good thinking," he said. "But I'm afraid we're going to have to head right back out into it."

CHAPTER NINE

ola Morofsky sat in one of her oversized office chairs, her feet dangling well above the floor, her five-foot, hundred-pound body making her look like a small child who had stumbled into a giant's living room. Lola adjusted her half-glasses on her long nose as she read the rap sheet Harry had just given her.

"Nasty fellow," she said. She turned a page and raised disapproving eyes to Harry. "You realize, of course, that you have juvenile records here, as well as adult records—juvenile records that you are *not* supposed to have."

Harry feigned surprise, without any attempt to be convincing. "Must have been a computer glitch."

Lola looked at him over the half-glasses, her soft brown eyes incapable of anything more than a mild reproach. "Yes, I'm certain it was," she said, her Brooklyn accent weighty with sarcasm. "What does your person of interest do for a living?"

"He's come home to Jesus," Harry said.

"What does that mean?"

"He's a minister . . . ordained by his minister father. He works in Daddy's evangelical church."

"Quite a change for him," Lola said as she went back to the rap sheet. "Let's see, we had three instances of possession, along with several burglaries as a juvenile, which are charges that often go together. It seems that all were treated with in-house arrest and probation, except for one stint in a boot camp. Then, as an adult—he didn't seem to learn anything in boot camp, which is often the case—we have several bad check charges, all dismissed after restitution was made."

"Probably by Daddy," Harry interjected.

Lola nodded. "Probably. It's not uncommon for parents to open their wallets when young adults get into trouble. But it's usually just a Band-Aid, not a solution, to the underlying problem." She read on, nodding her head as she did so. "Next we have a possession charge which was dropped when he agreed to cooperate with a police investigation of his supplier. Then we have a conviction for fraud, where one Robert Joseph Waldo fleeced a retired couple out of ten thousand dollars in a phony home improvement scheme. This one Daddy couldn't buy him out of and he was sentenced to a year. Since then nothing."

"His jail record shows he had some trouble inside," Harry said. "I don't have anything in writing on this—it's all verbal from people in corrections. But according to them Bobby Joe accused two inmates of sexual assault. Claimed they attacked him in a laundry room where they were all working. But the accusations never went anywhere. Three other inmates supposedly witnessed the attack, but claimed they didn't see anything, so it became Bobby Joe's word against the two men. Corrections, of course, took the easy way out. The two assailants got hit with some minor administrative punishments, loss of privileges, that sort of thing, and Bobby Joe got placed in an isolation unit. Down the road it was probably a factor in his early release—he got out after doing six months." Harry offered up a shrug. "The sheriff doesn't like news stories about inmates getting buggered in his jail, and the word going around is that he pushed to get Bobby Joe out early after he agreed to keep his mouth shut. The sheriff knows Bobby Joe's father, although I'm not certain how well, beyond the fact that there's a picture of them shaking hands on a wall in the minister's office."

"And, of course, you're thinking that Darlene Beckett escaped more serious charges because the victim, after an agreement was reached with his parents, refused to testify against her." Lola extended one palm up. "It's an interesting coincidence, Harry. But as a motive for murder it is very, very thin."

Harry nodded. "As thin as it gets, but I have to start somewhere. What do you think of Bobby Joe as a suspect?"

Lola gave him a noncommittal shrug. "His background certainly points toward him being a sociopath, but I'd need harder evidence to put that label to him. From what you've told me I suspect that his father is quite domineering. That could very well be the root of his psychological problems, but again that would require analysis, perhaps even long-term analysis."

"So I've got nothing," Harry said.

"You have a suspect, Harry. That's always something."

When Harry returned to the office he found Anita Molari, the exotic dancer known as Jasmine, going through driver's license photographs of the men who had visited Darlene's home. She was seated in the conference room next to Pete Rourke's office, which now housed the additional members of the task force. One of the newly assigned uniformed deputies sat across from her.

Harry placed a hand on the man's shoulder. "Go grab some coffee," he said. "I'll take over for a while." When the deputy left Harry gathered up the photographs. "Let's move out to my desk," he suggested. "I'm expecting some phone calls I don't want to miss."

Anita Molari was a different person away from the Peek-a-Boo Lounge. The last time Harry had seen her she was wearing only a thong and a see-through beach robe that put her very shapely body on open display. Today she was dressed in an oversized T-shirt and loose-fitting shorts that made her seem small, almost frail. Her short, dark hair was damp, as though she had rushed straight from her shower, and the vivid blue eyes Harry remembered from the Peek-a-Boo Lounge simply looked tired. She reminded him of the saying: Rode hard and put up wet.

"Do any of the photographs look familiar?" he asked, as they seated themselves at his desk.

"Not yet." She looked at him, head tilted to one side. "I don't really understand why it's important for me to look at these pictures if you already know these guys were at Darlene's house."

"I want to know if anyone who visited her home might also have followed her to other places."

"You mean like a stalker?"

"That's right. Anyone who might have been obsessed with her, or who might have been stalking her because of something she had done to them, or to someone else."

"Like that kid they said she molested?"

"That's right."

Anita gave a small shake of her head. "I never understood that. I always wanted to ask her how she could do something like that, but we never got close enough where I felt I could." She gave Harry a questioning look as though he might know the answer. "I mean she was beautiful, really beautiful. There aren't many women who look like that. And the way men stared at her . . ." She shook her head again, then shrugged. "I get those looks when I'm up on the stage, practically naked. Darlene would have got them if she walked in wearing a burlap bag. And you know something? She wasn't a bad person. I don't know if she was a good person. I mean I talked to her and all, but not that much."

"But enough to know she wasn't a bad person," Harry said.

"Yeah, that's right. Somehow it just doesn't make sense."

"Many things don't." Harry opened his notebook to the last page he had used and started to turn to a fresh one.

Anita leaned forward suddenly and pointed at the notebook. "You've

got the name of a church written there. I'm sorry, I couldn't help but see it
. . . it just sort of jumped out at me."

Harry looked at the notebook. *The First Assembly of Jesus Christ the
Lord* was written in large capital letters and underlined. "What about it?"
he asked.

"I know that church," Anita said. "I mean from work."

"How so?"

"One of their cars scratched mine in the parking lot."

"The Peek-a-Boo Lounge lot?"

"Yeah." She gave him a small shrug. "Whenever I park my car there,
when I'm going to work, I write down the make, model, and license plate
numbers of the cars on either side of me. I mean guys leave there pretty
sloshed—hell, most of them get there pretty sloshed—and I want to be
sure if somebody clips me I have a way to know who it was."

"So you got clipped by a car belonging to the church?"

"I sure did." She leaned forward. "I probably shouldn't tell you this,
but I got a friend of mine who's a cop to run the plate. And it comes up
belonging to that church. So I called there and eventually got to talk to
one of the ministers."

Harry felt a rush of excitement. "You remember his name?"

Anita screwed up her face. "It was a funny name, real Southern. You
know what I mean?"

"Bobby Joe?" Harry asked in return.

"Yeah, that's it. Bobby Joe Waldo, I remember now." There was a big
smile spread across her face, and Harry thought it made her look like a
schoolgirl who had just gotten a difficult question right. "It was funny. He
was real nervous when he got on the phone, and when I told him where
the car was parked and that I was one of the dancers who worked there,
he was even more nervous. He said the head minister at the church would
be real upset if he found out, and that he'd like to handle it privately, no

insurance companies or anything, just to tell him what it cost to fix the car and he'd get the money to me."

"Did he send you a check?" Harry asked.

"No. It was only a small dent, and he told me to get an estimate on how much it would cost to fix it. I did and called him back the next day and he had the cash delivered to me the day after that."

"Who delivered the money?"

"I dunno. Just some guy. I was working days that week and he met me in the parking lot of the club like we had arranged. I remember thinking that I'd seen him before someplace, maybe the club. But I couldn't be sure. Unless a customer asks me for a private dance I don't pay much attention to individual guys."

"Can you describe him?"

Anita wrinkled her brow. "Sure, I guess I can. Let's see, he was tall, not real tall, more like you. But real thin; there wasn't any heft to him at all. The thing I remember most was his hair and eyes. His hair was down to his shoulders and real light, kind of a fake blond, like maybe a dye job. It was the same with his eyes. They were sort of a cold blue, not really natural. They kind of made me wonder if he was wearing those tinted contact lenses."

"How old?" Harry asked.

"Oh, maybe late twenties. At least that's what I thought at the time."

She had just described Bobby Joe Waldo, and it was a description that would be good enough for any jury. Harry kept that information to himself. He didn't want to be accused later of prejudicing a witness."

"Did he give you his name?"

Anita shook her head. "He just said Reverend Waldo had sent him and handed me an envelope with the money in it."

Harry slowly nodded, digesting what she had told him. "I need you to hang around just a bit longer," he said at length. "I want to put together a photo lineup—that's just a handful of mug shots—so we can see if you can pick this guy out."

Anita glanced at her wristwatch. "My kid doesn't get out of kindergarten for another two hours, so I guess I've got time."

Twenty minutes later Harry had eight photographs lined up on the conference room table—all men in their twenties, all with long, blond hair. Anita picked out Bobby Joe Waldo on her first try and Harry told her he might want to do a live lineup sometime in the near future. But not quite yet, he thought. First he would do some serious digging into Bobby Joe Waldo.

Pete Rourke pensively tapped the side of his nose as Harry gave him a rundown on Bobby Joe, his father, and the First Assembly of Jesus Christ the Lord Church. When he finished he warned the captain that down the road he might be asking a judge for a warrant to seize church records and to search Bobby Joe's home, car, and personal effects.

Rourke leaned back in his chair and raised a warning finger. "Before you do that, you better be pretty damned certain what you're gonna find. And I mean ninety-nine percent certain. This is still Florida, Harry, and asking a judge to sign a search warrant for a church or its minister is like saying you want him to piss in the holy water font." Harry smiled at the image, making Rourke raise the cautioning finger again. "I mean it, Harry. Don't take this lightly, or your ass will be in more trouble than you ever dreamed of."

"I know, cap." Harry conjured up Bobby Joe's father sending forth a proverbial river of outrage.

There was a knock on the door, interrupting them. Vicky came right behind the knock, pushing the door open and stepping up to the desk. Jim Morgan followed her, seeming a bit nervous over the sudden intrusion.

"Sorry, cap, but you and Harry need to hear this right away," Vicky said.

Rourke glared at her. When he spoke, his voice rose steadily in volume and ferocity with each word. "This better be damn good, *detective*. One of the joys of being a captain is having a private office that people *cannot* barge into when the goddamn door is closed and somebody is sitting in the goddamn visitor's chair."

Vicky was unfazed, Harry was grinning, and Morgan looked as though he wished he were somewhere else.

Vicky gave Rourke a little girl smile that almost broke Harry up. "Trust me, cap," she said wide-eyed and innocent, "this is something you need to hear forthwith."

Rourke narrowed his stare. "Speak," he growled. "And make it good."

Vicky extended a hand toward Morgan, who still looked like he wanted a place to hide. "Jim really deserves the credit on this," she began. "Turns out he's a wizard with computers."

Rourke threw an unhappy eye at Morgan just to let him know that, wizard or not, he'd stepped in the same pile of shit that she had. Harry wondered if the eager young deputy saw his future in the detective division hanging on Vicky's next words.

"Jim came up with the name of the person who signed out the cars that ended up in Darlene's driveway," she explained. "The records were altered so it looked like the sign outs were never recorded, but they were still in the hard drive and Jim was able to get them out." She threw an admiring glance at Morgan. "I have no idea how."

"The same person took both cars out?" Harry asked.

"You betcha," Vicky said. "And hold on for this. It was one of the detectives working this case, Nick Benevuto."

Rourke stared at her, then groaned out the words, "Oh, shit."

Harry gave a small shake of his head, almost as if driving off some annoying insect. "When were the records altered?" he asked.

Vicky glanced at Morgan.

"The day the body was discovered," he answered.

"Before or after the body was discovered?"

"After. It was done right after the end of shift," Morgan said.

"So somebody changed the records the day after the murder and *after* the body was discovered," Harry said, as he jotted the information in his notebook.

"That's right."

Rourke pulled a folder from his desk and opened it. "Benevuto was off duty the day Darlene was killed."

Harry stared into space. "It doesn't make sense," he said at length.

"What doesn't?" Rourke asked.

"Benevuto altering department records," Harry said. "First, he couldn't have known that we had a witness who took down one of our tag numbers until the *second* day after the murder, because that's when *we* knew, that's when our witness told Morgan that there was one plate number that he didn't turn over to me. So what would prompt Nick to alter the records a day before there was even a hint that we might tumble to the fact that he'd been to Darlene's apartment? Unless . . ."

"Unless he killed her and was covering up the fact that he knew her," Vicky said.

Harry nodded slowly. "That's right. And if he was the murderer why wait to cover it up until *after* the body was discovered? Why take the chance that someone would come across those records before he could change them?" Harry shook his head. "I just don't see it. And I don't see Nick as a realistic suspect."

"Why not?" Vicky asked.

There was an edge to her voice that Harry picked up on. "Look, I can see Nick running into Darlene Beckett and deciding he wanted to try to get into her knickers. I can even see him taking the initiative and seeking her out for the same reason. Hell, there aren't many women who Nick

Benevuto would take a pass on and certainly not one as sexually appealing as Darlene."

"But?" Vicky pressed.

"But while Nick may be many things, stupid isn't one of them."

"I'm not getting your drift," Rourke said.

"My drift is simple, cap. Nick's been a detective for a long time, and he's pretty well known in the police community. Darlene was supposed to be on a short leash and she was being watched not only by the probation department, but by the prosecutor's office and certainly by the media. If one prosecutor, one reporter, one anybody saw her with Nick, they'd be all over it."

"Like flies on shit," Rourke added.

"And Nick would know that. So I can't see him getting heavily involved. A quick toss in the hay, sure, but nothing more. And for him to be the murderer, it would have to have been a lot more."

"How so?" Vicky asked. The edge in her voice had become defensive now.

Harry softened his own voice. "If we're thinking of Nick as a legitimate suspect, the only logical motive I can come up with is that he became seriously involved with Darlene; that he followed her from the Peek-a-Boo Lounge, caught her having it off with another guy, and killed them both in a jealous rage. And that just doesn't make sense to me." Vicky started to object but Harry raised a hand, stopping her. "I can see him altering records to hide the fact that he was seeing her, but I even have some trouble with that because of the time line."

"So who altered the records?" Morgan asked. "Who else would have a reason to alter them?"

"Good question." Harry shook his head. "It doesn't make sense for anyone but Nick to have altered them. So we'll ask him. One thing for sure, I don't want him on the team anymore."

"That's a given," Rourke said. "I'll put him on restricted duty—duty unrelated to this case—until this computer records business is resolved. As of right now, the whole matter is in the hands of Internal Affairs."

Harry winced. "I wish you'd hold off on IAD. I don't need them climbing all over this investigation."

"No can do, Harry," Rourke said. "Whether you like it or not, IAD will be part of it until we know what happened to those records."

Nick Benevuto looked more curious than concerned when he entered Pete Rourke's office. Harry studied him closely, looking for a tell. As far as Harry could see, Nick had no idea what was coming.

Rourke laid it out slowly and deliberately, and with each sentence Benevuto's face moved from mild embarrassment, to concern, to outright anger. But beneath it all Harry could detect fear as well.

"So I spent some time with her," he said when Rourke finished. "Where's the fucking crime?" He glared in turn at Rourke, Harry, Vicky, and Morgan. "It was purely business, and as far as anyone in this room is concerned, and *for the record*, I never laid a hand on her. If you're looking at me as a suspect in her murder, you're either desperate or you're out of your fucking minds." He turned his attention to Morgan and sneered. "And as far as your big theory goes that I altered department records, you listen up, junior. I wouldn't know *how* to alter a fucking computer record. I know how to turn it on and type up a fucking report and that's it. You don't believe me, you ask my partner. We need anything done on a computer, he has to do it."

"Just calm down, Nick," Harry said. His voice was soft and steady.

"Calm down, shit, Harry! You know me. You think I killed her?"

Harry ignored the question. "How did you meet her?" he asked instead.

Nick studied his shoes for a moment. "I was interviewing a dancer at that club, the Peek-a-Boo Lounge. I thought she might have witnessed a murder when she was working in a joint in our jurisdiction. It was the Bruder case, Jeffrey Bruder. Happened late last January and this dancer disappeared right after I started my investigation. I finally caught up with her in early March. The case is still open. You can read my daily reports and cross check 'em in my notebook."

"So where does Darlene Beckett come in?" Rourke asked.

Benevuto shook his head and let out a breath. "She was at the bar. I saw her and recognized her, and when I was finished with my witness I struck up a conversation." He shook his head again. "Her case had just finished up in court and it wasn't very hard to recognize her. Hell, she was all over TV and the papers. *And* I knew she had gotten probation with some pretty heavy restrictions, so I asked her if she was supposed to be there."

"Just being a good cop, right?" Vicky threw in.

Benevuto looked at her as though he wanted to grab her throat and hang on for at least a week. "That's right, *lady*." The final word was spoken with pure venom.

"Alright, knock it off, both of you," Rourke snapped.

"What happened then?" Harry asked, throwing a look at Vicky.

"Well, she tells me there are no restrictions on her going to a bar, or restaurant, or anything like that. She says she's just restricted about where she can live—like not close to a school, or playground, or anything like that. And she can't hang out in places where kids hang or teach anymore." He shrugged. "It was bullshit, of course, bars are always a no-no."

"So you just kept chatting her up," Vicky said, ignoring Harry's silent admonition. He threw her another hard look.

Nick glared at her. "That's right. And I even got her phone number and address, and told her I'd give her a call sometime. She seemed interested in the idea."

"And it never registered with you that she was on probation and not a suitable social contact for a cop?" Rourke asked.

Nick looked him straight in the eye. "I wasn't imagining her as a social contact. You think I was gonna start diddling some broad who fucks kids? I wanted her as a snitch."

"Oh, Christ," Vicky said.

Nick rounded on her. "Fuck you, lady."

"Knock it off," Rourke roared. "This is the last warning for both of you."

Harry held up a hand. "So you called and dropped by her place," he said.

"That's right."

"How many times?"

"Three, four, I'm not really sure."

"We have you for two, both times in department cars," Rourke said.

"It was more than that. Your neighbor missed one or two."

"Was she wearing an ankle monitor the three or four times you saw her?" Harry asked.

Nick looked off as if trying to remember, then slowly shook his head. "I don't know. I think she was wearing slacks each time I saw her."

Harry held his gaze. This time the tell had been there and he wanted Nick to know he had seen it.

"So did she agree to be your snitch?" It was Rourke this time, skepticism dripping from every word.

Benevuto either didn't hear it, or chose to ignore it. "Yeah, after a fashion," he said. "The second time we met—that was the first time I went to her apartment—that's when I hit her with the idea of working as a confidential informant. She wasn't hot for the idea, but when I pressed her, told her I might be able to do her some good with her probation officer if she ever got jammed up, she said she'd keep her ears open and call me if she heard anything. I let it go at that, for the time being. Later I pushed her to see what she could find out from this dancer I interviewed at the Peek-a-

Boo. The one I thought knew something about the Bruder murder."

"Did Darlene agree to do it?" Harry asked.

Nick nodded slowly. "Yeah, she did, but not with a lot of enthusiasm. She said she didn't want to get the dancer into any trouble. You all know what it's like. Snitches'll tell you stuff they hear, but they can think up all kinds of reasons not to go in and ask questions. They know doing something like that is risky. Usually you can only get junkies to do it, and only when they need some fast cash to score." He shrugged. "Anyway, Darlene probably got iced before she ever had a chance to talk to this dancer."

"But you're not sure of that," Harry suggested.

"Well, no. I can't be sure of it, but I don't think she did."

"What are you thinking, Harry?" Rourke asked.

"Another possibility we have to pursue. Right now it's just a *what if*."

Rourke finished the thought for him: "What if she did ask the dancer some questions and the dancer went back and told somebody else."

"Like the person who iced Bruder," Benevuto said, grasping the offered straw.

"Oh, come on," Vicky said. "That's just a touch sketchy."

"Yeah, it is," Harry said. "But I don't want to ignore it and then find out later we walked right by Darlene's killer."

"John and I can check it out," Nick offered.

"No, you can't," Rourke said. "As of right now you're off the case and on administrative duty. That means you'll be riding a desk until this is cleared up. I need your reports and your notebook on the Bruder murder and I need Weathers in here to tell us about your computer skills. In the meantime I want your gun. You get everything back after Harry and IAD clear you."

"IAD? This is bullshit." Nick tossed his head toward Morgan. "Just because computer boy comes up with some bullshit theory that I altered department records, I get put on the rubber gun squad and my ass gets thrown to the fucking wolves."

"It's the way it has to be, Nick," Harry said. "You know that. I promise you we'll clear up our end as fast as we can. But as far as IAD goes, it would be the same story for any one of us. Cap's hands are tied."

"Bullshit," Benevuto barked. He placed his gun on Rourke's desk and glared at each of them in turn. "You'll have the reports and notebooks before I leave today." He spun around and headed out of the office.

"Tell John I need him in here immediately," Rourke said to his back.

After John Weathers had confirmed that his partner's computer skills began and ended with the power button and the keyboard, they left Rourke's office and returned to the conference room.

"So where does that leave us?" Harry asked when they were seated around the table.

"I think it leaves us with Nick as a prime suspect," Vicky said.

Harry looked at Morgan. "And what do you think, Jim?"

Morgan paused, taking time to study the top of the conference table. "All I know is that altering those records wasn't a big deal," he said, looking up. "Even if Nick didn't know any more about computers than he said, if he had come to me I could have walked him through it in five minutes. Look, I hate this crap. I hate dropping a dime on a brother cop. I just didn't think I could sit on the information when I came across it."

He had spoken the words with passion, but Harry didn't believe a word of it. Morgan was an ambitious young cop and Harry had little doubt he'd take whatever came his way if it gave him a leg up on a detective's shield. "So you're saying that Nick could have gone to any computer whiz and gotten it written down step by step," Harry said.

Morgan looked pained by the question. "That's about it," he said.

"Well, it's bullshit." It was Weathers, his eyes ice now. He turned them on Vicky. "I don't know what your problem is with Nick. Yeah, sure, sometimes he's an asshole and he comes on a little strong. And maybe he even did that with you. But I've worked with him for three years and he's a good cop, and there's no fucking way he'd ice some broad because she turned him down. Hell, if that was the case half the women in the county would be dead by now."

Vicky held his eyes. "What if he really fell for her, John, and then found out she was picking up guys in bars? And what if he followed her one night and found her getting it off on a beach?"

"That's a load of crap," Weathers snapped. "Nick never falls for any woman. All he ever wants is what they have between their legs. I don't think he even likes women. He told me once that if they didn't have pussies we'd hunt them like deer."

"Alright, let's leave it there," Harry said, holding up a hand. "Right now we don't have any choice. Nick's a suspect until we clear him. I personally think we will, but even then we'll have IAD to deal with before he's back working the case. In the meantime, John, you team up with one of the uniforms—you pick who you want—and keep working the case just like you were with Nick. You're probably going to lose a lot of time talking to IAD, but that can't be helped. I'll keep on with the church angle."

"You still think that's the strongest lead?" Vicky asked.

"Yeah, I do. At least for now."

"You want Jim and me to keep investigating Nick?"

Harry noted the skepticism in her voice. "That's right. And come to me whenever you develop anything new. No matter which way it goes, pro or con. IAD is going to want to look over your shoulders. How much you work with them is up to you, but do not let them impede this investigation."

"Are you going to work with them?" Weathers asked. His eyes were hard on Harry now.

"I'm going to avoid them like the plague," Harry said. "If they want me they're going to have to find me."

CHAPTER TEN

It was five-thirty when Bobby Joe Waldo left his father's private office. The outer office was already empty, the secretaries gone; the lights were turned off, but even in the faint light that filtered in through the windows Bobby Joe's face looked drained of color and a nervous tic was visible at the corner of his mouth. His father's office staff always left at five sharp so he doubted anyone had heard the old man's angry shouts. But what difference did it make; they had heard them often enough in the past. He exited his father's suite and headed to his own office farther down the covered walkway. Bobby Joe's accommodations as associate minister were little more than a twelve-by-twelve-foot box and lacked any of the amenities his father enjoyed. The view outside his one small window was meager; there was no gracefully landscaped pond to look out upon. Instead there was a remaining patch of the dusty scrub pine woodlot that had dominated the land long before the church complex was built. The office furnishings, while comfortable and adequate, were also run-of-the-mill, a mass-produced desk and chair from a nationwide office supply chain, visitors' chairs and lamps that could be found in any Wal-Mart, and durable low-end carpeting from Home Depot. It was something that normally rankled Bobby Joe when he left his father's office and entered his own. Today he ignored it as he slumped into his chair, his hands trembling slightly with a mixture of anger and fear.

His father was way over the top about this cop poking his nose around. And the old man didn't know the half of it yet. Billy Joe shook his head as that thought settled in. That was the operative word: *yet*. Because he was pretty sure the old bastard would find out every bit of it. And then all hell would really break loose. Especially when he learned that one of the church's cars had been in an accident in the parking lot of a Tampa titty bar, and that his own son had paid off the dancer whose car had been hit. Paid her off and never told the old man what happened. And when he put together the fact that the bar had been a regular hangout for Darlene Beckett, well, then the shit would really start to fly.

Darlene. It always seemed to come back to her. The woman was more trouble dead than she'd been alive. But you had to give it to her. The whole thing started because she decided to get into that kid's pants, and then pulled off a real winner by somehow getting the kid to clam up so she could pretty much beat the rap. His father had been off the wall about that, and then when the kid refused to repent before the congregation, it really set him off. He smiled momentarily at the memory. The kid's mother had pretty much told the old man to stuff it when he came up with all the repentance bullshit. And the kid's father looked like he was ready to rip somebody's head off, if not the old man's then Darlene's for sure. Repentance shit. Every man in the congregation would have given their left ball to fuck Darlene—everybody except his fat, limp-dick old man. And truth be told, maybe even he would, the phony old bastard.

He sat back and smiled as he recalled the first time he'd met her. He'd followed her to the titty bar, and after checking out the room to make sure nobody he knew was there, he'd slid into the seat next to her. She'd turned to him right off, looked him up and down and smiled. And he knew right there that even with all that incredible beauty the woman was nothing but good, old-fashioned trailer trash.

As he thought back on it now, it all seemed to make perfect sense. He'd followed her because his father had made it clear that he wanted someone to get something on her, preferably someone in the congregation: "See to it that she gets her just desserts" was the way old man had put it. So he'd gone on the Internet and checked out the sex offender registry and found out where she lived. Then he'd parked himself outside her apartment and right away it paid off. That first time he'd followed her she went straight to the Peek-a-Boo and he thought he'd hit pay dirt. Then she'd turned those big baby blues on him and he knew there was no way he wanted her back in the slammer. God, sex came off that woman like sweat, and he'd just lapped it up, his dick so hard he'd been afraid to stand up. She saw it, that bitch, and she reached over and gave it a nice little squeeze.

And that was after he'd told her he was a minister. He still didn't know why he'd done that, except that maybe it was a way to challenge her, or maybe he was still trying to do what Daddy wanted. Shit, that wasn't it. He'd known that as soon as he'd looked down into that scooped-neck top she was wearing, known right off there wasn't nothing bad he was gonna do to those beautiful tanned tits that were staring back at him.

Funny thing was that she seemed really turned on by the fact that he was a minister, and she'd asked him if he'd ever read a book called *The Scarlet Letter*. When he'd told her no, she just laughed and said maybe he was just a closet Reverend Dimmesdale. Then she'd taken him home and fucked his brains out. Score another one for Darlene—a fourteen-year-old boy and a goddamn minister.

He'd gone home that night and searched the name on his computer and found out that the Reverend Dimmesdale was this minister in this story who'd gotten boned by this good-looking married woman named Hester Prynne. Just reading that had gotten him hard all over again, and he'd known right then and there that he was gonna ball that woman every time she'd let him.

He spun his chair around and stared out the window at the dusty patch of scrub pine. And he'd done just that; gone back to her every time he could. And that's when the shit started for him, and now he was drowning in it.

* * *

It was seven-thirty when Harry got back to his house, a duplicate copy of the murder book tucked under his arm. He'd planned to spend several hours reviewing everything they had, but when he walked through the door he found Jocko Doyle sitting on the couch.

"Maria made a big batch of roast pork and an even bigger batch of rice and beans." He ginned up at his adopted son. "So . . . of course . . . she sent me over with a ton of it. She's certain, with this big case, you can't be eating right. And since you have no woman to take care of you . . ." Laughter cut off the sentence. "Well, you know the rest."

Jocko had never referred to himself as Harry's father, nor his wife Maria as his mother, even though they had always thought of themselves that way. It was space they knew Harry still needed.

Harry grinned back at him. "She's right . . . on all counts."

"She always is," Jocko said. "The food is in the kitchen, we just need to throw it in the microwave."

"Let's do it," Harry said. "Have you eaten?"

"Yeah, but I can always be talked into a small bowl. You know how I love Cuban food."

Jocko was tall and slender, and despite his fifty-five years his body was still as rock hard as the cattleman's son he had once been. He had a long nose and receding salt-and-pepper hair and eyes that were the same soft blue as a Florida morning, eyes that always seemed to have a smile hiding inside.

When they were seated at the kitchen table Jocko's eyes clouded and he looked like he was holding back on something he wanted to say. Harry suspected that he knew what it was.

"I got a call from a friend of mine," Jocko finally began. "A dick who worked your mother's case."

Harry nodded. "I got a call too. A guy I know up at the prison."

"Nobody from the Hillsborough state's attorney's office called you?"

Harry shook his head.

"Those pricks," Jocko said.

"Just business as usual. Don't let the victims get in the way of the paperwork."

"Yeah, it never changes," Jocko said. "How are you handling it?"

Harry shrugged, then drew a long breath. "As best I can."

"It must be a bitch, you up to your ears in this Beckett murder at the same time. How's that going?"

"Slower than I'd like."

"Anything I can help with?"

Harry thought that over. "You did a stint in community relations, right?"

"Yeah, about a year; mostly going to lunches and holding hands with community leaders. It was the longest year of my life."

"You ever come across a Reverend John Waldo?"

Jocko furrowed his brow, thought a minute. He slowly began to nod his head. "Yeah, I remember him. He ran a small store-front church on Alternate 19, just up from Gulf to Bay, back about twenty years ago. As I remember it, the Scientologists wanted the property—that's back when they were buying up as much land as they could get in Clearwater, and Waldo and his little church really cashed in. I don't know what happened to him after that."

"He built a bigger church—a real big one—up on Keystone Road, not far from the Hillsborough County line."

"I'm not surprised. The Scientologists were paying top dollar. And they usually got what they wanted. Hell, they ended up with that whole area of downtown."

"You ever come across his son, Bobby Joe Waldo?"

Jocko stared off, thinking again. "I don't think so. He have a sheet?"

Harry nodded.

"You think he and his old man are tied into this Beckett murder?"

"I do. I'm not sure exactly how, though my gut tells me they're in there somewhere. But I'm all alone in that. Right now everybody else who's working the case is looking hard at somebody else."

"Who?"

Harry told him.

Jocko sat at the table shaking his head. "That's bullshit. I know Nick Benevuto. He worked for Clearwater P.D. before he jointed the sheriff's department. The man's a complete ass but he would never do that. Even if he was banging her and got pissed off because she was stepping out on him, there were a dozen ways he could have set her up. And there are plenty of guys who would have busted her for him. Hell, we all know how easy it is to violate a parolee or probationer. And the way the media was all over that woman, even a hint that she was out of line and she would have found herself dodging bull dykes in the shower at county jail." He forked some rice and beans into his mouth and continued to talk around it. "Your theory about those ministers makes a lot more sense to me."

They talked about the Reverend Waldos, father and son, as they finished their meal. It had been more than a month since Harry had eaten one of Maria Doyle's Cuban dinners and he wolfed down two platefuls. When he finished he found Jocko grinning at him.

"What?"

"I was just thinking how happy Maria is gonna be when I tell her how much you enjoyed your dinner. It won't be long before she has me back here with another care package."

"Care packages are always welcome."

Jocko smiled again, but the smile slowly faded. He leaned forward, elbows on the table. "Let's talk about your mother and what's going to happen over the next few weeks." He paused. "Or better yet, what you want to happen."

Harry stared at him and for a moment Jocko saw the small boy he had taken into his home all those years ago.

The moment drew out. Finally, Harry spoke. "All I know is that I don't want her out. I don't want her to be part of my life again. I don't want to have to deal with her every day, or every week, or every month."

"If she goes up for parole, and gets it, you could ask the parole board to make that a condition . . . that she not have any contact with you . . . and if she tries, that it violates her parole and she goes back into the slam."

Harry began to slowly shake his head. He stared down at the table. "Every year, on the anniversary of . . . of what she did . . . I go to the cemetery where Jimmy's buried and I tell him that she's still inside . . . and then . . . then I promise him that I'll make sure she stays there." Harry did not tell him that he also went to the prison, but he suspected that Jocko knew.

"If that's what you want then you're going to have to fight for it. You're going to have to request to be heard before the parole board, and you're going to have to present a case, with evidence, that she shouldn't be released. But remember, you'll probably have doctors—shrinks who've treated her—saying she's not a danger to you or anyone else, so you're going to have to make a pretty strong case." He paused. "And she'll be there too, Harry. And I wouldn't put it past her to try to steal the show by telling you how sorry she is and how much she needs your forgiveness."

Harry's eyes hardened. "She won't steal anything. I have her letters. The ones she's written to me every year. And all of them, every single, fucking one," he hesitated to take a deep breath, "say how glad she is that Jimmy is with Jesus, and how she wishes I was there too." He shook his head. "The woman's just as crazy as she ever was, and if she ever gets out it won't surprise me to wake up one night and find her standing over my goddamn bed with a butcher's knife in her hand." Harry's fists clenched tightly. "And what am I supposed to do then? Grab my gun and send her straight to hell where she belongs?"

Jocko reached across the table and covered one of Harry's fists with a large hand. The boy said he didn't want her to be part of his life anymore. Not for a day, or a week, or a month. But she was already there, just as strongly as if she were standing in the room with them right now.

Jocko sat back and stared across the table at his adopted son. "Over the years she wrote to Maria several times, and a couple of times to me. For the life of me, I don't know how she ever found out who we were. Foster care and adoption records are supposed to be secret. But crazy people always seem to be able to find those things out."

Harry sat up straight in his chair. "You never told me that she wrote to you too."

"I know. Maria and I talked about it, and we decided the letters you got from her were enough, more than enough. We saw what they did to you and we didn't want to add to it." He raised a hand and let it fall back to the table. "The letters she sent to us, well, they were crazy letters, Harry, and over the years they never got any better. I don't see how anybody can say that woman is ready to be out on the streets again. If you want, Maria and I will appeal to the parole board too. We can add our letters to the ones you have."

Harry stared at him. "What did her letters say?"

"Mostly, that we'd have to pay someday for what we did."

"And what was that?"

Jocko stared at the tabletop and then raised his eyes back to Harry's. "That we kept you from Jesus."

Harry leaned back in his chair and shook his head. "You think the parole board will listen to any of us?"

"They'll listen. I'll make sure of it. Whether they hear us or not . . . well, that's another matter."

Harry nodded and took a moment to think about it. "I appreciate the offer. I'll let you know what I decide to do."

Jocko stood, walked to Harry's side of the table, cupped his head with one hand, and pulled him against his chest. "I gotta go," he said. "Maria will be waiting for a full report on how you look, how you feel, whether you are wearing nice clothes, whether there's any sign of a woman at your house, and how much of her food you ate."

Harry laughed. "Make sure you tell her my socks were clean."

"I will." Jocko paused. "Are they?"

"Yeah, they are."

"Good. I hate to lie to her. Whenever I try, she knows."

"Yeah, I remember. Sometimes it was spooky how she always seemed to know when I wasn't telling her the complete truth."

"It's not just Maria. It's a woman thing," Jocko said. "They're wonderful, but they're also scary as hell."

Jocko stepped out the front door and headed toward the sidewalk. The air was thick with tropical warmth, cut by a light but steady wind coming in off the gulf. Above, the sky was already dotted with stars and a crescent moon hung over the water in the shape of a cat's smile. As he reached the sidewalk, Jocko sensed movement on the other side of the street, and when he looked he saw a head and shoulders slip down in the driver's seat of a parked car.

He stopped and stared at the car, and as he did it lurched forward, cut into a sharp U-turn, and drove away. Fifty yards down the street it turned right on Mandalay Avenue and he could hear the engine rev as it sped away.

He turned back to Harry, who was standing in the doorway. "Was that car here when you got home?" he asked.

Harry shook his head. "No one was parked on that side of the street."

"I think whoever it was may have been watching your house. It was a Chevy Malibu, blue or black, the same car your department uses for unmarked units."

"I noticed."

Jocko offered a small shrug. "It could be Internal Affairs. Once they open an investigation on someone in a unit, they like to look at everyone in the unit. But you better check out Benevuto too; see if he kept his car, even though he's on desk duty. Who knows, I could be wrong about him. I was wrong once before." He paused, his face cracking into a slow, easy smile. "I can't remember when it was, but I'm sure it happened. It probably had something to do with you." He grinned momentarily at Harry; then the grin faded and his eyes hardened. "And from now on, make sure you watch for a tail."

CHAPTER ELEVEN

Bobby Joe Waldo looked one shade paler than death as he entered his father's office and took a seat next to Harry Doyle. It was ten o'clock on a clear, balmy Florida morning; the only storm clouds those that had gathered in the eyes of the Reverend John Waldo. The stout, unsmiling minister now turned those eyes on his son.

"Detective Doyle tells me that one of our cars was involved in an accident a couple of weeks back, and that it took place in the parking lot of some strip club in Tampa. You know anything about that Bobby Joe?"

Harry would have bet against the probability, but Bobby Joe's complexion became even paler.

"I do," Bobby Joe said in a soft, raspy voice, each word a separate croak.

"I think you better tell us about it."

Bobby Joe nodded. "I guess I should of tol' you before."

"Yes, you should have. So let's make up for it now." His father's eyes were still hard on him.

"I'm not sure exactly when it happened, but it wasn't all that long ago," Bobby Joe began. "The church got a phone call that one of our cars had been in an accident and the receptionist who took it passed it in to me." There was a film of sweat forming on Bobby Joe's upper lip despite the air-conditioning in his father's office.

"When I took the call I realized that the woman was an exotic dancer, and that the place she claimed the accident happened was the parking lot of a strip club." He gave his father a small, weak shrug. "Well, I decided the best thing for the church was to just pay this woman off." He glanced first at Harry, then back at his father. "I mean there was no way to know who had taken the car, and if they had taken it to where she said the accident happened."

Harry leaned forward in his chair. "Was the car damaged? Your car, I mean?"

"There was a scratch on the right front fender. It's still there. It was so small I haven't gotten around to getting it fixed." Bobby Joe used his thumb and index finger to wipe the sweat from his upper lip.

"What about the dancer's car?" The question came from Reverend Waldo this time.

"She said there was a scratch on the driver's door of her car. From what she told me the paint left on her car matched the color of paint on ours. She told me she always wrote down the license plate numbers of cars parked next to hers because the club has so many customers who leave drunk. Everything she said seemed legitimate, so I just told her to get an estimate. She called back when she got it and I took money from the automobile maintenance account and paid her." He looked anxiously at his father for some sign of approval. "Daddy, I just thought it best that we get rid of this as fast as possible. There was no way of knowing who took the car." He turned to Harry. "The keys to all our cars are kept on a peg in the outer office."

"The two ladies who work out there didn't remember who took that particular car?" Harry asked.

Bobby Joe twisted in his chair. The tells were falling off him like raindrops. "People come in for cars all the time," he said. "There's really no way of them knowing who takes what car. They just kinda make sure anybody taking keys is authorized to take a car. And that would be any of the associate ministers, both lay and ordained."

"What about assistant ministers and teachers in the school?" Harry asked.

Bobby Joe shook his head. "They're not supposed to take cars out. They're not covered on our insurance policies, and Daddy's secretary and the receptionist watch it pretty close."

"Is the office locked after normal business hours?"

"Yes."

Harry got up from his chair, went to the door, and opened it. He studied the lock and looked across the outer office at the door leading out on to the covered walkway. "It looks like you have the same type of locks on both doors," he said.

"We have the same locks on all the doors in all our buildings," Reverend Waldo said.

Harry nodded and returned to his chair. "You might want to consider dead bolt locks for your doors. Especially in areas you want to keep secure. The ones you have now can be slipped. What I mean is they can be opened with a flexible piece of plastic, even a credit card, by slipping it into the door frame and manipulating the lock."

"So anybody who knew how to do that could've got to the keys," Bobby Joe said, jumping at Harry's statement as if it were a lifeline thrown to a drowning man.

Harry turned to Bobby Joe, preparing to push him back out into deeper water. "We're concerned about one of your cars visiting the strip club because Darlene Beckett was known to visit the place on a fairly regular basis."

Bobby Joe glanced back and forth between Harry and his father. "I don't think I understand," he said, although the look in his eyes told Harry he understood completely.

Reverend Waldo leaned back in his executive chair. "I think what Detective Doyle has done is he's added two and two—our car and that

club—and he's come up with five, all because that woman went there too."
He turned his still unhappy eyes on Harry. "I'm sure that when this car
business is all sorted out we'll find that one of our parishioners called to
complain that her husband was visiting this club, and one of our people
went there to tell him to get himself home."

Harry gave the minister a long, blank look. Then he smiled. "You think
it's possible that one of your assistants took your admonition against Ms.
Beckett to heart and started following her around to see what he could dig
up on her?"

Reverend Waldo returned Harry's smile, his distinctly patronizing. "We
don't have any detectives in our ministry. I don't think any of our people
would know where to begin if it came to following somebody around."

Harry momentarily studied his shoes, thinking of the person who followed him home the previous night. When he looked up his smile was
back. "I'm sure you're probably right, Reverend Waldo." He paused. "But
just in case you're not, I'd like a list of all the people authorized to take cars
so I can speak to them."

The minister's eyes hardened again. He looked sharply at his son.
"Bobby Joe can get that together for you. I think you'll find everybody you
need to talk to is here this morning. And when you're finished with the
detective, Bobby Joe, please come back. There are some other things we
have to go over." When the minister turned back to Harry, his smile had
returned. "I hope we were of help," he said, his tone clearly a dismissal.

Harry got little more than blank stares when he asked members of the
church's staff if they had driven a church vehicle to the Peek-a-Boo Lounge
during the past month. He hadn't expected an admission. He was simply
looking for clues, but in each instance he came up empty. Yet when he
asked their opinions about Darlene Beckett, the church staff proved far
more forthcoming. Words like *sinful* and *child molester*, *harlot*, and *wick-*

edness dropped from their lips almost as though they were programmed responses. There was a genuine anger about Darlene, a remorseless anger that did not vary from one person to another, and it led Harry to conclude that the Reverend John Waldo had a staff of true believers unlike any he had ever encountered.

The last person Harry interviewed was Justin Clearby, the church's first assistant minister. Clearby surprised Harry both in his physical appearance and his demeanor. He was a tall, solidly built man somewhere in his mid-fifties who carried around the well-battered face of an aging prizefighter. There was also a sense of rigidness about the man, accented by sandy brown hair cut in a military buzz and pale blue eyes that could only be described as very hard, very cold, and very angry. Clearby also had huge, powerful hands and when Harry shook one he felt as though his own had been swallowed. There was no question in Harry's mind that Clearby would have the ability to wield a knife with enormous force. Harry also noted that just standing near him seemed to put Bobby Joe Waldo on edge.

"I know the area you're talking about," Clearby said, when asked about Nebraska Avenue. "Before being saved I had a thirty-year career in the Marine Corp, most of it spent as a seagoing Marine." His back seemed to stiffen with pride as he spoke. "Back then Tampa was a popular liberty port largely because of that area. So I know it." He paused to offer up a cold smile, then added: "Although I haven't been there in many years."

"How did you feel about Darlene Beckett?" Harry asked.

Clearby paused a long time before answering. When he did his eyes seemed to give off a steady chill, and as he leaned in to bring himself closer to Harry, his voice became little more than a gravelly whisper. "I wish I had been in heaven the day she died, so I could have borne witness to Jesus Christ casting her into hell," he said.

* * *

Bobby Joe watched Harry's car leave the church parking lot and head east on Keystone Road toward the Brooker Creek Preserve. The asshole had gotten nothing from all his questions. Everybody he had asked about the Peek-a-Boo had just looked at him like he was out of his mind. Even Clearby shut him down cold. And the big detective, he just stared back at them all the while they talked like he was gonna get something out of the tone of their voices, or the way they stood, or how they made eye contact. He was just like every cop he had ever met, thinking he was gonna be able to divine something, just like he was talking to one of those Greek oracles he had read about in school.

Now he had to go back to his father and listen to his shit for however long it took to smooth his feathers. But he better do it, and he better do a good job of it, or he was gonna lose this piece-of-cake job and find himself out looking for something in the real world, the very thing Daddy always threatened to make him do. Yeah, fat chance. Not with his record. Somebody got a look at that, they'd say so-long, goodbye, have a nice life, kid.

When Bobby Joe entered the office his father was seated behind his desk stone-faced. His tone matched his look, dark and simmering with anger.

"What happened with the detective?"

"Nothin' happened, Daddy. He talked to everybody and nobody knew nothin' about that accident."

Reverend Waldo leaned back in his chair, his large belly rising up above the desktop like some sea creature coming up for a gasp of air. His eyes narrowed as he continued to stare at his son. "Nobody said nothin' because the person who was driving that car was standing right next to that detective. Isn't that so, Bobby Joe?"

Bobby Joe shuffled his feet. He knew it was useless to lie to the old man. He wouldn't believe anything he said no matter how good the story was. And he didn't have a decent story anyway.

"I was just following her, trying to get somethin' on her. Something we could use to see that she finally went to jail," he said.

His father remained silent, the only sign he had even heard him an increased narrowing of his eyes.

"I didn't even know I had scratched that woman's car. But I knew I couldn't risk having anything that would show a church car was ever there. That's why I paid that woman off so quick."

"You were sleeping with that filthy harlot, weren't you?"

Bobby Joe began to rapidly shake his head as though it might drive the accusation away. "No, Daddy. No, no, no."

"Don't lie to me. Don't you dare."

The old man's voice thundered throughout the room and Bobby Joe could swear it made the photographs on the wall shake. His hands began to tremble. "Daddy . . . Daddy, I tried hard to resist her."

The older minister leaned forward, elbows on the desktop, hands pressed together in front of his face as if he were preparing to pray. His voice was little more than a whisper now.

"You tell me how you sinned with her. You confess it to me, boy. You tell me all of it. Every . . . last . . . detail. Then you tell me if anybody else knows about it, or even suspects it happened. And you hear this, boy: I don't want you to leave anything out. And when you tell me all that, then I'll tell you what you're gonna do next to make sure this here church doesn't pay a price for your sin."

It was two o'clock when Harry returned to the squad room. Since he arrived at the church that morning he had run into one stone wall after another and he was not in a good mood. The fact that he was followed home the previous night and hadn't even spotted his tail had dropped his mood another notch.

He slid into his chair at the conference room table and opened his notebook to review his interviews at the church. They hadn't proved use-less, but they were running a close second. Every question he had asked had been answered, but the information given had been minimal or non-existent. Justin Clearby had been the only plus, and that had been purely a gut feeling. But when he had run a criminal record check on him, he had drawn a blank there as well. All of it left Bobby Joe Waldo as his only suspect.

As he considered his next move someone slid into the chair opposite him. When he looked up he found Vicky looking at him intently. Jim Morgan stood in the doorway behind her. Harry acknowledged him with a nod and Morgan raised one finger to his forehead in a salute.

"How are things going with the church?" Vicky asked.

"I think I'm learning why churches are made of stone," Harry said.

"That bad, huh?"

"That bad. And the entire staff of ministers and assistant ministers—all except for my boy, Bobby Joe Waldo—is the biggest collection of Bible-thumping religious zealots I've ever come across. But, what the hell, this is Florida. How are you and Jim doing?"

Vicky jerked her head toward the squad room and when Harry looked past her he could see Nick Benevuto seated at his desk in a far corner. "It's a little weird when the suspect you're investigating is sitting across the room from you." She paused, hesitating to say more.

"You haven't come up with anything that might clear him? Or at least raise some doubts?"

Vicky gave him a steady look. "No, Harry. Not a thing. Are you still convinced the killer is someone involved with that church?"

Harry nodded and watched Vicky shift her weight in her chair. When he looked past her he saw that Jim Morgan had lowered his eyes. Harry smiled for the first time that day.

"Hey, guys, this is what homicide is all about. You follow every lead, every gut feeling. And when it's all over, with a bit of luck, you end up with the right guy."

Vicky stood and stared at him. "So it's not just the dead detective's well-known instinct for getting inside a killer's head. Or all that mysticism about victims talking to him." She returned his smile, but hers was cold and hard, her voice dripping sarcasm. "I think the captain actually believes in all that. I think he's even counting on that bit of homicide voodoo to get Benevuto off the hook."

Harry stared at her, allowing the bitterness in her voice to hang between them. He continued to hold her gaze as he leaned back in his chair. "Let's get back to work, partner."

Harry's use of the word *partner* hit her like a slap, and Vicky realized they probably wouldn't be using that word between them for a very long time.

Harry gathered his things, including the old mug shot of Bobby Joe Waldo. He had decided to show it to Darlene Beckett's neighbors and friends to see if anyone could place the young minister with her in the weeks preceding her death. As he left the conference room Nick Benevuto approached him.

"Harry, I gotta talk to you."

Harry nodded and stepped back inside the conference room. "What can I do for you, Nick?"

Benevuto's eyes kept darting toward the main door of the squad room. "It's your partner and her new sidekick. Especially Stanopolis. She's really out for my ass, Harry, and she's really bought into everything this kid Morgan claims he found." He shook his head. "Okay, maybe I was off base tryin' to dick that Beckett broad. And maybe I was stupid using one of our unmarked cars when I stopped by her place. But sweet Jesus, Harry, I never snuffed her, and I sure as hell never tried to alter department records to hide the fact that I was in an unmarked car when I went to her place. Shit, I wouldn't know how to alter a computer record."

Harry looked steadily into Benevuto's eyes. "Did you ever see Darlene Beckett's body?" he asked.

"No, Harry, I never did."

"She looked scared, Nick. But the fear came later, when she realized she was going to die. First she looked surprised, and that sense of surprise never completely left her face. I think it was a surprise that came from something she saw. Like maybe she knew her killer, or she was surprised that someone like that would *be* a killer, because maybe he was a minister, or a cop, or a kid, and it surprised her that someone like that could have just cut her throat. So it's like I told you before, Nick, the squad has no choice; they've got to check you out."

Nick shook his head vehemently. "Those two, your partner and this Morgan kid, aren't just checking me out, Harry. They're out for by sweet dago ass—every pound of it. And they're not gonna stop until they see it hanging from the nearest goddamn palm tree. Every time they look at me I can see it in their eyes. They're gonna make their bones on my goddamn back. And all of it's based on some computer bullshit that this kid dreamed up. But your partner, Stanopolis, she acts like this Morgan kid is some kind of genius detective, not some wet-behind-the-ears punk right out of a patrol car."

"I still don't get what you want me to do, Nick." Harry, too, was now glancing toward the squad room door and this time he saw two suits enter. They had to be the people Nick had been anticipating. Harry could almost smell them from across the room. "I think we've got company," he said.

Nick followed his gaze. "Shit," he muttered.

"Look, I'll do what I can. But it's not gonna be much. I can't tell them to back off."

"I know you can't. But Jesus, Harry, reign in this Morgan kid and his computer bullshit. Explain that it's another cop's blood he's after."

Harry nodded but made no promises. Benevuto was scared and, as a cop, he wanted to believe him, at least as far as Darlene's murder was concerned. But he wasn't about to impede another cop's investigation. He started across the squad room and found himself braced by the two suits coming toward him.

"You're Harry Doyle, aren't you?" the larger of the two said.

"That's right."

"My name's Dwight Jimmo." He nodded toward his partner. "This is Barry Brooks. We're from Internal Affairs and we need a few minutes of your time."

As Jimmo was talking, Brooks looked past Harry and called out to Benevuto who had started back across the room. "Don't go anyplace, Benevuto. We need to talk to you too."

Harry stared at each man in turn, the contempt clear on his face. "You'll have to catch me later."

Harry started to move past them when Brooks stepped in front of him. "We need to talk to you *now*."

Brooks was a big man, most of it fat built up from sitting behind a desk. A small, cold smile gathered on Harry's lips. His voice was just one level above a whisper. "You step in front of me like that again, and I'll dump you on your fat ass—"

"Maybe you didn't hear us," Jimmo interrupted. "We're from Internal Affairs and we want to talk to *you*."

"And like I said, you'll have to catch me later. Right now I'm working an active homicide, so you can set up an appointment with my captain, and when he tells me to drop what I'm doing and talk to you, I will. In the meantime, you can take your Internal Affairs creds and shove 'em up your ass sideways." This time Harry stepped past them without any interference.

"You'll be hearing from us," Brooks called after him.

"Be still my heart," Harry called back.

Bobby Joe insisted that he hadn't told his daddy everything, and the man he was now talking to believed him.

"Your daddy seems to scare the hell out of you. Why is that?" The man asked the question casually, almost as though he didn't care about Bobby Joe's answer.

"I'm not afraid of him," Bobby Joe said. There was a slight quiver in his voice as he spoke. "I just know what I can tell him and what I can't."

"You think he won't stand by you if you tell him you did something that offends him, something that goes against his beliefs?"

Bobby Joe snorted.

"Maybe he won't," the man said. "Maybe his beliefs are too important to him, or maybe he's just all used up with all the stuff you've pulled over the years."

"Yeah, well maybe I'm used up with him." Bobby Joe paused. He didn't want this man going to his father and telling him what he had said. "No, I don't mean that. I'm not used up with him. It's just that sometimes he's a hard man to get along with."

"He's a wonderful man."

Bobby Joe shook his head. "Yeah, maybe he is to you. But I know one thing you don't. He's a hard man to have as a father."

The man gave him a cold, distant smile. "I wouldn't know about fathers . . . never had one; not a real one anyway. I just had a string of creeps my mother hooked up with from time to time, before the state sent me off to foster care." He let out a barking laugh that sounded hollow even to him. He shook his head and continued. "The creeps, they only wanted one thing; they just wanted me out of the way so they could . . ." He let the sentence die. Then he smiled again. "Well, you know why they wanted me out of the way." The smile widened, turning colder as it did. "If Darlene had a kid, you probably would have wanted him out of the way for the same reason."

They were seated in the man's car in the parking lot of Frank Howard Park, and beyond the low wall in front of them they could look straight out into the calm waters of the gulf. It was seven o'clock; sunset was still more than an hour away, and only a handful of people dotted the beach.

"I love the Gulf of Mexico," the man said. "It always has a calming effect on me." He turned slowly to look at Bobby Joe again. "Did you know that Darlene was killed on a beach? In fact, it was very close to where we are now. She was with a man she'd just picked up. He was killed too. I suppose it could just as easily have been you, Bobby Joe." He looked back toward the water and his voice became distant and dreamy. "But that's not really relevant. That's just the luck of the draw." He cocked his head to the side as if considering what he'd just said. "Anyway . . . whoever gave Darlene what she deserved moved her body after she was dead; took it to Brooker Creek. But the man's body was left behind. A park maintenance crew found it a day later." A glimmer of a smile began to form then faded away. "Pretty ripe by then, what with lying out in the sun all that time. Crabs too. They can find a body faster than anything."

"You seem to know a lot about it," Bobby Joe said.

The man nodded slowly. "Well, I would, wouldn't I?" He continued to nod his head. "I mean I was doing what your daddy asked us all to do. I was watching her . . . just like you were."

"I wasn't watching her that night." Bobby Joe twisted nervously on the seat.

"You weren't?"

"No, dammit. I was nowhere near her that night."

"Can you prove that, Bobby Joe?"

He was silent for a moment. "No, I can't."

"Too bad . . . be better if you could. The detective you've got hanging around your neck seems to be looking at you pretty hard. Man's like a dog with a bone. And I don't think he's about to give it up. If I were you I'd get myself an alibi."

Bobby Joe stared out the window. "You could say I was with you . . . like we were doing something for the church."

The man shook his head as though Bobby Joe's suggestion was the dumbest thing he'd heard in a long while. "Now given my situation, why would I shine that kind of light on myself? Why would I put myself in the middle of *your* problem? Don't you think I've got enough of my own?"

"But you were watching her too. Don't you forget that. We even ran into each other at that club that one night." Bobby Joe's voice had become sharp and petulant.

The man turned to face him. As he did his arm slid along the top of the bench seat until his hand was behind Bobby Joe's head. "But I didn't keep going back inside that club. And I wasn't sleeping with her behind everybody's back. Only you were doing that. Only you had that kind of *personal* relationship with that slut."

"Still . . ."

"You're not threatening me, are you, Bobby Joe?"

The man's eyes had turned so cold and so hard it sent a shiver through the young minister.

"No, no, of course not."

"Good. Because it would be a terrible mistake if you ever decided you could threaten me." The man moved in close, his face only inches from Bobby Joe's.

Bobby Joe leaned away until his back was against the passenger window. "You know better than that." There was a noticeable tremor in his voice.

"Yes, I know better. The question is, do you?"

"You don't ever have to worry about it. Look, I don't want any trouble with you. I need your help, that's all."

The man placed his hand on the back of Bobby Joe's neck and he could feel a trembling that radiated up from his shoulders. "You're on your own in this, Bobby Joe. Just make sure you never drag me into it. You understand what I mean?"

"Yeah, I understand." The trembling intensified. "Listen, you don't have to worry about it. Really, you don't."

The man watched Bobby Joe's eyes and he knew there was no way he could trust him. He was weak and foolish and when it came down to it, he'd only think about saving his own skinny backside. But you don't know everything, Bobby Joe. And there's one thing you sure don't know. You don't know you're already a dead man.

CHAPTER TWELVE

By the time he finished the canvass of Darlene's neighbors, Harry had three positive IDs on Bobby Joe Waldo's photo. All were reasonably sure they had seen him entering or leaving Darlene's apartment. Joshua Brown, the elderly neighbor who had provided Harry with the list of license plate numbers, was the most certain. Brown claimed that Bobby Joe had nearly knocked him down as he hurried out of Darlene's apartment one evening.

"I 'member him 'cause he was in such a rush to get away," Brown said. "Even tol' me to watch where I was goin' with my damn dog. That's what he said: 'your damn dog.' Little pissant. And I 'member thinkin' at the time that he musta parked his car on another street so nobody would see it here. I even thought maybe I'd follow him and get his plate number, but he was movin' too fast for me to keep up."

Harry drove the short distance to the Peek-a-Boo Lounge. He already had a positive ID from Anita Molari, but now he wanted to see if any of the other dancers could place Bobby Joe in the club.

The interior was just as it had been on his earlier visit, the air still permeated with the same unpleasant mix of stale liquor and human sweat. He spoke individually to each of the twelve dancers working that night and three were sure they had seen the young minister at the bar. Of the three, two were even certain they'd seen him sitting next to Darlene Beckett, with one insisting that Darlene had been "giving the kid her best moves," and that the next time she'd looked they were gone.

The call came into Harry's cell phone just as he was crossing the parking lot headed back to his car, and minutes later he was speeding toward Pinellas County with lights flashing and siren blaring.

The trailer park was on a small lake just off Keystone Road, a neat, quiet, secluded community with a scattering of large shade trees that kept the sun off the tin structures. Jim Morgan was standing beside an unmarked car; Vicky was thirty feet away helping a crime scene officer set up a laser to determine the trajectory of the bullet that had smashed through a trailer window.

Harry walked up beside Morgan and raised his chin toward the trailer. "Your place?" he asked.

Morgan nodded. "It used to be my aunt's. She left it to me when she passed."

"Were you inside when the shot was fired?"

Again, Morgan nodded. "I'd just gotten home and I was in the kitchen making a sandwich and I hear this thud as the bullet hits my refrigerator."

"Just the thud? No sound of a gun being fired?"

Morgan shook his head. "That's the thing, Harry. There wasn't *any* sound. I mean, even if it had come from inside another trailer I would have heard *something*."

"Did you hear a car?"

"I don't have any recollection of a car. But that wouldn't be unusual. There are almost a hundred units in the park, and there are cars going in and out all the time, so I wouldn't have paid much attention if I heard one approaching. I also hit the floor as soon as I realized what was happening, so I could have missed the sound of a car pulling away. The first thing I thought of when I was laying on the floor was that it's too thick in here for a bullet to have come from a long distance, so I got my own weapon out, called it in on my cell, and crawled to the back door so I could work my way around the house. Of course, there was no one there by the time I did. I don't want to be dramatic about it, but the only thing I can think of is that whoever did this used some kind of suppressor."

"You seem pretty calm given what happened."

Morgan gave him a boyish grin. "Yeah, *now* I am. With all you guys here. You should of seen me right after it happened. I had to check to make sure my pants were dry."

Vicky approached holding a plastic bag. She held it up. There was a mangled bullet inside.

"It's a .38. But as far as ballistics go, the slug is useless. The laser shows a trajectory that indicates the shot was fired from the same height the shooter would have been at if he was seated in a car."

"No chance it came from a trailer across the road?"

"Only if the shooter was lying on the ground in front of the trailer directly across from the window."

Harry turned and studied the trailer on the opposite side of the narrow road. He turned back to Morgan. "Who lives there?"

"An elderly couple, late seventies, early eighties. I can't see either of them being able to handle a weapon."

"We'll check them out, but I agree, it doesn't sound very likely." Harry studied the ground for a moment. "Any enemies from past police work? Or anything personal?"

Morgan shook his head. "Nobody I can think of."

"There could be one," Vicky piped in. "But not from the past; from the case we're working on now."

Harry had already thought of Nick Benevuto, but was waiting for someone else to voice the suspicion. "Let's work the scene here first. If we don't find anything we'll brace Nick." He turned to Morgan. "Vicky and I will do it. I don't want you there. He's pretty hot about you and the computer stuff you found, and I don't want to aggravate the situation."

Morgan seemed suddenly agitated. "You're not taking me off the case, are you?"

"No, don't worry about that," Harry said. "I just don't want you there when we interview Nick about this."

The canvass of the trailer park produced nothing. No one in the immediate vicinity of Morgan's trailer had heard or seen anything untoward. Reluctantly, at ten p.m., Harry moved on to Nick Benevuto.

Nick lived in an older condo complex in Countryside, a densely populated residential area on the northern fringes of Clearwater. Twenty-five years earlier it was among the first to fall victim to the real estate boom, its sprawling orange groves and horse farms seeming to disappear overnight. Now the only country left in Countryside was its name.

Nick's car was parked outside his unit. Harry placed his hand on the hood. It was hot to the touch. Vicky gave him a questioning look.

"It's been driven recently," he said. He watched a small smile begin to form at the corners of her mouth, and added: "For whatever that's worth."

"At least we know we're not wasting our time," she said.

It took Nick almost a full minute to answer the door, and when he did he had a drink in his hand. His eyes told Harry it had not been his first. Harry saw suspicion flood Nick's face. It only hardened when his gaze switched to Vicky. He looked back at Harry.

"I guess it's not a social call." He raised his chin toward Vicky. "Not if you need your partner with you." His voice was steady, no slur that Harry could detect.

"Wish it was. Can we come in? It won't take long."

Nick was dressed in khaki shorts and a T-shirt that emphasized the belly he had earned through a lot of hard drinking. He gave Harry a long stare; then a small who-gives-a-damn shrug. "Sure, come in. After dealing with those rat bastards from IAD, how much worse can it get?"

Nick's apartment was as rumpled and disheveled as his life. The living room he led them into was furnished out of a Rooms To Go catalog with a leather sofa, two matching chairs, an ottoman, and glass-topped coffee and end tables. All the glass tops had water rings and food stains, and through an archway Harry could see several days' dishes piled in the sink. He didn't want to see Nick's bedroom.

Nick picked up a dirty shirt and shorts from one of the chairs, told them they could sit if they wanted, and offered them a drink, which Harry and Vicky both declined.

"So what's this about?" he asked as he took a seat at one end of the sofa, stretching out a leg so no one could sit next to him.

"Do you own a .38, Nick?"

Nick raised his eyebrows. "Sure, what cop doesn't, especially if he's been on the job as long as I have? I've got my first service revolver, the one I carried when I was on patrol, and a snub-nosed Chief's Special, that was my first piece as a detective. That was in the good old days, before we switched over to Glocks. But you're too young to remember those days, right, Harry?"

"I remember, Nick. I grew up in a cop's house."

"Yeah, that's right." He paused a moment. "You know Jocko knows me. You tell him about this bullshit they're tryin' to pin on me?"

"I told him," Harry said.

"And . . . ?"

"He said he thought it was a crock."

Nick nodded as if that should settle the matter.

"Can we see the two .38s?" Harry asked, bringing him back.

"What for?"

"Somebody took a shot at Jim Morgan tonight. Whoever it was used a .38. I just want to rule you out."

"Morgan okay?"

"He's fine."

Benevuto nodded but said nothing more.

"So? Can we see them?" Vicky pushed.

Nick glared at her. "Yeah, you can see 'em. There in my locker at work. When I had it, I kept my Glock here. As far as the other weapons go, I didn't want to take a chance of somebody breaking in and walking off with them. Too many people around here know I'm a cop."

Harry nodded. "I'd like you to go to the office with us so we can have a look."

"Tonight? It can't wait until tomorrow?"

"I'm afraid not, Nick. By the way, what time did you leave work?"

"Around four, right after those humps from IAD left."

"You come straight home?"

"Yeah. Why?"

"Your engine's hot, like the car's been driven recently." Harry glanced at his watch. "It's been six hours since you left work."

"I ran out of bourbon and went out to the liquor store. You'll find the empty bag with a receipt inside on the kitchen counter." A sneer came over his face. "But hell, maybe I stopped on the way to squeeze one off at Morgan."

"I'll take the bag and the receipt with us," Harry said, ignoring the comment. "You okay to drive?"

"Yeah, I'm fine."

"Then just follow us down."

Nick stood in front of his locker, his shoulders shaking with what could have been rage . . . or fear.

"They were fucking here, damnit. They were here this morning."

Harry stepped around so he could look into Nick's face, see what was there.

"Are you sure, Nick? Do you specifically remember seeing them this morning?"

He stood there thinking about what Harry had asked. "If you mean, could I swear to it in court and not worry that I might find out later they'd been missing for three days . . . no, I couldn't." He shook his head. "Shit, Harry, they were covered with that cloth you see on the top shelf. I mean I might not have noticed they were gone until I actually looked for them."

Nick reached for the cloth but Harry laid a hand on his arm, stopping him. "I want to have the inside of the locker dusted, Nick. If anyone took them, they would have been sweating the idea of a cop walking in here, so they probably did it in a hurry."

"And they might have gotten careless," Nick said hopefully.

"Is there any chance you left the locker open?"

Nick shook his head. "Never happen. Hell, you know as well as I do, cops steal."

"I was thinking more along the lines of the maintenance people. They're in here late at night cleaning up."

"Yeah," Nick said, hopeful again, "and it would be easy to have one of them standing watch outside while the other went through lockers seeing what he could find."

Vicky stared off, clearly annoyed. "That's a really big stretch, isn't it? Alright, maybe a maintenance guy would pick up a loose gun, figuring he could sell it, but almost all of the people who come in here are cops. Why would another cop wanna steal Nick's weapons?"

"What if it isn't theft?" Harry asked.

Both she and Nick stared at him, openly confused.

"We're assuming the weapons, or at least one of them, *might* be involved in the shooting at Morgan's house. But the bullet was so mangled, even when we find Nick's guns, there's no way to prove or disprove that one of those weapons fired the shot. And maybe Nick's missing guns had nothing to do with any of it."

"What do you mean?" Vicky asked.

"Maybe somebody took them for an entirely different purpose. Maybe IAD searched Nick's locker and took them to see if they could tie them in to something else."

"Then there'll be a warrant," Vicky said.

"Not necessarily. This is sheriff's department property—the building, the room, the locker. Who's to say they can't go inside a locker just with the okay of a boss? They do it every time a cop dies, or gets fired. It's department property."

Nick's features darkened. "Those fuckers. I never even thought of them. They coulda been looking for evidence that would tie me to Darlene; noticed the two .38s and just grabbed them to see if they could score a hit on something else."

"So we'll ask them," Vicky said.

Both Harry and Nick looked at her as if she were out of her mind.

"Okay, dumb idea," she conceded. "What do you suggest?"

"We'll wait, see if their prints show up."

Harry got home at midnight. Checking his mail, he found a letter from the Florida Parole Board. It was formal notification that his mother had been granted a hearing on the following Tuesday. He had expected the letter; had known it was coming, but it didn't stop his stomach from churning. He read the letter again, noting the time: nine a.m. Then he read it a third time. Finally, he threw the letter on a table, went to the kitchen, and poured his nightly orange juice. He went out on the lanai, headed for a long beach walk, and found Jeanie Walsh curled up asleep on one of the chaise lounges. A sense of relief flooded him, and he sat down next to her and gently stroked her face. She smiled in her sleep, then her eyes fluttered and opened.

"I was just dreaming about you stroking my face."

"The power of positive dreaming," he said.

"Mmm, that's a nice thought." She smiled up at him. "If it works that way maybe I'll go back to sleep and dream about you doing something else."

"Are you trying to seduce me?"

She closed her eyes again and smiled. "Sure am."

"I'm not that easy," he said.

She laughed. "Oh, yes you are."

He scooped her up in his arms and carried her into the house.

"Sir, where are you taking me?"

"I'm taking you to my bed, where I intend to ravish you until you can speak nothing but gibberish and your eyes roll around in your head." He leaned close to her ear and whispered: "Yes, I'm that good."

Jeanie threw her head back and laughed. "You better be, mister. Especially after a buildup like that."

The bed sheets lay in a twisted mass about their feet and their bodies were covered in a thin layer of perspiration.

Jeanie turned on her side and rested her head against Harry's chest. "I don't know what got into you, mister, but I hope it gets into you again."

Harry slipped his arms around her and pulled her even closer. He brought his mouth to her hair and lightly kissed her. "You are one great way to end a lousy day."

"Mmmm, I like that idea. I think I might take it up as a hobby . . . helping Harry Doyle recover from very bad days."

Harry lightly ran the tips of his fingers along her back. "That could take up a lot of your time."

She ran her own fingers through the hair on his chest. "I have the time," she said simply.

They lay quietly for several minutes before Jeanie spoke again. "Harry, you don't have to tell me if you don't want to. But what upset you . . . Was it something at work . . . or something closer to home?"

"Work is always the same. They throw a murder at you and it's either clear cut, or it's a big puzzle. This one's a puzzle, and right now I don't like the way it's going. Darlene has stopped talking to me. But that's not surprising. Victims always do. They only know so much. And I can only hear them for a short time after their deaths. But in this case I'm afraid there are going to be more victims."

"Will they talk to you?"

"I hope so."

"Don't the victims always talk to you?"

"No. They only talk to me when they have to; when they have something to say. Sometimes their deaths were just a terrible surprise and there's nothing they *can* tell me." He paused, thinking about how he could explain without sounding as if he had a loose screw. "With Darlene . . . everything I felt from her shouted out religion right from the start. But after that it stopped; there wasn't anything else." He paused. "Maybe she just didn't know anything more."

"So now you think there will be more victims and they might tell you more?"

"Yes. But that's part of the problem. There'll be more victims because I haven't caught the killer with what I already know."

"And that's what's bothering you?"

"That's most of it, yes."

Harry let another minute pass. Finally, he sighed and blurted the rest of it out. "A letter was waiting when I got home. It was from the parole board. My mother's hearing is at nine a.m. next Tuesday."

"Are you still planning to go?"

"Yes."

Jeanie pulled herself closer. So you have two monsters to deal with, she thought. A woman who sexually abused children, who you hope will whisper secrets to you about her killer, and that other monster who killed you and your brother all those years ago, and who hasn't stopped whispering to you since. She squeezed him lightly. Oh, Harry, you poor, sweet man. What an emotional nightmare you've been dealt in this life.

CHAPTER THIRTEEN

Bobby Joe Waldo started to sweat before Harry finished his first sentence. By the third sentence his floral Tommy Bahama shirt was clinging to his back.

"Look, you got this all wrong." Bobby Joe stood up from his desk, went to a wall-mounted thermostat, and lowered the air-conditioning by several more degrees. It was a beautiful Florida morning, warm and sultry with cloudless blue skies overhead. None of it found its way into Bobby Joe's box of an office. The room was already cold; soon it would be freezing.

"Alright, so why don't you just tell me how wrong I've got it," Harry said.

Returning to his chair, Bobby Joe propped his elbows on his desk, formed a steeple with his fingers, and began speaking through it. "I don't care what those women say, detective. They were just plain mistaken. I wasn't in that bar and I sure wasn't in there with Darlene Beckett." He gave his head a solemn shake to emphasize the point. "For God's sake, I'm a minister in a respected church."

The self-righteous pose forced Harry to fight back a smile. "You don't look like you slept very well," he said, smoothly changing tact. "Are you having problems here at the church?"

Bobby Joe gave him as hard a stare as he could manage. "I slept fine. And I don't have any problems at the church."

Harry lowered his voice, making the conversation more intimate. "Look, Bobby Joe. We know somebody from the church was at that bar.

We can prove that one of your cars was in a minor accident in the parking lot. We can also prove that you resolved that problem for the church. Now, that doesn't mean you were the person involved in the accident, but it's sure a possibility."

"My daddy told you how that probably happened . . . somebody from the congregation complaining that her husband was going to that bar, and an assistant minister going out to see what he could do to help a sinner."

Harry smiled. "Yeah, I know what your daddy said, Bobby Joe. The funny thing is that you're the one guy who keeps popping up. First it's you paying off the accident in the parking lot—and paying off without telling anybody here at the church what you were doing—and now again with these dancers telling me they saw you in the bar, and not only in the bar, but in the bar with Darlene Beckett. And they're also telling me that you're sitting there with her and that she's coming on to you pretty strong. How did they put it?" Harry stared off as if trying to recall the dancer's exact words. "Oh, yeah, that she was 'usin'' all her best moves' on you." Now Harry shook his head and put an extra good-ol'-boy twang to his words. "My Lord, Bobby Joe, a woman who looked like Darlene did, who had a reputation like Darlene did, and she's just sittin' there in that titty bar, puttin' her best moves on the guy sittin' next to her. Now that surely would be a temptation, wouldn't it, Bobby Joe?" He dropped the twang and let his eyes harden. "And all that's a big contradiction from what you're telling me, Bobby Joe. And it makes it real hard for me to believe you."

The door to Bobby Joe's office swung open and his father wielded his great bulk through the door. A step behind him was a tall, slender, balding man with a solemn expression spread across his face. He was dressed like someone who had just been dragged off a golf course.

The Reverend Waldo stretched his lips in a closed-mouth smile. "Sorry to interrupt you, detective, but you seem to keep comin' back to visit us, so I thought it was time to bring in the church's lawyer. This here's Walter

Middlebrooks. From here on he's gonna sit in and advise anyone you need to question."

Harry glanced at Bobby Joe. He seemed confused, his eyes showing relief, then fear, and then relief again. Harry decided it was time to wipe away that sense of relief. He looked up at the older minister and slowly nodded. "Then I guess we'll have to change our procedures a bit." He turned his gaze to Middlebrooks. "I was trying to keep everything informal for now, but that seems not to be working for you folks. So I'm going to make a call for some deputies to take Bobby Joe down to headquarters and we'll continue down there."

"Are you charging him?" Middlebrooks snapped.

"Not for now. Right now he's a material witness. We have other witnesses—please note the plural there, counselor—who have placed Bobby Joe at a certain topless bar in Tampa in the company of our murder victim, shortly before her death."

Middlebrooks ground his teeth. "And I suppose this will involve flashing red lights, handcuffs, and perhaps a leaked story to the media," he snapped.

Harry inclined his head to one side. "Well, as you know, counselor, cruisers have to leave their red lights flashing when they enter a building on a call, and handcuffs, are department procedure when transporting a suspect. For a material witness, it's kind of up to the deputies doing the transporting." He ended the line with a false smile. "As far as leaks to the media go, that is definitely not department procedure. And I'll do everything I can to make sure it doesn't happen." Harry closed it off with a faint smile.

Reverend Waldo swelled up like an angry toad. "What does all this mean, Walter?"

Middlebrooks put a calming hand on his arm. "It means that if we want a lawyer present during questioning, he intends to name Bobby Joe as a material witness and take him in for formal questioning, rather than do it quietly here. It also means that other deputies will arrive here at the church with the red lights on their cars flashing, and they'll put Bobby Joe in handcuffs and take him away with them. Informally, it's known as a perp walk, a form of embarrassment the police like to inflict on people." He turned toward Harry. "Does that sum it up, detective?"

"That's pretty much right, counselor, except for the embarrassment part."

"Well, I don't want that," Reverend Waldo snapped. "I don't want that at all." He glared at his son. "I won't have the church put in this position."

Middlebrooks patted his arm again. "Let me talk to the detective a moment, John."

The lawyer walked across the small office and took a seat next to Harry. "Now exactly how reputable are these witnesses who placed Bobby Joe with this murdered woman? I mean it is a minister we're talking about here."

Harry nodded, fighting off a smile. "I know that, counselor. But the witnesses both identified Bobby Joe from his old mug shots." He watched the lawyer wince at the words. "But, of course, we'll do a formal lineup at headquarters and let them identify him in the flesh."

The Reverend John Waldo began to sputter, but Middlebrooks raised a hand asking him to hold off any comment. "And who exactly are these witnesses?" the lawyer asked.

"They're both topless dancers at the Peek-a-Boo Lounge," Harry said. Middlebrooks began to object, but now Harry raised a hand and continued speaking in a slow, methodical voice. "And . . . they were both close acquaintances of Darlene Beckett. And . . . they also both say that shortly before Darlene's murder, they saw her sitting at the bar engaged in some rather heavy flirting with Bobby Joe, and that after a time . . . Bobby Joe and Darlene appeared to leave together." Harry let his words sink in before going on. "In my book, counselor, that's enough to make him a material witness."

"Well, we shall have to see about that," Middlebrooks intoned in his best lawyerly voice.

At that point Reverend Waldo stepped forward and smiled down on Harry. "Now look here, son. What's say we take a step back and decide not to get our lawyer involved, maybe just go on like before? We do that, can we maybe do away with the need for the flashing red lights and the handcuff business?"

Harry took a moment to feign consideration. He glanced over at Bobby Joe, who seemed suddenly hopeful. He looked at Middlebrooks, who now seemed annoyed at having his golf game interrupted. Then he looked up at the Reverend John Waldo, his plump cheeks again spread into a cherubic smile.

Slowly, Harry shook his head. "I'm sorry, reverend. I'd like to help you out here, but I think we've gone a bit too far."

Harry watched the reverend's smile turn into quick, red-faced rage, before he turned to his son. "Bobby Joe, I'm afraid we're gonna have to take a ride down to headquarters."

Harry took out his cell phone and called for transport.

CHAPTER FOURTEEN

Bobby Joe sat in the interrogation room breathing in hot, stagnant air, looking very much like a lost soul. Harry entered the room with Walter Middlebrooks and immediately came up short.

"Damn, the air-conditioning seems to be on the blink again. Let me go see what I can do to get it back on." Harry turned and left the room, the door automatically locking behind him. A uniformed sergeant was waiting for him.

"When do you want me to turn the air back on?" he asked.

"Let them sweat for about twenty minutes; then turn it on. I'll go back in ten minutes after that. It'll be nice and cool by then."

The sergeant laughed and Harry headed for the soft drink machine.

When he returned a half hour later the sergeant was still standing outside the door grinning. "That lawyer started pounding on the door about ten minutes after you left, but nobody could hear him; kept on pounding until the air went back on. It should be cool now, but I don't know how hot he's still gonna be."

"I'm sure the Reverend Bobby Joe explained that we all have crosses to bear," Harry said as he reached for the door handle.

Walter Middlebrooks was glaring when Harry entered the room.

"Sorry it took so long," Harry said. "Our maintenance guy had slipped away on a coffee break." He raised his hands at his sides as if testing the air. "It sure feels good in here now, though."

Middlebrooks looked at him through narrowed eyes.

Don't blame me, Harry thought. You talk to your fat preacher client. He looked down at Bobby Joe. "First thing we want to do, Bobby Joe, is get these two women who placed you with Darlene to get a look at you in the flesh. All they saw was a mug shot and that was a couple of years old."

Bobby Joe twisted in his seat, looked up at Middlebrooks, and asked, "Do I have to do this?"

"No, you don't," Middlebrooks said.

Harry shrugged and gestured to a large mirror on the wall. "You know what's behind the mirror, right?" He waited while Bobby Joe nodded. "These two ladies . . . We could have brought them in there to have a look at you through the one-way mirror. I could also bring them out to the church tomorrow or the next day and wait for you to go to your car. What I'm trying to do here, Bobby Joe, is give you the best shot at being eliminated as a suspect."

Bobby Joe peered up at him, the distrust in his eyes so vibrant it seemed alive. "How do I know you're not settin' me up?"

Harry paused, surprised by the question. He decided to let it go unanswered and move on. "It's like this, Bobby Joe. Doing it this way gives you your best shot at shaking their earlier ID. What I do is I put you in a lineup with five other guys, all your size and age and physical description, and if these ladies can't pick you out as the one and only guy they saw with Darlene . . ." Harry offered up a shrug. "Then their earlier ID isn't worth anything and I'm back to square one."

Bobby Joe looked up at his lawyer.

Middlebrooks nodded. "That's all true, but this lineup isn't something they can make you do unless they charge you. It's also true that they'll find a way to do it anyway, and that way might not be as favorable to you." He turned to Harry. "But if my client agrees to do this I expect to be present and in the same room with these . . . *women* . . . when they try to make a positive identification."

* * *

The lineup room was just off the booking area on the first floor. It was actually two rooms, separated by a large viewing window made up of one-way glass. One room was dimly lit and had a row of chairs where witnesses could sit and look into the second room without being seen by the people they were viewing. The second room was long and narrow with bright lights centered on the wall opposite the viewing window. That wall was lined and marked in feet and inches so the height of those being viewed could be noted.

A uniformed deputy led a line of five men into the room. Bobby Joe was the third man in line. The men were approximately the same age, all were white and between five-ten and six feet in height, and all had longish hair. The two dancers were seated behind the one-way window watching as the men entered. Harry had introduced them to Bobby Joe's lawyer only by their first names. Middlebrooks seemed confused by their appearance. Both young women were dressed modestly in shorts and T-shirts and neither was wearing makeup. They looked more like college coeds than exotic dancers and that fact obviously unsettled Middlebrooks. One of the women was, in fact, a junior at the University of South Florida, which was only a short drive from the Peek-a-Boo Lounge. She lived with her mother and used the money she earned to pay her tuition. She had also made the dean's list the past three semesters. Middlebrooks and Bobby Joe had been told none of that. Harry was saving those bits of information to further unnerve them.

The viewing room filled as five uniformed officers took seats between the two dancers, effectively separating them. Harry didn't want a reaction from one to influence the other. As a deputy directed the men to take numbered spots along the wall, Harry gave paper and pen to each woman and instructed them to write down the number of anyone in the lineup they could identify. As Harry moved to the back of the room, Vicky came up beside him.

"Which one is your guy?" she whispered.

Harry held up three fingers so the young women, whose backs were to him, wouldn't hear his answer.

The deputy in the lineup room went through the routine, asking each man to step forward and then turn to the left and the right. When he had gone through all five men, Harry repeated his instructions to each dancer.

"Each man has a number above his head. If you recognize anyone as the man you saw sitting with Darlene Beckett in the Peek-a-Boo Lounge, just write down the number."

Each woman scratched a number on the sheet of paper and Harry collected them.

"You both identified number three," he said. "Is that correct?"

The two women glanced at each other for the first time. The one on Harry's left shrugged her shoulders. "Yeah, number three," she said.

The other nodded. "Yeah, it was definitely three."

"Are you both certain he's the man?" Harry asked.

"Yeah, no question about it," the first woman said.

"Definitely, he's the guy I saw with Darlene," the second added.

"I'll need the names and addresses of these two witnesses," Middlebrooks chimed in. He kept his voice low and rumbling and filled with as much threat as he could muster.

Both women gave him a dismissive glance, and Harry decided the lawyer needed to do some serious work on his threatening voice.

Harry turned the two witnesses over to John Weathers with instructions that he take signed statements from each; then returned to the interrogation room with Middlebrooks and Bobby Joe. Vicky and Jim Morgan slipped into the small viewing room and took chairs behind the one-way window.

Morgan spoke without ever taking his eyes off Harry. "I hear that Harry's tops when it comes to questioning a witness or a suspect. Weathers told me he's got like a sixth sense for it."

Vicky thought about that, and about Harry's insistence that Benevuto wasn't their killer. Her eyes hardened and there was a tightening at the corners of her mouth. "I've only worked with him a few days, but from what I've seen, he's very good." She turned to Morgan. "But you are too, Jim. And we never would have had the plate numbers that led us to Benevuto if you hadn't gone back and questioned that old man who lived across the street from Darlene. Harry missed that one. I guess his sixth sense wasn't working that night."

Morgan nodded almost as though he hadn't heard the compliment. He continued to watch Harry. When he spoke his voice sounded distant. "I'm not as good as he is, not yet, not by a long shot . . . But someday . . ."

Harry took a seat opposite Bobby Joe and Middlebrooks. "Okay," he began, placing his palms on the table, "I guess we all know where we stand here."

Middlebrooks gave Harry a false smile. "I think we do. Shall I sum it up?" He stared at Harry, who shrugged agreement. "Let's see," the lawyer continued, "we have two exotic dancers who claim they saw my client—a respected minister—sitting next to Darlene Beckett in a darkly lit lounge a few days before she was murdered. My client insists they're mistaken. Now who is a jury of good, God-fearing Florida citizens to believe?" Middlebrooks shook his head. "I don't think the state's attorney will be too impressed with what you have."

Harry leaned back in his chair and nodded. "Those are some very good points, counselor." He glanced at Bobby Joe. There was a self-satisfied smirk on his lips, but he could still see the nervousness in his eyes. Harry leaned forward again, resting his elbows on the table. He turned his gaze back to Middlebrooks. "I think you're missing a few points, counselor. First, you've got Bobby Joe's criminal record."

"A juvenile record," Middlebrooks interjected. "Not admissible, as you are well aware."

"There were several arrests as an adult."

"But only one conviction," the lawyer said, interrupting again. "And one I believe a jury would accept as a regrettable and youthful mistake, one Bobby Joe made *before* he found Jesus."

"Quite possibly, counselor, but the arrests are still a matter of record." Harry flipped several pages in his notebook. "One charge involved possession of a controlled substance, which was dropped when Bobby Joe agreed to turn snitch for the arresting officers and provide information about his supplier. The supplier was eventually arrested and copped a plea, so Bobby Joe never had to testify. Another was a bad check charge, also dropped when restitution was made. And finally there was a charge involving a phony tree-trimming scam. Seems Bobby Joe tried to bilk an elderly couple out of several hundred dollars in that one. The couple got suspicious when Bobby Joe wanted half the money up front, so they called the cops. An investigation found that he had pulled the same scam on another couple a few blocks away. They paid him half the money up front and he never showed up to do the work, so the investigating officers busted him on that one as well as the attempted fraud on the second couple. The attempted fraud charge was eventually dropped two days after the couple met with the senior Reverend Waldo. We can only assume what happened at that meeting. The first couple refused to drop their charge and Bobby Joe did a year in county jail. But you're right, counselor. There is only one conviction. Still, it's not exactly a spotless record."

"He's a man of God now. And these two women you have as witnesses."

"Let's talk about these two women." It was Harry's turn to interrupt. "I'm sure if this matter proceeds you'll be hiring an investigator to check them out pretty thoroughly, just as we'll be checking out Bobby Joe pretty thoroughly." Harry glanced at Bobby Joe. The smirk had disappeared. He turned back to Middlebrooks. "Let me save you a little time." He flipped several pages in his notebook. "The first dancer, Sara Jones, she's pretty similar to Anita Molari, the dancer Bobby Joe paid for the scratch on her car. She's a single mother with a child at home." Harry paused and smiled. "She says she takes her little girl to church every Sunday, by the way. The other young lady . . ." he checked his notebook again, ". . . is Cindy Lewis. She's single. She's a junior at the University of South Florida—hopes to be an anthropologist one day—lives with her mother, and uses the money she makes dancing to pay her tuition." Harry paused and looked down at his notes for effect, although he already knew what was there. He looked up again. "Made the dean's list the last three semesters," he added.

The lawyer's lips tightened. "A very commendable young lady; the pro-verbial whore with a heart of gold. I'm sure the state's attorney will love throwing that old saw at a jury. Who knows? They might be into buying clichés on that particular day."

"Neither of these women is a prostitute," Harry said. "In fact, neither one has any criminal record at all." He shifted his gaze to Bobby Joe as he spoke. "Not juvenile, not even charges that were eventually dropped." He leaned back in his chair and stretched his arms out. "Look, we can go around and around on this without either one of us getting what we want. And in the end Bobby Joe gets himself locked up. But that doesn't have to happen. Let's say I'm willing to buy the argument that Bobby Joe didn't kill Darlene Beckett. Let's say I'm willing to accept the idea that he was at the Peek-a-Boo Lounge for some other reason—maybe I even buy Reverend Waldo's suggestion that some member of the congregation asked for help with a straying husband. So let's say I buy the idea that Bobby Joe goes there to try and help some sinner, and lo and behold, he just happens to sit next to Darlene Beckett. And the dancers see him, and all of a sudden he's in the middle of a murder investigation just because he was trying to do his duty as a minister of the Lord."

"You're forgetting, detective, Bobby Joe insists he wasn't there at all," Middlebrooks said.

"Yeah, well, that one I'm not buying. I've got credible witnesses who say otherwise. And I've got another witness who saw him leaving her apartment. You want the rundown on him? He's a retired security officer—a *bonded* officer who worked at a local bank for thirty years."

Middlebrooks let out a long breath. "So what is it you want?"

"First let me tell you what I *think* happened." Harry tilted back in his chair, playing the role of storyteller to the hilt. "The way I see it—the way the evidence points right now—the Reverend John Waldo was outraged that Darlene Beckett molested a child from his flock. He was further outraged that the boy wouldn't testify against her and that without that testimony Darlene ended up with little more than a slap on the wrist. He even gives a sermon telling the congregation to do everything they can to make sure she ends up in jail. They can do that, he says, by reporting any contact she has with kids, or any other violations of her terms of house arrest. In other words: keep an eye on this woman, and when she crosses the line—which she will, being the sinner she is—report her to the police. He even repeats that in a church bulletin. I know that. I have a copy of the bulletin."

Harry leaned forward again, propped his elbows on the table. "Well, I think Bobby Joe decided he was going to do his daddy's bidding, so he started following Darlene around. What he didn't count on was Darlene taking a shine to him, and before he knew it he's rolling around in her bed. And he gets himself seen not only at the Peek-a-Boo but also by her neighbors when he leaves her apartment."

Harry grasped two fingers with one hand. "But here are two reasons why I think Bobby Joe may *not* be her killer." He released his fingers and raised one. "First, even somebody as self-centered as Bobby Joe had to know that Darlene was nothing more than a fast roll in the hay, and that

she was willing to take that roll with anybody who had the right equip-
ment. So right there we rule out jealousy as a motive." He raised the other
finger. "And second, even Bobby Joe isn't dumb enough to let himself be
seen all over creation with a woman he planned to harm or kill. He's got
enough of a criminal history to know that a mistake like that is certain to
get his ass caught."

Middlebrooks jabbed a finger on the table. "So if you believe these
things, why are you harassing my client?"

Harry smiled across the table. "I didn't say I believed them, counselor.
I said I might be willing to accept them. What I do believe is that Bobby
Joe wasn't the only person from the church who was checking Darlene
out. And I think Bobby Joe knows who those other people are. So if your
client wants me off his ass, he's going to have to give up those names. But
even then, that doesn't mean I'm through with him. Down the road, if I
turn up more evidence that points to him, I'll be right back knocking on
his door."

"So the bottom line is, you want Bobby Joe to help you widen your
net?"

"That's one way to put it, counselor."

"And if he doesn't?"

Harry gave him a small shrug. "Given the evidence I have, that leaves
him as my primary suspect. And right now, I think the state's attorney
might feel it's enough to hold him."

Middlebrooks stared off for a moment. "We'll need to consult with
Reverend Waldo," he said at length. "He was leaving this afternoon on
church business. He'll be back the day after tomorrow."

"I believe they have this invention called the telephone," Harry said.

"I will, of course, talk to him by phone," Middlebrooks said. "But I'll
also want the three of us to sit down; perhaps even bring in someone who
specializes in criminal law. I assume Bobby Joe will be free to go with me."

Harry nodded very slowly. "I'll know where to find him if I need him." He glanced at Bobby Joe. The young minister's eyes were filled with as much fear as Harry had ever seen. His own eyes hardened. "And if you run, I will find you, Bobby Joe. You can make book on that."

Jim Morgan glanced at Vicky and nodded. "Pretty darn slick," he said. "Harry squeezed him like a ripe orange."

"Yeah, he did," Vicky said. "The kid looked like he was ready to wet his pants. I'd bet my next paycheck he'll give Harry all the names he can think of." She let out a small grunt. "Hell, he may even make up a few." She glanced at her watch. "We're supposed to meet Darlene's parents at the morgue. We better get moving."

After identifying the body of their daughter, Darlene Beckett's parents returned to the squad room with Vicky for a more thorough interview. Harry watched them from across the room. They were a couple not unlike many he had seen over the years: the nondescript people who filled Florida's trailer parks and crowded villas, lonely people who seemed to be living out their final days huddled under a dark cloud, each one destined for some tragedy they could not escape.

As they concluded their interview and started to leave Harry watched the mother, whose name was Betsy, precede her husband across the squad room. Withered was the only word he could find to describe her. She seemed drained, washed out, as if all the energy had been sucked from her body. Her hair, once blond, was streaked with gray, a thin, limp shank that fell to her shoulders. Her eyes were equally faded, as if any color that had existed simply dissipated over time, and they were set in a face that was a mass of broken lines and sagging jowls. He knew, from his investigation, that she was only fifty, although she carried herself like a woman ten or fifteen years older. The pale gray, calf-length dress she wore only added to that image.

Her husband Bert was a retired Navy chief who ran a small insurance agency that specialized in auto and boat policies, although he still had the look of a man who had spent his life working with his hands. He was dressed in baggy gabardine trousers and an open-neck white shirt, a short, stocky block of a man with large, rough hands. He had a broad, clean-shaven face with a flattened nose and a hairline that had receded well back on his head. What little hair was left was salt-and-pepper gray and cut short. His eyes, like his wife's, were lifeless and dull, and Harry wondered if it was due to the death of their daughter or the result of a hard, dispiriting life.

Harry had never interviewed Darlene's parents. Initially, that had been left to John Weathers and Nick Benevuto. Weathers had told him that, while hurt by her death, they had seemed almost relieved she was out of their lives. Harry thought that was the saddest commentary of all.

Now, with Nick suspended, the parents had been turned over to Vicky and Jim.

When Vicky had seen the couple out and returned to her desk, Harry approached her.

"Where's Jim?" he asked.

"He stayed behind to make sure all the paperwork on the release of the body was by the book . . . chain of evidence and all that," Vicky said.

"I saw the parents leaving."

"Yeah, it was pretty grim at the morgue. They had a funeral director with them to collect the body. They're planning to have the funeral tomorrow; short and sweet and quick. They want to avoid extensive press coverage, which of course they won't."

"I'm surprised they agreed to come back here with you," Harry said.

Vicky nodded. "I was too. I told them there were some things I had to go over with them; stressed it might help us find Darlene's killer. They're still in a state of shock and they came along like a pair of sheep."

"Did you learn anything?"

"Quite a bit, actually . . . even more if my *intuitions* are correct." She gave him a hard stare. "You're not the only one who has them, Harry."

Harry ignored the sarcasm. "Wanna share?"

"You're such a pushy detective." She paused a moment. "I'll make a deal. You tell me what's going on with your mother, and how it's affecting you on this case, and I'll tell you everything I learned, factual *and* intuitive."

"How do you know anything's going on with my mother?"

"Word gets around the squad room, you know how it is. Cops in Hillsborough hear something; they talk to their cop buddies in Pinellas. Suddenly everybody knows, even me. Do we have a deal?"

"You're asking for a quid pro quo. That could be construed as threatening to withhold evidence from a superior officer."

"And at my departmental trial I'll testify that your mental condition is precarious, at best. I could probably make a good case for that."

Harry looked off to the side and fought off a smile. "I bet you could," he said when he finally turned back. "She has a parole hearing coming up. My adoptive father—he's a retired Clearwater cop—has been in touch with a friend in the state's attorney's office in Tampa to see if they're planning to oppose it. So far he hasn't been able to get a straight answer."

"And you? Are you going to oppose it?"

"She killed my kid brother and she tried to kill me. I want her locked up."

"Have you heard from her?"

"The same letter I get every year, on the anniversary of my brother's death. She tells me how much she wants me in heaven with Jesus and Jimmy."

Vicky looked down at the floor. "That must hurt a lot."

Harry's jaw tightened. "It'll hurt a helluva lot more if she tries to send me there."

Vicky raised her eyes and kept her voice soft. "What will you do if she does?"

Harry stared at her for what seemed a long time. She wondered if he was trying to work the answer out himself. His eyes blinked, then he drew another long breath. His voice was cold and flat when he finally spoke.

"I'll stop her," he said.

Vicky studied his eyes but could find nothing revealing. There had been a note of finality in his voice, a hint of impending matricide, and she wondered if it was something he could really do. It certainly didn't fit the man she had come to know. But her years as a cop had taught her that people were sometimes forced to do things beyond the pale of what they would normally consider. It might be that way for Harry, and she wondered if he could emotionally survive if forced to commit an act so terrible. She knew she could not.

"Okay, you got your pound of flesh, now tell me about Darlene's parents; what they told you about her."

His question brought her back and she put her other thoughts aside. "Most of what I learned came from the mother. It was very interesting. You remember Darlene's claim that she was sexually abused as a child?"

"It was a big part of her defense, one of the excuses she gave for what she did to that boy."

"Yeah, it was. Well, the mother confirmed that abuse, but in an odd way. When she talked about Darlene's childhood, she claimed that even as a little kid she liked to sexually tease men. The mother said it started when she was only eight or nine years old; that even then she liked to sit on men's laps and when she did she would 'wiggle' around in a provocative way." Vicky used her fingers to place imaginary quotes around the word, indicating she thought little of the accusation. "She claimed Darlene would also put her head on their chests and give them long, lingering hugs."

"So she claimed that Darlene brought the abuse on herself."

"That's exactly what she wanted me to believe, although she never came out and said it directly. It was so damn obvious what she was doing. She was deflecting blame away from herself as a parent."

"Did she say who Darlene supposedly teased?"

"No, she didn't, it was all very general. She claimed it was just about every adult man she met."

Harry paused. "Why do you think she wouldn't be specific? Was it because the father was there?"

"Yeah, I think it was. Are you thinking that maybe the father might have been the abuser?"

Harry nodded. "It's always a possibility."

"Yeah, and that's exactly the vibe I got off the whole conversation." Vicky tapped the side of her nose. "The father was *very* quiet throughout the conversation. Mostly he nodded agreement to whatever his wife said. Whenever I asked for his opinion he deferred to her, claiming she was in a better position to know; that he was away a great deal of the time when Darlene was growing up. I gathered that his job in the navy took him out to sea for long tours of duty." Vicky bent forward as if preparing to impart some secret. "The mother said she tried to get Darlene to stop what she called 'this obvious sexual flirting,' which of course was nothing more than a kid imitating what she'd seen adult women do, either in person or on film or television. When I asked her if she'd had any success modifying that behavior, she said everything she tried failed, even though Darlene had been severely punished—those were her words." Vicky shook her head. "So what we had was a young girl who was getting a positive response from men when acting flirtatious and anger from the primary female in her life, her mother."

"But that experience alone couldn't have been enough to turn her into a child molester." Harry's voice had become incredulous.

Vicky vigorously shook her head. "No, of course not. I think it was a contributing factor, but no more than that. Look, I consider myself an expert on sex crimes, but I'm certainly no shrink. Based on what I've read of her history, it's no secret she was a very disturbed woman and I'd bet anything that her claim in court that she suffered from some bipolar disorder wasn't very far off the mark. And maybe we add some heavy abuse as a kid."

Harry was quiet for several moments, digesting what Vicky had said. When he spoke again his voice was soft and low and slightly raspy. "It still doesn't excuse what she did to that little boy."

Vicky studied Harry's eyes, wondering if they were still talking about Darlene Beckett. "No, it doesn't," she finally said. "Illness may explain why something happens, Harry, but it never excuses the act."

CHAPTER FIFTEEN

Bobby Joe listened to his daddy's voice rumble through the speaker. He was seated in Walter Middlebrooks's well-appointed office, his father hundreds of miles away in Atlanta, but even so he could still see the look on his father's face; feel the anger emanating from his eyes, just as if he were seated across the room listening to his son's stream of excuses.

"Who can you give this cop that'll get him off your back?" his father demanded, cutting him off. "And understand me, boy, I mean somebody who is *not* gonna lead him right back to my church."

Bobby Joe could not think of anyone who would not hurt the church. There was one whose involvement with the church might be overshadowed by other facets of his life. But he also knew what would happen if he ever offered him up, and he had no intention of paying that high a price for his daddy's fucking church.

"I'm not hearin' any answers, boy."

"I'm tryin' to think, Daddy. Almost all the people who were keeping an eye on Darlene were church people, at least in the beginning right after you sent out the call."

"There was no call, damnit. And don't you ever tell anybody there was. And stop callin' that harlot by her first name. I know you were sleepin' with her, but I don't have to hear her talked about like she was a good, God-fearin' woman. And certainly not one who was bein' persecuted by *me.*"

"Yes, Daddy." He musta forgot, Bobby Joe thought. He musta forgot how he preached it from his goddamn pulpit and had it written down in his goddamn church bulletin.

"So, who?" his father's voice shouted across the line. "Who are you gonna give up to this cop?"

"I'm thinkin', Daddy."

"Well, think faster."

Bobby Joe looked at Middlebrooks, his eyes begging for support. Middlebrooks turned away, just as older adults had turned away from him his whole life. Then an idea came to him. It was an audacious idea and a dangerous one, but there might be a way to pull it off if he got his daddy and Middlebrooks to do it for him.

"There was one person that Dar . . . that Mizz Beckett talked about. He really seemed to make her nervous."

"Who was it?"

"It was this cop who she said was pressing her to . . . to . . . well, you know."

"Yes, I know." His father's voice was riddled with sarcasm. "To do what my own son was already doin' with that strumpet."

The hope Bobby Joe had felt plunged to the pit of his stomach. "I guess it's a bad idea," he said.

There was quiet on the other end of the line.

"I just remembered it, and how she acted about it when she told me." Back then there had been no question in Bobby's Joe's mind that Darlene was already sleeping with that cop. He had known it as soon as she mentioned him. It was just her way of bragging about how much other men wanted her. She couldn't seem to help herself when it came to that.

"No, it's not a bad idea."

His father's voice jolted him, brought him back to reality. "It's not?"

"No, in fact it's a fine idea. We do it and we can take the accusations this detective is makin' about our church, and we can turn it right back on him. Put this Harry Doyle on the defensive for a change. What do you think, Walter?"

"I think it's an excellent idea, John. We can pressure the sheriff, demand to know why his detectives aren't investigating one of their own with the same vigor they're expending on a minister of the church."

"Exactly," Reverend Waldo said. His voice had a hiss to it that was almost serpent-like, and Bobby Joe could practically feel the look of satisfaction spreading across his daddy's face.

"I'll do it today," Bobby Joe said. "I'll call this Harry Doyle and I'll tell him straight away." He waited for his father or Middlebrooks to respond, knowing neither of them would trust him to do it right.

"No, you let me call him," Middlebrooks said. "He's going to have to earn the right to talk to you now."

"You listen to Walter, boy," his father said. "Always let a lawyer front for you when there's trouble. It's always the smart play."

The call came in from Jocko Doyle at four p.m.

"How long will it take you to get to St. Pete Beach?" he asked without preamble.

"Twenty, thirty minutes," Harry said. "Why, what's up?"

"An assistant state's attorney named Calvin Morris is going to meet us to talk about your mother's parole hearing. He wants to hook up at a joint called the Sea Hag. It's on Blind Pass Road at the marina where he keeps his boat."

"I know the place," Harry said. "What time?"

"Five. I suggest you get there about fifteen minutes early so we can talk."

"You got it. I'll leave in about ten minutes."

Except for the occasional high-rise condo, and the increased winter migration of elderly snowbirds from the north, St. Pete Beach was still the "traditional Florida" Harry had known as a child—wide, sandy beaches dotted with bars and restaurants, and a strictly laid-back lifestyle. It was a place where shoes gave way to sandals, shopping in bathing suits became commonplace, and the only mandatory activities involved sunsets or gathering for the weekly drum circle on Treasure Island, where hundreds of people celebrated the end of the day by dancing at the water's edge to the incessant beating of every imaginable manner of drum.

The Sea Hag fit its surroundings perfectly, a waterfront joint with a wide deck overlooking the Blind Pass Marina, with its complement of nearly 200 boats lining its docks, and attractive young waitresses dressed in short shorts and tight T-shirts, each one looking as though she had just wandered in from the beach, which several undoubtedly had, and a clientele that gave off a studied beach bum air.

Given that, Calvin Morris looked like a man from another time when he walked up to their table still dressed in a tan suit, white shirt, and a powder-blue power necktie. Jocko and Harry were wearing shorts and jeans, respectively, flowered shirts worn out to conceal their weapons, and boat shoes without socks.

Jocko gave the assistant state's attorney a long once-over. "You got a church meeting tonight, Cal?"

"No time to change," Morris said, ignoring the jab. He was a tall, slender black man with a neatly trimmed mustache and hard brown eyes, a seasoned prosecutor with ten years experience in the criminal courts, who knew how to use his wardrobe to intimidate adversaries.

As soon as he walked in Jocko and Harry knew they were just that—adversaries. Had Morris taken the time to go to his boat and change, or had he invited them out for a drink near his office in a roomful of suits, it would have been different. Here, in the laid-back atmosphere of a beach bar, his wardrobe let everyone know that he was the man in charge and there would be no arguments, thank you very much.

"So tell us about the parole hearing for Lucy Santos, Cal," Jocko be-gan. "Is your office going to oppose the parole, or just let it slide on by?"

Morris's eyes narrowed, a display of annoyance he tried to mask with a tight smile. He was a handsome man with a caramel complexion, strong jaw, and the firm, slender body of a former athlete who still kept himself fit. "We don't let any parole slide on by," he said in a mildly pompous voice. "We don't oppose them all, either. We review each one and decide which ones should be challenged."

"And my mother's parole?" Harry asked. "What decision has been made about that?"

Morris sighed heavily. He obviously knew the history of the case even though it was well before his tenure with the state's attorney began. "Look, what your mother did to your brother, and to you, is nothing less than a heinous act. But she's done twenty years of hard time and she's eligible for parole. Life without parole was never part of the sentencing deal. It should have been, but it wasn't. According to her case file, her attorney back then threatened to go to the mat if we pushed for it. And, frankly, if the case had gone to trial she probably would have been found innocent by reason of insanity, committed to the loony bin, and been back on the streets ten years ago. The state psychiatrists who have reviewed her case say she's sane and not a danger to anyone, so our office opposing her pa-role wouldn't do a damn bit of good." He began ticking off other reasons on his fingers. "She's also been a model prisoner, according to corrections officials. *And* she's become a spiritual leader for other women in the prison. *And* her former church has agreed to help her get ordained and then hire her as a lay minister." He stared into Harry's eyes, his own softening for the first time. "What have you got that will beat back the testimony of two state-appointed shrinks, the corrections department, and her minister?"

"He's got letters that show she's still a fucking fruitcake," Jocko said before Harry could answer.

Morris lowered his eyes and nodded slowly. "Then go to the hearing and present them to the board."

"You don't want to see them," Harry said.

Morris studied his hands, clearly embarrassed. "It wouldn't do any good. The decision has been made that we are not going expend the time and staff and expense to fight this one. I'm sorry. If she's granted parole you can ask that it be on condition that she has no contact with you, if that's what you want. If she does, they'll violate her and put her back inside. But I think that's the best you can hope for."

"That really sucks," Jocko said.

"Yes, it does." He turned his attention back to Harry. "I'm sorry. If I were in your shoes I'd feel exactly the same way."

Harry stared at him for several moments. "You have no idea how it feels to be in my shoes."

Out in the parking lot Jocko slipped his arm around Harry's shoulders. "I'm sorry, kid. But I gotta admit I'm not surprised." He tightened his grip momentarily then let his arm fall to his side. "There's just not enough good ink in it. You know how much those assholes like to see their names in the newspapers; the bigger the headline the better. This case, it's just too old to get more than a couple of inches on an inside page. To spend the kind of time and money and effort it would take, they want a bigger payback than that."

"Yeah, I know," Harry said. "I was just hoping they'd get on it so I wouldn't have to do that much myself, other than show up."

"Yeah, well, now you gotta do a little bit more. You gotta show the board those wacky letters and tell them they'll be putting you in danger if they let her out. And we can try to get some of our newspaper friends to call the board members and ask some pointed questions about turning loose a child killer. One thing about the parole board: they don't like *any* ink about anything they do. They like to operate strictly under the radar."

Harry gave his adopted father as strong a smile as he could muster, but it faded quickly. "I appreciate all you've done, Jocko. Now it's just between her and me. She may have done enough time for what she did to me, but it sure isn't enough for what she did to Jimmy."

Harry sat on the lanai listening to the surf move against the shore, the gentle, soothing lap of water against sand that masked all the carnivorous acts of violence only a few feet farther out. He had grown up on the water, Jocko being an avid fisherman, and the murderous nature of the sea had quickly fascinated him. As a young boy he had watched schools of bait fish being chopped apart by marauding game fish and dolphins, the sea birds swooping in to pick up the bits and pieces left behind. Later, he had learned to dive and had gone deep below to witness the even greater carnage that took place beneath the placid blue water of the gulf. It had been an inspiring and sometimes frightening sight. As his mind began to race he imagined his mother swimming out there with the other predators, his mother and Darlene's killer swimming side-by-side, each looking for prey—one trying to satisfy her perverse view of Jesus, the other pursuing some perverse form of revenge.

"Hi, Harry. Are you busy?"

Jeanie's voice brought him back. "No, I'm not busy at all." He rose from his chair and unlatched the screen door.

"You sure I'm not interrupting anything?"

"Not a thing. I've just been sitting here thinking about the gulf and all the killer fish cruising along beneath the surface."

"You think too much about killing, Harry. Think about the beautiful things out there, like dolphin."

"They're one of the biggest killers . . . very organized, very methodical." He watched her shake her head and smiled at her.

"You're impossible," she said.

"Yes, I am."

He returned to his chair and she surprised him by slipping onto his lap. "Feeling a bit forward tonight, are we?"

"Yes. Does it make you feel threatened?"

"Not a bit. There's nothing like a good, forward woman after a hard day at the office."

"And any forward woman will do?"

"I didn't say that. I might have thought it, but I did *not* say it."

Jeanie jabbed a finger into his ribs making him jump. "You keep that up and I won't sleep in your bed tonight."

"Then I'll stop immediately."

She placed her head against his shoulder. "Are you sure everything's okay?" she asked at length.

"Everything's fine. Better now that you're here."

"Good."

Bobby Joe visibly shuddered when he looked through the spy hole in his front door and saw the man standing outside. He lived in a small apartment above the garage at his father's home. It had been one of the conditions of joining his daddy's ministry, being close by so he could be watched. It was something about which the old man had been very forthcoming. And on top of it, he paid his father rent for the privilege.

Bobby Joe looked through the spy hole again and thought about not opening the door, but his car was outside, the lights in the apartment were on, and he wouldn't put it past the man to just kick the door open if he tried to ignore him. He put a smile on his face and swung the door back.

"Hey there, I was just about ready to climb into bed."

The man brushed past him, ignoring what he had said, then turned and hit him with an icy stare. "Tell me what you told the cops today."

"I didn't tell them much of anything. They told me stuff, like how two of the bimbos at the Peek-a-Boo were able to eyeball me as somebody they saw sittin' at the bar with Darlene."

"Nobody asked you to give up any names?"

"Well, yeah, that detective, Harry Doyle, did. Somebody gave him a copy of the church bulletin where my daddy was callin' on everybody to keep an eye on Darlene, so he figures it was somebody from the church who killed her." Bobby Joe was talking fast, his nerves kicking in. He wanted to say less, say as little as possible, but this man just made him too nervous. "My daddy came up with an idea. You see, Darlene once told me about this cop who was pressing her to put out, and how much he scared her, so Daddy thinks it would be good to lay that name on Doyle, even maybe on the sheriff himself, and ask why Doyle is investigating me and other good, God-fearing church people and nobody's investigating this cop. He's gonna have the church's lawyer call him on it."

"Who's the cop?" the man asked.

"All I remember is that his name's Nick, and that he's a homicide detective."

The man nodded slowly. "That's very clever. Your daddy is a very smart man." And he just bought you another day on this earth, he thought.

CHAPTER SIXTEEN

Harry arrived at the office at seven a.m., hoping to get a jump start on the day. As soon as he slipped behind his desk a message stared back at him, bringing a smile to his lips. It was from Jim Morgan asking for a meeting in the late afternoon and saying that he was headed out to check some leads and would meet up with Vicky in an hour. The time on the message was six-thirty a.m. He glanced across the room at Nick Benevuto's empty desk. Benevuto would be in sometime later to slog through the paper shuffling he'd been assigned while on desk duty. He'd essentially become Diva Walsh's assistant, although without a voice in who was assigned what cases. It was a humiliating assignment, performed each day under the eyes of his peers, a punishment police departments freely handed out to anyone who fell into disfavor.

He took some time to reconsider Benevuto as a suspect. Vicky and Jim were so certain he was good for the murder, and he certainly had motive and opportunity and had even tried to conceal his connection to the victim. But something about it didn't speak to Harry. It was all too easy. If a homicide cop killed someone it shouldn't be that easy to spot him. He knew exactly how the investigation would proceed; where the investigating detectives would look. And Nick was one of those investigating detectives, so hiding his involvement should have been a piece of cake.

The phone rang, breaking his train of thought.

"Harry, is that you?"

It was Jeanie, her voice filled with panic. Thoughts of her husband jumped into Harry's mind. "Yeah, babe, what is it?"

"Somebody broke into the house, Harry. I woke up and found him going through your stuff, your police stuff, files and things."

"Are you okay?"

"Yes. But he had a gun, Harry. He told me to get back in the bedroom or he'd kill me. When I turned to go, he hit me with it, knocked me kind of loopy." She sobbed into the receiver.

"Is he gone?"

"Yes."

"Are you sure?"

"Yes."

"Call 911. Tell them whose house it is. The Clearwater cops will get there fast."

"I already did."

"Okay, I'm on my way. I'm also calling my dad. His name's Jocko. He only lives ten minutes away."

"Please hurry, Harry. I'm scared."

"I'll be there in twenty minutes, maybe less."

He ran into Pete Rourke on his way out and explained where he was going. Before he reached the parking lot he had already connected with his adoptive father. He hit the back door and sprinted through the parked cars. When he reached his own car he saw his twelve-year-old gangsta protégé coming toward him.

"Wassup, Doyle? Where you runnin', or is somebody chasin' your ass?"

"Get in the car," Harry snapped. "I got a job for you."

Rubio Martí jumped into the passenger seat as Harry slid behind the wheel. "This a payin' job?" he asked.

"Is there any other kind?"

Rubio scratched his chin and grinned. "Well, for you, I might work for free. I'd prefer not to, but I might."

"I'll take care of you."

"What I gotta do?"

"I want you to stay with this lady friend of mine." He quickly explained what had happened. "She's a little shook up. I just want her to know there's somebody watching her back."

"She good lookin'?"

Harry shot him a look. Rubio grinned back at him.

"Hey, I was only wonderin'."

When Harry arrived two Clearwater patrol units were parked in front of his house, along with Jocko's ancient MGB, a car he loved almost as much as he loved Harry's adoptive mother, Maria.

When he entered the house he found Maria seated on the sofa, holding Jeanie's hand as the police questioned her. She had just met Jeanie and she was already mothering her.

"What took you so long," Maria demanded as he approached them. It was typical of her. He had been ten miles farther away than she had, but she had expected him to get there ahead of her.

"Traffic," he said.

Maria was a heavyset woman with warm, brown eyes that now offered up a disbelieving stare. "I came with your father; we had traffic too. You have a siren," she added, "and flashing lights. Maybe you could use them."

He nodded agreement, it was the only way around the verbal onslaught. He squatted down in front of Jeanie, taking her other hand. "How are you?" he asked.

"I've just got a lump on my head."

"It's a bad lump," Maria interjected. "I don't know why you live in this crazy beach house. It's not safe."

Jocko sat next to his wife. "Maria, hush," he said.

"Don't hush me," she snapped. "What I say is true."

Harry smiled at Jeanie. "She thinks the only place that's safe for me is in *her* house on the other side of the intracoastal."

Jeanie held back her own smile. "You should listen to your mother."

"See?" Maria agreed.

"Tell me what happened," Harry said, ignoring her.

"I woke . . ." She glanced at Maria. "I was in the other room and I heard noise out here, and when I came out this man was going through your things . . . your police things . . . from the folder you keep here."

Jocko caught Harry's eye. Taking evidence home was against police procedure.

"It was mostly duplicates so I could work at home in the evenings," he explained.

"Mostly?" Jocko asked.

"And some stuff I was still checking out; stuff that hadn't become evidence yet." Harry knew he was talking about a fine line, but bending procedure was something that had never been a problem for him. He stood and turned to the two Clearwater cops. "Let me look through what's here and figure out what, if anything, this clown took. If you leave me a number I can call it in later for your report." Harry glanced around the room, and then stepped into his small kitchen. "All the appliances seem to be here, so it doesn't look like he got anything. Jeanie must have scared him off."

"Yeah, well, the lady said he was wearing latex gloves, so I doubt we're gonna find any prints," the taller of the two cops said.

"It looks like it might be related to a case I'm working on, so if I want prints taken I'll have my people do it," Harry said.

"Good enough for us," the Clearwater cop said. He handed Harry a card. "Just call in and let us know what's missing . . . for our report. And when the lady feels up to it, you can arrange a time for her to look at our perp book, see if she can ID this guy."

"You got it," Harry said.

"Oh, by the way, the guy got in through your lanai. Cut the screen and came in through the sliding glass doors to the house. It doesn't look like he had to force them."

"Sometimes I forget to lock them," Harry said.

"Bad idea," the cop said. "Your mother's right about this neighborhood. There's a lot of creeps on the beach early in the morning. Some of them sleep out there at night."

When the two officers left, Harry knelt back down in front of Jeanie. "You sure you feel okay?"

"Yes, I'm fine."

"Okay, tell me what this guy looked like."

Jeanie thought about the question, something Harry always liked to see a witness do. "Well, he was tall, maybe an inch shorter than you, or maybe an inch taller. It was hard to tell."

"But approximately my height.

"Yes."

"What about weight?"

"He was slim, but strong looking; muscular, rather than flabby, you know what I mean?"

"Maybe a hundred and seventy-five, a hundred and eighty pounds?"

"I'm not good about weight with men, but that sounds about right."

"Hair?"

"That was hard to tell. He had a bandana over his nose and mouth and a baseball hat pulled low over his eyes, but I feel like his hair was a light color, blond or sandy brown, something like that. But I couldn't swear to it. I spent most of my time staring at his gun. It was a big, square one, just like the one you have."

Harry nodded. "No facial features at all?"

Jeanie shook her head. "Just his eyes. They were blue, and I only re-member that because they were very hard, very scary eyes, like he was maybe a little crazy or something. It seemed like he was outraged that I was here, that I was interrupting him. I know it sounds crazy, but it made me feel that he knew I didn't belong here." She glanced at Maria with a look of nervous regret.

Maria just patted her hand.

"The Clearwater cops said he was wearing latex gloves."

"Yes. Just like the ones you have around here. Maybe he just took some of yours when he saw them."

Harry nodded, his thoughts drifting to Bobby Joe Waldo, and then to Nick Benevuto. "Are you sure the guy was thin?" he asked.

"Yes."

The door opened behind him and Rubio strutted in. He was dressed in an oversized Magic basketball shirt, baggy jeans falling off his butt that he held up with one hand, and a cockeyed Tampa Bay Rays baseball cap. Harry had told him to wait in his car until the Clearwater cops cleared the scene and left.

"Who the hell are you?" Jocko said.

Harry smiled at the boy. "This is Rubio. I hired him to be Jeanie's bodyguard."

"What?" Jeanie said.

"He's good," Harry said. "And I trust him. I want him to hang with you for a couple of days, or until I catch this clown."

"You think this guy might come back looking for me?" Jeanie asked.

"No, I don't," Harry said honestly. "But I don't want to take the chance." He looked back over his shoulder. "Rubio, come here."

Rubio swaggered toward them. "Wassup?"

* * *

Harry spent the next half hour going through the duplicate files he had at home. Nothing he could think of seemed to be missing, although he had a nagging feeling that something was. If so, he knew it would come to him later.

He left Jeanie and Rubio in the care of his mother, who had decided to take both of them home with her, "where it's safe," and "where I can make them a nice lunch." She promptly ordered Jocko to take his MGB home and get their "real car," so they all could fit inside.

Before leaving Jocko threw a glance a Rubio and offered to stay at the house with Harry.

"No, I'll be fine," Harry assured him. "This clown won't risk coming back."

"You got any idea who it was?" Jocko asked.

"Yeah, I do," Harry said.

It was well past noon when Harry got back to the squad room, half the day wasted. Rourke called him into his office as soon as he noticed he was back.

"We got a problem," he said, even before Harry had taken a seat. "But first, tell me how everything turned out at your house."

Harry told him, assuring him there was no evidence at the house that shouldn't have been there.

"You have any idea who did it?"

"Nothing solid right now," Harry said, "just a hunch. What's the problem?"

"The sheriff had a call from a lawyer named Walter Middlebrooks. I guess you know him. He represents that church you're looking into."

"And the head minister's son, who's my prime suspect right now. What did that weasel lawyer want from our great and glorious leader?"

Rourke gave him a warning look. "Seems like your boy, the minister's kid, remembers Darlene talking about a cop who was pressuring her to put out. He also remembers that he was a homicide dick and that his first name was Nick. The lawyer says the kid withheld the information because he was afraid we'd set him up if he pointed a finger at one of our guys. So he wants to know why we're pushing so hard on a kid minister, just because he may have strayed a bit, but we're ignoring one of our own who was doing the same thing."

"What did you tell the boss?" Harry asked.

"I told him the minister's kid *and* our guy are both under investigation, and that I'd send him copies of the daily reports to back that up. I also told him Nick's assigned to limited duty until the case is resolved, or at least his part in it is resolved."

"What did he say?"

"He said to suspend him forthwith. He said it could be a suspension with pay, but he wanted him out of here before the shift ended."

Harry looked over his shoulder and noticed that Nick's desk was empty.

"I told him a half hour ago," Rourke said. "He came in late this morning." Rourke hesitated and gave Harry a look that said, late enough to have been at your house.

Harry nodded, but didn't take the bait. "How'd he handle the suspension?"

"He was upset, but he knows my hands are tied." Rourke drew a long breath and shook his head. "Harry, I don't make him for this. And it's not just because he's a brother cop."

"Neither do I. But there's enough evidence pointing at him that we can't ignore him, either."

Rourke thought it over for several moments. "Who do you think broke into your house?"

"Bobby Joe Waldo," Harry said. "The same minister's kid that lawyer was yapping about. It was either him or somebody very close to him. But I can't prove it. Not yet, anyway."

"Why would he take a chance like that?"

"The same reason they're trying to deflect attention toward Nick. He probably heard Nick's name from Darlene. That part of it's probably true. But he's just using it; grasping at anything he can to take the pressure off. He knows I'm closing in on him. That's why he broke in. He wants to see what I've got on him and he knows he can't get in here. I think he was hoping to find exactly what he found, copies of reports that I was working on at home. Somebody was watching my house the other day and he took off when Jocko spotted him."

"Are you talking about your father, the retired Clearwater sergeant? He saw this guy too?"

Harry nodded. "Neither one of us made the connection then. Jocko couldn't make the guy out, but it was obvious he was watching the house. Hell, maybe he followed me home one day. Or maybe he followed me two or three days. I wasn't exactly looking over my shoulder. But if he did, and he saw me bringing home some folders, it wouldn't take a genius to figure out what they were."

"So what are you going to do now?"

"I'm going go have a talk with the young Reverend Waldo."

"Be careful," Rourke warned. "The sheriff doesn't want to piss off the faith community. This is still the Bible belt, and he's still running for reelection."

When Harry got back to his desk there was a note to call Walter Middlebrooks. That would be a demand to stay away from his client. He decided he would see Bobby Joe first and save the pleasure of Middlebrooks for later.

Bobby Joe wasn't at his church office, his secretary explaining that "the minister called in sick." To Harry's surprise the short, plump, and extremely prim woman was more than happy to hand over Bobby Joe's home address. "He lives above the garage at his daddy's house," she said, as if that solitary bit of information told Harry everything he needed to know about Bobby Joe.

Harry kept his back to the spy hole in Bobby Joe's front door. He wanted the benefit of surprise when the young minister opened it and realized who was standing there; wanted to see what tells Bobby Joe would give up. No matter how proficient the lair, there was always something that would show if a cop remained patient and watchful. The problem wasn't that some suspects were so clever. It was that there weren't enough patient cops.

Harry turned as the door opened and was met by a look of abject fear in Bobby Joe's eyes, a look that turned to sudden relief when he saw who it was.

Somebody is scaring the hell out of him, Harry thought. And it isn't me.

"Expecting the bogeyman?"

Bobby Joe stiffened. Harry took advantage of the momentary confusion and walked past him into a disheveled living room.

"Hey, didn't Middlebrooks talk to you?" Bobby Joe said, following him inside.

"Talk to me about what? Are you referring to Nick Benevuto?"

"Is that the detective? Darlene just called him Nick, a real scary homicide detective."

Harry turned to face him. "Scarier than me, Bobby Joe?"

Bobby Joe swallowed hard. "Look, Middlebrooks already talked to the sheriff and he was supposed to talk to you. My daddy wants to know why you're all over me about this, all over our church, and nobody's lookin' at this cop who was threatening Darlene?"

Harry made his mouth form a slow smile. "We're looking at him, Bobby Joe. In fact, we've been looking at him almost as long as we've been looking at you. But you know what, Bobby Joe? I don't make him for that murder. I make you for it."

"That's crazy. I didn't kill anybody." Perspiration had begun to form on his upper lip despite the cold blast of air-conditioning that filled the apartment. "Alright, I admit I slept with her. I was seduced. That woman could seduce anyone. But I didn't kill her."

"Somebody in your church killed her, Bobby Joe, and if it wasn't you I think you know who it was."

"I don't. All I know is this Nick guy."

"Bullshit!" Harry shouted. "You either did it, or you can point a finger at the person who did." Harry jabbed his own finger into Bobby Joe's chest. "And you better tell me, you little shit, or you're going down for it."

"All I know is Nick—"

"We've checked Nick. We've checked him inside out. And you know what? You're not gonna be able to hang this on him. But I'm gonna be able to hang it on you. And your lawyer and all his bullshit stories about Nick Benevuto aren't gonna let you weasel out of it. So you better tell me what you know."

Bobby Joe tried to light a cigarette, but his hand was trembling and it took several attempts before he succeeded. "If I could help you, I would," he managed.

"Who else was watching her? Who else was trying to do what your daddy asked everybody to do . . . to get something on her?" As he asked the question, Harry realized what had been taken from his house. It had been the copy of the church bulletin, the one in which Reverend Waldo repeated the call he had made from his pulpit, the call to his flock to go out and get something on Darlene, to make her pay for her sins. He was now 90 percent certain that it hadn't been in the file when he checked it this morning. It was the only thing that had been missing. He glared at Bobby Joe, thinking about the pistol whipping Jeanie had sustained. "Did you break into my house this morning?" He waited while Bobby Joe just stared at him. "Answer me!" he shouted when the minister failed to speak.

"No. No. I don't know what you're talking about."

"Somebody broke in and went through my files. If it wasn't you, then you know who it was."

Bobby Joe's face was dead pale. "You're tryin' to get me killed," he croaked.

Harry grabbed him by the arm. "Who would kill you, Bobby Joe?"

Bobby Joe pulled away. "I'm not sayin' anything more. I want you out of my house. I want you out of here right now."

Harry returned to his car and sat, staring up at the apartment. His instinct told him to sit on Bobby Joe, to see who he went to see, or who came to see him. But first he had to find out if his memory was correct, that the church bulletin was really missing. He tried to call Jeanie on her cell phone, but there was no answer. He called Jocko's house and Maria told him that Jeanie had left with Rubio, saying they were going to a movie to try and get her mind off what had happened. She said Jocko had gone with them, but that she decided to stay home and cook everyone dinner. She asked if he was coming to eat. Harry said he would try; then ended the call before Maria could begin an extended guilt trip. He had no choice. He had to head to his house and check the file. He'd also have to check the office to make sure it wasn't there. In the meantime he'd have to try and get a patrol unit to drive by Bobby Joe's apartment and keep track of anyone who showed up.

CHAPTER SEVENTEEN

Bobby Joe paced the floor trying to figure a way out. He called Walter Middlebrooks and got a token pat on the hand, complete with lawyerly assurances that things were being taken care of, the underlying message being: sit tight and let the adults handle things. He lit a cigarette and did another circuit of the room. Fuck you, Middlebrooks, he thought. You don't have to face the consequences if the adults screw everything up. And right now that smartass Harry Doyle is the least of those consequences.

Bobby Joe slumped into an overstuffed leather chair, stared at the cell phone on the adjacent end table, then stood and began to pace again. He had to call him, had to call and tell him what was happening. If he didn't and that mean son of a bitch found out later, he'd do just what he'd promised. The other alternative was to get his sorry ass out of town. Go to the bank and withdraw every cent, even the money stashed in the safety deposit box from his days of dealing blow. Get it and head north.

Yeah, sure, he told himself. Do it and that asshole Doyle will put your name out on the wire to every dickhead cop in the country; say you're wanted in a murder investigation. Then what do you do? Spend every dime you've got getting good, usable ID and some plastic surgeon to change your face? He stopped at a mirror by the front door. No way, he thought.

He walked back across the room and stopped, hands on hips, listening to his ragged breath. So tell the man what he wants to know; get him off your ass once and for all. Help Doyle arrest that crazy son of a bitch, lock him up for good, or maybe even kill him. Oh, yes, that would be even sweeter. He raised his eyes to the ceiling and let out a nervous rush of breath. Yeah, and then what do you do about Daddy when Doyle lays the murder at the doorstep of his goddamn church. Well, shit, that's where it belongs. If Daddy hadn't sent out the call to punish that bitch, nothin' ever would've happened. Truth be told, he did it to himself with his holier-than-thou, big fucking mouth.

A wrap of knuckles on the front door brought him back. That had to be Doyle, back to bust your chops again, maybe even take you back down to his office. Go ahead and give him what he wants; get him off your ass for good.

Bobby Joe strode across the room and swung the door back without even checking the spy hole. His face collapsed, all the resolve he had conjured up melting away when he stared into the man's face.

A slow smile formed on the man's lips but never carried to his ice-blue eyes. "You don't look happy to see me, Bobby Joe."

The man walked past him, and with the flat of his hand pushed the door closed even though Bobby Joe was still holding the door knob.

"I'm just surprised. I thought it was that detective. He was here a little while ago and I thought he'd forgot somethin' and come back."

"I know he was here."

"You do?"

"I was watching. Once I found out you weren't going to work I thought I better come on by and check on who you might be meeting. I parked on the other block and came in through the trees behind your daddy's house, and lo and behold, there was Detective Doyle coming out your front door." The man's blue eyes seemed to turn even colder. "You two have a nice conversation, Bobby Joe?"

Bobby Joe began to rapidly shake his head. "I didn't tell him nothin'. Not a thing." He looked into the man's eyes again and a shiver went down his back. "In fact, I told him to get the hell out."

The man's smile returned. "*You* told Detective Doyle to get out . . . and he did." He looked past Bobby Joe as if addressing some imaginary person standing behind him. "Now what's in that picture that doesn't work?"

"I did, it's true. I told him to get the hell out and he went right out the door. You see, my lawyer—"

"You curse a lot, Bobby Joe. And I truly find it offensive when you do. I'm certain the Lord finds it offensive as well."

The shiver returned to Bobby Joe's spine. "I'm sorry. You're right. I'm just nervous. Bein' pushed by that cop and now you not believin' me. My nerves are just a damn . . . My nerves are just a mess."

The man slipped his arm around Bobby Joe's shoulder and began walking him across the room. "No need to be nervous, Bobby Joe. Did you give him that other detective's name, the one Darlene told you about?"

Bobby Joe's head began to nod rapidly again. "I did. I did. And my lawyer called the sheriff and demanded to know why the cops aren't investigating one of their own people. Why they were tryin' to pin everything on a minister of the church, instead. He did it. He did it just like Daddy told him to, and he said the sheriff assured him he was gonna do somethin' about it."

"But Harry Doyle still showed up at your door, didn't he?"

Bobby Joe searched his mind for a reason. He felt like a man who had fallen into a raging river and was reaching out for anything he could find to keep himself afloat. "I don't think the sheriff had gotten to him yet. He seemed surprised when I told him that Walter . . . that's the lawyer . . . had called him."

The man continued to walk him slowly around the room, one arm still draped around his shoulder.

"What else did you tell him, Bobby Joe?"

"Nothin', nothin' at all."

"Did you tell him about me?"

"No, of course not. I didn't tell him nothin' else, not a damn thing."

The man shook his head. "I asked you to stop cursing, Bobby Joe. You're a minister of the Lord and you're cursing like some common riffraff."

"I'm sorry. I don't mean to. I really don't."

With a movement so deft and quick Bobby Joe never felt it happening, the man slipped behind him, slid one arm across his throat, and pressed his body against his back.

"If you move, I will break your neck," he hissed in his ear.

Bobby Joe said nothing, and the man could feel his entire body trembling against him. In a way it felt oddly erotic, reminding him of how he had felt when he killed Darlene, how she had begged when he put the knife against her throat, how she had promised to do anything he wanted, give him anything he wanted; how that terrible erection had come, tempting him until he had drawn the blade across her throat and seen her blood gush out into the sand of that sinful beach. He pushed the memories away and realized that his breath had become as ragged as Bobby Joe's. He removed the six-inch hunting knife from the sheath stuck under his belt at the small of his back and placed the blade under Bobby Joe's chin, moving it slowly down until it had replaced his arm, allowing him to grab a handful of the young minister's long hair. He felt himself becoming aroused and pushed Bobby Joe away from his body and pulled his head back exposing the entire length of his throat.

"This is the same knife that killed the whore. The same knife that cut into her throat and spilled her blood, the same tip of the blade that wrote the Lord's judgment on her forehead. Do you know what she said when I told her she would receive the Lord's judgment, Bobby Joe?"

Fear had stolen all the breath from Bobby Joe's lungs and he found himself struggling to speak. He tried nodding his head instead, but the blade of the knife bit into his throat and he felt a small trickle of blood run down his neck. His voice finally returned, breathless and weak. "Oh, please, please don't hurt me."

"That's *exactly* what Darlene said, Bobby Joe. And I'll tell you the same thing I told her. I'm not going to hurt you. No, I'm not. But the Lord *is* going to judge you. And in a few minutes you're going to be standing before Him, just as Darlene did, and His judgment will hurt you far more than anything I could do."

"No, no, no. Please, no. I'm not bad. I'm not."

He drew the knife firmly across Bobby Joe's throat and saw the dark, rich, arterial blood gush out in a long stream. Bobby Joe tried to scream but it came out as a loud gurgle; then his hands flew to his throat and the blood began to pulse through his fingers. The man released him and pushed him forward, stepping back as he saw the young minister stagger away. He stepped even further back as Bobby Joe regained control of his body and turned toward him, not wanting his clothes to be washed in the young minister's spraying blood. Bobby Joe took two steps and then collapsed to his knees. He looked up at the man, his face filled with the horror of his own impending death. Then his eyes began to cloud and he pitched forward, and fell facedown on the carpeted floor.

The man felt the erection pressing against his trousers and was repulsed. It had been the same when he killed Darlene and it made him ashamed of his weakness. He pushed all thoughts of his arousal away and concentrated on Bobby Joe, waiting for the blood to stop pumping from his body. When it finally slowed to a trickle he moved in, turned the body over, and brought the tip of the knife to his forehead. When he had finished he looked down at the young minister and gave a slow, approving nod, then he returned to the front door and retrieved a bag he had left outside. A smile kissed his lips. Now there was only one thing left to do.

Harry had checked his house and determined the church bulletin was indeed missing. Back at the office he went through the official file to make certain he hadn't inadvertently left it there. Jim and Vicky came into the conference room just as he was finishing his search. Vicky went straight to the chair across from Harry and Jim took the seat next to him.

"It's four o'clock, any chance you can give me a few minutes," Jim said.

The written request Jim had made for a four o'clock meeting came back. "Yeah, sure, what's up?" He glanced across at Vicky.

She glanced out into the bullpen at Nick Benevuto's empty desk. "Where's Nick?" she asked.

"Suspended with pay, by order of the sheriff," Harry said. "It seems my suspect, the kid minister, remembered that Darlene felt threatened by Nick. His lawyer called the sheriff and the big boss decided he should not even be in the office." He shrugged. "Rourke had no choice. Nick's gone until we wrap up the case and either charge him or clear him." He peered at Vicky, letting her know that in the end he still expected Nick to be cleared.

"Harry, we'd like to bring Nick in and formally interrogate him," Jim said.

Harry winced.

"It's no more than what you did with your suspect," Vicky chimed in. Her tone was sharp and held the unspoken comment that he was wasting his, and the department's time, with Bobby Joe Waldo.

The tone grated, the unspoken comment grated even more. He let it pass. They were right, of course. They had the right to interrogate Nick as many times as they felt were necessary. "You plan to cuff him when you bring him in?"

"That's procedure," Jim said.

Harry looked down at the top of the conference table. It was the same treatment to which Bobby Joe Waldo had been subjected, and he knew that doing any less with Nick Benevuto would only open the task force to criticism, possibly even jeopardize any future case against Bobby Joe. Still,

Nick was a brother cop, and one he considered innocent. Bringing him in wearing cuffs would rankle every member of the department. He glanced at Vicky and Jim . . . except two.

"Do what you think you have to do," he said. "It's your investigation."

"But you don't approve . . ." Vicky said, the sarcasm still heavy in her voice.

He stared at her longer than necessary. "What the hell difference does that make?"

They all knew that as lead investigator Harry could direct their actions. But they also knew that his decisions could be appealed to Rourke, who was in overall command. There was little question in anyone's mind who would win in this instance, especially after the sheriff's decision to formally suspend Nick.

"When do you plan to bring him in?" Harry asked.

"As soon as we can locate him," Jim said.

"I'd like to observe the interrogation, so keep me posted on it."

"No problem," Jim said.

"And try to bring him in when there are no media types around," Harry said. "We don't need to fan speculation that we've got killers working in homicide."

Jim nodded. "Of course. Vicky and I will go out and find him. We'll let you know as soon as we do."

"I don't think you'll be going anywhere right now."

They all looked up and saw Diva Walsh standing in the doorway.

She looked directly at Harry. "Bobby Joe Waldo was just found stone-cold dead in his apartment. His daddy's housekeeper went looking for him and found more than she bargained for. First unit at the scene said the M.O. was identical to Darlene Beckett—throat cut, face covered with another Mardi Gras mask. This time it was a leering devil. You all better get yourselves out there."

CHAPTER EIGHTEEN

One phone call from Harry had set the scene for the investigation. A uniformed officer was posted at the top of the garage stairs leading to Bobby Joe's apartment. Crime scene tape had been run in a wide circumference around the entire structure. And the housekeeper who had found the body was isolated in the rear of a patrol unit in the company of a female deputy. Harry also issued a direct order that no one be permitted inside the taped perimeter. This was met by repeated demands from the Reverend John Waldo that he be allowed to go inside and pray over his son. He was told he'd have to speak to the detective in charge.

When he arrived at the crime scene, Harry went straight to the cruiser that held the housekeeper, after sending Vicky and Jim to make sure the remainder of the scene was still secure.

The housekeeper was somewhere in her early fifties with graying hair, brown eyes, and a light brown complexion. Harry guessed she was Mexican, probably illegal—although he had no intention of pressing the point—and thoroughly shaken by what she had seen.

After telling him her name was Dolores Sanchez she stared at him with trembling lips and watery eyes. "He is dead?" she asked.

"Yes, Mrs. Sanchez, he is." Harry saw a sense of warmth enter the woman's eyes when he spoke to her with a tone of respect. The words also seemed to relax her. "Tell me why you went to Bobby Joe's apartment and everything you saw when you went inside."

She shook her head as if his words had brought back a horrific image, although Harry was certain the image of what she had seen had never left her, and would not for a very long time.

"I went because his father wanted to talk to him and he did not answer his telephone. His *padre*, he was getting very angry. He say, 'Go get him,' so I go."

"And what happened then?"

"Well, I knock on the door, but nobody answer. Then I try the door, but it no open. But I have keys for cleaning," she patted a pocket on her apron, "so I open the door but I no go inside. I can see him right from the doorway. Blood is everywhere, all over everything, and that horrible *diablo* mask is on his face."

"Did you touch the mask?"

She shook her head. "No, I no go inside."

"Then how did you know it was him?"

"He's wearing the same clothes I wash and iron for him," she said.

Harry nodded. It was a practical answer from a practical woman. "Did you see or hear anyone or anything unusual before you found the body?"

Dolores thought before giving her answer. "There was someone in the backyard maybe two hours before."

"Did you see someone?"

She shook her head. "*El perro*, next door, he start barking. He always bark when there people in the backyard. I thought maybe the reverend go out to smoke a cigar. Dog always bark when he does. It always makes the reverend angry. But then I saw him inside. So I look, but nobody's there."

Harry thanked her and told her that he would send someone to see her shortly to take a formal written statement that she would have to sign. "It won't be long. Then you can go home," he said.

The woman looked relieved.

Jim and Vicky were waiting for Harry at the foot of the stairs that led to

Bobby Joe's apartment. He led them up and told the uniform standing watch to allow no one else in except the forensic unit and the medical examiner.

When Harry swung open the door, the heavy coppery smell of blood assaulted their nostrils. Bobby Joe's body lay on its back in the middle of the room, the devil mask covering his face. He was still wearing the same clothing Harry had seen him in just hours before. Otherwise nothing was as it had been. The room was literally bathed in blood, the walls, the furniture, the floor, all washed in an arterial spray. The body had bled out before the heart had stopped beating, and Harry was certain the autopsy would show that all but the smallest amount was drained from the corpse. Still standing in the doorway he could see one set of bloody footprints leading away from the body. The first officers at the scene had checked the room to make sure the killer was not still there, but had remained far away from the body. The housekeeper, Mrs. Sanchez, said she had never entered the apartment after seeing the body from the doorway. Harry opened his crime scene case, removed his camera, and photographed the blood-stained path leading away from the body so they'd be able to separate those footprints from any new ones that were made in the course of the investigation.

The trio slipped on shoe covers distributed from Harry's case, then entered the room single file staying away from heavy blood splatter. The first thing Harry noticed were the stark similarities to Darlene Beckett's murder: the deep wound in the throat; the cut made by someone so powerful it almost opened the neck to the spinal column; hands carefully, even prayerfully folded; the mask placed over the face and left untied.

Harry went immediately to the body, took two photographs in situ, and then carefully raised the mask from Bobby Joe's face. He stared at the word *Fornicator*, carved into the forehead. He stood, took two more photographs with the mask removed; then knelt back down and stared into Bobby Joe's bloodless face.

"I should have stayed outside and watched you," he said softly.

"Did you say something, Harry?" Vicky asked.

He shook his head. "Nothing." He glanced at his watch. "I was here three hours ago. I rattled him pretty good and I even thought about staying parked outside to see if he went to anyone, or anyone came to him. But I decided there were other things I had to do first. I requested some unit drive-bys. Either that didn't happen, or they missed whoever killed him."

"I'll check it out," Vicky said. She went back outside to check with the uniform at the door. The first unit at the scene would also have been doing any drive-bys.

Harry picked up Bobby Joe's wrist, then reached out and manipulated his jaw with a latex-covered hand. Rigor had not begun, but given the heavy air-conditioning in the room the process could have been delayed. He reached inside his shirt and felt under his arm. It was still warm to the touch, indicating he had been dead for less than three hours.

"I should have stayed and watched," he said to no one in particular.

"Whoever killed him was probably outside watching *you*, waiting for you to leave," Jim said.

The words startled Harry. He had forgotten anyone else was still in the room. But the point was well taken, and he wondered if Bobby Joe's killer was the same person who had searched his home and pistol whipped Jeanie. Maybe you were looking in the right direction but at the wrong person, he told himself.

Jim's words interrupted him again. "If you don't need me here I'd like to go and check where Benevuto was when this murder went down. Superficially, at least, it looks like the same killer who did Darlene, and if Nick has an alibi for the last three hours that kind of lets him off the hook."

Harry looked back at Jim and nodded. "That's good thinking, and its fine with me if want to check it out, but touch base with Vicky first and make sure she doesn't need you. She worked Darlene's crime scene, along with that cowboy who got himself killed, so I want her to stay and work this one too. She's liable to spot any similarities that I miss."

"I'll tell her," Jim said.

Harry turned his attention back to the body. He studied the hands. They were covered in dried blood, indicating that Bobby Joe had used them in a vain attempt to staunch the flow from his throat, but otherwise there were no signs indicating a struggle. That told Harry that Bobby Joe knew the man well enough to let him get in close, and that the killer had not only been powerful, but also quick. He had moved in and had gotten behind Bobby Joe before the young minister realized what was happening. Military training? Justin Clearby leapt to mind. The first associate minister had told Harry he joined the church after a lengthy career as a Marine. And there could be others as well. He'd have to begin checking military records for everyone affiliated with the church.

He studied the wound. Like Darlene's it appeared to have been administered in a right-to-left motion, which, if Bobby Joe had been taken from behind—which is the only way such force could have been applied—would indicate that the killer used his left hand.

"How does this person get so close to people before he kills them?" Harry asked aloud. "Does he just inspire so much fear that his victims are afraid to move? Or is he that fast, that nimble?"

He looked into Bobby Joe's eyes. They had not become milky and clouded yet. There was still fear in them, Harry thought. The same fear he had seen when Bobby Joe had opened the door to him that afternoon—a fear that disappeared when the minister realized it was not the person he had been expecting.

"Who was that? Who were you waiting for?" Harry stared down at the corpse, almost as if he expected Bobby Joe to return to life and answer him.

The door to the apartment opened and Vicky came in. "The same unit that was called to the crime scene had your earlier request for a drive-by. Unfortunately, there was a traffic accident on McMullen-Booth and the drive-by never happened."

Harry nodded slowly. "I should have stayed and watched him. He was all unwound. I could feel it in my gut. He was either going to rabbit, or reach out for somebody. He even told me that what I was pressing him to do could get him killed. And he wasn't running a game on me. Whoever he was talking about scared the living hell out of him."

"What were you pressing him to give up?" Vicky asked.

"The name of anybody else he knew who was watching Darlene, who was trying to get something on her that would violate her probation."

"So you still think it was somebody in the church who did this." Vicky's voice held all the incredulity she felt.

Harry just looked at her and then turned his attention back to the body.

"Why won't you even consider Benevuto?" she demanded. "Is it because he's a brother cop?"

Harry kept his eyes on the body. "I wouldn't care if he was the man in the moon," he said. "Nick just doesn't look good for this kind of killing."

"Why not, why doesn't he look good for it?" She spoke the last four words with an edge, mocking the idea.

Harry pivoted slowly to face her. He inclined his head toward the body. "Look at him. Look at the way he was killed; the way the body was mutilated. Then think back to Darlene's body. This is the work of a religious head case, and that's not Nick Benevuto. You were in his apartment. There wasn't one iota of religion in it. Whoever killed Darlene thought she was evil—not a sick woman, not a deviant—but evil. Hell, Nick wouldn't think twice about a woman spreading her legs for anyone—even a kid. He might think it was stupid, and he'd definitely think *she* was stupid to do it the way she did, as an open invitation to get caught. But he wouldn't be declaring it evil and be so outraged that he'd carve that message in her forehead." He swung a hand toward Bobby Joe's face. "And do you think Nick Benevuto is so down on fornication that he'd cut up a body like this?" Harry shook his head and glared up at her. "He'd brand anybody who *wasn't* a fornicator as an asshole."

"Did you ever consider that he's just trying to throw us off? He's a good investigator. He knows how a good investigator thinks. He knows how you think, Harry."

"Okay, let's say I give you all that. Let's look at the choice of weapon. Our killer used a knife, and a fairly good-sized one. Why? Was it because this was some kind of religious sacrifice? I don't know. But I do know that Nick would not have chosen slicing somebody's throat as the best way to kill them. He might use a knife, but he would have used it with a few well-placed stabs to the heart. He wouldn't want to bathe the room in blood. Nobody who's ever worked homicide would want a crime scene like this. Not if he had to walk out of it. It's too damn hard not to leave evidence behind, or take evidence away with you."

"People do stupid things when they're in a jealous rage."

"These weren't impulsive acts. These murders were well planned. Remember, Darlene's body was moved, and it was moved for a reason that we haven't figured out yet. But whatever it was, it was worth the risk of moving her. And in both murders the killer came prepared to deliver a message."

"Prepared how? He had the knife with him?"

"He brought the masks with him too."

"I don't buy it, Harry. I just don't buy it. I think it's all part of his game to throw us off. Just like he altered the computer records so we wouldn't be able to trace his department car. He was involved with Darlene. He fell for her, and he fell for her hard. But she wanted to bounce from bed to bed. She needed to know that she was wanted by a lot of men; it's the only thing that satisfied her. God, she even needed to know that young boys wanted her. And Nick couldn't stand that. He wanted her for himself. Hell, Harry, you saw her. A man couldn't ask for a more beautiful, more desirable woman. And Nick Benevuto didn't want to share that with anybody. Period, end of story; motive and opportunity all wrapped up in a neat little package. And to top it off, the best cover in the world. He's a cop. And better yet, a detective who just might get to investigate the case. And that, my friend, is why Darlene's body was moved. To make sure the case stayed in our jurisdiction. If her body was found in Tarpon Springs, the case might have been snatched up by Tarpon P.D."

Harry swiveled back to the body. "Those are all excellent points. And you've got a very dirty crime scene here and no reason for Nick Benevuto to ever have been in this room. So let's work the room and then you can see if anything we find here ties him to the crime scene."

Vicky's jaw tightened. "And if we don't find anything, what does it prove? Just that he's as smart a cop as I think he is."

Harry loved the woman's tenacity. He smiled up at her. "Lady, you're like a dog with a bone. But the bottom line is this: we've got to put the killer at the scene of the crime. If we can't do that, we've got a lot of evidence and no one to tie it to."

Mort Janlow, the assistant M.E., finished his examination and turned the crime scene over to the forensic unit before joining Harry and Vicky on the small landing outside the front door. "Looks like the same killer—superficially at least," he said. "I'll be able to tell more once I get him on the table. But the killer was a strong son of a bitch. The cut went back so far it nicked the spinal column." He raised a finger. "But that nick in the bone should let us ID the knife as the murder weapon if we ever get our hands on it."

"You see anything else that we might pick up from the autopsy?" Harry asked.

"Are you talking about fingerprints on skin, something like that?" He watched Harry nod. "Nothing that's obvious right now. The body looks fairly clean. There's some loose hair on the scalp and some more on the shoulders. I suspect the killer held him by the hair to pull his head back just before he cut into the throat."

"Yes, I saw that," Harry said. "He didn't do that with Darlene. He held her close to him when he cut her; pressed up against him. You could tell that from the disturbance their feet made in the sand on that small beach and by the blood splatter evidence from the initial cut."

Janlow nodded. "But he may not have wanted to do that with a man, to keep him close to him like that."

"Why is that?" Vicky asked.

Janlow gave her a cautionary look, almost as if he thought his next words might embarrass her. "I don't know anything for certain, but according to the literature I've read on the subject, it's not uncommon for a killer to become sexually aroused when he kills with a knife, or by strangulation, or anything that brings him in close physical contact with the victim. Maybe in this case our killer didn't want to be close to another man when he began feeling aroused."

"He didn't want it because it was sinful." There was a faraway sound to Harry's voice, almost as if he was speaking to himself.

"That could very well be," Janlow said.

"Maybe he just didn't want to get blood on himself," Vicky said with a snide edge in her voice.

Janlow took in the exchange, a small smile forming on his thick lips. "Are we having a professional spat, children?"

"Just a disagreement about who our primary suspect should be," Harry said.

Janlow grinned at them. "More than one suspect strong enough to be a primary? Be grateful when your cup runs over, kiddies."

"Except you just got through examining *his* primary," Vicky said.

Janlow raised an eyebrow. "The young minister?"

Harry nodded.

Janlow smiled again. "I've heard the department folklore that the dead speak to you, Harry, but with this poor devil you might be asking a bit too much. His voice box is all chopped up." He let out a low cackle, then turned to the sound of footsteps coming up the stairs.

Vicky and Harry also turned and saw Jim Morgan coming up toward them.

"Any luck with Benevuto?" Vicky asked.

"He didn't answer the door at his apartment, and his car wasn't in the lot," Jim said. "I tried his cell phone, but didn't get any response there either."

"There are a couple of bars he hangs out in," Harry said. "I'll give you the names and addresses." He paused. "Do you intend to bring him in for questioning?"

"That's the eventual plan," Jim said. "Right now I was just going to see if he had an alibi for tonight."

"Take Vicky with you. If you find him, bring him in. Let's get the interrogation out of the way when the office isn't full of his peers. But don't start questioning him until I get there." Harry glanced at his watch. "I shouldn't be here much longer. When forensics finishes I'll connect up with you."

Vicky gave him a long look. "If we find him and decide to bring him in, do we cuff him?"

Harry let out a long breath. "It's your call. If he was my suspect, I wouldn't. He's still a cop. But he's also not supposed to be carrying, so pat him down and make sure he isn't."

Marty LeBaron, who headed up the CSI unit, pointed to the prints that marred the light tan carpeting on the apartment floor. "We've got a beautiful blood footprint leading out the door. The shoes are an eleven-C, and you can see a nice pattern in the heel of one print. They won't be hard to identify when we find them. Blood gets absorbed into the soles and heels; you never get it all out. So unless our perp tosses them, we find them, we nail his ass to the wall."

"So find the shoes, we find the killer. Sounds simple," Harry said.

Marty grinned at him. "It is simple, so why don't you get your ass moving and do it."

"You notice anything under the victim's fingernails, any fingerprints on his skin, defensive wounds?" Harry asked.

"The body was pretty clean. There were some fibers on the back of his shirt. Probably left there when the perp first came up behind him; also some hairs that weren't his. But it was less than we usually find. We'll sort it all out back at the lab. As far as skin prints go, nothing. It's my guess the perp wore latex gloves."

"So you'd say it was a pretty clean crime scene? Like somebody who knew what they were doing?"

"What are you trying to say, Harry?"

"I want to know if the crime scene looks like it was handled by someone who knew how to keep the level of evidence down."

"Like a cop?" Marty's eyes narrowed.

"Some people are looking real hard at a cop," Harry said.

"I can't say that, Harry. And I sure as hell wouldn't testify to that."

"Ease up, Marty." Harry placed a hand on his shoulder. "I'm not trying to nail a cop for this. I just want to be able to answer any questions that come up."

Marty looked away momentarily. "It could have been someone who knows crime scenes," he conceded. "For everything except the footprints, that is. It took a real asshole to leave footprints like that. The clown never even made an effort to clean them up. If he had, we probably never would have gotten that heel print."

"Maybe something scared him off," Harry speculated.

"The way this guy killed these two people, he doesn't strike me as the type who scares easy."

"You wouldn't think so," Harry said.

Vicky and Jim found Nick Benevuto in one of the bars Harry had suggested, a Hooters wannabe joint located on 66th Street just off Ulmerton Avenue. Nick was seated in an obscure booth nursing the same drink he had ordered when he arrived an hour earlier. He was dressed in a black silk short-sleeved shirt, open at the collar, and tan slacks with a razor crease. Vicky thought he was living up to his nickname: Nicky the pimp.

"What the fuck do you two want?" he asked as Vicky and Jim stopped at his table. "Or are you just here to feed off what's left of me? Fucking vultures."

"We need to know where you were earlier tonight," Vicky said.

Jim had placed himself so he blocked Nick from making a quick exit from the booth, and Vicky was off to his side so she had a clear field of fire. Nick looked at each of them; saw the way they'd positioned themselves.

"This a bust?"

"We just need to ask you some questions," Vicky said.

"Ask away."

"Where were you tonight?"

"I was home. I just came out about an hour ago, wanted to have a couple of drinks. No big surprise. They suspended my ass today."

"Jim went by your place about two hours ago. Nobody answered the door."

"I never heard the door." He glanced up at Morgan, contempt filling his face. "Maybe your rookie partner went to the wrong door."

"Your car wasn't in the parking lot," Morgan said.

"Then I'd already left, asshole. What else can I tell you?"

"So you were at home between two and five this afternoon?" Vicky asked.

"That's right."

"Was anybody with you?" Jim asked.

Nick held up his right hand. "Yeah, Mary Fist. I'm sure you know her well, jerkoff."

"That's not necessary," Jim said. "We're treating you with respect; you can treat us the same way."

Nick let out a barking laugh. "I got a problem there, boyo. I don't respect either one of you. So I guess I'd have to fake it."

"Then fake it," Vicky snapped.

"Fuck you," Nick snapped back.

"On your feet and assume the position," Jim said.

"What? Are you out of your fucking mind?"

"Do it," Jim ordered. "Do it or I'll charge you with resisting the lawful command of a police officer."

"You arresting me?"

"You're going in for questioning," Vicky said, seizing control back from Morgan. "Let us pat you down for weapons and we won't use cuffs."

"Why you cunt . . ."

"Now," Morgan growled. His raised voice made several patrons turn to watch them.

The sudden attention seemed to embarrass Benevuto. "Alright, alright," he said in a softer voice. "But can we do the pat down in the parking lot?"

"As long as you behave yourself," Vicky said.

Morgan gave her a look that told her he thought it was a mistake to grant Benevuto's request.

Benevuto reached into his pocket and then froze when he saw Morgan and Vicky tense. "I just want to pay for my drink," he said. He removed a wad of folded bills held by a money clip, pulled out a ten, and placed it next to his half-finished drink. "I suppose you don't wanna wait for me to get change."

"Leave the whole thing," Vicky said. "It'll make the waitress remember you."

Nick was alone in the interrogation room when Harry arrived at the office. Vicky and Jim filled him in.

"So he has no alibi for the time period when Bobby Joe was killed," he said when they had finished.

"None," Vicky replied. "And when we found him he was dressed in clothes that looked like they'd just come from the cleaner. I checked with Rourke and got an idea of what he wore to work today. It didn't even come close. I'd like to get a warrant to search his condo."

Harry held up a hand. "I don't think we have enough probable cause for a warrant. Let's interrogate him first, see what you come up with, and then we'll decide where we go from there."

"Are you going to question him?" Jim asked. There was an edge in his voice that Harry picked up on—as though he feared Harry might try to steal Benevuto away now that his own suspect was dead.

Harry shook his head, and glanced at each of them in turn. "I'll watch through the glass. The interrogation is all yours."

Vicky and Jim huddled outside the interrogation room, setting up strategy, as Harry entered the viewing area. He took a chair facing the one-way window. Nick Benevuto was seated no more than ten feet away, isolated and alone. Harry saw a lonely, beaten man, not the same pushy, thoroughly obnoxious detective he had worked with for more than five years. All the cockiness was gone from his eyes and Harry knew that any manifestation of it that he managed to force out would be little more than false bravado.

Nick's head snapped around to the sound of the door opening and he watched Vicky and Jim enter and take chairs opposite him across a small metal table. There was a mix of relief and irritation in his eyes. Harry understood it. Suspects did not like to be isolated, especially in a small, closed, windowless room. They felt threatened by it. But they were equally threatened by the interrogation that followed. It was a confusing mix of emotions. Nick showed that now. He glared at his fellow detectives with open disgust. It was a feeling, Harry knew, that would never fully disappear, no matter the outcome. And he had little doubt that there would also be a dose of it for him as well.

Speaking to no one in particular, Vicky gave the date, the time, the location, and the names of all persons present; then advised Nick that the interrogation was being tape recorded, and that he had a right to have an attorney present.

Nick waved the statement off. "I don't need a lawyer. If I decide I do, I'll tell you your interrogation is over."

"Fair enough," Vicky said.

"Let's start with Darlene Beckett," Jim began, indicating that he would take the lead in the interrogation.

It was a smart move, Harry thought. Nick's attitude toward women would keep him from dealing with Vicky with any degree of openness. On the other hand, by taking the secondary role, she could jump in and force an issue whenever an irritant was needed.

"Start wherever you want," Nick said. "You can start with Marilyn Monroe. I didn't kill her either."

"You already admitted that you had a sexual relationship with Darlene. Isn't that true?"

"I slept with her a couple of times. I was trying to get her to turn snitch for me, and I was trying to get close to her. I got a little too close. It was a mistake."

"How many mistakes did you make?" Jim asked.

Nick glared at him. "Do you mean how many times did I fuck her? It's okay, kid, you can say the word. Your tongue won't turn black and fall out."

Harry saw Jim's jaw tighten, but he kept his cool. "How many times?" he asked again.

Nick gave out a little snort. "Three, four, I didn't keep count. To tell you the truth, for all her looks she wasn't that great."

"Then why did you keep going back?" Vicky snapped.

Nick seemed pleased that he had irritated her. "I didn't say she was terrible. I might even go back to a bitch like you for a second or third roll in the hay. Who knows?"

"Not on the best day of your life, slimeball," Vicky retorted.

Jim raised a hand, calling for an end to it, and Nick laughed out loud. First round to the suspect, Harry thought.

"According to the younger Reverend Waldo you were pressing Darlene for sex, but it never happened," Jim said. "At least that's what she allegedly told him."

"And?"

"Who's telling the truth, you or him?"

"Was he fucking her too?"

"That's irrelevant."

"No it's not, rookie," Nick barked, taking charge again. "If he was fucking her, why would she admit that she was balling me too? She might say I wanted to fuck her to make him jealous, but why tell him she'd already spread her legs for me?"

"Jealousy, that's an interesting point," Jim said. "You didn't know that she was sleeping with him—with Reverend Bobby Joe Waldo?"

"I assumed she was sleeping with anybody who had a dick. That's the kind of broad she was. For crissake, she slept with fourteen-year-old kids, didn't she?"

"So you expected her to be promiscuous," Jim said.

"Shit, it was a fact of life." He leaned closer to them, lowering his voice in a mocking manner. "It was on TV, in the newspapers, it was no fucking secret. So, yeah, I expected it. I never went near the broad without a box of condoms in my pocket."

"So you weren't jealous of her other lovers," Vicky said.

"No," Nick shot back.

Harry looked at Jim. It was time for him to jump in. He did, and he came in hard.

"You're a liar," he snapped, his eyes cold and hard on Nick.

"Fuck you," Nick responded weakly. He hadn't anticipated the sudden turn, the hard edge to Jim's body language. He thought he was in control and it had taken him by surprise.

"You were jealous of every man who had ever been with her. She was beautiful, more beautiful than any woman you'd ever had. Men saw her on television and sat in their living rooms wanting her. And now *you* had her. You, Nick Benevuto, a short, fat, aging womanizer, who could only get a woman when he could browbeat or threaten her into it. And you weren't going to let this one slip away. You weren't going to share her with anybody. So you started following her, and when you caught her with that pathetic salesman, all dressed up like a cowboy, you flipped out and killed them both."

"Prove it. It's all bullshit!"

Harry watched Jim bear in, ignoring Nick's denial.

"And when you realized what you'd done, you knew you had to do two things. First, you had to move the body so it was sure to come under county jurisdiction, where you'd have some involvement in the investigation. And second, you knew people were watching her, and that somebody might have seen your department car at Darlene's house, might even have written down the license plate, so you had to cover yourself, you had to alter department records so they never showed you taking that particular car out."

"It's bullshit and you know it."

Again, Jim ignored him. "And then you found out that Bobby Joe Waldo knew about you and Darlene, so you went to him and threatened him, scared the living hell out of him. But Harry Doyle was on his case; had him named as a suspect because people had seen him at Darlene's house. And you knew Harry was good, you knew he'd break him down eventually, and that the little punk would give you up to save himself. So this afternoon you went to see him, didn't you?"

"What the fuck are you talking about? I was never anywhere near that dope-peddling little prick. I never even met the son of a bitch."

"You went to him and you killed him, just like you killed Darlene. You killed him because you knew he'd not only tell Harry about you and Darlene, about how you'd threatened her and blackmailed her into having sex with you, but that he'd tell him how you were threatening him to keep his mouth shut. You knew Harry would break him eventually, and so you had no choice. It was a ball rolling downhill and you couldn't stop it."

"The kid minister is dead?"

Harry noted the genuine shock on Nick's face. If he was acting, he'd missed his calling in life.

"Stop the innocent act, Nick," Vicky said. "If you want to show us you had nothing to do with this, let us toss your apartment, right now, tonight."

Harry could see the wheels turning in Nick's head. He was clearly thinking about what they might find there if he allowed a search. But it wasn't necessarily what they might find about Darlene or Bobby Joe Waldo. Harry knew if they tossed his apartment and found the duplicate evidence he kept at home, he might easily face a suspension. Very few cops, if any, were clean as the driven snow. If the department wanted to get something on you, there was always something they could find.

"Let me think about it?" Nick said.

"Think about it for how long?" Jim asked.

"A day or two," Nick said, knowing it was more than they'd agree to, but also knowing they'd have a tough time getting a search warrant any faster.

"Just enough time to clean out the place," Vicky said. "That's bull. Would you give a suspect a day or two?"

"So now I'm a suspect? I thought I was a brother cop."

"You're both," Jim said.

Nick leaned forward again, glaring at him. "If I wanted to toss a suspect's crib, I'd get a search warrant. Maybe you should do that, rookie."

"So you're refusing?" Vicky asked.

"You bet your ass I'm refusing. And as far as I'm concerned, this interview is over."

Nick sat back in his chair, stone-faced, hands in his lap. Harry noticed that his hands were trembling slightly. He was scared, and he should be scared. Harry was sure murder charges would never hold up. But Nick had to know they could be filed. Mistakes had been made before. Harry still didn't make him for either murder. It just didn't add up, and he'd fight filing charges against Nick. But at best the guy's career had been tarnished beyond redemption. Even if he remained with the department, it would never again be in a position of trust or authority.

"You still don't make Nick for either murder?" Vicky's tone was pure incredulity. "Are you going to back us on a warrant?"

"Go for your warrant," Harry said. "I agree he's a viable suspect. I just don't think he's our guy."

"And who do you think is?" Jim asked.

Harry studied his shoes for a moment, considering how much he wanted to say. "I still think it's someone connected to Bobby Joe's church. And I think he knew who that person was, and it was somebody who really scared the hell out of him."

"You said his father scared him to death," Vicky said.

"No, this wasn't someone who just intimidated him. This was somebody who made Bobby Joe believe he'd be killed if he ever talked. But his father was part of it. His father sent out a call asking his parishioners to get something on Darlene. Bobby Joe answered that call—that's how he met Darlene. But our killer answered it too, and Bobby Joe knew it. That's what eventually got him killed. The parents of the kid Darlene molested gave me a copy of a church bulletin where that call from Reverend Waldo was repeated. That's the only thing that was taken from my house when the killer broke in. That's the connection, that church bulletin. So I'm going to find out why it was important enough to make our killer risk breaking into my house. And when I do, I'll know who killed Darlene and Bobby Joe."

"I don't buy it, Harry," Vicky said. "It still could have been Nick Benevuto. Bobby Joe knew about him and his connection to Darlene. And Nick smells to high heaven on this. The only thing we haven't been able to do is place him at the scene. When we get our warrant, we'll do that. In the meantime, I need people watching his house to keep him from removing any evidence."

"I'll assign the two Tarpon detectives, Davis and Deaver. You two can alternate with them, take turns sitting on him. One at a time, six-hour shifts each."

"That's going to slow us down," Vicky complained.

"I can't help it," Harry said. "Give it thirty-six hours. If you don't get a warrant by then, you're not going to get one. But right now I can't spare any more manpower."

"You can't spare it for a suspect you don't believe in," she said.

Harry gave her a long, hard look. "That's right, Vicky, not for a suspect I don't believe in."

CHAPTER NINETEEN

It was ten o'clock when Harry finally made it home. Jocko Doyle was seated on the living room sofa, glasses perched on the end of his nose, a Stuart Kaminsky mystery in his lap. Harry noticed he had his old, off-duty .38 snub nose on his hip, a weapon he rarely wore since his retirement from the Clearwater P.D.

"Where's Rubio?" Harry asked.

"He's out on the lanai watching TV."

"Jeanie?"

"In bed, asleep," Jocko said.

Harry started toward the bedroom.

"Hold up a minute," Jocko said, stopping him. "There was a call from that assistant state's attorney, Cal Morris. He's got some info on your mother you need to hear." He raised his chin indicating a pad on the coffee table. "His number's there; he said you could call whenever you got in."

Harry immediately punched the number into his cell phone. Cal Morris answered on the third ring.

"I've got an odd situation here, Harry," he began. "First, let me explain that the prison called our office because they don't have an address or a number for you. They said you never filled out their forms to arrange contact with your mother, or with the prison."

"That's right. I didn't want contact."

"Well, it seems that's what has screwed up their notification about the parole. Now they've got something else. They contacted us as her prosecutor, because they couldn't reach you and thought we might be able to. Seems your mother has asked to meet with you prior to her parole hearing. It's not something you have to do, but I advise you to consider it."

"Why? I have no interest in meeting with her."

"If you're going to oppose her release I advise you to do it. Don't give her the opportunity to say that you haven't had any contact with her for umpteen years and therefore have no solid basis to try and stop her from getting out."

"I have her wacko letters," Harry snapped.

"Yes, but letters and personal contact are like apples and oranges. You need to be able to say that you've read her letters *and* seen her and feel that she's a danger to you. It will make your argument a great deal stronger. The prison has set a time—nine a.m. Sunday morning."

"How efficient of them," Harry said. "Tell me something, Cal. Why does the state seem so anxious to let her the hell out?"

"They're overcrowded, Harry, and overcrowding makes life difficult for them. Whenever that happens they look to see who they can cut loose. The people who've already done heavy time are usually the safest bet. That's how your mother ended up on the list."

Harry closed his eyes, let out a breath, and surrendered to the madness of it. "I'll think about it, Cal. I appreciate your call and your advice." He closed the cell phone and looked at his father.

"I know," Jocko said. "Cal filled me in when he called. I think you should consider his advice." He stood and headed for the door. "I'm going home. Think over what I said."

Harry nodded, but said nothing. It was Friday. The meeting with his mother—if he decided to go—was two days away. He walked into the bedroom and sat on the edge of the bed. Jeanie was lying on her side, facing him. He could see the bruise where the killer had hit her. It crept from her hairline out on to her forehead. He bent down and kissed the area lightly.

Jeanie stirred and opened her eyes. "Hi," she said, her voice heavy with sleep.

"How do you feel?"

"I'm fine. I had a great day. Your father and mother were wonderful, and Rubio is just a hoot. I'm learning a whole new language."

"Street," Harry said.

"Yes, that's what he calls it. He's pretty cute for a twelve-year-old."

"Twelve going on forty," Harry said.

"He thinks you're pretty special too. He says you can hear what dead people are saying."

"Only on Thursdays." Harry leaned down and kissed her forehead again, staying well away from the bruise.

"Come to bed," Jeanie said. "You look exhausted."

"I will."

CHAPTER TWENTY

Reverend Waldo's secretary looked at Harry as though he had just crawled out from under a rock.

"Do you realize what we're doing here?" she asked. "We are all in working early on a Saturday morning to prepare for Reverend Bobby Joe's funeral. We do not have time to waste satisfying the curiosity of a police officer."

She was a slender woman somewhere in her mid-fifties, with a flat chest and a pinched face. Her graying hair matched her dress and was worn in a tight bun, and her dull, brown eyes were obscured by rimless glasses. There was no wedding ring on her finger and Harry doubted anyone had ever given her one. The name plate on her desk said *Emily Moore*.

Harry placed his hands on the edge of her desk and leaned in toward her. He kept a smile on his face but it was not a warm one. Emily Moore inched her chair away from him.

"Ms. Moore, Reverend Bobby Joe didn't die of a heart attack. He didn't die of cancer, or as the result of an automobile accident. Someone came to his home and sliced his throat open with a very sharp knife. He was murdered, Ms. Moore, and I'm the police officer who's been assigned to find out who butchered him like a Christmas turkey. So you stop whatever you're doing, and you go find me a copy of that church bulletin, or I will slap handcuffs on you, put you in the back of my car, drive you to headquarters, and charge you with obstruction of justice, after which you will be strip-searched, photographed, fingerprinted, and put in a holding cell with some very unpleasant people. Do we understand each other?"

The woman's lips began to tremble as she tried to speak, but no words came out. Her eyes filled with tears. Harry leaned in a bit closer. "Now," he said. His voice was little more than a whisper.

Emily Moore began opening drawers in her desk; then the cabinet behind her. She rose from her chair and went to a small closet that seemed to hold an abundance of office supplies and began rummaging through them.

Harry thought about what he had said to the woman. He had little doubt Rourke would hear about it sooner or later. He always seemed to hear about Harry's indiscretions. He'd probably think that threatening a spinster church lady with a strip search was a bit over the top. A smile began to form on his lips. It probably made her whole day, he told himself.

Emily Moore came out of the supply closet with her eyes brimming with tears again. "I don't understand it," she said. "We always have copies left over, but there aren't any." She stared at Harry, as if she expected him to whip out his handcuffs.

"You think someone took them or tossed them out?"

"I can't think of anything else that could have happened. But they're not supposed to be thrown out. We always overprint so we have a supply. I also always keep a few back issues in my desk. But everything is gone."

"What about getting one from someone who still has a copy at home?"

"The issue is several months old, but it's possible. Some of our older parishioners do keep them. I could make a few calls and see if I could find one."

"I'd appreciate it." Harry tried a genuine smile, but Emily Moore still looked tearful.

You're an ogre, he told himself. His cell phone interrupted the thought.

"Doyle," he said.

Vicky's voice came over the line, sounding a bit shaky. "You better get over to Nick Benevuto's condo," she said.

"Why? What happened?"

"I just found his body. Oh God, Harry. He ate his gun."

Nick's body was slumped in a chair, his head thrown back, the ultra-suede upholstery soaked with his blood. Harry stepped in close. Nick's mouth was open, showing several broken teeth and badly burned tissue. A Glock 9mm automatic lay at his feet.

Harry had seen the bodies of other cops who decided to eat their guns; civilians as well. The back of Nick's head was gone, the exit wound having blown out a section of skull the size of his fist. He looked up at the ceiling. Blood and bone and brain matter were spread over a three-foot swath. He snapped on a pair of latex gloves as he studied Nick's face. Normally the face of a victim spoke to him; told him things. Not this time. Nick's features were distorted, the eyes bulging almost to the point of coming out of their sockets. The broken teeth and burnt tissue indicated he had placed the barrel of the Glock into his mouth, which had internalized the explosion of gunpowder to the point that it distorted his features. He looked down at the weapon, noting that it was still cocked and ready to fire, something the pistol did automatically whenever it was discharged.

"There's still a live round in the chamber. As soon as it's dusted for prints let's remember to put the safety on."

"You should come and see this, Harry." Vicky was standing next to a computer that was set up on a small desk. Even from across the room he could see a message printed on the screen.

"What is it?" he asked.

"It's a confession. It covers all three murders—Darlene, the cowboy, and the Waldo kid."

Harry walked to the computer, but before he started reading he checked a nearby printer, making sure it was loaded with paper. Using a pencil to move the mouse he hit the print tab. "I want a hard copy, just in case we lose what's on the screen."

The printer started whirring as Harry began reading Nick's confession. It essentially followed Vicky's theory that Nick had fallen in love with Darlene Beckett only to find that she cheated on him every chance she got. He began following her, the confession said, and when he came upon her on a small beach in Tarpon Springs he lost his temper and killed both her and her lover. He had then moved Darlene's body to the Brooker Creek Preserve to make certain county homicide detectives were called in to handle the case. Later, he learned that Bobby Joe had also been romantically involved with Darlene, and that Harry Doyle was pressing him for information. He was certain that Darlene had told Bobby Joe about him—about their affair and subsequent threats he had made against her. He went to see Bobby Joe and tried to coerce him into silence. But he soon realized how weak the young minister was and decided that sooner or later he would spill everything he knew to save himself. Bobby Joe had left him no choice. The confession ended with Nick's name printed at the bottom of the two-page statement.

Harry walked back to the body without saying a word. Vicky followed, a quizzical look on her face.

Harry removed the camera from his crime scene case and took photos of the body, the gun, and the blood splatter on the ceiling. He then began to carefully search the body.

"Harry, talk to me," Vicky said. "Tell me what you're thinking."

Harry turned to the sound of the front door opening. Jim Morgan stood in the doorway staring at the body. He looked shaken and Harry wondered if it were due to the fact that he had never seen this type of head wound before, or if it was because he was seeing it on a brother cop, someone he had known.

"I called Jim and told him what happened," Vicky said.

"Put on gloves and shoe coverings before you come in," Harry warned. He looked at Morgan closely. "If you think you're going to be sick don't come in here."

Vicky went to Harry's case and retrieved the necessary materials and brought them to Morgan. "Are you okay?" she asked.

Morgan nodded absently. "Yeah, I'll be alright. I just feel responsible, like I helped push him into this."

"If you want to stay in homicide you better change that thinking," Harry snapped. "This state executes people. You can't do your job if you're going to worry about people ending up dead." He watched Morgan nod a weak agreement and turned back to his search of Nick Benevuto's body.

Harry removed and bagged all the items in his pockets; checked his wallet and bagged it as well. Vicky stood at his side writing each item in her notebook. Harry then began a close examination of Nick's clothing, carefully searching for any hairs or fibers he might want to point out to the forensic team that was now on its way. Nick was dressed in a T-shirt and baggy khaki cargo shorts. His feet were bare.

Harry caught a glimpse of something in Nick's gray hair. He leaned in closer to get a better look, holding his breath to keep away the smell of blood and brain matter.

"What is it?" Vicky asked.

"A feather," Harry said.

"Is it from the chair?"

Harry looked at the chair. "No. The chair's filled with foam."

"What do you think it means?"

"I'm not sure yet, but I don't like it."

Harry began walking around the room, taking a mental picture of his surroundings. "How did you find the body?" he asked Vicky.

"It was my turn on the surveillance. Jim had done the first six-hour shift and I came in and took over about five a.m. We figured we'd get our shifts out of the way first so it wouldn't interfere with other stuff we had to follow up on. Anyway, about seven-thirty this neighbor starts banging on Nick's door, but he doesn't answer. After she leaves, I went up to see what the problem was and I hear loud music coming from inside—I mean really loud, louder than any adult is going to want to listen to, and certainly nothing a person could sleep through. At that point I knocked too, and got nothing. So I asked the manager to open the door. As soon as it swung back the smell hit me and I knew. I went in, saw him, checked his pulse—pretty needlessly—turned off the CD that was playing, and called you. Then I secured the scene, radioed in a report, asked for uniform backup, and notified forensics."

Harry looked around the room again, found the location of the CD player. He didn't touch the machine, or any of its settings, leaving that for the CSI team. "The CD in there is the one that was playing when you came in?"

"Yes, it is." A note of concern crossed Vicky's face.

"What is it?" Harry asked.

Vicky shook her head. "It's gospel music. I just never figured Nick for gospel."

Harry went to the cabinet that held Nick's other CDs and began looking through them. "There's no other gospel here," he said.

"That doesn't prove anything in itself," Vicky said.

Harry let it go and began to look through the apartment. Nick had picked it up considerably since his earlier visit. He entered Nick's bedroom and immediately noticed that the television set opposite the bed was on and in a paused position. He recognized the format as a pay-per-view movie. He located the remote and using a pencil hit the play button. The TV restarted a Bruce Willis film that Harry had seen. Nick had been almost halfway through the film when he'd hit the pause button.

He turned and saw Vicky and Jim in the bedroom doorway. "He was watching a pay-per-view film and was halfway through it."

Vicky nodded. "So that means he paused the film, got up, went into the living room, wrote out a confession, turned on the CD with the volume way up to cover the sound of a shot, and then sat down and blew his brains out. Doesn't make a lot of sense, does it?"

"What do you mean?" Jim asked. "Nobody came in here during the six hours I was watching."

"Well, about five-thirty I did drive up to that all-night gas station to take a pee." She looked at Harry and Jim in turn. "Hey, I can't pee in a bottle like you guys can."

"So you were gone how long?" Harry asked.

"Fifteen, twenty minutes tops."

Harry turned to Jim. "And you're certain nobody could have gotten in while you were outside?"

"Sure, it's possible if they came in and went out through a rear window. We were concerned about Nick leaving with evidence, so I was positioned where I could see his front door and his car. I wasn't worried about anybody climbing in."

"Did you talk to the neighbor who was knocking on the door?" he asked Vicky.

"No. There hasn't been time."

"Let's do it now. Jim, you stay on the front door, make sure nobody comes inside except the CSI team. When the uniforms get here tell them to secure the scene, including Nick's car in the parking lot. Show them which one it is."

"You got it," Jim said.

The neighbor's door was answered by a woman in her mid-thirties, who looked as though she had not had a good night's sleep. She was a tall, slender blonde with large, clearly augmented breasts, and Harry wondered how many times Nick had hit on her during the time they'd been neighbors. The woman gave her name as Terry Hogan and said she had lived in her condo for three years and had known Nick well.

"Yeah, that was me pounding on his door," she said. "All of a sudden this music started, like real loud, you know. And it wasn't even dawn yet. I tried calling him, I mean he'd given me his number and all, but I couldn't get an answer."

"What time was it when the music started?" Harry asked.

"It was like three a.m.," she said. "I put up with it for a couple of hours, threw a pillow over my head, and went back to sleep, but it kept waking me up. Finally I just went over there and started pounding on the door, but he never answered."

"Did you go outside, or look out the window when the music first woke you?" Vicky asked.

"No, should I have done that? I mean did Nick get robbed or something?"

Harry found Pete Rourke standing over Nick's body when he returned to the apartment.

"This isn't the way I wanted this case to end," he said. "Not with a confession and suicide by one of my own men."

"I'm not sure it's a suicide, or that the confession is legit," Harry said.

Rourke's head gave a quick jerk and he threw a questioning look at Vicky.

"I'm not sure it's legit either. I want to wait for CSI to have a look, but I agree with Harry. It just doesn't smell right," she said.

Rourke turned back to Harry. "Talk to me."

Harry went through the evidence he'd found at the scene. Rourke nodded as Harry explained each contradictory piece. When he had finished Rourke shook his head.

"Harry, I'd give anything to have it not be one of my guys, but if we can't prove this isn't a suicide, we're not going to be able to ignore a written confession found in a locked room with a cop who blew his own head off. Let's see if CSI can come up with anything that will nail this down as a homicide."

Marty LeBaron arrived with his CSI team a half hour later. He listened to Harry's concerns, did a quick turn of all the rooms, and then motioned Harry to follow him outside.

"I see what you're getting at, Harry. You're right on every point, except one."

"The surveillance," Harry said.

"That's it. Now unless Nick didn't shoot himself until Vicky was on watch, and went off to have a piss, we've got a situation where a killer would have had to break in through a rear window. There is an open window in Nick's bedroom, but I can't imagine Nick laying there watching a movie and not doing anything when some asshole starts climbing in his window."

"He could have been in the bathroom," Harry said. "He could have gone into the kitchen for a beer. There are several viable scenarios."

"Yeah, there are, Harry. But each one's a stretch." Marty rubbed his chin. "Nick was a cop and a good one. If some asshole climbed in his window, my bet is he'd either be in cuffs, or stretched out in a morgue wagon."

Marty and his team spent the next two hours going over Nick's condo and car. Mort Janlow arrived when they were halfway through the crime scene and began a thorough examination of the body. Harry decided to wait for preliminary results from each of them. Janlow finished first.

They left the body to the morgue attendants and went out to Harry's car. Janlow rested his considerable bulk against the left front fender.

"I love being called out on a Saturday morning," he groused. "I work sixteen hours a day, five days a week, and half the time I end up working part of the weekend."

"Yeah, but you get the big bucks," Harry said.

Janlow gave him a fish-eye. He toed the ground and began to study his shoe. "Harry, why do you think this isn't a suicide?" He raised a hand. "I'm not rejecting the idea. I just want to hear your reasons."

"You noticed the feather in his hair, right?"

"Yes, I did. But he was lying in bed watching a movie before he . . . died. We'll have to compare that feather to the type of feathers in his pillows."

"They're foam pillows," Harry said. "I already checked them."

Janlow nodded, conceding the point.

"It also bothers me that the next-door neighbor, who was already awake because of the music, didn't hear a shot," Harry said. "A 9mm Glock is a noisy weapon. But if you place the barrel in somebody's mouth and a pillow over the receiver, the noise can be reduced significantly."

"Did you find a pillow with gunshot residue, or scorching?"

"No."

"So you're thinking the killer took it away with him—another assumption we can't prove."

"That's right."

"What else?"

"The neighbor was awakened by the loud music, that we assume was turned on to cover the sound of the shot. Why cover the sound of the shot if this was suicide?"

Janlow nodded, but said nothing.

"Nick had just ordered a movie on pay TV, so if we buy into a suicide scenario we have to assume that he reached a decision to kill himself in the middle of a movie he was watching, that he left his bedroom, turned on the CD player at high volume, and ate his gun."

"It's possible."

"He *paused* the movie, Mort . . . just like someone would if they had to go to the bathroom, or to the kitchen to get themselves a beer."

"It's still possible he did it that way. I mean suicides can be irrational, but okay, that's another point in your favor."

"And finally there's the confession. It's too well written, Mort. I've read a lot of Nick's reports over the years, and frankly, like a lot of cops, he wasn't that articulate. The confession doesn't say anything about the masks that were used to cover the faces of the victims, or the words carved into their foreheads. Nick was a homicide detective, Mort, and homicide cops don't like loose ends. He would have told us why he did what he did; he would have told us all of it."

Mort Janlow issued a heavy sigh. "Alright, you've made your point. There are some legitimate concerns so there won't be any rush to judgment on my end. I'm scheduled to do Bobby Joe Waldo's post early this afternoon, and I'll do Nick's right after that. You're welcome to be there, or you can check in with me about four o'clock."

"I'm going to send Jim Morgan down to observe the posts. Vicky and I are going to canvass the neighbors, and then I've got to get Pete Rourke to buy us some time. If news about this confession leaks to the media, all hell is gonna break loose."

When Harry returned to the condo Nick's body had already been loaded on a gurney. He told the morgue attendants to take a break so he could make a final examination of the body, then undid the straps holding down the covering sheet and pulled it back.

Nick's features were even more grotesque lying on his back. His bulging eyes had begun to cloud, and the facial features seemed even more distorted. Beneath the clouding in his eyes Harry thought he could detect a strong sense of fear. He leaned in closer studying them more carefully. Yes, it was there. He was certain of it. He had seen many suicides by gunshot. Fear had been there when the fatal wound was to the victim's torso and death was not immediate. But not when death came quickly. Not when death came from a head wound. Everything he had read, every psychologist he had ever questioned about suicide, agreed that a great sense of calm came to the victim when that final decision had been made. From that point fear was seldom a factor. But Harry felt fear here. Nick had not been seeking his own death. It was not something he welcomed.

Who was it, Nick? Who scared you before you died? He placed his latex-covered hands on Nick's chest but no sensation came to him. He looked up and saw members of the CSI team watching him. Marty LeBaron was smiling.

"Doing your dead detective thing, Harry?"

Harry ignored him, turning his attention back to the body. Staring down at Nick's swollen, deformed face he recalled the first time the cop had been braced about his relationship with Darlene Beckett. He had been peppered with questions from the four of them—Rourke, Vicky, Jim, and Harry, himself. The questions had produced concern, embarrassment, and anger. But beneath that montage of emotions there had been a hint of fear as well. It was the same fear Harry had seen so many times with suspects he was out to nail, suspects who had come to the realization that nothing they said or did would get them off the hook.

Was that it? Was that what he was seeing in Nick's dead eyes? He wondered if it was that simple—that in the last moments of his life, Nick had realized that there was nothing he could do to stop his own killer. It had to be, Harry decided. If Nick had taken his own life, his final emotion would have been a sense of resignation, perhaps with a touch of relief—a final release from all the pressure that had driven him to that end. But fear? There would have been some, certainly, but fear would not have been a major part of that final equation.

* * *

Harry and Vicky came up dry with Nick's neighbors. Only a few had heard the late-night music and only the woman who lived next door had made any attempt to stop it. The music apparently had only been loud enough to disturb people in the adjoining apartments—and to cover the sound of one very loud pistol shot.

When they returned to the crime scene the CSI team was just packing up their gear. Mary LeBaron approached Harry with a handful of Polaroid photos in his hand.

"Something new?" Harry asked.

"Yeah, one more complication you're not going to like," Marty said. "Or maybe you will." The photos showed a pair of brown wing-tipped shoes shot from every conceivable angle. "We found them way back in Nick's closet. I haven't compared them to the photos from the Waldo murder scene, but I'm pretty certain they're going to match."

"Are the shoes the right size?" Harry asked.

"Eleven-C, the same as Nick's other shoes."

Vicky took the photos and began looking through them. "So if these are the shoes from the Waldo crime scene, it means he wore them home and saved them for us to find, rather than drop them in some dumpster, right?"

"Right," Marty said.

"If he wore them home there should be some blood on the driver's-side floor of his car," Harry said. "Is there?"

Marty LeBaron gave him a slow smile. "I happened to check that. There was no blood evidence in Nick's car."

"So the shoes were planted," Vicky said.

"I can't prove that, but it sure would be my guess."

Harry thought over what he had been told, letting various possibilities run through his mind. "I'd like you to hold back on this for a day," he finally said.

"Why?" Vicky and Marty spoke the word in unison.

"I want to keep this between us—you and me and Marty and Mort Janlow. It will just be for a few days. But right now I don't want to tell Rourke or any of the other detectives on the team. I don't want even the smallest chance that any of this will leak to the press."

Pete Rourke sat behind his desk and listened to Harry's plea for more time. Vicky sat next to Harry, uncharacteristically quiet.

"Why don't you buy it as a suicide, Harry? All the physical evidence fits."

"We don't know that yet. We haven't gotten a CSI report, and Mort Janlow still has the autopsy this afternoon."

"Harry, I haven't talked to Mort or Marty LeBaron, but I gotta tell you, as of right now everything I've seen points straight at Nick. Plus, there's the confession."

"Unsigned, just sitting on a computer," Harry argued. "Nick was a good detective, Pete. He knew that type of confession wasn't very solid. He could have easily printed it out and signed it. The printer was working and loaded with paper. But he didn't."

"Maybe he just didn't give a rat's ass," Rourke said. "Maybe he just wanted out of this world and didn't give a damn what he left behind."

"Then why confess at all? Why rent a movie and watch half of it? Why blast gospel music to cover the sound of the shot?" It was Vicky, and hearing her suddenly list Harry's concerns startled both men. "There's even the question of a pillow that might have been used to help silence Nick's Glock."

Rourke nodded slowly. "Who's covering the autopsy?"

"Jim Morgan," Harry said.

"Alright, if Mort has even the slightest doubt, I'll hold the confession. Just keep your fingers crossed that somebody else doesn't release it for me. What are you and Vicky doing in the meantime?"

"I'm going to check in with Mort and then I want to take another look at Bobby Joe's church."

"Why take another look at Waldo's church? You still think there's a tie between the killer and that church?"

"It's the only thing that makes sense," Harry said.

"What makes sense, Harry, is that you just don't like churches," Rourke said.

"Do I get the time I need, or not?"

Rourke scratched his chin. "For once—and maybe the *only* time in your police career—the brass is on your side. They don't like the idea of one of our own being tagged as a damn serial killer, so when I told them that you didn't buy Nick for the murder, they told me to give you time to prove it." He watched a smile form on Harry's lips, then wiped it away with his next words. "You've got seventy-two hours, Harry, and not a minute more. And that's straight from the top. When it's up, no matter what Mort comes up with, Nick's confession goes to the media."

CHAPTER TWENTY-ONE

Jim Morgan looked a bit queasy, his well-tanned face now showing a hint of gray.

"First autopsy?" Harry asked as he stepped up beside him.

Jim nodded, but didn't speak, afraid his voice might crack if he did.

"I don't like them much myself," Harry said. "I've seen dozens and each one is as bad as the first."

Mort Janlow was leaning over Nick Benevuto's open body cavity preparing to remove the heart. He looked up at the two detectives. "No puking," he said with a faint grin. "You have to puke, you go outside." He looked at Harry and the grin widened. "That especially goes for you, Harry."

Janlow began removing each organ in turn, weighing it, examining it for abnormalities; then setting it aside for further examination later.

"Anything?" Harry asked.

Janlow nodded. "Nick had an enlarged heart. If his brain hadn't been vaporized by that 9mm slug he probably would have dropped dead the next time he chased some kid down an alley. Even without that kind of strain, I doubt he would have lasted another five years."

"But no cause of death other than the head wound."

"No."

"And the feather we found in his hair?"

"It doesn't match with any of the pillows in the condo, but that doesn't mean he didn't pick it up somewhere else. Maybe he visited a lady friend in another condo and had a roll in her hayloft. But it also means a killer could have used a pillow to silence the shot, and then taken it with him. We just don't know yet."

"Killer . . . Aren't we talking about suicide here?" There was a look of complete bafflement on Jim Morgan's face.

Janlow threw Harry a look and Harry gave a small shake of his head in return. The medical examiner turned to Morgan. "We're just exploring all the possibilities. It's what we do here."

"I'd almost be relieved if it turned out to be murder," Morgan said.

"Why?" Janlow asked.

"Because right now I feel like I hounded him into killing himself."

Harry looked at the concern etched into the young deputy's face. There was nothing he could do about it. If Nick's death turned out to be suicide, Morgan would have to live with it. And if Harry was right and Nick was innocent of the other murders, Jim would have to live with that as well. Homicide cops make mistakes. You just try not to make too many. He placed a hand on Morgan's shoulder. "Go get some fresh air. I'll cover for you here."

When Morgan left Janlow gave Harry a questioning look.

"Marty found some shoes hidden in Nick's closet. There was blood on the soles and heels and Marty feels pretty certain they'll match the blood footprint in Waldo's apartment."

"Was there blood evidence on the floor of Nick's car?"

"No."

"So Marty thinks they were planted," Janlow said.

Harry nodded.

"And you're keeping a lid on it?"

"I am for now. I need a few days to work this angle without the press climbing all over me."

"What about the knife? From the wounds I examined my guess is that the same blade was used on both Darlene and the Waldo kid. From the marks made on the spines I'd say you're looking for a fairly substantial hunting knife with a nick in the blade."

"No sign of that either," Harry said.

"It doesn't make sense to get rid of the knife and leave blood-soaked shoes in your closet." Janlow thought about what he had said for a moment, then added: "So who's in the know about what you have and don't have?"

"You, Marty, Vicky, and me."

Janlow's eyebrows went up. "That's it? Not even Rourke?"

"Not even Rourke," Harry said.

Emily Moore was still working on Bobby Joe's funeral arrangements when Harry and Vicky returned to the church.

"Reverend Waldo wants to see you. He told me to send you over to the sacristy if you came back."

"I'll see him before I leave," Harry said. "First tell me if you came up with any copies of that church bulletin."

"No, I didn't, and I don't understand it. They just disappeared. This has all been one ongoing tragedy. And it started with that evil woman abusing that poor boy."

Vicky's head snapped toward the woman. "Why did you use that word?"

"What word?"

"Evil," Vicky said. "Why did you describe her as evil?"

Emily Moore looked confused. "Well, that's what she was. And it wasn't just Reverend Waldo who said so. Even that poor boy's father said she was. He said she was the most evil woman he'd ever met. And he wanted her punished just like Reverend Waldo did. I heard him say so myself. He said his son had been badly hurt and he wanted that woman to be hurt just as bad. It was his wife who wanted it all to end without that Beckett woman getting what she deserved, not the father. I felt sorry for him. He'd been a volunteer youth minister here for about a year, and he always seemed like such a kind man."

Harry was jolted by the information. He thought back to his interview with the boy's father, Joe Hall. He pictured him in his mind, a big, burly construction supervisor with a surprisingly gentle voice and demeanor. The man had said he'd only come to the church because of his wife. Now he was being told the man had volunteered as a youth minister. He had also said he'd only been tempted to harm Darlene on one occasion—when she smiled at his family as she had left the courthouse. But according to the church secretary there had been at least one other time as well.

"I need you to give me the name of the printer," Harry said. "I want to see if he still has a copy of that bulletin."

The secretary opened her Rolodex and copied an address and phone number. "And please don't forget that Reverend Waldo wants to see you."

"I'll see him before I leave," Harry said.

Outside, Harry searched his notebook until he found his notes on his interview with Joe Hall, then told Vicky exactly what Hall had said. "I want you to interview him again. Brace him on what this church secretary said, and if he admits it, press him on why he told me he had only thought about hurting her that one time in court. Also ask him why he never told us he volunteered as a youth minister."

"What if he denies it?" Vicky asked.

"He's a suspect as far as we're concerned. He's not just the father of a sex crimes victim. Go after him like you would any other suspect."

"That's all I wanted to know," Vicky replied. "And you're headed for the printer, right?"

"As soon as I see what Reverend Waldo wants."

* * *

The sacristy was empty, the only light coming through the large stained-glass window behind the stage. The two massive projection screens that hung above the stage displayed the image of a slender, young woman pushing a small boy on a swing. Reverend Waldo was seated alone in the first pew, but his head was bowed, his eyes staring at the floor. As Harry approached him he could see that the man's cheeks were stained by recent tears. On the seat next to him was an electronic device.

"Reverend?"

The minister raised his head at the sound of Harry's voice. He did not look well. His eyes seemed to have sunk into his heavy cheeks, and he had the look of a man greatly in need of sleep. "Thank you for coming." Reverend Waldo's voice was barely above a whisper, and it made Harry feel as though he was the first guest to arrive for his son's funeral.

"Your secretary said you wanted to see me."

Reverend Waldo raised his eyes to one of the screens above the stage and began to weep again. "Bobby Joe was four then," he whispered. "That's his mother pushing him. She joined our Lord in heaven seven years ago—cancer."

He touched a button on the electronic device on the seat next to him and the little boy and the woman began to move. Harry watched the home movie along with the weeping man. The child and the woman were both laughing, the little boy calling out that he wanted to go higher.

"He was always a good child, precocious but good. It was only later, as a teenager, that he got mixed up with a group of kids who were doing things they shouldn't—drugs and liquor, even stealing on occasion. And there were, of course, always the loose young women hanging around them. It was the time right after his mother died, a time when he needed guidance most, a time when I had thrown myself into my work. You see, all I could feel was my own pain over my wife's death, and to free myself of it

I became consumed with my work. I told myself I had to make this church bigger, more influential in the faith community, and I worked at it night and day; brought it to the point it's at now. But what I really needed to do was take care of my son. He was suffering then, but I was too busy with my own suffering to see it."

"A lot of kids get into trouble as teenagers, reverend. Most of them work their way out of it."

John Waldo began to slowly shake his head. "No, my son went far astray, and I helped lead him there." He turned and looked up at Harry. "Do you think Bobby Joe killed that woman?"

Harry took a moment to decide how much he wanted to say. "No, I don't. But I think he knew the killer, and I think that person scared the hell out of him, scared him so much he was afraid the tell anyone what he did know. And I think that person killed him to make sure he never would."

"How would he even know such a person? I know he had gone astray, but not that far, never that far."

Harry wanted to tell the man what he believed—that the killer was someone connected to his church, that the killer was a sick son of a bitch, a walking religious time bomb who had only needed the right situation and the right person to set him off, and that Darlene Beckett with her flagrant immorality, and the Reverend John Waldo with his righteous, God-fearing indignation had provided him with everything he needed all wrapped up in one tight little package. Instead, he looked the minister in the eye and said: "I don't know."

The minister stared at the floor for several long moments before he began to speak again. "I talked to the sheriff about you. This was before my son died, when I thought you were persecuting him. He told me what a good detective you are, and what happened to you as a child. He also told me there are some people in the department who think the dead speak to you because they recognize you as one of them. Is that true? Do the dead speak to you?"

"It's more an intuition about what they felt just before they died," Harry said.

"I believe that's a form of speaking." Reverend Waldo paused, almost as if he were afraid to ask more. Finally he seemed to gather his courage. "Did my son speak to you after his death?"

Harry slowly nodded his head. "In the sense you and I are talking about, yes, he did."

The minister's lips began to tremble. "What did he say to you? Please tell me."

"He told me about his murderer." Harry stared at the man, wondering if he'd understand. "When the dead speak to me, reverend—if that's what they in fact do—that's all they ever tell me . . . things about the person who took their life from them."

"Do they tell you who that person was?"

Harry smiled faintly. "I wish they would, reverend. They only tell me what their killers made them feel in those last moments."

The minister's lips kept trembling as he prepared to ask the question Harry did not want to answer. "What did Bobby Joe feel?"

"Do you really want to know?"

"Yes."

Harry nodded in resignation. "He felt terror . . . terror that what he had feared for so long was finally happening."

Waldo sat shocked for several moments. "So that's why you think he knew his killer."

"Yes, reverend. That's the primary reason why."

Waldo looked up with beseeching eyes. "Please catch him," he whispered. "Catch the person who killed my son."

"I will," Harry said.

* * *

Vicky sat on the small lanai where Harry had first interviewed Joe Hall. She stared at the burly construction supervisor contrasting his size to the soft, gentle demeanor he presented. Then his eyes lingered on her legs longer than necessary and she decided to give him a quick dose of reality.

"How badly did you want to hurt Darlene Beckett for what she did to your son?" she began, jolting him.

He hesitated, deciding how he should answer. "Real bad," he said at length. "You know, there were these people at work who used to joke about it. They had seen her on TV, seen how beautiful she was, and all they could talk about was how lucky the kid was who had gotten into her pants. Then, when they found out it was my kid she was having it off with, well, then it got real personal. The suck-ups would say he was a chip off the old block, and the others . . . the others asked if he ever told me whether she was good in bed, as if some fourteen-year-old kid would know the difference. But none of those clowns ever had to come home with me and see a kid who used to be full of fun sitting in his room not wanting to come out, a kid who was afraid to turn on the TV or the radio because he might hear something about it. They never heard him crying through his door when the goddamn school system said he had to go to a different school, had to leave all his friends behind, had to go someplace where he didn't know anybody, just because some parents thought he'd be a bad influence on their kids, or that the school could hide what had happened by getting him out of sight. So, yeah, I wanted to hurt her for all that, for what she did to my son, for what she did to my wife and me." He drew a deep breath. "It just wouldn't end, not once the newspapers and the TV people got ahold of it. And she seemed to love it. She seemed to glow every time a camera was pointed at her."

Vicky marveled at the fact that the man's voice never rose in anger, that his breathing never increased, his face never flushed. Throughout it all he seemed calm and controlled.

"You told my partner, Detective Doyle, that you wanted to hurt her that one time in court when she smiled at your family. Do you remember saying that?"

Hall folded his arms across his chest, creating a barrier between them. "Yeah, that's right," he said. "It was after she'd been given that slap-on-the-wrist sentence and she just walks by us and looks down at us sitting there, and she just smiles like she's looking at a collection of fools. And yes, right then and there I wanted to put my hands around her throat and choke her until her eyes popped out of her head. But I didn't. I didn't do anything then, and I didn't do anything later. She hurt my son and she got away with it, and I didn't do anything to make her pay for what she'd done."

Vicky stared across at him. "Somebody made her pay big time, Mr. Hall."

He nodded slowly, almost absently. "Yeah, but not me. I gave her a pass. Somebody hurts your kid you're supposed to make them pay. But I didn't do that. And my wife didn't either. She didn't even want the courts to go after that damn woman. The only people who wanted that woman to pay for her crimes were that fat minister whose church we went to, and some of the people who worked for him, and a whole bunch of people in the congregation. They all wanted her hung out to dry. And they put a lot of pressure on us. But my wife and son didn't want that. They just wanted it over with. So we stopped going to the damn church." He offered up a bitter smile, almost in resignation. "Now how's that? What that damn woman did even took my family's church away from us."

Vicky let a few moments pass, again taking time to study the man. The church had clearly been more important to Joe Hall than he was willing to admit.

"How active were you in the church?"

"Not very. A few years back I coached the Little League team the church sponsored. My son played on it, so when they asked me to help I said I would. I ended up being the coach." He shrugged. "You know how those things go."

"We were told you were a youth minister."

"Who told you that?"

Vicky hesitated, not sure how forthcoming she wanted to be. "It was someone who works for the church."

"Everybody who helps with the kids on a steady basis gets referred to as that. They're very big on handing out religious titles. It sort of keeps the kids in line. But, believe me, they're more honorary than anything else. All I did was coach baseball."

"Do you own a hunting knife, Mr. Hall?" Vicky dropped the question out of the blue and then waited for the tell.

Hall's eyes narrowed. "I didn't kill that woman, detective."

"Do you own a hunting knife?" Vicky repeated.

"Yeah, I own a hunting knife. It used to be my father's. I don't hunt, but I kept it for sentimental reasons and to use when I go fishing."

"Would you allow me to take it in for analysis?"

She could see anger coming to Hall's eyes for the first time. On a man his size it was an awesome sight.

"What's going on?"

Vicky turned to the sound of Betty Hall's voice. She had come into the lanai unnoticed and had picked up on her husband's anger.

"This cop wants my dad's hunting knife for some kind of half-assed analysis," Joe Hall answered.

Incredulity filled Betty Hall's face. "What?" she finally managed. "After all we've been through because of that bitch, now you're coming around suggesting that Joe had something to do with her murder?" She shook her head violently. "Oh no, not on your life. You get the hell out of here, lady.

And if any of you cops want to talk to *anybody* in this family again, you better have some kind of court paper that says we have to do it."

Vicky stared back at the woman, cool and calm. She didn't want to add to this family's troubles, but right now she knew she had to play the game out. She turned back to Hall. "Does this mean you won't surrender the knife for analysis?"

"Get *out* of here!" Betty Hall shouted.

"I think you should go," Joe Hall said. He no longer looked angry, only resigned.

"I may be back with a warrant," Vicky said. "If I have to do that, we'll go down to the office to talk. That won't look good to the neighbors, Mr. Hall—seeing you loaded into the back of a police car."

"Get out!" Betty Hall shouted again.

"You do what you have to do," Joe Hall said.

Rawlings Custom Printers was located in an industrial area of Tarpon Springs inhabited by equally small but clearly prosperous businesses. Ed Rawlings, the owner of the shop, had agreed to open the business when Harry reached him at home. Rawlings was a tall, slender, balding man in his mid-fifties with pale gray eyes and a faint Southern drawl.

"My daddy started this business when I was just a boy," Rawlings said, as he ushered Harry into the main office. "Back then we mostly printed up business cards and stationery, some wedding invitations, stuff like that. When I took over the business thirty years ago I switched gears a bit. We still do business cards and stationery and all that, but the bulk of our work now is custom printing jobs like the church bulletin you're looking for, some community theater programs, school programs—graduation programs, PTA bulletins—sports schedules, jobs like that. We employ fifteen people full time and two part-timers, which is up from the five who worked here when I took over."

Rawlings led Harry behind a customer counter and fired up a computer. Within minutes he had brought up the church account and checked the inventory of finished materials on hand. "As you can see, everything we printed was sent on to the church. You know, it's funny, but after you telephoned I remembered that I had a call from someone at the church asking about this same bulletin."

"When was that?" Harry asked.

"Just last week. Pretty insistent too. Asked me to go into the stock room and make sure I didn't have any overruns on hand. I told him print quantities were tightly controlled, but when we had any overruns we always shipped them to the customer. He still insisted that I physically check, so I did. We didn't have any."

"Was this a man or woman who called?"

"It was a man. He identified himself as one of the assistant ministers. Said his name was Stark, Starkey, something like that. I must have gotten it wrong, though, because when I called back the person I spoke to had no idea who I was talking about."

"Why'd you call back?"

"Well, after I hung up I started thinking that maybe he needed another small run of that bulletin, a hundred or so." Rawlings gave Harry a decidedly boyish smile. "Can't afford to lose business. And since I had the printing proofs it would have been easy to set up a small run and accommodate them."

"You have a proof copy of the bulletin?" Harry asked.

"Of course," Rawlings said. "We always keep proofs on file for at least a year. That way we have it if a job has to be repeated, or someone wants to see what was done the previous year for a Christmas program, or if there are any complaints about errors or omissions."

"But you didn't tell that to the man who called?"

"No. He caught me at a busy moment and I didn't think of it. Later, I did, and decided to see if there was any additional business available."

"I'd like to see those proofs," Harry said.

Vicky and Marty LeBaron faced Harry across the conference table. Vicky had just briefed them both about her interview with Joe Hall.

"I'd like to get my hands on that knife," Marty LeBaron said. "If it's old, like he said it is, the blade would have some pretty distinctive markings."

"We'll get a warrant if it proves necessary," Harry said. "But first I want you both to take a look at these printing proofs." He slid a manila folder across the conference table. "Take a look at page three," he added as Vicky picked it up.

Her eyes began to scan the page and then suddenly stopped. When she peered up at Harry her face looked stunned. "I don't believe this," she said. She handed the folder to Marty LeBaron. "How did we miss this?"

"We had no reason to look for it," Harry said. "None at all."

"Well, we do now," Vicky said.

Marty LeBaron put the folder down. "You think he could be our killer?"

"I do," Harry said. He looked at Vicky. "I want you to run a complete background check. And I mean complete—all the way back to when our friend here was in diapers." He turned to Marty. "In the meantime, I'll get you a warrant to go through our friend's home, cars, workplace, the whole shot. I want it done before anyone outside of us knows it's happening." His jaw line hardened. "This is one suspect who's not going to get a chance to lawyer up or deep six any evidence." He paused and looked at each of them in turn. "I want it done before I get back tomorrow afternoon."

Vicky's eyebrows shot up. "Get back? Where are you going?"

"I'll be out of the loop in the morning. I've got to go to the Central Florida Women's Correctional Facility. It'll probably be mid-afternoon before I get back." He looked Vicky in the eye; held it. "I have to meet with my mother. It's something they say I have to do if I want to fight her parole, and there's no other time."

"I understand," she said needlessly. "I'll handle things while you're there." She paused, trying to decide if she should wish him luck. She just nodded instead.

Harry returned her nod. If you understand, you're one up on me, he thought.

A Clearwater patrol car was parked in front of Harry's house, and a second four-wheel-drive unit was on the beach with a view of his rear yard. Harry checked in with both before going inside.

Jeanie was sitting on the lanai with Rubio when Harry entered the house. He kissed the top of Jeanie's head, gave Rubio a shoulder squeeze. "How are you?" he asked Jeanie.

"I'm fine," Jeanie replied. "Rubio is great company."

"I think she's hot for me," Rubio said.

Harry jabbed a finger at him, then explained that he had some papers to go through to prepare for a meeting he needed to attend the next day.

"Hey, my man, before you go off, I gotta tell you somethin'," Rubio called out as he started to leave.

Harry glanced back and saw Rubio grinning at him. "What's that?"

"I jus' want you to know that you don't need all them cops outside. Not when you got Rubio Martí *inside*. And that's truth, my man."

Harry glanced at Jeanie and saw her smiling at Rubio's macho act. He brought his eyes back to the twelve-year-old gangsta. "Yeah, I know that, my man. But my dad, Jocko, he's an old time copper, and you know how that is. They think there's never enough backup." Rubio gave off a little snort and Harry turned away before he could see him smiling. "Give me a half hour," he said as he walked away.

Returning to the living room, Harry retrieved the box that held his mother's letters and placed it next to him on the sofa. The letters stood on end, the box serving as a makeshift file cabinet, each letter sorted by the date it had been received. There had never been more than one letter per year, each arriving on the anniversary of his brother's death. He knew the letter he wanted. It was the eighth one he had received, arriving only a few days after his eighteenth birthday. It was also the only letter he had repeatedly read.

My son,

Your brother, Jimmy, has been with Jesus for eight years now. How I wish you were with him too. Last night Jimmy came to me in a dream and told me how happy he is in heaven, sitting at the foot of our Lord, seeing Him in all His heavenly glory. It was a beautiful dream. In it Jimmy told me that he talks to you and that you hear every word he says. Jesus told him it is a power you have had since you were a small child. The dead speak to all of us, of course, but only a few people have the ability to hear what they are saying. I have this power, and now I know that you do too. I hope you will write to me and tell me what Jimmy has told you. It is important for me to know this. It is my right as a mother to know.

I also hope you will tell me what other dead people say to you. What the dead say is very, very important. They see things that are hidden from us. The dead see everything because Jesus has opened their eyes to all the things the living cannot see. If only we knew the things the dead know. If we did all the mysteries of life and death would fall away and we would have the knowledge of the angels. That is what I want. I want that heavenly knowledge that will allow me to continue to do the bidding of our Lord. You can help me do this if you tell me what the dead are saying . . .

Harry saw that his hands were shaking and he put the letter aside without finishing it. His mother's madness overwhelmed him, but it also struck something deep inside. He wondered if this was where it came from, this sense of hearing the dead speak. Did it come from this insane letter he had received when he was an eighteen-year-old boy? He had always described what happened in his work as nothing more than intuition. But was it more? Was it a piece of a mother's madness passed on to her son in a prison letter? He doubted he would ever know the answer.

Harry folded the letter and placed it back in the box. All that mattered now was keeping his mother behind bars. He would go and see her tomorrow, and then, on Tuesday, he would take the letters to the hearing and let the parole board members read them. He'd even read the letters to them if he had to. He had made a promise to his brother and he had repeated it each time he visited his grave. And, yes, Jimmy had spoken to him. He had asked him to keep his promise; keep his mother locked away so she could not hurt anyone else.

If she gets out she'll kill you, Harry. She'll send you to be with me.

Harry put the box of letters away. He would not need them again until Tuesday. And after that, no matter what happened, he would never need them again.

CHAPTER TWENTY-TWO

The heavy barred steel door slid open with a loud rumble as Harry left the reception area and entered the main body of the prison. He could feel sweat gathering in the palms of his hands and he wiped it away as discreetly as possible on the sides of his lightweight tan sports jacket. A correctional officer walked ahead of him and came to a stop before another solid steel door. The officer glanced back at Harry, pressed a buzzer set into the wall, and then lowered his mouth to an intercom and identified Harry and the name of the prisoner he was there to see. Above them the light on a closed-circuit security camera blinked on so other officers could see who was at the door. Moments later there was a solid click and the correctional officer pushed the door open.

"The prisoner you're here to see should be brought in within a few minutes," the officer said. "You can sit anywhere you want. This isn't a normal visitation time so you have the place to yourself." He gestured toward a row of cubicles each separated by a thick glass partition, with telephone receivers on both sides of the glass. "They told me you were a cop," the officer added.

"That's right," Harry said.

"Then you know the routine. Just hit the buzzer by the door when you're finished."

"This won't take long," he said.

Harry's hands trembled as the door on the other side of the glass opened.

He watched his mother enter the visitor's room and wondered if his eyes were playing tricks on him. What he saw was the same young woman who had stood in their kitchen all those years ago, a broad smile on her beautiful face as she listened to Jimmy do his comic imitation of the small boy who lived next door.

Lucy Santos slid into the chair opposite him, her hands going to the glass partition that separated them, stroking it as if the glass were his face. He stared at the hands. They were old hands, cracked and work worn, not the soft hands of his mother. He looked up at her face and saw lines and creases he had not seen when she entered the room. Then the creases slowly disappeared, the lines smoothed out, and the face was young again. He fought for control and grabbed the handle of the telephone receiver that would allow him to speak to her, jabbing with the index finger of his other hand at the receiver on her side of the glass, indicating that she should pick it up. She obeyed, bringing the phone to her lips.

"Harry, my darling Harry," she said.

"Be quiet and listen to me," he snapped.

She jerked her head back and her eyes widened in surprise. "Harry—"

"Just listen. Don't speak." He glared at her with unforgiving eyes. He saw her lips begin to tremble but felt nothing. Her face was soft and young and beautiful again and he fought the image off. "When I was eighteen you sent me a letter and asked me if the dead spoke to me, if Jimmy spoke to me. I never answered your letter, never answered that question because I didn't want to; didn't want any contact with you at all." Harry leaned forward still glaring into the young/old woman's face. "Now I want to answer you. Now I want you to know what Jimmy has told me, year after year after year; I want to tell you what other dead people have told me."

"Oh, thank you, Harry. Thank you, thank you. You give me a beautiful gift. You give me the knowledge of the angels. Tell me, tell me what Jimmy says? Tell me, my son, what your brother says to you."

Harry's jaw tightened. "He says that Jesus is waiting for you . . ."

"Oh, yes, yes . . ."

"He says that Jesus has told him that when you get to heaven you will see Him in all His glory . . ."

"Oh, yes, thank God, in all his glory . . ."

"And when you see Him you will also see all that awaits the pure of heart; all the beauty that will be theirs for life everlasting. You will see everything that Jimmy has now. And Jimmy says that after you have seen it, after you see all the beauty and the glory that awaits those who have pleased the Lord, Jesus will raise his hand . . ."

"Oh, yes, yes . . ."

" . . . and He will cast you straight into hell."

Lucy Santos's back stiffened and the telephone receiver fell from her hand. Her eyes were wide and terrified and her face was lined with sharp fissures and sagging flesh. She was an old woman now.

Harry got up and walked to the door, pressed the buzzer, and waited for it to open. He did not look back.

Chapter Twenty-Three

Harry called Vicky from the prison parking lot. She answered her cell phone on the first ring.

"I was hoping it was you," she said. "How'd it go with your mother?"

"It went," Harry said. "I told her something she needed to hear. Now I'll have to wait for the parole hearing on Tuesday . . . Do you have anything for me?"

"I do."

"Are you able to talk without being overheard?"

"Yes."

"What happened with the background check?"

Harry sat in his car and listened to a story of childhood abuse that had been inflicted on their new primary suspect. As he listened Harry marveled at what now lay before him. He had just visited one child-abusing monster, his own mother. At the same time he was investigating the murder of a different child-abusing woman. And that investigation had now revealed one more monster, this one molded years earlier by the hands of yet another. He was silent for several moments when Vicky finished.

"Harry? Are you there?"

"Yes. Sorry. I was just thinking about everything you dug up. I'm starting to feel like we're surrounded by monsters."

"Yeah, I know what you mean."

"Have you heard from Marty LeBaron?"

Vicky let out a long sigh. "Marty got a warrant and searched his house and both his cars, but he hasn't located the murder weapon yet. He did come up with positive blood evidence in his work vehicle. Blood that matches Darlene's type that he found in the trunk, along with some on the driver's-side floor mat of his personal car that we haven't matched yet. It could be transfer evidence from one or more of the crime scenes, something that came off the shoes he was wearing. It'll take some time for DNA to prove everything beyond doubt, but Marty's pretty sure he's good for these murders."

"Get that stuff all on paper for me," Harry said. "I'm about two and a half hours away, but when I get back I want to run this stuff by Lola Morofsky before we lay it out for Rourke and decide how to set him up."

"It'll be waiting for you when you get here," Vicky said.

Lola Morofsky sat in her overstuffed chair, her short legs dangling way above the floor. The preliminary reports that Vicky and Marty LeBaron had prepared were resting in her lap as her index finger moved from point to point like a computer mouse.

"I would very much like to interview this man."

"I imagine you will in time."

"Is the arrest imminent?" There was a clear look of concern on her face.

"We need to force a move on the perp's part," Harry said.

"Force a move?"

"We don't have the murder weapon yet. It's obviously stashed somewhere that we couldn't find. But . . ."

"But?" Lola pressed.

"The killer has gone after everyone who's become a problem, and excluding Nick Benevuto who had to look like a suicide, the same weapon has been used in each murder. If another problem suddenly comes up, I think it will draw the killer out, murder weapon in hand."

"Harry, please listen to me. You are dealing with a tormented killing machine here, someone whose mind was badly twisted by something that goes far back into his childhood. It would not surprise me to find that he has killed other abusive people over the years. This may or may not have begun with the killing of Darlene Beckett. We know that was an act of retribution for what she did to that young boy. But there may also have been other acts of retribution in the past. And understand this. Unlike some serial killers, this person does not want to be caught. For this person the act of killing is truly messianic in nature and any attempt to stop those acts will be met by the harshest of responses."

"That's what I'm counting on," Harry said.

Lola let out a long breath. "Be very, very careful, Harry. This killer knows you and hates you. Not as a person—although perhaps that way as well—but definitely for the danger you present. That makes your life meaningless—meaningless to the point that ending it would not produce one iota of guilt. It would simply be a means to an end."

Harry and Vicky walked toward Harry's car at six-thirty that evening. They had just met with Pete Rourke in a restaurant parking lot. Harry glanced at his watch.

"He should be home by now," Harry said. "Call him as soon as you get back to the office. If he's not home leave a message with his wife. Make it very specific."

"What if the kid answers and the mother and father aren't home? Do I leave the message with him?"

Harry thought that over. "Yes, I hate to do it that way, but I don't think we have any choice."

"Are you coming back to the office with me?"

Harry shook his head. "As far as anyone else is concerned, I'm out of town. I'm going to need the next couple of hours to set the rest of it up."

Vicky nodded. "Good luck. Hopefully I'll see you later tonight."

* * *

Vicky looked across the conference table at Jim Morgan. She glanced at her watch. It was seven o'clock. "Time to put a little pressure on our suspect," she said.

Morgan nodded. "You want me to make the call?"

Vicky shook her head. "I want to do this myself." She opened her cell phone and punched in the number. It was answered on the third ring.

"Hello, Mr. Hall. This is Detective Stanopolis. I'm calling for Detective Doyle." She paused, listening. "Yes, he's the other detective who interviewed you. He needs to do it again. He can come to your house before you leave for work tomorrow, or he can see you at work. It's your call." Again she listened. "It's about a church bulletin we've been trying to locate. Detective Doyle found a copy and there's something in it that he needs to discuss with you." Another pause. "No, I can't tell you what it is. I haven't seen the bulletin. Detective Doyle has been out of town all day and he has it with him." She listened. "I know what you said. If it's necessary, Detective Doyle can bring a warrant with him." Another pause. "I'm glad you feel that way. Thank you for your cooperation."

Vicky closed her phone and peered off in the distance.

"Where's Harry been?" Joe Morgan asked, bringing her back.

"Visiting his mother," she said. "She's up for parole on Tuesday. Twenty years ago she killed his six-year-old brother. She also killed him, but some Tampa cops were able to bring him back."

"His mother? God, I didn't know." Morgan thought over what she had said. "So that's why they call him the dead detective. It's because he was dead once. I thought it was all that nonsense about how he can talk to murder victims."

Vicky stared across the conference table. "He doesn't talk to victims," she said. "They talk to him."

CHAPTER TWENTY-FOUR

A misting rain turned the street into a shiny black mirror, the gleaming surface reflecting the lighted windows that faced the street. A steady breeze came from the west, bringing the noise of the surf up from the beach, the low distant rumble obliterating the sound of a car that pulled in from Mandalay Avenue and glided silently to the curb. It was ten-thirty and the only other sign of life was a young boy rolling toward the intersection on a skateboard, his baseball hat askew on his head, his long, baggy basketball shirt flapping about his legs.

When the boy reached the corner he glanced back, then seemed to lower his head to his hand before rolling off into the avenue.

The car remained at the curb for several minutes before the driver's door opened. A tall figure slipped out and moved quickly to the shadow of a large hedge of sea grape. Again, there was no movement, the driver remaining perfectly still, eyes fixed on a house directly across the street. The house was dark except for the faint flicker of a television screen.

The driver had cruised the area for the past hour, seeking out the patrol units that had guarded the house in recent days, making certain they hadn't been replaced by unmarked cars. Now the driver's eyes scanned the windows of the other houses, watching for the rustle of a shade or curtain or blind that would indicate some watcher. There was nothing.

Harry sat in a leather recliner positioned so it offered a clear field of vision of both the front door and the entrance to the lanai. The dead bolt for the front door had not been secured; the lone lock that now held it closed was one that could be easily slipped with a credit card. The exterior door to the lanai had been left unlocked. A walkie-talkie sat on the table next to his chair. Moments before, Rubio Martí's warning that someone had entered the street had squawked over the receiver, a simple warning that the killer may have arrived. Harry's hand moved to the stock of the 12-gauge sawed-off shotgun that lay across his lap.

The driver moved quickly down the street, heading toward the beach. Once there he cut into the dunes and dropped to his knees. There was no moon and the beach and the water beyond were hidden by an impenetrable darkness that obscured all but the few yards of sand closest to the buildings that faced the gulf. The driver's left hand tightened on the handle of the large hunting knife. There had been no intention of using it again and he had considered throwing it away. Now it was needed one more time . . . all because of Harry Doyle. Now it was time for Harry Doyle to die . . . again.

Harry heard the screen door creak as it was eased back on its hinges. The sound was followed by complete silence. Someone was standing on the lanai, waiting, listening. A faint smile played across Harry's lips.

"Come on in, Jim. I've been expecting you."

Long moments passed before Jim Morgan stepped into view. His eyes found the shotgun in Harry's lap, noted his finger resting on the trigger guard.

"Looks like you're loaded and ready for bear," Jim said. "I thought I'd come by and help, cover your back in case Joe Hall came at you from the beach."

"Joe Hall's not coming," Harry said. "The phone call Vicky made . . . it wasn't for him, Jim. It was for you." Harry's eyes dropped to the hunting knife that Jim held along his left leg. "Is that the knife you used on Darlene and Bobby Joe? I was hoping you'd bring it with you. Marty and his boys couldn't find it when they searched your house and your cars yesterday. Oh, but they did find Nick's missing .38s. They even found the suppressor you used." Harry watched Jim Morgan's eyes harden. "Altogether they found more than enough evidence, Jim . . . Blood in the trunk of your patrol car, still more blood on the floor mat of your personal car, even some fibers that we expect will match up with the clothing Darlene was wearing. And of course we have that church bulletin with that wonderfully obscure reference to your work there as a youth minister."

Jim smiled bitterly and shook his head. "Reverend Waldo just couldn't help himself. He just had to see that everybody got a title. He didn't even know who I was. Bobby Joe handled the youth ministers." He let out a little snort. "All I did was work with the kids one night a week. But I still got a title. Seems like everybody but the janitor got one."

Jim took a step forward and Harry raised the shotgun, leveling it at his chest. "Not one more step, Jim."

"Aren't you going to disarm me?"

"Not yet, Jim. You know how it is. Always give a cop killer a chance to go for his weapon." He smiled at Morgan. It was a cold, clearly threatening smile. "Not a good chance, but a chance."

"I *was* sorry about Nick, but it couldn't be helped." He shrugged. "Besides, he wasn't much of a cop. He was even less of a Christian."

"Were you sorry about Darlene Beckett?"

Morgan's face twisted obscenely. "She got what she deserved. I'm sure the Lord's punishment was even harsher."

"Why do you think so?"

"You have to ask, after what she did to that boy? I thought the great Harry Doyle could see that. Or are you going to tell me she didn't deserve to be punished? Are you suddenly some great defender of women who abuse children? Are you, Harry . . . the same Harry Doyle who was murdered by his own mother?" He shook his head vehemently. "No, she was nothing but a tramp and she used that kid to satisfy her filthy cravings. She deserved just what she got. Reverend Waldo saw that. He couldn't say it just that way. He couldn't say right out what needed to be done, but he saw it, he saw it, Harry."

"Did Darlene remind you of Betty Higgins, Jim? Was that it?"

Morgan's head jerked back as though he had been slapped. "How did you find out about her?" His voice sounded almost like a growl.

"There were others too, weren't there, Jim—other abusers at all those foster homes you were sent to one after the other when you were just a little kid?"

Bitterness filled Morgan's face. "That's what kids are for. Don't you know that, Harry? They're for the satisfaction of sinners. Darlene Beckett understood all that. And . . . that's . . . why . . . she . . . had . . . to . . . die." He pressed the knife tighter against his leg. "It was perfect, you know, the way I worked it out. I followed her for weeks—I even saw Nick messing with her. But I waited for the perfect chance. Then she went off with that clown in the cowboy clothes and he took her to that beach at Frank Howard Park. So I followed them in and killed them both." A small smile flitted across his lips and then disappeared. "I was off duty, but I lived close by. So I went home and changed into my uniform and drove back in my patrol unit. It was a perfect cover if anyone saw me. I loaded her into the trunk and took her to Brooker Creek. I had always intended to dump her body there, no matter where I ended up killing her. I was assigned that area for the whole month, so I knew when the body was found and the call came in—with any luck at all—I could be the first unit at the scene. And, of course, I was." His face broke into a wide grin. "And I did such a good job I even got an official attaboy from the great Harry Doyle." He let out a low, soft laugh. "From there on it was a cinch to make the team investigating the case."

Harry nodded slowly. "Tell me about Bobby Joe. Why did he have to die?"

Jim looked down at the floor and shook his head. "He was the only one who knew about me. He knew I'd been tailing Darlene, because he'd been doing the same thing. He'd started out trying to get back into the good graces of his daddy. But she seduced him, just like she seduced everybody. Later, when he saw that I was tailing her too, he approached me about it. He was worried I'd let his daddy know he was sleeping with her. But I told him not to worry, that she was the one I was after, not him . . . I guess I knew right then that Bobby Joe might have to go eventually. He was such a little coward he just couldn't be trusted to keep his mouth shut. He was also the only one who knew I was a deputy. I'd kept that from people at the church; didn't want the kids I worked with to know. Then one day I ended up pulling Bobby Joe over for speeding. I didn't know it was him, of course, and I let him go without even a warning ticket. But right then I told him he needed to keep his mouth shut about my job." Jim let out another small laugh. "You see, I had no desire to kill Bobby Joe. But you left me no choice. When you started in on him, I knew sooner or later you'd break him. He was just too weak . . . So it was your fault, Harry. You're the reason Bobby Joe had to die. You wouldn't fall for Nick as Darlene's killer, even when I gave you those computer records. You just kept on after Bobby Joe. You knew it was someone at the church and you were like a dog with a bone, you just wouldn't ease up and take what I handed you on a platter. And that's why Nick had to die, Harry. He was your fault too." Jim's voice began to rise. "I needed you to accept him as Darlene's killer. But you wouldn't do that! You wouldn't accept the evidence I'd put together about the doctored computer records. And that evidence was iron clad. I know it because I doctored those records myself. But they weren't good enough for you, were they? You just kept insisting Nick was too good a detective to let himself get caught that way. And even after I'd killed him and gave you his bloody shoes and a suicide note to tie it all together, you still wouldn't buy it." He tilted his head to the side and his voice became softer. "Why was that, Harry? Why did you refuse to look anywhere else but the church? Did that whore, Darlene, tell you it was someone at the church? Was it a case of the dead talking to you again, Harry?"

"Something like that."

"You're telling me that whore came back at me from the other side? Is that what you're telling me, Harry?"

The lanai door behind Morgan opened and Vicky stepped inside. She immediately dropped into a shooting stance, leveling her Glock at Morgan's back.

Morgan's head pivoted and the bitter smile returned. "Hi, Vicky."

"Drop the knife, Jim. Drop it or I'll drop you." She glanced at her partner. "Sorry, Harry. We lost him on the beach. It was so dark we couldn't be sure if he'd come into the house or not."

Suddenly Vicky realized her position in the room was all wrong. Harry was directly behind Morgan, right in Vicky's line of fire, just as she was directly in his. Neither she nor Harry could use their weapons without the risk of hitting each other. She began moving to her right, but Morgan had seen it as well. He lashed out with his left hand, the hunting knife slicing across Vicky's gun hand and sending her Glock clattering to the floor. In the same motion he lunged past her and crashed through the screen door. Within seconds he was out of the house and into the enveloping dark of the beach.

Harry leaped forward, barking into his hand-held radio as he hurried to Vicky's side, telling the others outside that Morgan was loose and escaping along the beach. He looked at the wound on her forearm. It was deep but not life threatening. "I'm going to call in an 'officer down' so you can get some medical help."

"Screw that," Vicky shot back. "Tell me where your bandages are and I'll be right behind you."

"We've got enough people out there."

"Just tell me," she snapped. "Then get the hell out of here and catch that cop-killing son of a bitch."

"The bathroom off the master bedroom," Harry shouted as he crashed through the screen door and raced to the dunes.

The dark closed around him and the crashing surf cut off all other sound. Harry lay in the dunes, his eyes searching for movement; ears tuned to any sound that might point the way toward Jim Morgan. He fought the tension that was infusing his muscles, tried to keep his body loose. Morgan would use the knife if he could to avoid the giveaway bark of his Glock and Harry knew he would need to react quickly. He also knew that Morgan could be lying only a few feet away and he'd never know—not until that hunting knife lashed out in the darkness. Farther out along the beach, flashlights came on as other members of the department began searching. Harry had turned off his radio when he'd entered the dunes. Now he turned it on again to warn the others that he was coming out on to the beach. The last thing he wanted was to be shot by one of his own men.

When the answering call came that his message had been received, he heard a brief rustling to his left, then the sound of movement heading south along the beach. Morgan, he realized, had indeed been lying in the dunes. Now, after hearing Harry's call to other searchers, he'd bolted and headed away from the probing lights.

Harry followed, keeping his body low to the ground, aware he was backlit by the lights of the buildings facing the gulf. Morgan, conversely, was hidden by the dark water and the moonless sky. Trying to reverse those positions, Harry gambled and raced toward the surf, turning back when he reached the water. Nothing came into view. He paused, turning in a slow circle. Morgan had either flattened his body against the sand or had entered the water. Harry reversed their positions mentally, trying to decide how he would elude his pursuers if he were Morgan. Then it came to him and he raised the radio to his lips.

"This is Doyle. Are the streets covered?"

Pete Rourke's voice came back. "We've got a blanket out there, Harry; our people and Clearwater P.D. You have any idea where he is?"

Harry hesitated. If he was right, he knew he couldn't answer Rourke's question. "I think he may have gone into the water. You need to get some men into the surf, but tell them to watch the beach behind in case he slips through. We could use some big lights to illuminate the area."

"They're on the way," Rourke answered.

Harry entered the lanai, his Glock out in front, eyes scanning ahead. Sliding doors led to both the living room and the master bedroom. A trail of Vicky's blood headed back toward the darkened bedroom where the sliding door stood open. Harry entered in a shooter's crouch, weapon swinging from corner to corner. Vicky stood against a far wall, deep in shadow.

"Hello, Harry. Aren't you the clever one?"

Jim Morgan's voice seemed to float out from behind her, and as Harry's eyes adjusted to the dark Morgan gradually came into view. He was standing behind Vicky, back against the wall, and he had pulled her body tight against him. The hunting knife was in his left hand, the edge resting along her neck. One slicing move and Vicky's life would pour out onto the bedroom floor.

"It's time to give it up, Jim. There's no place left to go."

"Maybe I'll just go to Jesus," Morgan said, ending the sentence with a cold laugh. "Maybe I'll take Vicky with me. Do you believe in Jesus, Vicky? Do you believe in everlasting life?"

"Fuck you, Jim," Vicky rasped.

Jim pressed the knife against her throat, drawing a thin line of blood. "Uh-uh. Wrong answer, Vicky." He let out a disjointed laugh. "Besides, no one's done that to me since I was a small boy. Betty Higgins was the first, she and her husband. They took turns; first one and then the other. They took turns watching too. They liked to watch, you see. They said it was fun. But it wasn't fun for me, Vicky. It was never fun for me." His eyes seemed to glaze as he spoke.

"Drop the knife, Jim." Harry took a step forward. Carefully, he placed the sawed-off shotgun on the floor, pulled his Glock from its holster, and leveled it at Jim's head. His thumb disengaged the safety and his finger tightened on the trigger.

"Shoot the son of a bitch," Vicky said.

Jim slipped his head behind Vicky's, only one eye looking out just past her right ear. "Put it down, Harry. Put it down or she'll die right now."

Harry lowered his weapon and raised the radio to his mouth.

"Don't . . ." Morgan said, but Harry was already speaking.

"This is Doyle. He's in the house. He's holding Vicky hostage."

"Harry, are you sure?" It was Pete Rourke.

"He's five feet away from me."

Morgan glared at him. "That wasn't very smart, Harry."

"You're not going anywhere, Jim. That's the bottom line."

"Then Vicky's dead!" he shouted.

Harry took another step forward, until his legs were almost touching the bed that separated them.

"Stop!" Jim yelled.

Harry continued the conversation, grasping at anything that might distract him, anything that would keep him from slicing Vicky's throat. "Are you going to Jesus with an innocent woman's blood on your hands, Jim? She's not a sinner like the others. She hasn't hurt any children. She hasn't lusted. She's gone to church her whole life."

Jim shook his head vigorously. "No, no, she hasn't. She told me she stopped going to church. She's a sinner, Harry."

"What if you're wrong, Jim? What if she lied to you about that? Maybe she was afraid you'd laugh at her. No, Jim, you can't take the chance. You can't go to Jesus that way."

The words seemed to confuse Morgan. His eyes blinked several times, then suddenly hardened. "No!" he shouted. "No, no, no!" He jabbed the knife at Harry as he repeated the word.

Vicky felt his grip slacken and she slammed her heel into his instep, then drove an elbow into his solar plexus. Jim gasped and she threw herself to her right.

Jim recovered quickly and swung the knife, trying to catch her fleeing body, but Harry had already launched himself over the bed and grabbed his wrist, slamming it against the wall as he drove his Glock into the side of his head. Jim crumpled to the floor with Harry on top of him, one hand still holding his wrist, the Glock jammed up under his chin.

Vicky moved in and pried the knife from Jim's hand. From the living room they both heard a key twisting in the lock securing the front door. Moments later Pete Rourke was in the bedroom, a small army of deputies behind him.

"Looks like the gang's all here," Morgan said from the floor.

"Lock your fingers behind your head," Rourke ordered.

Morgan complied and Harry grabbed him by the collar of his shirt and helped him stand.

Rourke frisked him, quickly removing his Glock from a holster at his waist and a backup revolver in an ankle holster. As Rourke pulled out his handcuffs, Harry stepped in front of him.

"Not yet," he said. He brought a right hand up from somewhere around his waist and it caught Morgan flush on the jaw, buckling his knees and sending him back to the floor.

"Damnit, Doyle, what the hell are you doing," Rourke roared.

Harry ignored him and crouched down to Morgan. "That was for Jeanie," he said.

"Who's Jeanie?" Morgan wheezed.

"The woman you pistol whipped when you broke into my house."

CHAPTER TWENTY-FIVE

T **he size of the room surprised Harry.** It was small with a long table dominating its center. There were chairs for witnesses lining three walls, and a lone chair, positioned just inside the door and set several feet back from the table, clearly reserved for the inmate seeking parole. Everything—the walls, the floors, even the furniture—was institutional green, a near sickening color that gleamed under the harsh neon ceiling lights.

Walter Lee Hollins had met Harry when he arrived at the prison. His tall, slightly overweight presence had been a welcome sight. He saw Harry to the hearing room, explaining that the board would arrive together.

"It's their way of avoiding witnesses. They only want to hear from them when they're in session, only when the hearing is underway," Walter Lee said.

"What do you think her chances are?" Harry asked.

"You want me to be honest, Harry?"

"Yes, I do."

"The prison's overcrowded, Harry. Hell, all the prisons are overcrowded. The administration, and I mean the big boys in Tallahassee, are pushing them to free up some space." Walter Lee finally raised his head and looked Harry in the eyes. "I think her chances are damn good, Harry. And I don't think what you or anybody else says is gonna make a damn bit of difference."

Harry said nothing. Minutes later the door opened and the members of the board entered, a mix of everyday men and women who would decide whether or not he would live his life with his mother's shadow hovering over him. They were followed by two prison guards, a state psychologist who Harry had seen testify in court, and Calvin Morris from the state's attorney's office. Morris positioned himself on the opposite side of the room, distancing himself from Harry. It was not a good sign, Harry thought.

The board chairman called the meeting to order and introduced the other members, along with Morris and the psychologist, who he identified as Dr. Edgar Meeks. He then turned to Harry and asked his name for the record.

"Harry Santos Doyle."

"And what is your relationship to the prisoner?"

"I'm her son . . . Twenty years ago I was the other child she murdered."

The board chair glanced around uncomfortably; the latter part of Harry's statement had taken him by surprise. "We have received some evidence, some letters written by the prisoner, Lucy Santos, to a John and Maria Doyle. Are they related to you?"

"They're my adoptive parents," Harry said.

The board chair made a note on a legal pad set before him, then looked at the other board members. "Are we ready for the prisoner?"

The other board members either nodded or mumbled that they were. The chair nodded in turn to the prison guards who had stationed themselves on either side of the door. They left immediately to collect the prisoner.

Lucy Santos entered the room minutes later flanked by the two guards. She was dressed in an orange prison jump suit that hung loosely over a seemingly frail body. Her hair was heavily streaked with gray, and her dark eyes darted nervously around the room, passing over the board members, Meeks, and Morris, and settling on Harry. She stared at him intently, and when she seemed certain it was him, her eyes suddenly brightened and her mouth spread into a wide—and to Harry—near maniacal smile.

"Harry, Harry," she said, her voice barely audible.

"The prisoner is to be seated," the chairman said.

Lucy Santos glanced back at the chairman as though she didn't understand what he had said. "It's my boy. It's my boy, Harry." She looked back at Harry and again the smile returned.

"The prisoner will *sit down*, or the prisoner will leave the room," the chairman said.

Lucy's hands fluttered in front of her face. "Oh, I'm sorry. I'm sorry." She hurriedly sat in the chair. "Forgive me. It's just that I've been away from my boy for so long."

Harry stared at his mother, his stomach tied in a twisting knot. She wasn't the woman he remembered from childhood. She didn't even seem to be the same woman he had seen two days ago, and he realized that his mind had been playing tricks on him during that short, angry visit. Now she just seemed old and even more badly worn by the years. Two days ago he had seen flashes of her as he remembered her, as she had been when he had last seen her as a boy, a pretty woman, young and lively at thirty-three. But the subsequent twenty years in prison had not been kind.

The chairman began speaking though Harry had difficulty filtering his words through his own thoughts, his own memories. He continued to stare at his mother, trying to see the woman he remembered standing in the kitchen of their home twenty years ago. She had been laughing then— laughing at Jimmy as he mimicked the small boy next door—and he could almost hear the rhyming words that came from his brother's mouth, words that told the story of a spider climbing a water spout, his mother laughing at those words, laughing at her small son, all the time knowing that within minutes she would be dragging his drugged body into the garage so she could start the engine of her car and leave him there to die. And she did the same to you, Harry told himself. She did the same to you.

". . . *and your actions led to the death of your six-year-old son James, and your ten-year-old son Harry. Only the timely intervention by Tampa police allowed your son Harry to be resuscitated. Your son James, largely because of his age and small size, was not as fortunate.*" The chairman stopped reading from the papers before him and stared down the long table at Lucy Santos. "You have served twenty years of a life sentence for murder and attempted murder. The prison administration has listed you eligible for parole, due to time served and your lack of disciplinary problems while in custody. Dr. Meeks has found you mentally fit." The chairman glanced at the state psychologist and received a confirming nod. "The state's attorney's office has raised an objection based on the heinous nature of your crimes." This time he looked at Calvin Morris and again received a confirming nod. It was little more than a pro forma objection, Harry noted. The chairman turned back to the prisoner. "At this time, can you offer us any reasons why your parole should be favorably considered?"

Lucy sat mute for several long moments. Gradually her lips began to move, although no sound came from them at first. Her hands twisted in her lap.

"I committed sins, very terrible sins," she began. "At the time I thought I was doing good. But now I see that I was wrong. Now I want to make up for my sins." Her eyes turned to Harry. "I want to make up to my son the terrible thing I did to him." Her eyes then brightened, almost dancing with pleasure, and her face broke into a beaming smile. "As you can see, my son is here to support me." She placed a hand over her breast. "This fills my heart with joy and hope. It is a gift from God."

The chairman raised a hand, stopping her, and turned to Harry. He turned to Harry. "Normally we wait until the prisoner is finished until we hear from the victims. But your mother has raised a point I would like to clarify. Do you, indeed, support your mother's parole, Detective Doyle?"

Harry peered at the man as though he was mad. "No," he said. He stood abruptly and stepped toward the table the board was gathered around, and placed the box containing his mother's letters at the chairman's elbow. "These are letters the prisoner has written and mailed to me over the past twenty years—one each year on the anniversary of my brother Jimmy's death. I only came here today to give you these letters. You read them and then tell me if she deserves to be on parole." Harry stared at the board chair and then each board member in turn. Then he started for the door.

"Mr. Doyle, do you want these letters returned to you?"

Harry didn't break stride. "I never wanted them in the first place."

As he moved past his mother, Lucy's hand shot out in a beseeching gesture, her fingers brushing the sleeve of his shirt. Harry pulled back his arm as if something vile had touched him.

"Harry, Harry . . ." Her voice was plaintive and he knew he would hear that voice for a very long time. He pushed his way through the door and left the room.

CHAPTER TWENTY-SIX

A week had passed and the media coverage of Jim Morgan's arrest had finally begun to fade. It was late evening and Harry was holding Jeanie's hand as they strolled along the beach. It would be a good sunset with no cloud banks marring the horizon. Harry tried to remember when he last enjoyed a sunset. It was before Darlene Beckett's body had been found, of that he was certain. He had visited Darlene's grave earlier in the week, the mound of dirt that covered it still appearing fresh and recently turned. He wasn't certain why he had gone. Perhaps because he had come to recognize that she was a victim too—a victim of her own illness, as well as a victim of someone who was even sicker than she. Perhaps he had gone to see if she would speak to him again. She did not.

"My husband came by to see me this morning," Jeanie said, bringing him back.

"And . . . ?"

"He wants to get back together. He said all the right things . . . that he was sorry . . . that he'd been a fool . . . that he realizes now how much I mean to him."

"And . . . ?"

"I told him it was too late."

Harry looked at her and saw that she was smiling. Jeanie was not a truly beautiful woman . . . except when she smiled. "You sound proud of yourself."

"I am," she said.

Harry slipped his arm around her waist and pulled her closer as they continued walking. "You should be."

They headed down to the beach for several minutes before Jeanie spoke again. "You never told me how Vicky is."

"She's got a week off to let her arm heel, two weeks if she needs it. She's happy as a clam."

"Are clams happy?"

"I never heard one crying," Harry said.

"What's going to happen to Jim Morgan?"

"Don't know, but I suspect they'll find him mentally unfit to stand trial, which will mean a hullabaloo in the media, probably a slew of editorials demanding that all cops get psychological evaluations."

"Doesn't sound like a bad idea," Jeanie teased.

"Except that it could put me out of work," Harry came back.

"Did he ever explain why he killed those people, why he carved those words in their foreheads and covered their faces with masks?"

"In the end his explanations were all religious gibberish," Harry said. "Lola Morofsky thinks it goes back to the abuse he suffered in foster care, but who knows? It's easy to abuse kids. They're trusting and they're vulnerable and they can't do a lot to defend themselves. They're easy targets for people who want to hurt them. And it always changes the way they look at the world."

They walked on again in silence for another minute or two until Jeanie got up the courage to ask the one question she knew she had to ask.

"Have you heard anything about the parole board's decision?"

"Yes, my friend Walter Lee Hollins called yesterday. The board approved her parole. My mother gets out as soon as the paperwork is finished." He thought about the trip he had made that day to his brother's grave. He had stood there for a long time, working up the courage to tell Jimmy that he had not kept his promise, and that he was sorry. They were the hardest words he had ever spoken.

"They released her even after they read the letters she wrote to you?" Jeanie asked.

Harry looked out into the gulf. "Walter Lee said they never read the letters. They gave them to the guards and told them to get rid of them. The prisons are overcrowded."

Jeanie stopped and slipped her other arm around Harry's waist. She held him, hoping she was providing some comfort, certain she was not.

"Life goes on," he said. He wanted to smile, but found that he could not.

Chapter Twenty-Seven

Two weeks later

Lucy Santos stood on Mandalay Avenue staring at the side street where her son's house was located. The parole board had ordered her to stay at least one hundred yards away from him. But she knew they didn't really mean it. Oh, for a time they'd insist that she stay away, but soon Harry would tell them he wanted to see his mother; soon God would intervene and show him it was necessary. And then, when God told her it was time, she would finish her mission.

Earlier that day she had gone to Jimmy's grave. She had talked to him as only a mother can, told him how she knew that everything Harry had said to her was a lie, how Jesus would always love and protect her, how He would never cast her into the burning pit of hell. She had even told him about her plan. But it had not been a very satisfactory visit. A cold breeze had come off Jimmy's grave that she did not understand. It was probably Harry's doing, but she would have to pray about that; she would have to understand it before she continued. Right now she just needed to see where Harry lived, see what kind of aura his house gave off. Yes, that would be good to know.

She stepped off the curb and headed for Harry's street. She knew she wouldn't see him today. No, not yet. But soon, Harry. I'll see you very, very soon.